ENIGMA

DAW Books Presents
C. F. Bentley's
The Confederated Star Systems:

HARMONY

ENIGMA

ENIGMA

The dramatic sequel to *Harmony*

C. F. BENTLEY

DAW BOOKS, INC.

DONALD A. WOLLHEIM, FOUNDER

375 Hudson Street, New York, NY 10014

ELIZABETH R. WOLLHEIM
SHEILA E. GILBERT
PUBLISHERS

http://www.dawbooks.com

This book is dedicated to a number of people who keep me going
when the going gets tough:

For Deb and the wonderful what ifs.

For Lizzy for the amazing dreams.

For Bob and all the science stuff.

For Maggie anchoring me in reality.

For Judy for showing me a new way to pray.

ACKNOWLEDGMENTS

Many years ago I sat on a panel discussion at Baycon in San Jose, California on the etiquette of First Contact. This was so long ago I don't remember much about the discussion or the people involved. But one comment stuck in my brain. "When we meet someone on the Internet, we don't invite them to our home. We make that first face-to-face meeting in a coffee shop across town. Neutral territory."

I took that statement home and wrote a short story, "The First Contact Café" by Irene Radford (one of my pen names). Many thanks to John Helfers, editor at Tekno Books for including it in the anthology *Space Stations;* DAW Books 2003.

When I began developing *The Confederated Star Systems* series, I knew I needed a space station. Since I already had one, I stole it from my pseudonym Irene Radford. Then I had to make the thing work. A little redesign and much advice from Bob Brown, a health Physicist for the Hanford Nuclear Reservation, and I bring you the new and improved version of the First Contact Café. Two other short stories centered in my space station are available on the Bookview Café: http://www.bookviewcafe. com.

Creating a book of the scope of *Enigma* involves many more people than just the author. My family gets many hugs and much gratitude for putting up with me in my workaholic moods, scanty meals, nonexistent housework, and minimal conversation. My friends who read the book before I dared submit to my editor, Lea Day, Deborah Dixon, Bob Brown, and Lizzie Shannon, deserve more than I can give them for their invaluable advice. Variations and inconsistencies are mine not theirs. As always, I am in deep awe of my editor Sheila Gilbert who can always find ways to make my work more complete and meaningful.

And last but not least I want to thank Judy Gregoire and The Dance

Connection in Welches, Oregon for providing me a place of sanctuary and refuge, and showing me that dance too can be offered as a prayer.

C.F. Bentley
Welches, Oregon
December 2008

Small rituals when combined with ancient tradition remind us day-by-day, minute-by-minute, of our connection to the Divine.

✦ ✦ ✦ ◇ ✦ ✦ ✦

PROLOGUE

FREEDOM. SAFETY. Within sight. An end to this endless flight. A beginning of truth.

The seeking, ever the seeking, will there ever be an end?

I feel the ending in my bones and in my heart.

If only I can survive a little longer, I will know who it is that I seek. Who can resanctify the rituals.

Will the search begin again with only one new clue, or will this truly be the end?

What am I without the search? What are we without the sacred rituals?

$$\text{✦ ✦ ✦ ◇ ✦ ✦ ✦}$$

CHAPTER ONE

"**S**TUPID, USELESS, SONS of a Denubian muscle cat. Why can't Ambassador Telvino and Lord Lukan just sign the damned treaty! Then we'd have access to Badger Metal and could defeat the Maril once and for all." Colonel Jeremiah Devlin tossed aside the coded communiqué from Admiral Pamela Marella, the spymaster of the Confederated Star Systems. Pammy thought she should be Jake's boss. Ambassador Telvino claimed him as well. Lord Lukan, Ambassador from Harmony, thought he belonged on his delegation.

Jake slammed his fist into his thigh. His blow bounced off hard muscle, a side benefit from hours spent in the heavy grav gym trying to work himself to exhaustion so he could get *some* sleep.

Jake rubbed his bleary eyes, and the secret words swam before his mind.

The Marils are changing tactics. After their defeat at Harmony Six by the combined fleets of Harmony and the CSS, the Maril amassed a new fleet and attacked our border at Haven IV, our closest outpost to Harmony. We hold them off for the present. Prepare to depart your current assignment with six hours notice to rejoin our defense forces.

Damn, damn, and damn again. If he left the space station, he'd also have to leave Laudae Sissy, High Priestess of Harmony, to the mercies of the ambassadors and Admiral Marella. None of them had the frail young woman's best interests in mind. Only their own agendas.

Our enemy also now makes forays to frontier worlds on the rim. Worlds beyond our protection, either by choice or by distance. We

have reports that planets that surrender or put up only token re-
sistance are absorbed into the Marillon Empire. Serious attempts
are made to convert humans to the religion and culture. Rumors of
DNA manipulation so they can interbreed are spotty and unreli-
able but worth investigating.

Worlds that resist are wiped out, as the Maril have always done.

Jake knew that as well as anyone. He'd lost both his parents and his
brother when Maril bombs shattered all traces of civilization on their
home planet. But that was back when he was Cadet Jake Hannigan at the
CSS Military Academy. Under his new identity as diplomatic liaison between the CSS and Harmony delegations on this cursed and lonely space
station—after a six month stint in deep cover as a spy on Harmony—he
wasn't supposed to feel that loss.

But he did. And the words of the memo still imprinted upon his memory, blotting all else from his consciousness.

The Maril still seek a new source for Badger Metal. As do we.
We suspect they will open a new battlefront near Harmony, the
only source for Badger Metal, when they have augmented their
forces with human troops.

Returning to First Contact Café soonest.

Seeking solace from the turbulent thoughts Pammy's words evoked,
he fell to his knees before his makeshift altar in the corner of his pie-
shaped quarters. His hands folded and his head bowed automatically
into respectful prayer. Unconsciously he flexed and relaxed his muscles,
counting sets of seven. Ever seven, for the seven gods of Harmony and
Her seven castes. Always seven.

"Words. They fight over words while our alien enemies build new
fleets and man them with our own people." He bowed his back until
his forehead nearly touched the altar, silently begging the line drawing
of Goddess Harmony and her divine family for guidance. He wanted to
light the purple candle stub and saucer of incense to speed his prayers.
But no way would he violate the most sacred law of life on a space station
by igniting anything.

If he had a crystal, any crystal, he could make it chime and get the attention of Someone out there who could acknowledge his seven prayers.

He stared long and hard at the crude picture. The blank eyes of Harmony, her Consort Empathy, and their children, Nurture and Unity,

stared back at him almost in accusation. They embraced their stepchildren, Anger, Fear, and Greed, as part of the balance of nature that banished Discord. He'd seen the original painting in a mural deep within the funerary caves on the planet Harmony.

All he could think of was the blasted memo. Or if he put that aside for a few moments, he daydreamed of a life with the love of his life. A woman he could never have.

He stood up and jumped to the crossbar he'd set in his closet. Twenty-one pull-ups barely strained his shoulders. Forty-nine, he began to feel the stretch and burn.

Fifty-six . . .

I need you. A thought brushed across his mind. Something weird and very frightened flared within him. Then it was gone.

He glanced at the line drawing rather than give in to fantasies and wishful thinking.

The figures on the drawing shuddered. So did the station bulkheads. Just the slightest vibration where none should be.

Come. Now. The plea for help became more urgent. It had a feminine quality.

Jake cursed. Only one person in all the universe had that kind of hold on his mind and his heart.

Under the mental noise of people in distress the distant keen of an alarm rose and fell.

Which had come first?

He swung off the bar, landing halfway to the exit hatch. Long strides took him to the circular lobby of level M2 in the CSS diplomatic wing of the space station. With every step the klaxon grew louder, more insistent.

The lift, moving platforms three meters apart on a conveyor belt, rotated up to the zero-G hub and back toward the heavy-G end of the wing in their placid rhythm. The double spiral staircases around the lift looked empty.

Three long corridors, running between groups of quarters, stretched toward the hull. The rest of the circle showed firmly closed doors to diplomatic suites and high-ranking crew quarters.

Each tubular wing stuck out from the vastly larger cylinder of the station core. Station spin gave the outermost ends of the wings heavier gravity and made the core appear "up" from any given location. Smaller tunnels stretched between adjacent wings for stability and maintenance robot access. From outer space the entire complex looked like a tin can with thirty strands of spaghetti sticking out of it in clusters of three or four.

Frightened voices, screams, bangs, and thuds at the end of the corridor directly ahead drew his attention.

He skidded to a halt in front of a maintenance access hatch. This two-meter-diameter tunnel connected his wing to the living quarters of the delegation from Harmony. Designed primarily for maintenance robots, only a few highly trusted, heavily screened personnel were allowed to use it. Only one of those had a key.

It was locked to all others. An override from Control could open the hatches in case of emergency evacuation. Otherwise, people were prohibited from using them as a shortcut.

As special liaison and military chief of staff Jake had keys that would open any door or hatch in the seven wings assigned to Harmony and the CSS. Lord Lukan from Harmony and Ambassador Telvino of the CSS had limited emergency keys.

Jake invoked special diplomatic privilege and beamed a coded signal from the comm unit strapped to his wrist to the panel. The locking mechanism took its own sweet time accepting his authorization. It wanted another password, then a thumbprint, and finally accepted a retinal scan.

The voices behind the hatch reached hysteria.

At last the light blinked a benign green.

Using all of the strength he'd gained from those hours in the gym, he applied his weight to the latch. The bolt grunted and heaved as loudly as he did. Then it slid back slowly, protesting and grinding every centimeter of the way. Rust should not have developed on a new station! At last it pushed free. Then he had to spin the bolt to open the hatch.

"Archaic, redundant, miserable . . ." He exhausted his litany of abuse on the thing before the hatch gaped a scant ten centimeters.

Now he recognized the coded alarm in the background. Three short blasts, a long one, then three more short, repeated again and again until someone in Control could override it. *Hull breach. Losing atmosphere.*

That tiny shudder of the goddess in the line drawing should have warned him. Instead, he'd ignored Her.

A wind grew behind him, pushing itself into the crack of an opening. Atmosphere trying to equalize.

He needed help. But first he had a wing full of people to evacuate. He prayed that the Labyrinthe Corporation had implemented full safety protocols in their hurry to complete the station before the CSS and Harmony delegations arrived.

Bracing his feet on the bulkhead, he pulled the hatch open with both hands. The reluctant hinges gave up their mission to remain closed. The two-meter-diameter door swung free suddenly and flung Jake away. He landed against the wall and slid down hard on his butt, legs sprawled, back screaming in protest at such abuse.

He ignored the stabbing pain to the left of his spine beneath his shoulder blade. Dimly he knew that a free fall grip might have penetrated his skin. At the least, he'd have a bruise in the morning. No time to think about that now.

The klaxon continued. Discord! Where in the seven hells were the maintenance bots, a dozen of them in different sizes and functions, designed to flood the area and fix the damage?

A tangle of arms, legs, and lavender clothing clogged the hatch opening. He sorted them out, drawing free first a small blonde girl, then an older, dark-haired one.

"Suzie!" He hugged the younger girl close as he dragged Mary free of the confining tunnel. He inspected both girls from head to toe. No bruises, still a good sparkle in the purple circle Temple caste marks on their left cheeks. "Is Laudae Sissy safe?"

In another life Mary and Suzie might be his daughters, instead of merely acolytes to the High Priestess of Harmony.

"I don't know where she is!" thirteen-year-old Mary wailed, clinging to him. "She told us to come to you. I can't see who's behind. Most of the lights aren't working. Dog and Monster herded us into the tunnel faster than we could think." She mentioned two of the mutts that followed Laudae Sissy everywhere, along with a clowder of cats, birds, lizards, and other critters seeking a home. She'd brought most of them with her from Harmony, then sent all but the two dogs and three cats home when they didn't adapt to the confined life on station.

"Easy, Mary. I need you to take Suzie so I can help the others. Can you be brave for just a few more moments?" He forced himself to speak calmly, authoritatively, to still the girls' panic.

Mary gulped back her tears and nodded.

"Now, as I get people free, I need you to direct them to the central tram. Send them to the Conference wing." He pulled another girl in a lavender nightgown free of the hatch; Sharan, the littlest, but not the youngest, of Laudae Sissy's acolytes.

"Trams in the core don't work. Bulkheads closed at the top to contain the breach." Mary spoke the unfamiliar vocabulary carefully. "Our in-wing lift stopped too. Everyone's got to use the stairs to get to this escape route."

"Damn." He checked the lift on his level. Sure enough, it had stalled with only one platform visible about one and a half meters above the deck. "Okay. Mary, I need you to bang on the fifth door down to the right. Keep banging until Ambassador Telvino wakes up and knows what's going on. Can you do that?"

Bella and Sarah tumbled out together, clinging to Martha's hands. All six of the girls safe. Sissy's girls. His girls. He breathed a little easier.

No sign of the dogs yet.

He hadn't seen the briefest glimpse of Sissy's bright purple clothes either. Nor the neutral brown of her young siblings, Marsh and Ashel.

If she lost those two remaining of her once large family, she'd shatter, and with her the entire Harmonite Empire.

"Yes, sir," Mary replied smartly.

"Good." He swallowed his panic. Useless emotion. Time later to indulge in screaming fits. "When the ambassador has taken charge, you can gather Laudae Sissy's girls in my room directly across from the end of this corridor. The door is unlocked." He reached into the tunnel and brought forth strangers in blue that matched their Noble diamond caste marks.

A single handcar trundled along the tracks at the bottom of the tunnel. Jake turned his attention to check on the girls at the same time he reached into the tunnel blindly to assist.

"Unhand me, you barefaced troll!" A lady batted his hands away from her august personage.

"Sorry, Lady. But if you don't get your Noble butt out of there quickly, on your own so others can come free, I'll just have to drag you out," Jake replied, clamping both hands around her swollen ankles.

"I'll have your head for your impertinence."

✦ ✦ ✦ ◇ ✦ ✦ ✦

CHAPTER TWO

THE HAUGHTY NOBLE FEMALE looked down her long nose at Jake, quite a feat since she was sitting in the hatch at his waist level.

"You can't have my head on this space station," he said around half a grin. "You left behind you on Harmony the authority to execute without trial anyone below you in rank."

"Uncivilized brute. Oh, it's you, Military Jake." She huffed and allowed him to pull her free.

He recognized Lady Jancee, wife of Lord Lukan, the Harmonite Ambassador. He should have known her by her tirade. Tall, long-legged, with a magnificent bosom, this blonde autocrat was deemed the most beautiful woman on Harmony.

Jake reserved that title for Sissy.

"Just keep moving, My Lady. Someone up the corridor will help settle you into temporary quarters."

"I knew Laudae Sissy trusted you with her life for a reason."

Yeah, I protected my Sissy from an assassin hired by your mother-in-law, My Lady.

Jake had kept his red square caste mark after returning from Harmony because it remained his only link to Sissy. Now it acted as a bridge between his world and hers, smoothing troubled communications.

Lady Jancee waddled less than gracefully in the direction he pointed. She looked about six months along in her seventh pregnancy. Good reason for her to use the only handcart in the tube. He wondered briefly who had propelled it with the hand pump for her.

He noted that the six lavender-clad acolytes had formed a sort of reception line, guiding people toward Ambassador Telvino at the staircase. They knew how to do ceremony. They'd found a familiar ritual and applied it to an emergency, turning tragedy into something sacred to be remembered and honored for the lessons learned.

Jake returned to the hatch. Fewer people pressing from behind now, mostly with the brown X mark of the Worker caste. They'd all been ennobled—adding a blue diamond outline to the caste mark. A couple of Professionals sporting a green triangle encircled with Temple purple, lauded medics, accountants, lawyers, and such. Then a squad of Military slid through, also lauded so they could serve Temple people. They took orders easily from Jake and deployed to communications and directing traffic. Their solid presence kept panic to a minimum.

People came free of the hatch more smoothly now, in less haste and panic.

Still no sign of anyone wearing deep purple. Or of Marsh and Ashel. The dogs wouldn't leave Sissy.

The next man through propelled himself easily along the handgrips at waist level along the walking ledge above the 'bot tracks at the bottom. Ambassador Lukan.

"Where's Laudae Sissy?" he asked before he'd set his feet firmly on the deck.

Like a good lord, he'd looked after his people first, bringing himself to safety last.

No one came behind him except Dog. The brown mutt of extremely mixed lineage whimpered in fright as he crawled along the tracks, completely surrounded by the transparent walls.

"It's like swimming, Dog," Jake whispered reassuringly. Dog had finished his herding job. But without the job to do, the vast openness around him, without visible walls bewildered the beast.

"I haven't seen Laudae Sissy, My Lord," Jake called over his shoulder while coaxing Dog with gentle murmurs and beckoning gestures.

"Discord! I directed her through first. Harmony cannot afford to lose her avatar."

Jake knew in his heart that one slim woman born to Worker caste parents but with all seven caste marks, who had grown into the spiritual leader and head of Temple caste, was all that held a fracturing society together.

He wasn't too sure he'd come out the other side whole and sane if he lost Sissy or any of her charges.

"Sissy's girls came through first, safe. Did you actually put the High Priestess into the tunnel? With her brother and sister?" Jake pulled Dog free and sent him to circle Sissy's acolytes.

"No . . . damn. I've got to go after her."

"That's my job, My Lord. You help Ambassador Telvino organize things on this end. Here's my override key. You can get the lift moving. You'll have to open some light-grav quarters to accommodate everyone. You can't get to the other wings yet by tram. Oh, and you might try calling Control to get them to override the bulkhead to the trams."

With that, Jake swung one leg up and climbed into the access. "And will someone please turn off that damn alarm."

In response, it grew louder yet.

✦   ✦   ✦

Jake walked gingerly along the narrow ledge above the tracks, hauling himself from one grip to the next. He dared not hurry through the transparent carbon fiber tunnel toward the noise and red pulsing lights several kilometers away. The central tracks at the bottom sometimes carried electricity to power the 'bots. Sometimes not. Nothing seemed to be working precisely as dictated in the instruction manual.

The network of tubes helped stabilize the otherwise independent wings of the space station as well as giving those tardy maintenance 'bots and workers easy passage between, without detouring to the trams at the nul-grav center of the spinning station—properly called Labyrinthe VII.

These stabilizing tunnels were necessary, yet invisible from a distance.

Locked into an orbit around a young planet just beginning to explode with bacterial life, the station's spin exposed it to alternating sunlight and darkness, controlling the heating and cooling rate from the local sun.

He grunted as his foot slipped off the ledge. A momentary jolt flashed through his boots to his spine. Yep, the tracks carried power again. He clung to the wall grip with two hands while he caught his breath. Then he gulped. Only a thin layer of transparent carbon fiber separated him from vacuum. Vast constellations spread out around him. Nothing between him and eternity.

He froze, staring in awe and terror of the endless universe beckoning him outward. "If only I was out in a fighter, I'd know what to do with all that black."

Why hadn't the interior lights come on to aid him? If he had light, he could blot out the allure of the vastness outside.

The alarm grew louder, more insistent. Discordant. He imagined it yelling, "Pay attention to me!"

Laudae Sissy would sing those jarring tones back into harmony. If she still lived. He had to find her.

He counted his movements to keep from screaming. Seven paces at a time. Forty-nine, then ninety-eight, and onward.

"Sissy, where are you? You'd better not be dead. Not after all I went through to keep you alive," he muttered.

At last the opening at the end of the tunnel grew from a pinprick in size to a thumbnail, to something he might fit through.

The pulsing red lights disappeared behind a shadow.

"What in the seven hells?"

"Jake," a tiny voice whispered.

"Marsh?" He moved faster.

"Thissy won't come," the little boy lisped. "An' Ashel wants to stay w' 'er. Monster too. The cats ran up to the tram afore the alarm closed 'em."

Great. Cats loose on the station, free to crawl into any crevice they decided was warm and safe. Without proper supervision and separation, they'd breed and overrun the place in a matter of months.

Serve the Labyrinthe Corporation right.

"I'm coming, Marsh. I'll take care of your sisters." He jumped to the deck, sparing the boy a brief hug. Then he swung him up into the tunnel. "Stay on the walkway, Marsh. The tracks aren't safe. Go to Mary. Stay with her so we can find you later." Breathing definitely shallow here. They were losing air and pressure.

"But . . ."

"Do it, Marsh." He closed the tunnel hatch. But only for a moment. The power plant would push some atmosphere and pressure from the CSS wing through the tunnel to this wing, replenishing some of the air that drained away in the hull breach.

Pressurized atmosphere moving toward the vacuum of space sucked down the lift shaft. He climbed onto a staircase railing and let the wind push him, and the increasing gravity pull him, down ten levels into the heavy-grav section at the outer reaches of the wing.

"What new disaster has found you, Sissy?"

The klaxon kept blaring. The few working lights continued pulsing red. He felt as if he moved through heavy water in a surreal and distorted parody of an orderly and safe space station.

When he was still Major Jake Hannigan, hotshot fighter pilot and undisciplined brawler, he preferred the known dangers of a space station to the uncounted variables dirtside. After six months on Harmony with Sissy, he'd come to appreciate solid ground under his feet and *natural* wind in his face.

A shift in the wind told him to jump off at level HG30. He paused to assess the situation. An empty level, too heavy for human occupation—as was a good half of each wing. No partitions divided this level into rooms; it was just a vast circular space broken in the middle by the lift system. A few sturdy columns stabilized floor and ceiling.

According to the specs, the long continuous lift had been put in place during construction to facilitate the movement of equipment and materials. After completion the lifts should have been divided into three sections with a sealable bulkhead across each shaft. That last safety measure had been cut short. Something was terribly wrong here. Something that endangered all the inhabitants of the wing.

He gasped at the sight of the bridge of a small cargo ship penetrating the hull. Almost half the length of the cigar shaped vessel protruded through the bulkhead. Two bizarre creatures, all tentacles and heads, stared deadly out of the cockpit. A small woman in purple nightdress and bare feet pounded desperately at the bio-plastic windshield with the blunt end of a fire extinguisher.

Her seven caste marks arranged in a circle on her right cheek seemed to glow in the baleful light.

Her younger sister, in brown coveralls and with a single brown X caste mark, beat at the other side with some kind of wrench.

Monster, the huge, shaggy, black water dog, ran around them both, barking in rhythm with the obnoxious alarm.

As Jake watched, Sissy gasped in what little air was left and belted out one crystal-clear note born of angelic choirs. The sweetness overrode the klaxon and brought the alarm into her harmonic circle. The clear windshield clouded over with a spider web of cracks. A second note and it splintered inward.

A wave of water gushed outward, knocking both Sissy and Ashel off their feet.

A wail of pain and despair burst from the interior of the ship, louder than the alarm. It came from behind the watertight partition of the bridge. It stabbed into Jake's brain with psychic urgency.

✦   ✦   ✦

A wave of salty water rushed over Sissy's head. Instinctively she held her breath. For a brief heartbeat of time she wished she'd made the effort to learn to swim before leaving Harmony.

No time, no privacy then. And she would not subject herself to the embarrassment and humiliation of discarding *all* of her clothes in front of the Crystal Temple population for that luxury.

Her next heartbeat reminded her that Ashel could not swim either. She flailed about in a desperate effort to reach her sister. The salty water—warmer than the freezing air—stung her eyes. But she had to keep them open, her only chance of finding the child.

Pressure built in her chest. She desperately needed to gasp for air or cough out water. She didn't know which. Either would kill her.

Nothing must happen to Ashel or Marsh. She couldn't allow it. Not after losing the rest of their family in an assassin's massive explosion intended for her. Only she could get Ashel to safety.

Then out of nowhere, strong hands grabbed her shoulders. She fought the restraint. But he dragged her free of the lethal ocean of water.

"Jake," she breathed as her head popped above the water into the rapidly thinning air. Barely enough left to fill her lungs. The atmosphere had mostly bled out into space. "I knew you'd come."

He grunted something and dove down into the murky depths, even as they slopped and drained away.

"Sissy!" Ashel wailed the second she cleared the water. Monster held the little girl's collar in his mouth as gently as if he'd retrieved a fallen bird. She sounded weak, far off, though only a few yards separated them.

Jake surfaced right beside them. He pushed Monster's hindquarters toward the stairs.

"I'm here. I'm safe," Sissy gasped. Her heart sounded overloud in her head, beating too fast, too shallow without enough air to push it.

They had to get out of here soon.

The sharp, piercing mind scream of a trapped passenger inside the ship called again. Someone was stuck inside that small spacecraft, wailing in despair and agony. Sissy swallowed her distaste for even looking at the mangled alien pilots. Thinking only of getting to those that lived, she jumped and clasped the edge of the broken windshield.

She had to hang there too many long moments, gathering enough strength and air to continue.

Jake grabbed her around the waist and pulled her back to the deck. Only a few inches of water rolled against her ankles now. The movement in the pulsating and uncertain light and the lack of air sent her senses reeling. She had to cling to him to remain upright. She had to ignore the warmth and vigor of his hands on her chilling body.

"Let me go. I've got to help them."

"Not you. I'm here now, Sissy. I'll do it." He clutched her close against his chest.

His heart beat strong beneath her ear. Oh, to stay here. To linger with him, to allow him to protect her. As he always had.

Then he pushed her away.

A vast and icy barrier of three inches separated them.

"Go. Take Ashel to safety. Now. Your clothes are freezing on your bodies. You are too valuable to risk."

"But . . ."

"Now."

"No. You can't do it alone." She turned back to the damaged ship, seeking hand and footholds to climb. "Our strength of purpose will unite our power and compound it. Such is the work of miracles." Her voice echoed through the thinning air.

Did she really say that? She hadn't thought the words before speaking.

Hands on her waist interrupted her musing. Not Jake's. She didn't know this touch, this pinching grip.

Panic made her hands clutch the protrusion on the craft tighter.

"I will handle this. Take her to safety. Now." A stranger's voice. An alien accent she'd only heard once before, from the mouth of the station owner. A strange creature no taller than herself, with huge ears that could cover his entire face and larger spectacles with communications and monitors built into them.

Same accent, different voice. This one was higher in tone, almost female, and yet it *felt* male.

"Take her." The alien lifted her free as if she weighed nothing and passed her to Jake.

"You need help . . ."

"No, I don't. Believe me, I can handle this better than you. Now go. At once. Before you lose the ability to breathe. The water is draining out and freezing in the cracks. It will slow the loss of atmosphere. I hope I have time to break through the cockpit barrier to the air breather behind."

Jake threw Sissy over his shoulder, grabbed Ashel under his other arm and sloshed toward the stairs. Monster ran ahead, checking for more dangers.

Jake put Sissy down to maneuver up the narrow spiral. She glanced back at the damaged ship. A gasp of surprise, horror, and defilement escaped her throat. The alien being spread two extra arms and two extra legs from beneath the folds of his voluminous clothing. These had pincers instead of four-fingered hands. Then he scrambled up the side of the craft as if each of his eight appendages had sticky pads embedded on the ends.

"Jake, look." She couldn't take her eyes off the monster. And yet he'd been so kind and gentle—like her dog Monster. So, how could he invoke horror?

"I'll be damned. He does exist," Jake whispered.

"Who? Who is he?"

"A phantom. A ghost. A legend. Every station has one. But this one is different. The stories are too specific, too close to the observer."

Even as they watched, the being squeezed himself inside the broken windshield.

Jake pushed Ashel up toward a safe exit. Then he grabbed Sissy's hand to drag her behind him.

She looked back one last time just before clearing the deck of the next level.

The alien emerged from the broken ship, a long figure in white dangling from his two lower arms. A strange radiant glow from a cloud of nearly white hair, pale skin and a gleaming gown engulfed them both. Sissy couldn't see a definite edge to the injured passenger.

The thin air must be hindering her sight.

Then the alien jumped into the nearest stabilizing maintenance tube and disappeared.

✦ ✦ ✦ ✧ ✦ ✦ ✦

CHAPTER THREE

AM I IN HEAVEN, *soon to see my angel father? Or is my rescuer a demon whisking me off to hell?*

Pain fills my body. Confusion clouds my mind. There is no truth here. Only a continuation of my agony. My physical pain equals my spiritual emptiness of not knowing. I cannot succumb to the pain, I must keep searching for the one place where the rituals can be resanctified; where life can return to its origins.

✦ ✦ ✦

Mac settled the weight of the injured passenger easily into his secondary limbs. With the pincer at the end of his secondary leg he flipped a switch, cutting power to the tracks. He had to pause and close the hatch behind him. The sensitive pads on his feet located and fixed the lock without the aid of his eyes. A few of the photo- and motion-sensitive cells embedded in the walls blossomed into life.

He had no need of the lights. Even if he did not know every passage in the station by smell or by feel. He gathered enough starlight through other sensors to find his way.

He liked the way the humans called his station the First Contact Café better than the family name of Labyrinthe VII.

His half brother, Number Seven, had no right, talent, or enough intelligence to run the place.

With the hatch closed and the air safe for the being he carried, he moved forward, sedately, careful not to jostle fragile bones. The broken ones were in danger of penetrating lungs and liver.

Such an inefficient structure these bipeds had. An exoskeleton like his own protected the body much better.

His father's species—responsible for his unique bone structure, his

extra limbs, bulbous lower body, and his ability to survive vacuum—
would have let this delicate creature die. His mother's people would hold
her for ransom. He shouldn't have risked exposing himself to the humans
to rescue her.

But something about her yearning for truth called to Mac from her
soul to his. A being out of time and place. A being who belonged in no
world and yet offered so much to every world.

Just like him.

He paused a moment to catch his breath and gaze at the majesty of
space beyond the protective walls of the tunnel. His heart yearned to go
out there, explore, see more of life than just this station, a smaller version
of Labyrinthe Prime but built on the same design. As much as he loved
the station, considered it his own, he knew there had to be more to life
than his shadow existence, always hiding.

He'd like to visit some planets to see how different they smelled from
this station. He'd like to talk to other races. He'd like to find his father's
people. Would they accept him as one of their own? Or would they shun
him as his mother had because he was different, neither Labyrinthian
nor Arachnoid.

Slowly, he worked his way toward a place of safety. As he progressed,
he noted the places he'd deliberately left dark, making sure the blun-
dering maintenance 'bots hadn't fixed them. At the same time he found
places showing wear, in danger of breaking down—shoddy construction
finished in too much haste. They must be fixed before they endangered
the station.

His circuitous route took him through bulkheads, around living quarters, past kitchens and storage facilities, where he commandeered food
and medical supplies for himself and his charge. He couldn't take her
to the central MedBay. They'd shoot him full of drugs and dissect him
on the spot. As for the female? He couldn't trust any of his brother's
employees with her. Their greedy sloth reflected the station manager's
personality. This woman was unique and special. He could tell that at
first glance.

She was also desperate and illegal. No one else would take passage in
a cargo hold sealed off from the rest of the water breathers' ship. No one
else would trust the aging vessel held together with rubber bands and
chewing gum.

Keeping to tunnels with full hydrogen-nitrogen-oxygen atmospheres,
he approached the final obstacle in his journey: a wide expanse of deserted cargo bay. His brother had lowered the air, pressure, and heat here

to save money and power. Mac had emptied it. He had no need of them for an hour at a time. The lack of amenities kept snoopy security personnel from finding his nest on the opposite side. A purloined wall partition and safety hatch made his home look like the natural curved walls of the hull.

With three deep breaths, he filled the extra air sacks hidden beneath his jowls, and he wrapped his charge in both sets of extra limbs to keep her as warm as possible. At the last moment, he clamped his mouth over hers, dribbling his air into her.

Then he ran as rapidly as he could to the only safe haven in all seven of the Labyrinthe Stations.

✦   ✦   ✦

"How did this happen?" Ambassador Telvino demanded the moment Jake dropped from the maintenance tube to the deck in Sissy's wake.

Lord Lukan pressed hard on Telvino's heels with his own questions.

Like I'm responsible? Jake thought.

Before he could formulate a reply, a flurry of lavender flocked around Sissy.

She drew each of her six acolytes and her brother and sister into one massive hug. High-pitched chatter and wails filled the corridor.

"If you will excuse me, Ambassador, My Lord. Let me settle Laudae Sissy and her charges safely, then we will speak, privately. In the meantime, you might want to summon Mr. Labyrinthe, the owner of the station." He ducked away from the two men, arms extended to herd the Temple refugees into his quarters.

"Laudae Sissy, you need dry clothing right now," he ordered, deeply concerned about her barely disguised chattering teeth.

He needed some himself. Deep chills raked his body.

"Where can we find a blanket for her?" Mary asked.

"When did I become the leader of this motley crew?" he muttered to himself. A year ago he'd asked when he'd become the dad of this hodgepodge family.

"They look to you for leadership because you make a point of knowing more and staying calm when all around you scream in panic," Sissy whispered back. Her voice sounded strained, a little echoey.

"That a prophecy?" He grinned at her, not letting conversation slow him down in pushing her toward his quarters.

"No. I . . . I lost my connections to the Goddess Harmony before I left the planet." She hung her head sadly.

"You didn't have to come," he said quietly.

"Yes, I did." She looked up at him, jutting her chin stubbornly. "You know why."

The dying prophecy of her murdered acolyte Jilly said it all. *The Covenant is broken. It can only be restored out there, among the stars.*

He knew better than to argue with Sissy when she set her chin like that.

"Colonel Devlin," Telvino snapped.

Jake jerked to a halt. The ambassador had been his admiral in another lifetime. The habit of obedience died hard. Not that it had been very strong in Jake at any time, under any of his identities. Not until Sissy's gentle persuasion had taught him there was a place for rules and ritual and chains of command.

"Yes, sir?" Jake fought the need to salute.

"I think Laudae Sissy will be more comfortable in my quarters."

"Um . . . With all due respect, sir, I figured you'd want to take Lord Lukan and his family there." He continued onward.

"Then perhaps you should settle the Laudae in Admiral Marella's quarters," Telvino reprimanded without actually saying accusatory words. "Larger and more comfortable than yours."

"Pammy's off station, sir, and even I can't pick the locks on her doors." Jake flashed a grin. No one in the Confederated Star Systems got away with calling the spymaster by her first name, let alone an intimate and impudent sobriquet.

Except Jake.

Not that everyone knew Pamela Marella was spymaster for the CSS. But Telvino knew. And the ambassador knew that Jake had worked for Pammy during his time on Harmony.

Hastily he ushered the High Priestess and her girls into his cabin: larger than some but still crowded and . . . um . . . intimate when filled with a High Priestess, six female acolytes, two children, two dogs, and himself.

"My Laudae, you may sleep here." He pulled a top bunk down from the wall. "Suzie and Sharan, bottom bunk. Martha and Mary, see if you can scrounge some extra pillows and blankets for the rest of you. Supply closet in the cross corridor to the left."

"I will attend the meeting with Labyrinthe," Sissy pronounced.

"I suppose you will," Jake sighed. "I'd feel better with you safely locked in here. Even Pammy can't pick my locks."

"Jake," Sissy said on a giggle. "This was not an attempt on my life. You don't need to look for conspiracy in every accident."

"Yes, I do." He drew in a deep breath and coughed it out again. His lungs rebelled at working after so long in super-thin air.

She stared him down. Eventually he looked away. "Okay." He should know better than to try to out-stubborn his Sissy. "You come with me as soon as I get some dry clothes on. I've got some jeans and a sweatshirt you can wear; roll up the sleeves and cuffs. And a pair of socks until your feet warm up and you can go barefoot again." He yanked clothes for her and himself out of the closet and turned his back while she changed. He stripped out of the salt and ice encrusted uniform and changed, trusting the girls to look away.

This wasn't the first time he'd been forced into close quarters with Sissy and crew. Privacy became a thing of the mind. His spacious room that seemed too big for just himself suddenly felt warm and crowded and comfortably homey.

"You stay within arm's reach, Laudae Sissy, and you don't let anyone else in the room get close to you," he ordered. "If I say 'gun,' you drop to the deck, cover your head, and don't move until I say otherwise."

"Yes, Jake," she replied with false meekness.

Jake rolled his eyes. He knew beyond a shadow of a doubt that she'd forget his orders the moment they stepped outside the door.

"You don't have your veil," he reminded her. "Your people aren't used to seeing you without . . ."

"I don't have formal robes or shoes or a toothbrush either, at the moment. Neither does Lord Lukan. We will make do. Now go to sleep, girls, I have work to do."

Six girls ranging from ten to nearly fourteen in age bowed to her in unison. Then they all looked to each other in some silent, feminine communication.

"You will stay here," Jake ordered.

As one, their heads jerked toward him.

"Do you understand me?"

"Yes, Colonel Jake."

Satisfied with their compliance, he checked the entire lobby before allowing Sissy to follow him. The crowds had thinned. Mostly blue-clad Nobles wandered aimlessly from group to group, wringing their hands, looking over their shoulders nervously. Jake snagged a female Worker just as she settled to the deck, her back against the wall.

"Can you get them organized?" he asked. He pointed out supply closets. "There are unoccupied quarters in the light-grav sections."

"Yes, sir." The anonymous woman bowed and insinuated herself beneath the attention of Lady Jancee. From the way the Noble woman rubbed her swollen belly, he wondered if tonight's alarms would send her into premature labor.

Great. They needed to get the lifts and trams operating quick to open a path to MedBay.

Telvino and Lukan awaited him at the lift. They'd gotten it working again at least.

Lukan returned his key. But he refused to budge from his solid stance in front of the moving platforms until Jake had stepped safely onto one.

Damn it! They should be the ones giving orders. High-ranking ambassadors earned their authority. Couldn't they do anything besides yell at each other in meetings?

✦ ✦ ✦ ◇ ✦ ✦ ✦

CHAPTER FOUR

❝ I MUST LEAVE YOU NOW, my little bird. You will be safe here," Mac whispered to his charge.

A delicate hand shot forth from her white draperies and grabbed his shirtfront with amazing strength. "How can I be safe anywhere? I am lost between worlds, beyond the sight and protection of the Gods," she said, eyes still closed. The rest of her body remained still, as if frozen by the vacuum. "We have lost the sacred ritual places. We have lost everything."

"No one will hurt you while I protect you." Mac shook his head in wonderment at her rambling and meaningless sentences. "You can find your gods later," Mac reassured her. "There is food and water within reach. Blankets too if you need them. I will not be long."

He'd stolen air from a dozen different conduits for his nest, channeling in the composition he needed at the time. As he spoke, he increased the oxygen and the heat to make her more comfortable.

He hoped the female truly was a natural NHO breather. She looked as much human as anything, but there was something different about her. That difference could mean she came from a world with an exotic atmosphere.

"Go with the angels," she said, stronger than before.

"First time anyone has bothered to send me off with a blessing. Usually it's a boot to the rear. If they can catch me." His own mother had spaced him at birth, not knowing that exposure to radiation and vacuum was the natural way of his father's people.

Mother had wanted to kill him for the crime of not looking exactly like her. Instead, she had made him stronger and forced his Arachnoid DNA to become dominant.

Keeping his extra limbs hidden within his blousy shirt and trousers, he drew aside the curtain covering the air lock to the cargo bay.

Once clear of his home, with the hatch firmly closed behind him, he released his limbs and scuttled rapidly up the wall to his favorite listening post. Inside one of the connecting tunnels he sat quietly, knowing that the other end opened just outside the door to his half brother's penthouse wing. An unplanned chance of acoustics made conversations in his brother's home perfectly audible at this one position in the tubes.

Labyrinthe VII, the name his brother took upon promotion to manager of the seventh station, occupied an entire wing. His apartment and space for his personal servants took up all the mid- and light-gravity levels at the "top" of the station. The heavy-gravity levels contained storage for special supplies reserved for Number Seven.

"You were only Number Seven son. I was Number Three." Mac addressed his brother bitterly, though he knew his words would not be heard, or acknowledged if they did filter through the layers of transparent carbon fiber and bulkhead. "You got the name of our race as your own and an honored position. I got exile and ignominy. All because you look exactly like our mother, with your only augmentation from your father a heavier bone structure to withstand variable gravity. You got the mind and manners of a Glug. I have the cunning and intelligence of our mother."

Every one of Mother's twenty-six children, by twenty-six different fathers of twenty-six different races, looked exactly like her, indistinguishable from each other to clients, friends, and enemies alike. Most could not differentiate gender among them.

Except for Mac. He'd committed the unforgivable sin of allowing his father's Arachnoid features to dominate. The DNA had become firmly fixed during his first journey into vacuum. If his mother had bothered asking for information and kept him close, nursing him in atmosphere, the Arachnoid features would have atrophied and eventually dropped off.

She hadn't appreciated the irony of her actions.

So few Labyrinthes remained, their genes corrupted by pollution, inbreeding, and radiation, that they could no longer breed among themselves and had to combine their DNA with other races.

A buzz rippling along the bulkhead alerted Mac to his intended task. He spread his ears wide to collect every nuance of sound. The voices continued softly, almost whispering in stilted and archaic Earther.

"Poverty and radiation," he cursed in his mother's language. The one trait he wished he had inherited from the legendary A'bner Labyrinthe was her ears. She'd used them almost as extra appendages: to fan herself, to fold over her face to hide her emotions, to drape backward in elegance and poise, to secrete small items within their ripples, to listen closely to the tiniest fragment of voices over long distances. Mac could bring his ears forward only far enough to touch his flat nasal slits. Spread wide they barely reached as far as his shoulders.

"Concentrate," he admonished himself. Earther had been one of his favorite and best-learned tongues. Illogical and redundant compared to most languages, Earther could be manipulated and twisted, made to serve several purposes at once without lying. Other races only dreamed of such flexibility.

But this slow and drawled version spoken on Harmony did more than that. It cloaked insult in politeness and made threats look like compliments.

"Laudae, please sit here, in the place of honor," Labyrinthe Seven said. His voice cut through the chaotic sludge of noise. "Now, what seems to be the problem?"

"Problem!" Ambassador Telvino shouted.

Mac could almost see the broad-chested man's high color deepen and his eyes narrow. If he wasn't careful, he might send his heart into full arrest.

"Problem?" Ambassador Lukan snarled. That tall and elegant man could flay skin from Glugs with his sarcasm. "There's an outlaw cargo vessel crashed into the heavily restricted and isolated diplomatic wing. We were forced to evacuate."

He didn't add that his people had been contaminated by contact with "others." He didn't have to. His tone said it all.

"The tunnel hatch was locked on the inside as well as outside at the opposite end," Telvino continued.

"The maintenance 'bots did not respond," Colonel Devlin added. Ah, the good Military man who bridged both worlds with calm logic and daring compromises. "The specs I was given on the station suggest that the lifts are supposed to travel only one third the length of a wing, so that airtight bulkheads can close above and/or below them in case of hull breach. You did not replace the single construction lift with the three safety lifts. The entire wing was compromised because of your negligence."

"If not for the quick thinking of Colonel Jake, my people would all have died," Laudae Sissy completed the thought in a voice so soft that Mac had to strain to hear her.

From the silence on the other end, he suspected the others did too. He quirked a smile. Sometimes a quiet whisper had more impact than a shout. He could learn much from her.

If she'd only look directly at him. Her gaze had slid away from him in revulsion.

"We had to rely on your phantom to save the survivor of the crash," Jake said.

"Phantom? What phantom? We have no unauthorized personnel aboard Labyrinthe Station," Number Seven insisted. "If such a phantom exists, I will hunt him down and personally space him."

✦ ✦ ✦

Sissy longed for the concealment of her formal robes and headdress with its beaded veil. So much easier to pretend to authority with them. As if the trappings made her important, rather than her mutant caste marks and her former gift of prophecy.

She hadn't had a vision from Harmony since the explosion killed her family and damaged her hearing, long before she had left her home world to survive or fracture without her.

We can only mend the broken Covenant with Harmony out there among the stars, Jilly had said with her dying breath.

Sissy's residual tinnitus from the explosion continued to clang inside her head, sometimes loud and demanding all of her attention, sometimes soft, like the whisper of the Goddess. Always the noise inside her warred with the vibrations and hums of the power plants on the stations.

No Harmony within or without.

"The question, Mr. Labyrinthe, is not about the being who helped us. Rather it should be how did this tragedy happen, and what can we do to prevent a recurrence," she said.

Jake came to stand behind her thronelike chair. The narrow seat fit her legs perfectly and allowed her feet to rest flat on the floor. She lusted after it. All the standard chairs designed for humans were too high and deep for her frame.

She breathed easier knowing Jake would supply her with vocabulary and confidence when her limited education failed her.

If only his clothes fit her better, she'd have more confidence in her words.

But then, her bedraggled refugee trappings emphasized her plight. Now that she'd warmed up, she slipped his socks off and stuffed them in the pocket of her borrowed trousers.

"Let me talk to my people in Control." Labyrinthe Seven bowed deeply to her, nodded to the others, then turned his back. He mumbled as he touched various sections of the spectacles that covered half his face and extended almost as wide as his ears.

Sissy relaxed a little, now that she didn't have to look directly at this alien. At home, he'd have been killed at the moment of birth. A fate she had almost shared because of her abnormal caste marks. No one, absolutely no one, was allowed to have more than one, and it had to be positioned on the left cheek. She had all seven arranged in a tight circle on her right cheek.

Now she knew that the marks had been genetically engineered by the first *human* settlers of Harmony. They'd used the caste marks to set up a totally artificial society and culture—to enslave. She also knew that the genetic manipulation had begun to break down after seven hundred years. More and more people were born every year with variations and multiplications of the marks.

Just as the order and tranquility of Harmony had begun to break down. She'd bring it down faster if she dared.

But she couldn't leave the people she loved open to civil war and vulnerable to outside invasion when the balance of power in the galaxy teetered on the fine edge of a Badger Metal sword.

She now forced herself to accept and champion others when her cultural distaste wanted to shun them.

Lord Lukan, more liberal than his twin brother, Bevan, who now ruled the High Council, still shied away from anyone not born and raised on Harmony. He barely accepted Jake because the Military man had kept his caste mark from his months undercover on Harmony.

Even now, Lukan frowned at Jake's proximity to Sissy.

Ambassador Telvino paced furiously, hands clenched behind his back, while they waited for Labyrinthe to consult with his Control.

"Excuse me, I must tend to this myself." Labyrinthe turned and bowed deeply. "Please accept my hospitality in my absence. Servants will tend to your needs momentarily." He backed toward the door, ears drooping forward to hide his facial expressions.

"I'll accompany you," Jake said, moving determinedly to his side.

"That is not necessary."

"I think it is." Jake's hand hovered near his hip where he was accustomed to wearing a sword or a blaster. He wore no obvious weapons tonight.

Sissy had no doubt he had knives and such hidden on his person. He always did.

"I'll come too." Sissy bounced to her feet. Her toes caressed the thick carpeting in the luxurious apartment. Vibrations from the power plant trickled up her body to jangle with her unconscious awareness of the separate facility in the Harmony wings of the station. A headache threatened to tie her neck in knots.

On Harmony she had only the mother planet to attune her mind and body to.

Jake gave her a swift, assessing glance and frowned. "You should be in bed, My Laudae."

"We all should. But something is out of control here, and I mean to be with you when you discover the source. I may need to perform a ritual to bring it all back into balance."

"You don't have any crystals or incense, My Laudae," Jake reminded her.

"I have my voice. If I can sing a planetary quake to silence, then surely I can sing a space station into balance."

Lukan nodded in approval of the High Priestess.

"Superstitious nonsense." Telvino shook his head and paced more rapidly, his steps bringing him close to their host and the exit.

Jake frowned.

Sissy couldn't tell if the CSS ambassador displeased him with his belief, or if she brought on the frown because of her insistence on accompanying him. His frowns always made her want to soothe him with a gentle touch and compliance.

Tonight she had to stand firm. Her place was with these men, rooting out the source of the problem.

Someone should have noted the passage and trajectory of the alien ship. Someone should have sounded the alarm and started evacuation before the crash.

She felt chilled to her heels. "You may handle this your way, Colonel Jake. I will handle it mine." She marched in front of him and waved her hand before the door sensor. It shooshed open on silent sliders. "Please lead the way, Mr. Labyrinthe."

CHAPTER FIVE

JAKE JUMPED ON THE LIFT FIRST. He needed to make certain Labby didn't make a break for it once they reached the top and the trams. The station manager could easily use the screens in his spectacles and the communications embedded in his teeth to alert Control to cover up any mistakes.

Something was definitely rotten at the First Contact Café.

An empty tram car waited for them at the top of the lift. Jake stepped off carefully, to make sure he didn't drift too far from the others in zero G. Labby came up, one platform behind him. Jake took up a position beside him as they filed into the waiting tram cubicle, using the handrails to orient themselves.

Sissy paused a moment at the doorway—one entire side of the tram. She touched two fingers to her lips, then placed them atop one of the markings at the side.

Jake raised his eyebrows at her. She shrugged and moved inside. The doors slid closed behind her.

Out of his peripheral vision Jake saw Labyrinthe begin walking up the wall in preparation for heading "down" in the tram to Control at the opposite end of the station. Something seemed out of alignment. Maybe it was a shift in lighting. Maybe his brain was still starved for oxygen.

Jake grabbed the huge spectacles off Labby's face.

"I beg your pardon!" Labyrinthe exclaimed. He reached to take the tool back.

Jake held it behind his back and walked up the opposite wall, as comfortable in this weightless environment as Labby. "We want this to be a surprise visit," he said. "A surprise for the one who let an illegal ship, piloted by aliens not on the approved list of visitors, slip past his sensors. Not a surprise for us facing armed troops at the entrance."

"I do not employ armed troops." Labyrinthe stretched to his full length indignantly. His head barely reached Jake's shoulder.

Jake merely raised his eyebrows at him.

"You have severed all comms by disconnecting me from those spectacles." A touch of panic edged into Labby's voice.

"Have we now? No backup? Now that's unusual. Maybe negligent. What would happen if you tripped and the glasses broke? Would the entire station shut down?" Jake inspected the instrument, hoping he could intuit its workings.

Labby quivered in agitation, but he remained silent.

Telvino grumphed and growled. "Good work, Jake."

"What about the communications in his teeth?" Lord Lukan asked.

Jake peered through the spectacles a moment. "The sensors in his teeth are linked to the earpiece here." He pointed to the elongated knob at the end. "Can't use comms unless he's wearing the spectacles."

"May I see?" Sissy asked. She held out her hand politely. She too had taken a post in the proper alignment for the end of the trip along the central hub.

Jake handed them to her. She'd respect them and not let him, or Telvino, stomp on them in the next fit of anger.

She placed them on her nose and giggled. "Too many things to focus on at once. It's like looking through . . . through, you know, Jake, the child's toy that looks at changing patterns of fractured glass."

"Kaleidoscope," he supplied the word.

"Yes, kaleidoscope." She chewed her lip a moment, a habitual gesture when she memorized a word. "In time I could figure it out." The oversized spectacles spun off her head as she twisted about trying to peer into every section of the lenses.

Labyrinthe grabbed for them.

Jake beat him to it, by the sheer length of his arms. "Sorry, Labby. Until we get this all figured out, I'll keep custody of these."

"Ambassador Telvino," Labyrinthe stiffened indignantly. "Your man is out of line. You are in violation of your contract with Labyrinthe Space Stations, Incorporated. I can demand all CSS personnel depart within twenty-four hours if you do not curb him and return essential property."

"But your contract with the Harmonite Empire demands that this station remain clear of all but a few humanoid aliens." Lord Lukan looked at his fingernails. "First off, you are in violation of our contract in allowing aliens to breach the hull. Second, while we remain, you cannot open quarters and docks to others. You will lose over half your income when Ambassador Telvino departs with his people."

"And if you are found negligent in your operations of this station, I have the authority to confiscate the entire station in the name of the CSS," Telvino reminded them, in a deceptively mild tone.

"But . . . but . . ."

"Mr. Labyrinthe, would you care to have me bring my crystals and incense to Control to cleanse it of all negative thoughts and any imbalance of energies that might affect the behavior of your people?" Sissy asked mildly. She floated around them all, like some street punk fairy in her borrowed clothes.

How had she become so proficient in this alien environment in just a few months?

Then Jake remembered frequent outings and field trips with her back on Harmony. Laudae Sissy never was one to sit still and read a book when she could learn just as much by observing the world. He had few doubts that Sissy and her girls had explored every inch of the station.

Jake shook his head in amazement. Just when he thought Sissy could no longer surprise him, she did. Her capacity for learning proved how unjust and inadequate the caste system on Harmony had become.

But Harmony had to remain . . . Harmony . . . a while longer. When the CSS had the formula for Badger Metal, he'd gladly help dismantle the entire caste system and government. Personally. With his bare hands. For what they had done to Sissy and her family.

They completed the swift ride to the opposite end of the station in silence. Acceleration mimicked gravity, and they all kept their feet firmly in place on the new floor.

Weight and orientation ceased as the tram came to an abrupt halt.

The door opened slowly.

Jake held Labyrinthe back with an extended arm while Sissy led the two ambassadors into the micro-G lobby. Once more she kissed her fingertips and placed the kiss over a marking beside the door. Jake peered closely at a newly painted set of curved lines: the glyph of Harmony they'd found repeated in line drawings around the funeral caves on Harmony.

As he exited the tram last, Jake gave his own ritual kiss to the Goddess in thanks for a safe trip. It couldn't hurt to keep on Her good side.

Jake moved ahead with a bounce and glide through the minimal gravity and onto the first platform of the lift headed down to the Control levels. Sissy and Lukan herded Labby onto the next one, leaving Telvino to bring up the rear.

As they passed each level, a holo of the gravity designation and level number flashed on the moving platform. At Control central, the middle of the light-G levels, Jake jumped off and turned a full circle, hand hovering close to his hip and his hidden miniblaster.

Computers, observation screens and real-time windows spread out around him, filling the level to the bulkhead. All personnel had deserted their posts.

✦   ✦   ✦

Adrial roused from her fitful slumber. Too warm outside. Too cold inside herself. The air felt heavy and too full of moisture. She kept her breathing shallow.

Out of long habit she remained immobile, listening, absorbing the knowledge about her surroundings through her other senses. A faint citrus taste in the air caressed her nose and tongue. That meant she was aboard a space station or ship. She reclined on piles of soft and lumpy pillows rather than a mattress. Scratchy blankets over her without sheets. Not a medical facility. The smell of testosterone-laden sweat. A man's quarters.

Instantly she shifted her attention to her own body. No aches or stickiness in the wrong places. She hadn't been violated this time. The sacred breeding rituals had not been profaned. This last survey did reveal sharp pains along her ribs. Deep pain. Bone deep. Duller aches showed her where bruises formed on her hips and back.

Memory crashed through her mind.

Blaster fire whined above her head. She ducked and dodged into a narrow opening among the refuse of a back alley. Long-legged men in bright blue Law uniforms with equally blue feathers growing in a tall crest atop their heads paced after her. They moved with confidence and pride. They never failed to capture their prey.

One of the Law raised his arms high. Blue and white striped feathers decorated the folds of skin opening from the concealing flaps beneath those long, long arms. He ran six steps and lifted into the air. His head swiveled back and forth, surveying the hidden places in the alley.

Adrial pressed herself deeper into the shadows. Her white prisoner's gown gleamed in the faint starlight.

Why did these Messengers of the Gods punish her so? She had been spared by the avenging Gods and had taken their gift of life into exile. For fifteen years she had studied and prayed and searched for the spiritual center of the universe. She had done everything she could think of to find a true path back to the Gods, to make up for her lack of blood purity.

Still the Law sought her out and tested her faith time and again. What more did she need to do before the Gods finally accepted her as one of their children?

The flying Law's eyes riveted toward her. He chirped once. His partner chirped back in acknowledgment and aimed his blaster directly at Adrial's heart.

Certain she must die in the next heartbeat, she crouched in on herself, making her body as small as she could. At the same time she pressed even farther backward.

The wall behind her gave way. She tumbled into darkness.

The whining blast of energy struck the metal door as it closed behind her.

Adrial dug her palms into her face, trying desperately to erase that memory. At the same time she hoped to dig out what had happened afterward.

This was no Maril prison cell on a rim world. The Messengers of the Gods granted few comforts like pillows and blankets. The subtle vibrations of a power plant felt wrong for a Maril ship.

Where am I? What happened to me?

✦ ✦ ✦

Jake didn't wait for questions. Leave those for the ambassadors, the professional talkers. He dove into the chair at the center of Control. The dormant screens awoke at his touch. No security, no password required.

Dumb! Downright stupid as well as negligent.

He took a moment to familiarize himself with the screens. Different glyphs, but touchpads and keys seemed pretty standard. Touch here, slide a finger there.

Ah, he had communications, he had short-range sensors.

He had flashing red lights all over the damn place warning of the crash and hull breach.

Then he found an icon that looked like a miniature maintenance bot. He touched it. Nothing happened. He pressed harder. Still nothing.

Labyrinthe appeared beside him. His teeth chattered in agitation. A stream of harsh syllables erupted from his throat.

The screen to Jake's left brought up a visual of the diplomatic wing with sensor readings in a long column to the side. He stared in dismay at the icy mess of the crumpled craft and dead squid pilots draped across the nose. The ice seemed to have stopped the air and pressure leakage.

"I . . . I . . . I know nothing of how this tragedy occurred," Labyrinthe stammered.

Something on the communications screen bothered Jake. He touched a message glyph that flashed with urgency. The blankness dissolved. A page of a standard memo form blossomed before him. He read aloud the same paragraph in three different languages. "Due to budgetary concerns, Control staff is cut entirely during the nontraffic hours of 2300 hours to 0500 hours. Signed Labyrinthe VII."

Labby's eyes opened wide in horror.

"Not even one half-trained watcher for emergencies?" Jake asked.

"I did not send that message," Labby insisted.

"Got your signature."

"Anyone . . ."

"Not just anyone can send along that restricted path." Jake traced the memo back to the terminal of origin. It could only have come from the penthouse.

"I cut staff to minimum to save money. Your rents barely cover operating expenses, and your restrictions mean I cannot open most of the station. Seven wings out of thirty. You only occupy seven wings." Labby stood firm. "I did not authorize that message."

"Maintenance 'bots are turned off. Not just powered down." Telvino said settling into a post adjacent to Jake. "Another cost-saving measure?"

Jake found a routine for awakening the 'bots. Who knew how long it would take to get them working again.

"Whether you sent that message or not, you are responsible for the operation of this entire station. You have endangered our delegation and the negotiations between Harmony and the CSS." Lord Lukan sounded appalled.

"You've left the station vulnerable to Maril attacks. My sources say they have fighter squadrons prowling this sector looking for just such an opening," Jake snarled. Damn, he wished he had a fighter squadron attached to this station. With his own ship to lead them.

"Mr. Labyrinthe, I hereby exercise my diplomatic authority with the CSS—within whose space you operate—to confiscate this station." Telvino said. He stood at attention, every inch the admiral he used to be. "Colonel Devlin, take this person into custody. Do you have enough trustworthy people to operate this place for us?"

"Hell, no."

CHAPTER SIX

"**G**UILLIAM!" LAUD GREGOR, HIGH PRIEST of all Harmony and its six colonies, shouted for his assistant.

The senior acolyte had quarters right next to Gregor's. He should be within easy hailing distance. Guilliam was required to be within hailing distance. He'd been no more than a few steps away for fifteen years, ever since Gregor was elevated to High Priest.

His life had been structured and his assistant close by to aid him for fifteen years.

But then Gregor had made the huge mistake of elevating Sissy to become his High Priestess. Change had followed in her footsteps from her first utterance of prophecy. Change equaled chaos, which led to Discord.

"Guilliam, where in the seven hells are you?" Gregor yelled into the comm unit. He'd never had to use it to summon Guilliam before.

"May I be of assistance, My Laud?" a small voice came from the doorway between Gregor's bedroom and private sitting room. The young man's words cracked in the middle and rose an octave.

"Caleb? Why are you on duty and not Guilliam?"

"Mr. Guilliam is needed elsewhere, My Laud. How may I help you?" The youngest of Gregor's seven acolytes stepped cautiously across the threshold.

Mumbling and grumbling, Gregor pointed to his half-empty traveling trunk. "Pack that."

"Yes, My Laud." The boy scuttled toward the closet and lifted down three green shirts, still on their hangers. "How many days will you be away, My Laud?"

Gregor calculated the journey, a day to the jump point. Discord only knew how long the trip through hyperspace would be. Time ran differently there than on conventional clocks. Then another day to the space station. He hoped to conclude his business there in a few hours and return. A week at most.

But he could not count on Laudae Sissy's cooperation.

"Three weeks, Caleb. I'll need full formal regalia as well." The delicacy of his negotiations required that he maintain the aura of power and mystery inherent to his office. "And when you have finished, find Mr. Guilliam and make certain he is ready to depart."

"You travel with only one acolyte, My Laud?" Caleb's eyes grew wide with horror.

"You are correct, Caleb. I will need another assistant on the journey. Prepare yourself as well." Gregor turned to sorting books and papers he needed, including a full and accurate copy of the original covenant with the Goddess, as recorded on the stone tablets beneath the High Altar in the forecourt of the Crystal Temple.

"You will break the symmetry of seven, My Laud?"

Did he dare violate the oldest tradition of the Covenant?

"If I travel with a full seven acolytes, then Mr. Guilliam will refuse to accompany us unless his *wife* . . ." Gregor shuddered at the word. Temple caste had no business committing themselves to one partner. "I cannot afford to wait for Laudae Penelope and her six acolytes to prepare for a journey as well. Just the three of us will go. The shuttle launches in two hours."

"Y . . . yes, My Laud." Caleb bit his lip and shook his head as he added more clothes to the trunk. "If I might say, My Laud . . ."

"No, you may not. I am still High Priest here, and I decide these things." About time he took back control of Temple and Government.

Sissy might have run away from Harmony, but her influence lingered. Change and chaos ate away at the structure and peace of their world every day.

The Media considered themselves a separate caste now. The poor no longer existed, absorbed into the Workers. Every Holy Day service priests and priestesses read bits of the original Covenant to their congregations. And now Laudae Penelope integrated—tainted!—Worker and Professional children in the school system.

Add to that the hideous violation of tradition of clergy *marrying*, and Gregor wondered if life on Harmony would ever be harmonious again.

When Gregor returned from this trip, with his High Priestess in tow, life would return to normal and be under his control once more. All attempts to form an alliance between Harmony and the Confederated Star Systems would come to an abrupt halt.

And false reports of Maril incursions into Harmony space would cease to alarm the government and the people. The bird aliens didn't dare invade. The Goddess Harmony would see to that.

Will I?

"Who said that?"

No answer.

✦   ✦   ✦

"At last," Mac chortled. He watched the action playing out in Control from his own terminal hidden in yet another lair. This one occupied an empty heavy-grav cabin at the far end of the same wing Control occupied.

In the levels between him and Control the technicians and maintenance trolls cowered in their beds, afraid of unemployment in Number Seven's next round of cost-cutting measures.

Now that his brother had been deposed, Mac could scale back his interference, wait and assess how well the humans ran *his* station.

This was only the first step in his campaign to take over. He needed the humans to hand him the keys to the place of their own free will. A *coup d'etat* would only raise hostility, make them leave, and cut down profits.

Undoubtedly, most of the workers would flee on the next ship. Their contracts with Labyrinthe Corporation guaranteed them employment on other stations if this one should fail. In the eyes of every Labyrinthian, with the removal of Number Seven from power, this station had failed.

Let them go. He sent a message to the nearest Labyrinthian transport that they would take on passengers when they finished off-loading their cargo here.

Mac watched Colonel Devlin's movements closely as the military man tried to awaken the maintenance 'bots. Mac embedded a code into the signal that would rouse them and set them to working again, but slowly. Then he tacked on a call that would break through his firewall around the comm unit inside the maintenance workers' quarters. They must return to work now.

His audio sensors heard them grunt and groan as they dragged themselves out of deep sleep, cursing the interruption.

"We can't trust Labyrinthe's employees," Ambassador Telvino said, back in Control. He'd taken up a post on an auxiliary terminal.

Mac saw that the former admiral had begun prepping a vacant wing for the Harmony delegation. He allowed that action to proceed.

"No, you can't trust them," Mac agreed, though the humans would not hear his words. "They are lazy and loyal only to the highest bidder." He sent a memo to the workers' terminal offering higher paying employment elsewhere.

He had no idea if Labyrinthe II had places for them or not. He just needed them to desert the station.

"We have to trust them to get the repairs done," Colonel Jake said.

"Leave it damaged for now," Lord Lukan said. He peered over Telvino's shoulder. "Each wing can be independently powered and air-locked so it won't damage other, viable spaces. Send in Military Jake's people and my own Spacers in EVA suits to gather our personal belongings. We'll just move to this other wing."

"Good idea," Telvino laughed. "We'll have to buy the station from the Labyrinthe Corporation eventually. The damage should reduce the price, on top of the proven negligence. You keeping records of all the problems, Jake."

"Yes, sir." The colonel mumbled something else as he worked frantically at the screens. Mac heard the curses even if Jake's superiors did not.

"Lord Lukan, Ambassador Telvino, we can't just leave the pilots in the damaged wing. What are those creatures anyway?" Laudae Sissy butted in.

"They look like squids," Colonel Jake said.

The High Priestess nodded as she absorbed that information. "If the Squid people were smart enough to fly a spaceship, they were sentient. They deserve a respectful funeral," Laudae Sissy insisted.

None of the men in Control acknowledged her.

She stamped her foot. "If you will do nothing, I will send my own people in to retrieve the bodies."

"Not yet, My Laudae," Colonel Devlin said quietly. "Give us a few more hours to assess the situation. Please."

She crossed her arms and frowned. But she continued to watch over the colonel's shoulder, pointing out things he missed on the terminal.

"I must protest the confiscation of *my* station!" Number Seven dared raise his voice.

"Tsk, tsk, Mother would not approve," Mac laughed. "Rule Number 57 of Mother's etiquette book: 57A: No need to raise one's voice when greeting another species. 57B: No untoward noise while moving. That goes for voices raised in anger. Corollary Rule 43: Never show negative emotions in public." His younger brother was proving himself most unworthy of the name Labyrinthe. If only Mother had lived long enough to see this.

"How I run this station is between me and my siblings of the Labyrinthe Corporation. You have no right to just take over," Number Seven said, assuming a polite poise and demeanor. He must have remembered the etiquette book.

"We do have the right when your actions endanger the lives of all those who lease space on your station," Jake reminded him quietly. He must have read a different book.

"Just make a list of the changes you wish made. I will run them past the Corporation," Number Seven said. He looked oddly vulnerable without his spectacles.

"Can someone shut that whining annoyance up?" Telvino snarled. He pushed Number Seven away from the terminals.

"Done, and done." Jake punched one screen icon in triumph. A new icon he'd just installed while Mac had mused about etiquette. "My squadron is on their way here now. Armed and carrying restraints. What's the closest thing to a brig we've got here?"

"We have detention cells aboard the *Victory*," Telvino offered.

"Do we really want an alien aboard your flagship, Ambassador?" Jake kept his hands busy on the terminal.

Mac had trouble keeping up with all of his work, restoring the station to full operations. Where he could. Mac had a lot of overrides in place that needed to be reversed manually. Later. He'd release them one by one as he saw fit, not when Colonel Jake wanted them.

"Perhaps Mr. Labyrinthe can be confined to his apartment with an armed guard?" Laudae Sissy offered. "He is merely a deposed owner rather than a criminal."

"Criminal needs to be decided later," Lukan growled. "If we were on Harmony, I'd have had his head an hour ago."

"We may need information from him later," Jake mused. "No sense totally alienating him. Might as well let him stay comfortable. House arrest with two armed guards at all times."

"Disable all comm equipment in the apartment," Telvino added. "The guards all have portables. Control contacts them independently. Nothing through the central system."

"You can't do this to me." Number Seven looked agitated. His ears flapped over his face and back again. At the same time he twisted his hands and looked about rapidly. He kept bringing up his left hand to touch the spectacles he no longer wore. Lost. He appeared lost.

"I can't think of a more deserving person," Mac added.

Seven armed men in the ugly gray-green uniform of the CSS stepped off the lift platforms in three groups. Ungently they strapped electronic restraints around Number Seven's wrists and dragged him away. His screams of protest and fear echoed along the lift shaft. Only when the tram doors closed on them did silence return to Control.

"I need my crystals before anything else. I have to cleanse and rebalance the entire station," Laudae Sissy insisted. "If they haven't been damaged by exposure." She hung her head sadly, lips moving in some silent prayer.

A gentle hymn followed the prayer. Reverence, awe, and gratitude filled Mac for several long moments.

Mac prepared to retrieve the crystals, incense, formal robes, and elaborate headdress with beaded veil for her. He'd place them outside Colonel Jake's quarters once the traffic on that level quieted.

Forcibly he banished the sense of peace Laudae Sissy's music brought to him. He had no time for mystic nonsense. He had a station to acquire.

"On the list of things to do, My Laudae," Jake grumbled. "But that list is getting mighty long."

"Um, Jake," Laudae Sissy said hesitantly. "The survivor of the crash?"

"What survivor?" Telvino demanded. He searched Jake's visual of the damaged area. "How could anything survive *that*?"

"If anyone survived the initial crash, they are dead now," Lukan said. "Readings indicate minimal life support on the entire wing."

"But we saw one of Labyrinthe's people carry off a survivor. An air breather apparently, who was locked behind the water-filled cockpit. Someone dressed all in white. She looked human," Laudae Sissy insisted.

"She?" Jake asked.

"The screams felt female. In my head. I heard the energy of a female scream before the crash woke me."

Mac drummed his fingers on his terminal. He couldn't allow them to find his fragile little bird. Those distinctive white draperies could only come from a Maril prison. Special receptors keyed to Maril sensors were woven into the synthetic cloth. Even a Chameleonoid could not hide from the Maril wearing those clothes.

But she needed medical help beyond his abilities. How could he protect her and heal her at the same time?

"Heat sensors are registering an anomaly inside a bulkhead in cargo bay seventeen D," Jake said. "Flooding air, heat, and pressure in that bay now. Lord Lukan, you have trauma-trained medical Professionals in your Spacer caste. Will you please authorize them to suit up and do an emergency evac? Your Military should go with them in case they meet . . . anything unusual."

Mac abandoned his terminal without bothering to close it down. He had to move his little bird now, before the humans found her and handed her back to the Marils. Or worse, killed her outright. The Harmony Military were notoriously ruthless when dealing with aliens—not recognizing any creature without a caste mark as deserving of life.

No one. Absolutely no one had ever escaped a Maril prison alive before. His little bird deserved special protection and attention for that feat. Now that the avians were absorbing rather than annihilating the rim worlds, they'd pay dearly to retrieve the escapee. They might even agree to enter into negotiations with the humans for possession of her.

Mac wasn't ready to let that happen. Not until he had full control of the station and everyone in it.

◆ ◆ ◆ ◇ ◆ ◆ ◆

CHAPTER SEVEN

THE HOURS TRUDGED FORWARD. Sissy found jobs for herself and everyone else who didn't have a place to sleep. Anything to keep them busy—to keep them from thinking about how near death they'd all come.

"My Laudae, forgive me for intruding," a small, meek voice whispered from behind her.

Sissy clamped down on her annoyance at the interruption to her tally of people evacuated from the residential wing. "What do you need?"

She slipped the stylus into the handheld computer's slot and turned her full attention on the petitioner.

"My Laudae, this man says he cannot find his brother's family." A robust woman with a lauded Worker caste mark pointed to a man standing behind her, head hanging, feet shuffling. His brown X caste mark looked naked without a purple circle or blue diamond outlining it. He could not approach the High Priestess with his concern. The lauded Worker must speak for him.

Sissy cursed inwardly at the barriers within the caste system that prevented basic communication.

"What was your brother's quarters number?" Sissy asked the Worker directly.

He whispered something to the woman, still afraid to speak directly to a Temple. He must be employed in laundry or dishwashing, or some other vital job that required no out-of-caste contact.

"Sixteen-thirty-three D MG," the woman replied.

Sissy lifted the comm unit Jake had given her to her face. "Temple One to search crews," she said distinctly, still uncomfortable with remote communications and their arcane protocol. She wished she could be among the specialized crews working their way through the damaged wing, know personally what transpired.

"Search One here," a disembodied and distorted voice came back through the unit. The mechanics of the EVA suits altered timber and accent. She had no idea whom she spoke to.

"Search One, please check Worker quarters Sixteen-thirty-three D MG for . . . for . . ."

"Just exiting those rooms, Temple One. Sorry to report five bodies."

The Worker raised stricken eyes to Sissy. His mouth worked, but nothing came out.

Sissy wished she could have told him of his loss personally, in a gentler manner than hearing the abrupt words from a stranger over electronic equipment.

"Thank you, Search One. I'll arrange for funeral care of . . . of the lost ones. Temple One out."

The lauded Worker wrapped an arm around the grief-stricken man. Sissy rejected caste prejudice and added her own hug of comfort. "Go ahead and cry," she whispered. "We all grieve with you. Your loss is our loss as well."

She steered them toward a shadow near a narrow corridor that might give the illusion of privacy.

"Will . . . will you perform the Grief Blessing, My Laudae?" He lifted his gaze briefly, then dropped it abruptly at his presumption.

"Of course. That will be the first order of business, as soon as we have a temple set up in our new quarters."

How many times had she conducted that most sacred of rituals for her people?

Dozens of times. Thousands of rituals if she counted the mass funeral she'd presided over for the slaughtered inmates of an asylum in Harmony City. No one else thought the "Loods," or logs of wood, as the inmates were called, worth the bother of a religious ceremony.

Sissy, with her multiple caste marks, knew that she might well have been one of them. She might have become so desperate from the neglect, the filth, the abuse, and the starvation that she too would have thrown herself on a Badger Metal sword wielded by one of Jake's men rather than continue. She too might have become so desperate that she'd tear a Military limb from limb to get away from the asylum.

She would rather have been sent to Lady Marissa's factories in the desert, where death came quickly from overwork and dehydration.

But she had been saved from that because of her bond with Harmony that gave her the gift of prophecy.

That bond had been severed when Lady Marissa's agent had set off a massive bomb in an attempt to murder Sissy. The bomb had robbed Sissy of more than just her hearing temporarily. Lady Marissa had murdered almost Sissy's entire family and many of her childhood friends and coworkers.

Sissy had lost her gift of prophecy along with her connection to the Goddess. Her primary qualification to be High Priestess, Harmony's avatar, had vanished in an instant of blinding light and shaking ground.

She'd regained most of her hearing. The ringing in her ears had become a constant companion she could almost ignore most of the time. Nothing could restore her family.

Laudae Penelope, once her enemy in the Temple, had become her friend and had performed a Grief Blessing. Only after that ritual could Sissy begin to heal in mind, body, and spirit.

Lately Jake and her girls reported that Sissy spoke prophetically, even though she didn't remember doing it.

"I consider it an honor to grant you a Grief Blessing," she whispered.

"Thank you, My Laudae. You bring us hope," the woman said as she pushed the man to sit with his back against a wall. Then she stood with her back to him, blocking him from the view of others. He could grieve in private.

Sissy's comm unit beeped. Others needed her. She shouldn't linger to comfort this anonymous man. Still, she paused to squeeze his shoulder even as she answered the call.

"Temple One, we've finished with level sixteen. Moving to fifteen."

Despite her own bone-deep ache of fatigue, she proceeded with her head count of the evacuees. Making certain no one else got left behind.

Morning, by the station clocks, had come and gone.

She handed her computer with its neat charts to Lord Lukan, who stood beside the staircase that spiraled around the lift. He'd folded his hands inside his blue nightrobe and seemed to doze on his feet. He barely acknowledged receipt of the data with a nod, then returned to his doze.

Lady Jancee, his wife, fidgeted nearby. She'd had several hours of rest while her spouse helped sort out the confiscation of the station.

Sissy's conscience twitched uneasily. Did they have the right to take the station away from Labyrinthe? Certainly the man had been criminally negligent. He might face charges for murder when this was all over.

She was surprised they'd lost only the five Workers, a man, his wife, their two children, and the wife's sister. Undereducated Workers, who'd probably never been informed of emergency procedures because they were disposable. Or their supervisors considered them too stupid to re-member the drills.

Of all the seven hundred in the Harmony delegation, only the ninety-eight Spacers and seventy-seven Military had known what to do during the emergency. And they had been safe and snug in another wing, sepa-rated from the other castes, untainted. As all castes had remained sepa-rate for too long.

One squad of twenty-one Military had been on duty patrolling the residential wing at the time of the crash. Their cool heads and authorita-tive voices had organized the evacuation. But they hadn't known how many people needed to get out. They hadn't had time to search all the quarters.

This latest catastrophe was just one more example of why she had to break the caste system. Or at least whittle down some of the prejudices.

The lift platforms paused a few seconds while three strange figures in the bulky space suits with air tanks strapped to their backs stepped free. One of them gingerly carried a black wooden box.

Sissy stopped the first figure before it had gone more than a few paces. "Are they safe?" she asked breathlessly.

The anonymous figure remained silent as it handed her the box, bow-ing slightly—as much as the insulated suite would allow.

She cradled the box against her chest. "This is only my travel kit. What about the full array of altar crystals in the Temple?"

"Cracked beyond repair. You might be able to salvage some shards." The anonymous voice came through the suit, distorted with electronics.

She winced at yet another alien sound warring with all the others.

One-handed, she fumbled with the catch on the box. Another hand reached out to help her with the nearly frozen metal. Jake's ungloved hand with its calluses and scars protruded from the space suit.

"It needs to warm a bit, My Laudae, before it slides easily," he said gently, opening his faceplate.

"I . . . I need to do a Grief Blessing," she said quietly.

He blanched. "Who?"

She related the grisly find.

"Why wasn't I told about this?"

"They are—were—our people."

"Everybody on this station is now my responsibility," he growled.

She looked up to him in question.

"Both Lukan and Telvino confirmed it with their governments. They had the legal authority to confiscate the station. They appointed me to run the place, and the home worlds agreed. CSS also made me a general, if you can believe that."

"But is that the morally correct course?"

"I dunno. That's a question for you Temple folk. I've got to get back to Control. Your new quarters are almost warm enough. You'll be the first one in when they're ready. Bless and cleanse the place as you see fit. Then you can move the walls around to suit your needs."

She nodded, but she doubted he saw it. He'd already turned and stepped into the lift, barely looking to see if an upward bound platform had come into view. Separated from her by caste and by duty.

Would he ever have time to just sit and talk with her again?

"You'll be there for the ceremonies, Jake." She might as well have spoken to the vast empty vacuum of space. "I need you there to share in the Grief Blessing with me," she whispered.

"What about my jewels?" Lady Jancee asked belatedly. "If anyone has stolen my jewels . . ."

"Later," Lord Lukan snapped at her. "My Laudae, do what you need to do. I want you ready the moment General Devlin authorizes entry to our new quarters."

"What about the survivor?" she asked, remembering the one blank spot on her careful tallies.

"You know as much as I do. Last I heard they found a habitat hidden between bulkheads. Recently deserted."

✦ ✦ ✦

Sharp grinding pain ripped across Adrial's entire body. Her lungs burned so fiercely she dared not take more than the shallowest breath.

All of her manipulations for rapid self-healing became undone.

Her scream of pain sounded little more than a kitten's mew.

"Forgive me, Little Bird," the strange, eight-legged being said. "I must keep you safe."

Adrial whimpered. She'd endured different pains at the hands of the Messengers of the Gods. They meted out equally intense tortures in punishment for her sin of carrying alien blood in her veins. Not until she completed her path to Spiritual Purity could they accept her as one of the true race.

She must endure.

Bits and pieces of memory flitted through her mind.

A tank of salt water that filled one entire room of the basement refuge she fell into. Intelligent water creatures with eight legs and two longer arms peered through their glass container at her. One of them lifted an arm and flipped a switch on a translator box.

"Lost," he whispered. "You lost. Like us."

That described her situation as well as any. She didn't know where she needed to go, only that she must leave here immediately.

"Do you have a ship?" she asked. Somewhere in her wanderings, probably the library at Biblio III, she'd seen a holo of these creatures. Human experts thought them extinct.

"We have ship. Await cargo."

"Can you take me with you?"

"You do not ask where we go."

Adrial let her silence speak for her.

"We hear of one who collects the lost. Gives them refuge, direction, and life."

"Who?" Adrial breathed. This sounded like the person she needed to find.

"No name. At end of our journey. Our last journey."

"May I come with you?" Occasionally politeness earned her more than demands or coercion.

And so she'd come to this alien place seeking another fragment of the puzzle of enlightenment. Someone here . . . she must find the One Person in all the universe who held the next key.

She could not find that person if she died at the hands of yet another being who tortured her for spiritual cleansing.

The constant jarring of her pain-wracked body ceased. She breathed in a little deeper and pushed it out again immediately. The agony in her damaged lungs persisted.

A moment of blackness. Abrupt awakening. Angry voices.

"Put her down, beast!" someone shouted.

"Put her on the gurney right now or we'll shoot," another voice commanded.

"Please, I did not mean to hurt her," her captor said.

"You're killing her," the first voice said.

"No . . . I would never . . ."

"Put her down and we might be able to save her."

"Who?" Adrial whispered.

"Medical Professionals from Harmony."

"Harmony." That resonated in her pain-fogged memory. "I must find Harmony."

"You heard her, beast. She wants to go with us."

"Very well, I entrust her safety to you. Temporarily. But be advised I will watch over her."

A scream of agony ripped through her as her captor shifted her from his arms to the gurney. Instantly a layer of gel floats cradled her in a cocoon, as if she floated in zero G.

Then a scuttling sound akin to the click of an insect's feet dashing up the wall. A barrage of blaster fire.

"You can't kill me," the beast called back. "I will watch you. If anything happens to my little bird, you all die." Then the slamming of a hatch.

More blaster fire.

She cringed, wondering when the next whining bolt of energy would take her life. She hurt so much and struggled so hard for air that death seemed almost welcome. Almost.

She could not allow herself to die until she'd found Harmony. The One who collected lost beings and gave them light and life was here. She knew that to the depth of her soul.

◆ ◆ ◆ ◇ ◆ ◆ ◆

CHAPTER EIGHT

"THREE HOURS LATE, Mr. Guilliam. Explain yourself." Laud Gregor tapped his foot impatiently as they waited for the Spacer crew to finish loading the last of Laudae Penelope's luggage and that of her six acolytes.

Six, a mere six: another change Sissy had brought about, realigning the symmetry of seven. She claimed that Goddess Harmony had a consort and five children for a total of seven; therefore a priest or priestess should have six acolytes for a total of seven. Gregor maintained the old style of a priest and *seven* acolytes.

Penelope and her six were seven people too many on this trip.

"You know Laudae Penelope. She cannot travel light, and making the decision of which dresses to bring and which to leave is not a light matter." Guilliam shrugged. His square body rested easily against the padded seat beside Gregor at the front of the shuttle.

"I had numerous communications to send as well," Guilliam continued. "Our abrupt and unannounced departure left many loose ends that needed tidying."

Gregor grunted in reluctant approval. Guilliam may have developed an independent streak since Sissy began overthrowing conventions, but he did his job efficiently. He did his job better than anyone else at the Crystal Temple could. For that reason alone, Gregor had kept him as an assistant far longer than he should.

"Since your attention was occupied with other, more weighty matters, I took the liberty of redeploying the fleet with a deeper concentration around Harmony V. That is the sector with most activity reports regarding the Maril," Guilliam continued.

"You took protection away from Harmony VI!" Gregor shouted.

A subtle shift in the vibrations at Gregor's feet told him the shuttle neared launch. Did he have time to dash out and change Guilliam's orders?

"A difficult decision, I'm certain you have pondered long and hard, My Laud," Guilliam said, bowing his head. "Previously the Maril have been sighted most frequently around Harmony VI. Now they have changed tactics. We must as well."

"It's a decoy to force us to move troops away from their real target," Gregor lowered his voice so as not to alarm the others. Heat infused his face and sent his heart racing. A sharp ache spread outward across his chest toward his left arm.

Caleb fumbled for the packet of pills he always carried. Gregor took two of the little white pellets and placed them under his tongue.

The pains eased almost immediately, and his heart resumed a normal rhythm. He took several deep, calming breaths before continuing. "Everyone knows that the route from H5 to H Prime is convoluted and heavily fortified. They'd have a much easier route to our homeworld through H6."

"Perhaps. But they know we are waiting for them at H6, reluctant to move our forces from there. So they stab at the more vulnerable H5 to test our reactions. A strong response will force them to rethink their strategy."

"An unpredictable strategy," Gregor reminded him.

"A delayed strategy. We need time to build up our forces and get the treaty in place so that we have aid when the Maril choose their next target."

The vibrations increased as the engines boosted more power.

Gregor cringed and clasped the armrests tightly.

"Considering how you hate travel, My Laud, I'm surprised you did not delegate this mission to another," Guilliam said politely.

"Delegates tend to loose track of their mission. I cannot trust this to another. As it seems I cannot trust anything to you." Gregor firmed his resolve and did his best to ignore the flare of pain in his joints as the shuttle rolled forward, increasing its speed.

"Delegates do tend to lose themselves in Laudae Sissy's smile," Guilliam mused. He glanced to his right and gazed fondly at Penelope. Twin girls shared the seat beside her.

The prophetic twins, Gregor noted. The girls who, by rights, must be trained to replace Laudae Sissy.

Unfortunately, neither of them was old enough to take on the responsibilities of full ordination. He already directed much of their education, overriding the lessons suggested by Penelope, the Director of Temple Education. When the girls passed their tenth birthday, Gregor could legally separate them from their parents. Not before. Five more years before they made Sissy redundant and useless.

But he knew his way around the rules as well as or better than Guilliam.

The nose of the shuttle lifted, the wheels left the runway. The flight was committed. None of the passengers could escape now.

"I am immune to Laudae Sissy and her wiles," Gregor said, keeping his tone mild and conversational. "She will manipulate me no longer. Nor will she use you to circumvent my orders. The moment we reach the ship, I will commandeer communications and rescind your orders."

"If you say so, My Laud." Guilliam maintained his bland face that might agree or just as easily disagree. No way to read his feelings. The guise had proved useful to Gregor over the years. He'd miss the man's efficiency and his lack of ambition.

"When we return to Harmony, you will find it time to retire, Guilliam."

"I will not be separated from my wife, My Laud. According to the Covenant Tablets, you cannot separate us."

"No, I can't. But I have already signed the orders to transfer Penelope to an isolated funerary temple on the Southern Continent. You will be demoted to the resident priest's lowest acolyte. I believe the job entails filling incense burners and cleaning toilets. The twins will, of course, remain in Crystal Temple school and nursery."

Guilliam sat stiffly in shocked silence for several moments. Then, as the shuttle leveled out and gravity lessened, he gulped several times.

"If you wish to be rid of me, why did you bring me along on this trip?"

"So that you could not change the orders I left behind, nor work to find my replacement. And so you could not try to rule in my name without me. By the time I return with Laudae Sissy, docile or dead, I will have regained complete control over both Temple and Government, without your interference."

✦ ✦ ✦

Jake gladly shed the bulky EVA suit inside the tram. He'd rather have a flight jumper and helmet. Much more maneuverable and comfortable. Unfortunately, he'd left his old outfits behind when he took this transfer to the diplomatic corps. He contemplated borrowing one from a pilot stationed aboard or the *Victory*, currently docked at the CSS military wing of the complex. He had most of the pilots, along with their tech crews, already scheduled to work Control—they knew about docking and schedules and defensive grids. They wouldn't be flying for a while.

But he needed some of them to patrol the vicinity, make certain the First Contact Café had no blind spots in its sensors. If he was very, very lucky, he might schedule himself to lead one of those patrols.

Just a little stroll around the solar system to keep his skills active.

Unfortunately, he seemed to be needed in every crevice of the station at the same time. He'd better find time to change into a clean uniform. He probably didn't look very authoritative in jeans and a sweatshirt with mismatched socks and athletic shoes. Hmmm, he noticed one was white and the other black. No wonder his feet felt funny and off-balance.

One more thing to add to the list of things to do and acquire.

Top of the list was trained personnel. He'd take them from Harmony, or the CSS, or Prometheus XII, the pirate planet, if he had to. Anyone who could fill the roster. And not just Control people who knew their way around sensor arrays and computers. He needed medics, maintenance experts, merchants, tailors, cooks, and bartenders. And a partridge in a pear tree. A priest or two to serve the multitude of faiths wouldn't hurt.

And armed troops. No. He amended that to civilian security personnel.

Just by beefing up the civilian sectors he could increase trade and cargo transfers and fill the place in a month. Rents would go a long way toward paying salaries and supplies.

In the current tight political situation, the First Contact Café might become a haven outside the war zone. He'd almost bet that once word got out, traders would move their business here just to get away from the percentages that governed Labyrinthe stations and the security restrictions of military space stations.

Hmmm. Something more to think about.

He wondered how Labby could have interpreted the diplomatic lease so narrowly as to not allow much of anyone but the two delegations on board.

The place was a mess.

"Stupid," he muttered. His comm link interrupted before his words became a tirade. "What?" he growled into it.

"Incoming ship, sir," a female Spacer said respectfully.

"Are any ships expected?"

"Not on any ledger I've managed to access, sir."

That was another problem. Labyrinthe had so tightly encrypted and protected vital and random bits of information contained on the computers, no one could put it all together without the spectacles.

No wonder main terminals awoke to anyone without a password. A hacker couldn't find anything useful.

He pulled the spectacles out of the EVA suit's pocket and crammed them on his nose.

Instantly a dozen images burst into view around the periphery. His senses wavered, and his empty stomach threatened to revolt.

He had to close his eyes, think about what he searched for, and then look slowly into each sector separately. Not difficult as long as he concentrated on one image at a time.

But there was so much!

Ah, there was a glyph for schedules. He touched it on the outside of the lens with his index finger. A short list of ship traffic scrolled across the center of the left-hand glass.

"What's the ship's ID?" he asked Control.

"CSS light cruiser." Then the woman rattled off a string of codes.

"It's not on the schedule, but I recognize the *Champion* by her number. Admiral Marella should be aboard. Send her my compliments and ask her to meet me in her quarters as soon as she docks." Pammy didn't know it yet, but he was about to shanghai her entire crew.

"I wonder if there's a way to download what's in these spectacles into a more convenient terminal."

"What's that, sir?" the woman in Control asked.

"Sorry. Private musing. I forgot to close my comm. Who's the best hacker on station?"

"Harmony or CSS?"

"Doesn't matter. We're all on the same side now."

"I've broken my share of codes, sir. We specialize in that in the Harmony Military."

"Find someone to relieve you there. I've got a special mission for you."

One less thing to worry about.

"Oh, sir, Laudae Sissy tells me she expects you at the Dedication ceremony in one hour. Attendance at the Grief Blessing afterward is requested as well."

"Was that a request or a skillfully disguised order?" He grimaced. He didn't have time to attend to Sissy's every whim. As much as he wanted to be with her, he had other duties now.

Still . . .

"I think, sir, it was an order. She needs you to represent all of us on duty. *We* need you to represent us."

The tram chose that moment to glide to a stop. He made his weary way to the lift, then closed his eyes for the few moments needed to move down to Control.

He tossed the spectacles to the Spacer at the prime terminal. With his own undistorted vision he read her name tag.

"Mara du Danna." He automatically added "pu FCC." Everyone from Harmony was known by a first name, their same gender parent's name, and a locator, who they worked for or where they were stationed. "See if you can copy the information contained in those spectacles to appropriate terminals. And while you're at it, let me know how to add information to them. They're more useful than having to call someone every time I need something."

"Yes, sir. And, uh, sir, does my unit belong to you now?" Her gaze fixed on his caste mark.

"Not to me. The entire delegation now belongs to the First Contact Café."

"Shouldn't that be Labyrinthe VII Station, sir?"

"Nope. I just officially changed the name. Advise Admiral Marella of that too."

He turned toward the lift again.

"Where will you be, sir?"

"At the other end of my comm unit."

She glared at him but did not say that was unacceptable.

"Sir, the medical team that recovered the survivor of the crash has video of the encounter with the phantom. Would you like to view it?"

"Send it to the screen in my quarters. Got to grab a dress uniform for Laudae Sissy's rituals."

"Sir, Ambassador Telvino had your belongings moved to the apartment in the opposite wing at this level. There's a footbridge across the hub. You'll be within easy reach at any hour. Control personnel also have quarters in that wing."

"In other words, I have no privacy, and I'm on call twenty-four/seven."

"Privacy is a thing of the mind, sir."

"Don't remind me."

When he saw the extent of his new quarters, an entire level to himself, truly fitting for the station manager and rivaling Labby's place for luxury, he stopped and looked around. Never in all his years of living aboard stations and battleships had he known such comfort could exist. Telvino and Lukan didn't have this much room.

"Mara," he called through his comm.

"Yes, sir."

"Amend my request to Admiral Marella. Have her meet me in my private conference room."

"Yes, sir." Was that a laugh underneath her words? "The video is available on your office terminal now."

Ideas percolated from his mind to his gut and back again. He almost doubled over with the enormity of it. "When I left Harmony, I knew there had to be a better way. I think I may just have stumbled into it."

$\diamond\; \diamond\; \diamond\; \diamondsuit\; \diamond\; \diamond\; \diamond$

CHAPTER NINE

MAC PAUSED IN HIS terrified flight from the blaster fire. He kicked loose an omnisensor with his most powerful hind leg. Then he crunched it with his pincer. Pieces scattered.

He took little delight in its destruction. For every one he removed, he blocked the eyes and ears of Control. But he also lost his own means of tracking the inhabitants of his station. And as each one went blank on the computers, he left a trail of his progress through the ducts and tunnels.

That didn't mean he couldn't double back.

He crawled forward, skipped three sensors, turned off the next five. The sensors overlapped their range. The loss of one wouldn't affect Control's ability to monitor this duct for real damage. Random groupings of destruction would give him blind spots to hide in.

The hatch behind him opened. He caught snatches of conversation.

Time to move forward. No time to close down more sensors.

He uttered an oath in his mother's native language. If Control heard him, they'd not understand that he wished them all a long vacation on the Labyrinthe home world. That planet had died a long time ago. Continuously spewing volcanoes in a boiling atmosphere held in by toxic clouds was all that remained.

He ripped around a corner into a narrower duct. It abutted a docking level. This passage was intended only for maintenance bots, barely big enough for him to squeeze through.

His pursuers clanged behind him, pounding their boots as they crawled through the metal enclosure.

No space to turn around.

Mac stretched all eight limbs forward and back and expelled air from his bulbous torso. About half his original girth, he squeezed and pushed himself along. Darkness enfolded him. He oriented himself by the smell of disinfectant overlaid with evergreen. Ah, he approached the MedBay of the Harmony service wing.

The whine of a blaster interrupted his plans. He heard the weapon before he felt pain in his hind end. Numbness crawled down both his primary and secondary leg on the right side. He paused and gulped. If he could slide past this next spiral down and a jog to the left he could get beyond the line-of-sight weapon.

A second blast whined. Searing pain shot up his spine.

He stifled a scream. His left legs convulsed. He heard his claws click against the duct but couldn't feel them. Only a ripple of muscles up his back.

"If you kill it, it's stuck there and will stink up the place," a pursuer grumbled.

"If I kill it, we can get bots to cut it up and deliver it to the medics for autopsy," growled another one.

A third shot.

Mac's vision dimmed and narrowed to the center of the next hatch. He stretched and reached as far as he could. His fingers barely brushed the joint. Three more centimeters. He needed three more to grab hold and pull himself free.

Three more centimeters between him and safety.

✦   ✦   ✦

Jake fumbled with the tight collar of his class A uniform. The fabric refused to stretch around the increased muscle in his neck and shoulders.

"Discord!" he shouted to no one in particular as he dashed across his office.

Late. He'd be late for Sissy's ceremonies if he didn't get the blame thing fastened in a hurry.

Mara appeared in the doorway to his office. "Sir, do you need some help?" She set aside the sheaf of flimsies requiring his signature.

"Yes, damn it. I've been able to dress myself since I was three years old. Why can't I get this uniform to fit when I'm in a hurry."

"Because class A uniforms have always been designed by people who don't have to wear them, so they see no problem in requiring eight hands to fasten everything. You'll find the same problem with formal wear in any culture." With calm and efficient fingers she closed the upright collar and began work on his cuff links.

"Thank you, Lieutenant Mara," Jake sighed in relief. The chrono on his desk showed he had three minutes to spare if he caught a tram right away.

"Before you dash off, I really think you ought to take a look at the record of the survivor retrieval."

"Sorry, I don't have time."

"Make time." She stood between him and the door to the outer reception area. The grim determination on her face reminded him of Sissy. He knew better than to disobey. Arguing would take up three times the minutes he needed to view the record, and he'd still lose the argument.

Mara must have seen the resignation in his posture. She touched an icon on the desktop. The two-dimensional scene sprang up on the flat surface.

"Must be a Harmonite record, since it's not a holo," he muttered.

The bizarre eight-limbed creature came to life. Words came from the mouths of the alien and the person behind the helmet camera. He watched the gentle placement of the female in blazing white draperies with hair and skin almost as pale. Then her captor scuttled up a wall and out of view.

"What's so special about that?" Jake asked. He closed the screen and dashed toward the door.

"Think about it during the Grief Blessing," Mara called after him.

✦ ✦ ✦

Sissy bowed her head to the altar, letting the beads and crystals in her veil clank together. Their chord chimed in her mind, blending with the constant ringing in her ears. The music only she could hear spread peacefully through her veins. Different music from the resonance of her home on Harmony. Still music.

She breathed deeply, exhaling fully. The faint citrus taste of the air didn't fully mask the metallic tang of the unnatural atmosphere. She searched her mind for a way to make the clashing scents a part of the harmonic chord of her veil and her own sensitivities.

Dog and Monster slunk in to take positions on either side of her. Each animal pressed into her side, eager for her touch and attention.

She dropped a hand to each head, fondling ears and relishing their silky fur. The tactile stimulation blended with the music of her veil crystals. Monster moaned in near ecstasy. Dog whined and lifted his chin for a scratch.

There! The elusive combination settled in her mind. She drank it in, finding Harmony. She had only a few moments of meditation before she met with Nobles wanting a Temple Blessing and the weeping and grieving friends and families of the lost Workers needing a Grief Blessing.

A slight inclination of her head set the veil chiming again. She found a sympathetic note in the back of her throat.

The bare walls of the new Temple reflected and compounded the sound. Candle flames flickered. Delicate incense rose to fill the sacred space. The bare walls seemed to ache for decorative murals to enliven them and bring them into the balance.

Miniature crystals from her travel kit awaited the touch of her glass wand. Already they quivered with music.

The specially insulated box and cushioning had protected these precious crystals. Their larger brothers and sisters that normally graced the altar hadn't fared so well. She thought perhaps the shards should be fashioned into beads for other veils so that their life and place in ritual might continue.

A shift in air pressure told her that someone entered behind her. Her few moments of contemplative preparation vanished. She dismissed the dogs with a final scratch and a gesture. They retreated through her private entrance behind the altar.

"Welcome to Harmony's bosom. May our Goddess and Her family aid you in easing your grief."

"Amen," Jake whispered.

Sissy smiled to herself, not that the all-concealing veil would reveal her expression. Now she could proceed. Jake's coming completed her preparations. His presence granted her more calm and sense of unity than any amount of meditation. She turned to face him, arms raised, palms out in blessing and formal greeting.

He bowed low. A golden bird emblem glinted from each side of his upright collar. The dark green uniform tunic looked good on him with his dark hair and space-pale skin. His red square caste mark with its purple lauding seemed out of place with that uniform. It should be the red tunic of Harmony, which also looked magnificent on him.

"You need a new emblem, General Devlin. I believe the eagle is for a mere colonel." Polite small talk. Nothing more intimate allowed in public. She longed for the feel of his hand in hers, on her shoulder, a fingertip tracing her mutant caste marks. Any touch at all to connect them.

"Forgive me, My Laudae. I've had no time to search out a star insignia."

She needed to grant him some tiny gift in return for all he'd done for her over the months he'd acted as her bodyguard. He'd also acted as her tutor when the teachers in the Temple grew frustrated and short-tempered at her rudimentary education prior to coming to them. Jake became more a friend than her priestly coworkers, who disdained her Worker beginnings and humble birth.

Her vision splintered. Candlelight against crystal facets sent prisms arcing across the room. She gasped, trying to hold onto the moment, to glimpse Harmony in the unity of the universe. Strands of light connecting . . .

The almost-vision vanished as quickly as it had come.

"General Jake, will these suffice?" She unhooked the two star-shaped crystals that tipped the longest bead strands of her veil.

"Laudae, I can't!" Jake drew in a sharp breath between his teeth. "They . . . they're black crystals, they've got Badger Metal braided through the matrix. Worth four times my annual salary. Each!"

She didn't understand the physics of what Badger Metal did to crystals, only that outside of Harmony they were incredibly rare and special. Something to do with instant communications. She heard the term "avian precision" used in connection with the black crystals and navigation systems.

"A token of my gratitude for saving my life more times than I can count. If you must, you may return them when you get proper insignia." She pressed the stars into his hand, closing his fingers around them with her other hand.

Something about reforging the Covenant among the stars . . . "Please, Jake. I want you to have them. Make them into cufflinks or something." She giggled at the thought of him wearing a large fortune on his wrists.

"I shall treasure them always, My Laudae." He bowed again. Then he fumbled with the eagles on his tunic.

"Let me." She reached up and unfastened the emblem of his former rank. Then she inserted the attachment hooks for the crystals through the fine fabric. As she lifted her face, the bead strands fell away, exposing her to his gaze.

"Thank you, Sissy." He leaned forward, his face very close to her own.

She held her breath, not daring to hope he might kiss her. Surely one kiss did not break the laws against out-of-caste and out-of-culture relationships. Surely. If only he'd kiss her. Just once. All she asked of the Gods was one kiss from the man who held her heart.

Jake closed his eyes and straightened. A grimace of near pain crossed his face. "Forgive my impertinence, My Laudae." He turned on his heel and retreated to the bench in the far corner, facing the door, not her or the altar.

✦   ✦   ✦

A gentle note wiggled its way through layers of drug mist and mind fog. Half-remembered scenes of happiness with her mother brought Adrial a little closer to that lovely bit of music. Just a single note that needed others to swell into a full chord.

She tried to hum the tone that would complement it. Her mind thought it knew which note it should be. Her voice betrayed her. Flat. Atonal. Harsh.

"Wh . . . at?" That shrill bird's croak could not have come from her throat.

She waited, barely aware of herself. All she knew was the single, lost, and lonely note.

Then a second joined it. Not the one Adrial had sought, a better one. Together they swelled and became much more than the combination of the two. The beginnings of an entire family of notes.

She felt herself sigh. That small act of breathing loosened the layers of darkness from her mind and weight from her body.

A third note. *Yes*! The one she had thought of first.

Dull aches and sharp slices of pain intruded upon her appreciation of the peace and joy of the fragile music.

Not again, she sighed in resignation. A part of her remembered a cold and dark prison cell, bruises and burns on the most intimate parts of her body.

This was different. She'd dreamed of escape. The dream was so real she'd heard the whine of blaster fire, smelled the garbage in the alley she hid in. Felt the press of a metal door against her back, that door giving way. Tumbling into a dimly lit room with scabrous creatures huddled around a single candle flame and a giant saltwater tank . . .

She opened her eyes as the fourth note drifted around her, seeking its mates, climbing toward them until it blended and augmented.

Panel lights above her. Soothing blue walls with delicate murals of a peaceful woodland scene graced with blessing runes in front of her. She tried turning her head and found it immobilized by a soft collar that pressed against her chin. An annoying drip to her left played a counterpoint to the music that soothed her.

This was no Maril prison. She smelled hospital.

Flashes of memory returned. A strange creature carrying her. Extreme pain and weakness. Shouts, blaster fire. Blessed sleep and relief.

She still hurt, but in a different way that made no sense.

A fifth note circled around her.

Movement in her peripheral vision. She shifted her eyes as far to her left as possible. She caught fragments of ghostly figures in a tiny holovid processing across the bedside table that could swing across her body for convenience.

Definitely a hospital fixture.

Her hand flapped, trying to move the table and the holovid closer. The music originated there.

"Here, let me get that for you," a man said, barely above a whisper. He rose from the chair behind the table and moved into her line of sight. He wore a black uniform with extra pockets on sleeve and thigh and chest. But what riveted her attention more than the holovid and the music was the red square blotch on his left cheek. A single red line ran below it, the whole encircled with a blue line.

"I'm Lieutenant David da Jason pa Lukan Labyrinthe . . . er . . . make that FCC." He bowed slightly as he slid the table across her bed. The holovid now played between them.

"Quite a sight watching Laudae Sissy," he said. "That's her in the funeral black robes. High Priestess of all Harmony, and she's here on this remote outpost. She blessed the new Temple while you slept off the anesthesia. Now she's granting us all a Grief Blessing. Used to be those were private for family and close friends. Now she opens them to everyone, recognizes that we are all diminished by the loss of one of our own."

Adrial couldn't make a sound. Her gaze lingered on the anonymous figure in padded black and gold brocade with an elaborate headdress of the same material. Strands of sparkling gold, purple, crystal, and black completely covered her face. Anyone, even a man, could have hidden behind that costume. How did this David person, with a string of incomprehensible names, know that the High Priestess of all Harmony brought forth those magnificent tones?

Music that rivaled for beauty the stars singing to their planets!

Laudae Sissy tapped the next crystal with a tiny glass wand. A sixth note swelled forth to join the lingering tones of its fellows. She chanted something. Adrial had trouble understanding her dialect of the CSS standard language. But the lieutenant closed his eyes, and a blissful expression filled him.

The chord of six notes almost stilled, as if it held its breath in anticipation.

Adrial didn't dare breathe.

She watched as the priestess slowly touched her wand to the last crystal, a black one, bigger than its fellows, more slender, and flashing a wild prism of beautiful rainbows.

The crystal bellowed forth a deep tone that complemented and completed the other six, brought them into a full circle. Definitely celestial in orgin.

The chord seared deeply through Adrial's ears into her mind. The music rattled around and cleared her pain and hurtful memories.

All of her wounds seemed to fade in importance as complete and utter joy washed through her in a cleansing tide.

And then the priestess sang. Her clear voice rose above the clamor of all the machines on the station, unifying the crystal notes in a hymn more beautiful than the bird chirps of the Messengers of the Gods.

CHAPTER TEN

JAKE'S COMM VIBRATED silently on his wrist. He brushed it lightly. *Yeah, I heard you, but I'm busy.* It started up again almost immediately. He pressed the hold portion of the screen harder.

Blessed silence while Sissy sang her final benediction. As her voice soared up to the final satisfying note, the obnoxious comm vibrated again, so violently that he thought it would burn the hair off his wrist.

He bolted from the Temple the moment Sissy raised her arms in benevolent dismissal.

He didn't have time to linger and admire how much she'd grown in spirituality and authority since High Priest Gregor had dragged her out of the factory wreckage and tried to make her his puppet on the High Council.

He didn't have time to properly thank her for the gift of his new insignia.

"What?" he growled, the moment he was clear and had some sense of privacy.

"We found the beast," Lieutenant David da Jason pa Lukan/FCC said. He sounded anxious and excited at the same time.

"Aren't you supposed to be guarding the survivor?"

"I am, sir. The beast dropped into her room from a vent. He's badly wounded. And, sir, he's really, really strange. Stranger than I thought possible."

"Yeah. I noticed that. What do the medics say?" Jake jumped aboard the upward lift. He had to see this for himself.

"Um . . . Our physicians are just staring at it. They don't want to touch anything so . . . alien."

Jake spat a couple of curses he thought he'd forgotten.

"Sorry, sir, they had enough trouble working on the survivor—her name's Adrial, by the way. Seems like she's some kind of exotic half-breed they can't identify. Partly human at least. The beast doesn't appear to have anything human about it."

"I'm calling in a CSS trauma surgeon. See if you can get those xeno-phobic paranoids to at least make it comfortable. I want it alive for ques-tioning. On my way."

His mind replayed the record he'd watched with only half his attention an hour ago. Something . . .

Definitely something to think about.

He transferred from the lift to a waiting tram in a single weightless jump. As he cleared the open doorway of the tram, his fingers brushed the glyph of Harmony. No time to pause for a ritual kiss requesting a safe journey. No time to think. He keyed the tram to the MedBay on the Spacer wing on the Harmony side of the complex. His comm buzzed again.

"If that alien has died, Lieutenant . . ." he growled.

"What alien, sir?" Mara asked.

"Sorry. I thought someone else was calling." He forced himself to take three deep breaths, as Sissy had taught him. He remembered that last clear note of the Grief Blessing and found calm. "What do you need, Mara?"

"Admiral Marella awaits you in your private conference room, sir."

Pammy. Damn. He thought he'd have another hour before she came looking for him.

"Mara, I will make you my second-in-command if you will entertain the admiral for a bit. And while you're at it, see if she will send her ship's surgeon to the MedBay."

"I guess I can do that. You'd really make me your second?"

"If my plans come together the way I want, yes, I will. I want a fully integrated staff from both Harmony and the CSS." He touched the black crystal stars on his collar. A faint thrill of energy tingled against his fin-gers, sort of like a bell in the final phase of stilling after a hard knock with the clapper. "I think Laudae Sissy just started the ball rolling on that."

"I'll order the surgeon to meet you." She discommed without further explanation. Seconds later she came back on line. "And, sir, I think I've cracked the code on the spectacles."

"How soon can I start using them?"

"Unknown, sir. Cracking the code is only half the job. Downloading another, uploading to them a third."

"Get on it."

The tram slid to a smooth halt. Another flight through zero G to the lift. Rather than wait for it to make its ponderous way down fifteen levels, he hopped onto the stair railing and slid down through increasing gravity until he jumped clear in the last light-G level of MedBay. He followed the signs through a maze of rooms to Intensive Care and Post Op.

The knot of white-clad medics gathered around a door drew Jake like a magnet. "What are we looking at?" he asked mildly.

At least three of them jumped and held their hands to their chests as if to calm overactive hearts. Everyone looked about with wide, frightened eyes. They all wore a green triangle caste mark. One of them had been lauded with a purple circle, two ennobled with a blue diamond, and three more with the Spacer yellow star.

He noted that the Spacer medics were closest to the door.

Rather than answer, all of them backed away, making a space for Jake. He stared at the apparition sprawled on the floor of the typical hospital room. It looked like some giant mutant spider on steroids. Same voluminous blue shirt he'd worn yesterday. The green pants were different but contained enough fabric to disguise the seam at the center. His upper limbs, four arms Jake guessed he should call them, twitched and convulsed in a grasping movement. The lower limbs lay limp and useless. His round belly heaved with each breath.

But his head looked like a trimmed down version of Labyrinthe Seven.

"Get Labby down to MedBay ASAP," he growled into his comm.

"You," he pointed to the two medics authorized to work with Spacers. "Get in there and do what you can to make him comfortable."

"But . . ."

"Do it now or lose your augmentation."

They stared at him gape-jawed.

"Do I have to get Laudae Sissy down here? She can have you bare-faced and exiled in an eye blink."

The two men and one woman edged around him on tiptoe. Slowly, looking at the creature as they circled it. Finally one male knelt and straightened one of the secondary legs.

A high-pitched screech came from deep within the creature.

"He's not numb," he said. He pressed two fingers against the ankle, counting a pulse. Then he reached to compare it to the throbbing blood vessel plainly visible beneath his throat skin. "Limb pulse is slow and thready compared to neck. In a human I'd say spinal injury. Nerves intact but brain is not connecting. He can't voluntarily make them move."

"The men who chased him said he took direct hits from a blaster," Lieutenant David said from his post by the bed.

Jake grew cold, feeling as though all warmth and blood drained from his face.

He'd murdered enough innocents on Harmony in the name of quelling a riot and cleansing the populace of mutants. Just because the desperate inmates of an asylum had botched caste marks, they were treated worse than animals, reviled more than aliens.

On Harmony, no clean and remote blasters or even bullets. He'd had to kill *people* with his sword and dagger. An act of such extreme intimacy that he felt he'd died a bit too with every one of them.

"Then he fell about ten feet out of that vent," Lieutenant David continued. "I think his . . . arms? took the brunt of the fall. He nearly fell on the patient."

Jake noticed the slight figure resting in gel floats on the bed. She must have serious bone damage, hence the light G and the immobilizing padding all around her.

"Blaster fire," the kneeling medic said. "Okay. I have some ideas. We need to get him onto a table so we can work on him."

"What is the meaning of this, Colonel Devlin?" a stocky woman of middle years with a cap of board straight, iron gray hair said from the vicinity of the lift. She wore the everyday khakis of a CSS colonel with a medical caduceus pin next to her eagle insignia. Pammy's ship surgeon.

"It's General Devlin, and we have an injured alien. Thought you might have a bit more experience in helping station staff figure out what to do." Jake touched the stars on his collar. Again he felt that tiny tingle of energy from the Badger Metal grown in the crystal matrix.

"I don't care if they've promoted you to God, you can't order me off my ship." She stood firm, hands on hips, feet braced. But she craned her neck to peer around him.

Jake knew that medics rarely resisted a curious challenge. Except maybe those from Harmony. The Spacer docs had held true to his theory.

"As commander of the First Contact Café, all ships' personnel come under my authority the moment the docking clamps lock in place."

She still bristled.

"Please, Doctor. We need this being alive and talking. He seems to be the only one who might know how and why an alien ship crashed into the highly restricted Harmony diplomatic wing."

"Saw that from the monitors when we came in. Looks like one of your strands of spaghetti got overcooked and went limp."

A good analogy.

"Everyone get out okay?" She took one step forward, still looking curiously at the MedBay floor.

"No. We lost five, Worker caste. Two of them children. We almost lost Laudae Sissy. If she had died trying to rescue our other patient, we'd probably be at war with Harmony this very minute."

"Mariah Halliday." She thrust out a hand to shake his, but her attention remained on the medical puzzle. "I'll take a look at what you've got. First glimpse suggests Arachnoid in the mix. Maybe some Labyrinthe too."

"Never seen an Arachnoid. Heard bits and pieces though," Jake admitted as he stepped aside for Doc Halliday. He wanted to chuckle at the name. "Any relation to . . ."

"No, I'm not," Colonel Halliday snapped. Then she knelt beside the Spacer physician. Heads bent together, they consulted and ordered the others about.

Jake breathed a little easier. "Lieutenant David, is Adrial up to talking yet?"

"Not much, sir. She keeps drifting off to sleep. Sometimes in midword."

"Keep an eye on her. She goes nowhere without Military escort. Your relief will give you the password."

"Understood, sir."

Time to go meet Pammy. He backed away from MedBay and turned to face the lift.

Admiral Pamela Marella, spymaster and damned fine-looking woman, stood between him and the doors. At fifty-two and thirty pounds overweight, her personality seemed to fill any room she entered. The extra fullness on her round face and cap of curly brown hair only added to her cuteness and belied the cunning intellect and ruthless determination inside. She crossed her arms beneath her magnificent bosom and tapped her foot in impatience. The frown on her face would have made Telvino run for cover.

Jake had seen Telvino play chicken with his badly damaged heavy cruiser against an intact Maril battle wagon. The Marils, who knew no fear and suicided rather than surrender, blinked first and broke off the battle.

$$\blacklozenge \ \blacklozenge \ \blacklozenge \ \diamondsuit \ \blacklozenge \ \blacklozenge \ \blacklozenge$$

CHAPTER ELEVEN

"**D**O NOT CALL MY BROTHER,**"** Mac croaked. His throat grew dry from more than just his injuries. "I will not have Number Seven see me thus."

"Number Seven?" the female by the lift asked. She moved briskly to his side. Worry lines radiated from her eyes and mouth. A thick layer of cosmetics did not hide them from close inspection. "Old Lady Labyrinthe referred to her children by number. Are you one of her get?"

Mac nodded. He held the female's gaze with determination, though the pain in his back made him want to close his eyes and give in to oblivion.

He couldn't afford that. He had to make sure they treated his little bird correctly.

"Which one are you?"

"Call me Mac," he ground out. His birth order made no difference to anyone. Mother had died before Mac had proved his worth and brought down a favored son.

"Excuse me, Admiral, he's in no shape to talk. I've got to get him into a treatment room now." The older of the two physicians elbowed the other female aside.

"This being is a prisoner. I need to interrogate him." The admiral did not move.

Mac decided he did not like her. But others respected her. She could be useful.

"If you don't let Doc Halliday take care of him, we aren't going to have a prisoner to interrogate, Pammy." Jake grabbed the admiral by the collar of her civilian suit and hauled her to her feet.

"Put me down, Jake! I outrank you. I'll demote you and send you back to flying patrols around Prometheus XII."

"Nope. On this station I now outrank everyone but God, and maybe

Laudae Sissy. We've got other things to discuss. In *my* office." He dragged the female out of Mac's line of sight. They continued to argue all the way to the lift.

"Let's see, now. You're half Labyrinthe and half Arachnoid. Anything else I should know about your anatomy? Where can I find your previous medical records?" Doc Halliday asked. Her delicate fingers poked and prodded Mac.

"I do not exist." Mac tried to smile at her. "The other? My little bird?"

"Okay, no med stats. Is your half brother's blood compatible if I have to give you a transfusion?" She pointed to others in the room and showed them how to lift Mac.

No answer about their other patient. He had to know. He couldn't let them put him off.

Before he could form an answer, he found gel floats inserted around his limbs and against his back. Near instant relief.

Until they lifted him to a gurney. Fire lanced from the small of his back down all eight limbs. Endurable. He gritted his teeth. He knew he grimaced and tensed, but no scream escaped him this time. He'd not give them that pleasure.

If he had feeling below his belly, then his body had begun to heal itself. His exoskeleton had protected him well. If necessary he could lose his secondary limbs and regrow them. He'd done that with fingers and claws. But the primary limbs, the ones that hurt the most, obeyed his Labyrinthe DNA.

"Don't pass out on me now, Mr. Mac. What about your blood?"

Mr. Mac. He liked the sound of that. Respect. He'd never expected anyone to show him respect. Though he'd earned it.

"Your blood, Mr. Mac. Can I give you a transfusion from your brother?" Doc Halliday tapped his face lightly, demanding his attention.

"No." He'd take nothing from Number Seven even if it saved his life.

"What about hemosynth? Can you tolerate that?"

"Unknown." He had a sense of movement. They were moving him away from his little bird. He tried to reach toward her. The gel floats confined all of his limbs.

"Well, I'm not doing spinal surgery without something. We'll have to take a blood sample and clone it. Best way to deal with half-breeds anyway. But that will take time. Do you need drugs for the pain?"

"No drugs. I wish to be awake. I need to know that my little bird fares well." Every word cost him in strength and spreading fire inside his body.

"Little bird?" Doc Halliday asked.

Mac swallowed and licked his lips. He didn't have the strength to explain.

"He probably means Adrial. The sole survivor of the crash. She has delicate bones, like a bird's," the Harmony physician replied. "I'm John da Samuel pa FCC Spacer Battalion by the way."

"Someday someone is going to have to explain that string of names to me. Right now I need full three-D scans of Mac."

"It's very simple. John is my birth name. Da is for males, du for females. Samuel is my father—my sisters take our mother's name of Sadie. Pa indicates my locator, pu for females, in this case the First Contact Café, and that I'm authorized to work with Spacers." He almost giggled.

Mac took note of his explanation. It made sense. Much like Mother's designation of numbers for her children until they grew into a managerial position. Then they took the name of their station.

"About the female, is she half Maril?" Doc Halliday looked worried.

Doctor John shrugged. "I've never seen a Maril."

"I've only seen a couple of full bloods myself, and those were dead. But we're starting to see a lot of refugees from the rim worlds. Many of the women are pregnant with half-breeds. Takes some DNA manipulation for the cross to happen, more gene therapy to carry the baby to term. Not as much as I'd expect from true aliens though. I aborted several before the alien DNA turned toxic. But in others they carried to term with no complications and no further therapy. How old would you say that patient is?"

"In human terms, perhaps thirty, maybe a little more."

"Oh, shit. That means the Maril have been playing gene games for a lot longer than we suspected. We've got to find out where she came from."

"She's not fully conscious yet. Broken bones penetrated her liver, lungs, and pancreas."

"Go light on the drugs with her. Her metabolism is going to be strange."

Doctor John's eyes grew wide. Then he dashed out of the room, breathing raggedly.

Mac tried to rise and follow him. He had to protect his little bird.

Doc Halliday stopped his struggles with a single finger to the center of his chest. Then she busied herself with equipment.

Doctor John returned a few moments later. He breathed easier, moving directly to some elaborate equipment in the corner.

Mac breathed easier too. "Is she okay?" he asked.

"For now," Doctor John replied. "Will you show me how to clone blood, Doctor Mariah? I can foresee many uses for it on Harmony."

"You don't get many blood variations from what I hear," Doc Halliday mused. She moved a big machine on a swinging arm above Mac.

He glared at it, wondering what secrets it might reveal. At the same time, he remained alert. Information about Harmony, when he, as the patient, was all but invisible, might be worth trading to Ambassador Telvino later on. Or possibly Admiral Marella.

That one would pay dearly for the information, though. More dearly than the others.

"I've heard it theorized," Doctor John whispered, leaning across the bed conspiratorially, "that one of the reasons for the rising number of caste-mark mutations may be out-of-caste transfusions. Worker and Poor donations fill most of our blood banks."

Doc Halliday made a grunting noise. "I'll let you watch the lab techs do the cloning. I've got my own theories about caste-mark breakdown. And it has more to do with bodies rejecting DNA manipulation from centuries ago than any true difference between castes."

Another spark of information to add to his stockpile. Mac needed every bit of leverage he could gather to make this station his own. Disgracing his brother was only half the job.

$$\textcolor{gray}{\blacklozenge\ \blacklozenge\ \blacklozenge\ \diamondsuit\ \blacklozenge\ \blacklozenge\ \blacklozenge}$$

CHAPTER TWELVE

"I 'M SORRY, MY LAUD,** I cannot allow you access to the communications room," Captain Jonas da Jonathan du Spacer vessel Harmony 73258 said. He bowed his head.

"This communiqué is of the utmost urgency, Captain." Gregor looked down upon the compactly built man. All Spacers tended toward short, spare bodies with super efficient metabolisms. More of them could fit aboard a ship than the taller and rangier body types of other castes.

"We simply do not have time, My Laud. The delays in breaking orbit limit our leeway in accessing the jump point. I need you and your entire party seated and restrained immediately. However, if you will write out the message, I will see that it is sent as soon as possible."

Gregor pursed his lips in agitation. His heart raced and his lungs labored in the thin artificial air.

Caleb tugged on his sleeve and held out a handful of pills.

Gregor placed one under his tongue.

After a moment the pressure on his chest eased. "Very well, Captain. But I expect the encoded message to go through without any variation to my wording."

"Yes, My Laud. Now please take your seat. The rest of your party is ready to break orbit."

Gregor stumbled heavily to his assigned bunk. Damned artificial gravity!

With a great deal of fuss, Gregor made an enormous ceremony of finding a comfortable position on the narrow couch. At last, Caleb pulled the restraints around him and pressed more pills into Gregor's hand.

He nodded acknowledgment of the medication, available if he needed it during the passage. Then the High Priest slipped his other hand into the glove that would automatically administer sleep inducers before the ship entered hyperspace.

The Temple physician had warned Gregor that the drugs might put a severe strain on his heart. But Gregor had not imparted that bit of information to Caleb. Nor had he told anyone else in Temple just how fragile his heart had become in the last year.

Staying awake during the hyperspace crossing could prove just as dangerous for him.

"I've never seen ghosts in hyperspace before," Gregor muttered. All of his travel had been relatively short jumps to Harmonite colonies. This trip involved several much longer jumps. No need to worry. He had no ghosts to haunt him.

Surreptitiously he withdrew his hand from the glove.

He shared this cabin with Caleb and two crew members: all the space available on the short notice he'd given Admiral Nentares da Andromeda pa HQ HPrime, the head of the Spacer caste. He noted an empty bunk in the cabin, reserved for Laudae Sissy on the return journey.

Guilliam and Penelope filled another cabin to overflowing with her acolytes and their children.

Gregor wanted the twins and their prophetic visions with him in this cabin. But until the girls were older, he could find no precedent or excuse to take them away from their parents during the journey.

An annoying klaxon sounded seven blasts. "Warning, hyperspace in seven minutes. Sleep inducers available. Please administer now for best effect before entering hyperspace." The recorded message sounded harsh and authoritative. Anyone who disobeyed was foolhardy—or outranked the officer.

Gregor lay his head back against the three pillows on the bunk. He tested his breathing. He couldn't lie any flatter and still breathe properly.

In seconds his companions nodded off in deep sleep.

The klaxon came on again. Gregor counted the seven chimes, a different tone now. Gentler, more persuasive. "Entering hyperspace in one minute. Please administer sleep inducers if you have not yet. Last chance to administer sleep inducers."

Gregor counted off the seconds, waiting. He closed his eyes, not wanting to watch the strange shift in colors and angle of perception. He'd done that often enough over the years, any time he had to visit one of the six colonies.

When the lurch came, he felt it more intensely than any time he could remember. It grabbed at his gut and pressed hard on his chest.

His eyes flew open, half expecting to find some fallen piece of equipment hindering his ability to draw a deep breath.

Two transparent figures stood before him, fading in and out of clarity, like static on a radio.

"Go away," he told them querulously. Figments of his imagination. Neither the male in a black military uniform with a red square caste mark, nor the elderly woman in a flowing nightdress with a blue diamond caste mark obliterating her original purple circle, lived. They had no reason to haunt him. Their deaths had been necessary for the health of Harmony.

Both figures remained, becoming more solid with every strained heartbeat.

"Go away. I have no more business with either of you." He turned his face toward the wall.

Icy fingers touched his hand, the one he'd removed from the drug glove.

He jerked his gaze back to where Lady Marissa had placed her insubstantial hand over his. The communications officer flowed to the place at Gregor's feet.

The ghosts hemmed him in. He had no way to escape except through them.

No place to hide except in drug-induced sleep that might kill him.

"Your deaths were necessary for the safety of Harmony," he reassured himself. "Harmony required you to remove yourselves from life."

"Did your sin of murder bring safety or peace?" Lady Marissa whispered. Her ethereal voice was softer, more forgiving than he remembered her real voice.

"Your removal accomplished more good than the deaths *you* caused in your misguided need to assassinate Laudae Sissy," he insisted.

"One sin does not forgive another," the Military officer said quietly. "What have you accomplished?"

"How much safer is Harmony now than before you elevated Sissy to High Priestess?" Lady Marissa continued.

"You murdered me to keep me from contacting the worlds outside of Harmony. Now you have an ambassador talking to the galaxy at large," the Military said.

"You murdered me to bring Sissy back to Crystal Temple. But she ran away again, even farther," Marissa reminded him.

Gregor stared at them in horror. Everything he had touched spiraled out of his control.

His heart skipped a beat. Then two.

He fought to drag more air into his reluctant lungs. His airways refused to open and accept the life-giving oxygen.

Pain shot across his torso, up to his shoulder, down both arms.

He fumbled for the pills in his left hand. His fingers refused to open. He couldn't reach across his straining body with the other hand to grab them.

A frantic glance toward Caleb and the crewmen. They all slept peacefully.

"How long?" he whispered.

"You will die alone and unloved," Lady Marissa said with satisfaction as her body dissolved. "As alone and helpless as any prisoner awaiting execution."

"As alone as the inmates in the asylum who died from neglect and abuse," a chorus of voices crowded around him. Loods—logs of wood—every last one of them. Mutant caste marks, missing caste marks, multiple caste marks. They'd rioted when overcrowding and lack of food and medical care had driven them to desperation. Thousands of them died rather than continue living in the horrible conditions Gregor had authorized.

He hadn't laid a hand on any one of them, but he'd ordered the Military to put down the riot by any means necessary, including deadly force.

Every one of the ghosts that crowded around him showed signs of their death wounds from Badger Metal swords and daggers. Blood continued to spill from them, filling the room with red ooze, pouring into his mouth, robbing him of breath and life.

"Caleb," Gregor called with what little air he had left.

Suddenly it was important that he tell the boy how much he appreciated his loyalty, how much he trusted him. He needed to acknowledge Caleb as his son, though Temple folk had no need of such relationships.

"Caleb, help me."

The boy continued to sleep.

CHAPTER THIRTEEN

"**WHY DOES THAT LOOD** get quarters before us?" Lady Jancee whispered so loudly Sissy heard her one hundred paces away.

She flinched at the pejorative. Lood. Less than human and undeserving of life.

All her life she'd feared that someone in authority would discover her mutant caste marks and send her directly to an asylum or dump her in the Serim Desert, easy prey for carrion birds. She'd almost rather face an execution robot chained to a block, alone. The robot was programmed to take off a prisoner's head at any time within an hour. The fatal blow could come to the solitary and forgotten criminal in two seconds or sixty minutes. No way of knowing when. No family or friends to offer comfort and prayers.

Hiding her inner pain at the insult behind her veil, Sissy took the arm of the Military escort sent to guide her to her new apartment. Her acolytes lined up behind her, two by two, with Marsh and Ashel trailing at the end.

"I must find my jewels," Lady Jancee continued. "I need to make certain they have not been stolen by the lesser castes."

"Hush, dear." Lord Lukan tucked his wife's hand inside his elbow and patted it. "The babe sits uneasily today. You can rest in just a few moments. We must allow our High Priestess her honor."

"Honor, hmf," she sniffed. "No wonder Laud Gregor exiled her here. Serves him right for elevating a Lood hidden by workers. Should have executed her and her entire family . . ."

"You will be quiet!" Lord Lukan withdrew his hand. "I have indulged your complaints because this seventh pregnancy is difficult for you. If hyperspace were not so dangerous for the baby, I'd send you home on the next flight."

Sissy stood on tiptoe to whisper in her escort's ear. He made a signal to a sergeant standing at attention in the Temple doorway. That man went immediately to Lord Lukan's side and offered to escort them at the same time as Sissy.

Lady Jancee folded her hands inside her formal robe. "She gets a captain. I will not have an enlisted man."

Lord Lukan appeared at Sissy's side. Silent and grim, he took her other arm.

Thankfully, they reached her open doorway within two more steps. Her quarters occupied as much space as the Temple. The two spaces combined equaled half of this level. Lord Lukan and his party of sons and assistants and family and support staff took up the other half.

Only a narrow corridor to the maintenance hatch separated Sissy from the sacred Temple. She even had a private door from her office, across the corridor, into the Temple dressing room. The girls had a nice dormitory with enough beds for each of them. Marsh and Ashel had their own room beside Sissy's bedroom. She had an office, a private sitting room—which she intended to use for the girls' lessons—and a more public parlor, nearly as much room as her quarters in the Crystal Temple on Harmony.

Lord Lukan bowed and backed away, face carefully blank.

"I am sorry, My Laudae." The captain bowed formally as he released her into her quarters. "If I had known how distraught . . . the lady . . . is, I'd have arranged this little ceremony differently."

"You are not to blame." She raised her hand in silent blessing and dismissed him.

Immediately her girls gathered around her. They hugged her tightly, crying in their failure to understand deep-seated prejudice.

"Why is she so mean to us, Sissy?" little Suzy asked through her tears.

"We must make allowances for Lady Jancee. She seeks to honor the Goddess by giving to Her a sacred seven of children. She should not have tried to carry another child at her age."

Lady Jancee had conceived the child here on the station. And on the station she must stay. Everyone knew that hyperspace damaged unborn children. Sissy didn't know how, only that she was stuck with the woman's insults and prejudice for at least another three months.

"She only seeks to keep her husband in her bed and not another's," Mary snorted.

"Mary! You should not say such things."

"It's the truth. Everyone in the Noble enclave knows it."

"And how do you know of such things? You are only thirteen."

"Fourteen next month," Mary said proudly. "Besides, I grew up in Temple, expecting to seek bed partners in another year, two at the most. We do not hide such knowledge in our caste."

"That is changing, Mary. Laudae Penelope and Mr. Guilliam are seeing to that. Marriage and commitment to family must replace free intercourse with any partner on a whim," Sissy reassured herself. Centuries ago, Temple folk had rewritten portions of the Covenant with Harmony, declaring marriage and family for the lower castes only. Those with a purple circle caste mark needed to be above such things. Children were raised in communal nurseries. Women rarely allowed one man to sire more than one child on her. Then she sought another temporary mate.

Something about diversifying the limited gene pool, Laud Gregor claimed.

He refused to acknowledge that couples within his own enclave made commitments to each other and lived together as families.

When Sissy had demanded the original Covenant Tablets be dug out from beneath the High Altar, no one had anticipated how many changes had been made to them.

Laud Gregor's daughter, Laudae Penelope, and his assistant, Mr. Guilliam, had cast aside the cloak of secrecy and now proudly lived together as a married couple with their five children, right in the heart of Crystal Temple.

Sissy hoped her girls would grow up to share the same kind of joy.

She had little hope that she herself would. If she declared her love for the one man she wanted, she'd never be allowed to return to Harmony. She might be forced to step down as a priestess. She couldn't imagine herself with any other man. Nor could she relinquish her spiritual life.

"Mary, where are you going?" Sissy asked as the girl broke away from the group, cast off her veil, and headed for the door.

"I'm going to tell Jake what happened. He never would've allowed Lady Jancee to get away with insulting you, insulting all of us, when he was *our* Jake," Mary replied stiffly.

"Why wasn't Jake here?" Bella asked.

"Jake is no longer one of us," Sissy explained. Again. "This ceremony was for Harmony only."

"He came to the wing Dedication and the Grief Blessing," Martha retorted.

"Jake will always be one of us. He loves us," Sharan said. She rarely said anything.

Sissy sank into the nearest chair. The dogs crowded in on her, offering mute comfort along with a demand for a necessary walk in the gardens. "This is all too complicated. I just want to go home."

But when she thought of home, she thought of the small apartment where she'd grown up with her Worker caste parents, and brothers and sisters, and grandparents. Her aunts and uncles and cousins ran in and out. She thought of her friends in Lord Chauncey's factory.

All those were gone now. Wiped out in the single blast of a massive explosion set by Lady Marissa and her assassin. Lord Lukan tried to make amends for his mother's insanity and blatant violation of all that the people of Harmony held dear. Lady Jancee, it seemed, agreed with her deceased mother-in-law.

Then Sissy thought of the Crystal Temple, where she'd learned to be a priestess, and the funerary caves, where she'd learned more about being human and her relationship with the Goddess Harmony and Her family. A special place for a while. No one was meant to live there permanently, except the dead.

She had no home to run back to. She had only her girls, and Marsh and Ashel, and her pets. And Jake.

"I just wish we could find a planet so we didn't all have to live so close together." Mary echoed Sissy's thoughts as she glared fiercely at the closed door that separated them from Lady Jancee's insults.

"Yes. A planet. A new planet to make our home. Girls, you have the afternoon free to settle in and put your things in their proper places. I'll walk the dogs on my way to find Jake."

"Can we start murals in the Temple?" Bella asked. "It looks naked in there."

✦   ✦   ✦

"Music," Adrial said weakly, the moment she felt she could remain awake for more than a few moments. She'd drifted in and out for a long time. Sometimes she felt as if she heard and saw everything that happened in the MedBay but could not speak or move. Other times she knew she slept for long hours.

During those half waking moments she consciously manipulated her body. Once the priests had taught her to alter her blood chemistry, she rarely needed more than half the normal healing time. Extra protein to the muscles; flood the sites of organ penetration with lymph to fight infection; drain excess fluid from swollen tissue.

Ah, less pain and more strength already.

The beeping machines behind her recorded her every breath and heartbeat, signaling the nurses when she woke and slept. She calmed them with another thought, cherishing her privacy—time to observe and assess.

"What did you say, Miss Adrial?" a male voice asked. He moved so that she could see him standing beside her. In the same movement he raised his hand and beckoned to someone.

Only then did she realize her neck and head were still held immobile by the thick collar and the gel pads.

"I remember you. Lieutenant David?"

"Yes, that's me. I was here yesterday when you first woke up. Back again for the day shift. Important people don't want you left alone. Now what was it you said about music?" He leaned over her and smiled.

A handsome young man, except for the blemish of a red square with a stripe below and a blue line encircling it.

She attempted to smile back. That slight movement stretched tight muscles in her neck and back. She relaxed and tried again. It came easier.

"What happened to the music?"

"Oh, the Dedication and the Grief Blessing. They're all over now."

Disappointment nearly sent Adrial back to sleep. She did not think she could live long without hearing that celestial voice again.

"But they recorded it for replay throughout the station. Let me find it for you." He fiddled with something just beyond her periphery. "Here it is, Miss Adrial."

A holovid popped up on the table across the bed. In moments she heard the sound of an angel singing.

"Who is she that she graces this place with her voice?"

"Laudae Sissy. High Priestess of Harmony. I told you that. Guess the drugs made you forget. We're lucky to have her. Another priestess was assigned here, but at the last minute, our Sissy took her place. Hard to believe the Goddess Harmony would allow her avatar to leave the planet." He sighed and watched the holovid for several minutes. "But then, I've heard it said that Sissy belongs to the entire universe, not just Harmony. I can believe that."

"If She is here, then I must have found heaven at last."

"Not exactly," Lieutenant David snorted.

A doctor barged into the room and swept the table with the holovid aside.

Adrial tried to protest and found instruments attached to her arms and stuck into her mouth. The ethereal voice continued to sing in the distance, taunting her with mere glimpses of the next step in her quest that would never end.

She'd never know peace because the place where the sacred rituals began no longer existed. Life must continue to profane and defile the spirit.

But if she could keep that wonderful voice and music beside her, she might accept her fate with less anger.

✦ ✦ ✦ ◇ ✦ ✦ ✦

CHAPTER FOURTEEN

"**J**AKE, **PLEASE EXPLAIN** to the girls how the caste system became a part of Harmony's culture," Sissy said meekly when she cornered the new general while he inspected the hydroponics gardens.

She suspected he walked here to find a few moments of peace rather than to make sure the Labyrinthes had planted enough lettuce.

"My Laudae . . ." he paused and stammered with caution. He petted the dogs rather than continue his protest or look at her.

Monster and Dog accepted his adulation for only a moment before bounding off to complete their business at the compost pile.

"They need to know how and why the deep prejudice of Lady Jancee and her son Garrin came to be." She looked deeply into the overlapping petals of a plant labeled artichoke. Separating them out would prove as thorny and delicate as the caste system.

Jake straightened and motioned them all to take seats on the benches and paths between raised beds. "This is going to take some time."

"Just be blunt. We'll figure out the niceties and nuances later," Mary insisted.

Such a grown-up attitude! Sissy wondered if she herself would ever feel as mature as her oldest acolyte.

"Very well." Jake settled on the ground, cross-legged. He leaned forward a bit, as if including the girls in a huge secret. "Mr. Guilliam found some very old diaries and documents hidden in the library of Crystal Temple. He shared them with me. I pieced together that information with what we have on file in the CSS data bank."

"Okay, we trust you to have documentation. Tell us," Martha added impatiently.

"We don't want to have to put up with Lady Jancee any longer," Bella added.

Jake drew in a deep breath. "A long time ago, some people on Earth came together and founded a new religion. They called their goddess Harmony. When colonization became available, they took off, separated themselves from Earth. When they landed on the planet you call Harmony, they found a few Maril priests and mystics in residence. We think the Maril had been coming to Harmony for a long time for retreat and for burial."

"We know that. We spent more time examining the bones than you did," Sharan explained.

The dogs came back, circled the seated humans once to make sure they were all there, then wandered off, sniffing every plant and pathway.

"For a while your people lived in peace with the Maril. Then the planet became unstable. Quakes, erupting volcanoes, monster storms . . ."

"Just like when Sissy quieted the planet with her song," Suzie lisped.

"Exactly." Jake smiled at her. "Your people didn't understand that these disruptions were cyclic." He paused to make sure the girls knew the word.

Mary rolled her eyes. Of course they knew a lot of big words. More than Sissy did.

"They thought Harmony was displeased because the people had allowed the Maril to live there with a different religion and pantheon of gods."

"So they slaughtered the Maril," Sissy breathed. She saw again in her memory the first time Jake showed her the skeleton of a Maril child. The aroma of freshly disturbed dust and dirt still filled her nose. The blaring artificial lights deep within the funerary caves seared the images into her mind forever.

As if sensing her distress, Dog thrust his nose beneath her hand, eager and willing to comfort her.

"But the disruptions continued. A lot of people died in the war and from the planet's upheaval," Jake continued, glossing over the horror of all those deaths, human and Maril.

He gathered Monster beneath his arm. The big animal plopped down and rested his heavy head on Jake's thigh.

"How many died, Jake?" Mary asked quietly. She looked as though she needed one of the cats that had escaped into the station and gone feral.

"Many, many thousands. The number of humans was reduced to critical. They didn't have enough left to work the farms, rebuild their shelters, maintain the machines they brought with them."

"So how did they survive?" Martha looked about anxiously. Of all the girls, she had the best scientific knowledge and probably had hints about what was to come.

"When the children of Harmony first left Earth, they came on ships with a very primitive star drive. It was a long journey. Getting a large number of people from here to there was difficult. So they did what we no longer believe acceptable for people, but do for animals that don't travel well in hyperspace."

"Frozen embryos?" Martha asked, one jump ahead of the other girls in understanding. "Our cats and dogs did okay, in hyperspace because they could snuggle up to one of us. The other animals didn't like it. They nearly went insane. We had to drug them senseless and send them home. I can see why farm planets need to bring their sheep and cows and goats in as embryos."

Jake nodded and gulped. "The mother ship was still in orbit with most of the embryos intact. At first the colonists hadn't needed them; life on Harmony was peaceful and plentiful. But when only a couple hundred of them were left, they incubated the embryos from believers who couldn't come with them from Earth and filled the planet with enough people to carry on."

"What does that have to do with the caste system?" Bella asked, puzzled. She reached across Jake to pet Monster. He picked her up and deposited her in his lap. He had done that often enough back on Harmony.

"The first people on the planet had endured a lot of hardship." Jake spoke slowly fishing for polite words. "The new people hadn't. The older ones didn't think the new people should have as many benefits as them. So they tinkered with the embryos to give them caste marks. Most of the hard work fell on the created people, and they served the original colonists, who became Temple and Noble."

"They made slaves of the Workers, the Spacers, and the Military," Sissy insisted. Her anger had grown cold. Every day she plotted ways to break the system without launching a civil war. But who would believe the tale?

Most people on Harmony grew up accepting the caste system as part of life. They never questioned it or their lot.

Only when evidence of a breakdown occurred—like the riot in the asylum where people with mutant caste marks were thrown away—did the masses wonder if something had gone wrong.

"Actually, we now believe that Spacers didn't become a caste until the colonists decided to expand the empire," Jake corrected her. "Again they tinkered with unborn children of Worker and Military caste. They made Spacers smaller and lighter boned with very efficient metabolisms so they can fit more of them on board ships and use less supplies and life support. While they were at it, they added great spatial relationship skills. They'd already given Military extra height and muscle mass. We don't know if they did something extra to Professionals and Media."

"So the caste system came from our ancestors, not from Harmony?" Martha asked. She reached out to hold the hands of her two closest companions.

"Yes. But not everyone knows that," Sissy said in a mild tone that did not betray her roiling emotions. "Only a few that Mr. Guilliam has told. Lady Jancee and Garrin still believe that the Goddess created them superior to everyone else."

"There are people like that in every culture," Jake chuckled. "We call them pompous boors."

The girls laughed with him. Bella jumped up and began imitating Lady Jancee's waddling walk that threw her off-balance when she tried looking down her nose at the rest of the universe.

"On that note, I have to get back to work. A data gig of details awaits me in my office," Jake said, rising to his feet in one strong motion. He dusted off his uniform and glanced at his comm. "May I escort you ladies somewhere?"

"Back to the Temple. We have lessons and services to prepare," Sissy said.

The girls groaned in unison. "I thought this was our lesson time," Mary protested.

"All life is one long lesson," Sissy said. "We have to keep learning and growing or we become like Lady Jancee."

Or like the Harmonite Empire had become.

✦   ✦   ✦

"Explain yourself, Jake. I did not authorize you to assume command here. If anyone should have, it would have been me." Pamela Marella awaited Jake when he returned to his office. She assumed the chair at the head of the conference table as if she truly belonged there.

"You were not here. The ambassadors needed my organizational skills, my ability to manipulate Control screens, and my knowledge of the station. A little bit of leadership training as squadron leader didn't hurt. My position has been confirmed by both governments. Now get out of my chair, Pammy." He spoke mildly, leaning casually against the wall near the holovid window that showed a real-time spacescape near the jump point, the only decoration on otherwise naked walls.

He made a mental note to do something to spruce up the place, make it his own. A mural here and there wouldn't hurt. And glyphs of Harmony and her family . . .

He might have looked relaxed, but every muscle in Jake's body tensed, poised to launch into hand-to-hand combat if necessary. He'd sparred with Pammy during his training as one of her spies. She'd taken him down every time.

Since then he'd learned a few things about dirty fighting. He'd murdered dozens of desperate and rioting inmates from one of the asylums on Harmony and learned the horrible intimacy of taking another life, watching the spark in the eyes dim and glaze until his victim saw only death. He'd also helped clean up the aftermath of an assassin's bomb meant for Sissy.

Pammy wouldn't get the jump on him again.

He needed to be out and about the station. If he made Pammy walk with him, she'd see how desperate a situation he commanded. That knowledge would lessen his authority in her eyes. For now, all those supervisions and demands must wait. He must deal with Admiral Pamela Marella from his power base—this luxurious office.

The bureaucrats would make a politician of him yet.

His fingers caressed the grip of the Badger Metal knife on his belt, just one souvenir of his stint on Harmony. The blade was sharper than a razor and never dulled or broke. Pammy couldn't miss the implication that he was prepared to fight her in every way.

"You going to cooperate, Admiral, or do I confine you to the CSS residential wing without access to comms for the duration of your stay here?" He flashed her a feral grin, almost hoping she'd get argumentative or combative.

"You can't . . ."

"Wanna make a bet?" He edged the knife out of his scabbard.

"Very well. I concede you the trappings of authority. But never forget your ass is mine." She shifted to a chair in the middle of the table. She removed a layer of dust from the polished synthwood with a fingertip. "You need to get housekeeping up here."

"I'd love to. If I had a housekeeping staff. If I had any staff at all."

"What about Labyrinthe's people?" She looked surprised.

Jake hadn't thought anything could surprise Pammy.

"Labby cut his staff—and safety protocols—to the barest bones and then some to save money—or boost his profit margin, not sure which. Even if I could trust his people, I don't think there are enough to do half the jobs that need doing."

Jake took the chair recently vacated by Pammy. "I need a crew, and I need it fast. I can only borrow from the two ambassadors for so long. They have other duties, and many are due to be rotated out."

"What am I supposed to do about it?" Pammy sat back, arms crossed. She wanted favors for favors.

"You are more than just the spymaster, Admiral Marella. You have influence. You know which strings to pull, which favors to call in, which skeletons in the closets can be rattled. I need crew and a budget. Preferably shared by the CSS and Harmony."

"You don't ask for much," she replied sarcastically.

"I only ask for my due. The CSS has been trying to set up their own First Contact Café for a century, and the Labyrinthe corporation always moves into the area first. They've staked out locations next to all eight known major jump point crossings. Now's our chance." Jake leaned forward, eager to push Pammy to agree with him.

"Think about it, Pammy. At the moment, this place doesn't officially belong to anyone. You and I can make it our own, establish our own security protocols, set up trade routes. Use it as a base for unregistered travel." He threw in the last, knowing how hard she'd found moving her spies about the Confederation undetected.

"Fair enough. But you can't run this place for long." She smiled with secret knowledge.

"Why not?"

"Because we think we've found a planet for the CSS headquarters. I'll need you there."

"An unoccupied habitable planet *that no one claims*?" Somehow Jake didn't think that would ever happen.

"Got it in one."

"You've only been looking for twenty years. We've only been on this station six months."

"And now it's time to move on. Don't worry, Jake, I'll find someone capable to replace you here."

"Have you really found a planet?" Sissy asked from the doorway. In her simple purple dress, which hung discreetly below her knees, she looked far too young and fragile for the weight of the responsibilities she shouldered. She looked as though she needed the two dogs at her heels for protection.

Both animals curled their lips in silent warning as they caught a whiff of Pammy. Jake needed to protect her. Reluctantly he conceded that with his new schedule, the dogs would do a better job.

His heart flipped over. Then regret descended heavily. If he ever acted on the impulses of his heart, Sissy would be exiled from her home forever. He couldn't do that to her.

If he couldn't love her openly, he'd at least do his damnedest to grant her every wish.

"Jake, I need you to take me to this new planet. Today. This minute. I need to hear the natural rhythms of a world in harmony with itself. If I have to stay onboard this station, listen to the ceaseless cacophony of chaos one more minute, I'll go insane." She floated in, as graceful in gravity as weightless, eager and weary at the same time.

"Sorry, Laudae Sissy. Harmony hasn't signed a treaty with the CSS yet. Until then, our headquarters is off-limits," Pammy sneered.

$$\text{✦ ✦ ✦ ◇ ✦ ✦ ✦}$$

CHAPTER FIFTEEN

ADRIAL CAME FULLY AWAKE, minus the fog of drugs. She kept her eyes closed, listening, assessing, waiting. Her breathing and heart rate responded to her command to remain quiet, even, and slow. Sharp smells of antiseptic and the sour smells of sweat and fear told her she remained in the hospital. Comfortable, light gravity held her bones in place without straining them.

She tested her hips, knees, and feet with a gentle rotation. They all worked. Only her ribs remained unhealed. She could move if she had to. She'd managed greater pain than this and still kept running.

The constant drip and hum of machines annoyed her. She endured their presence as she'd endured so much.

Ah, the breathing of her constant guard in the corner. A quick peek revealed Lieutenant David. He paged through a reader, absorbing the information with a smile. She allowed her eyes to flutter open as if slowly reviving from slumber.

The machines responded with increased humming and beeping. They recorded her wakefulness when she deemed it safe. A little reprogramming and she'd make them record her presence when she chose to absent herself. She never knew when she needed time to escape.

"The one who saved me?" she whispered. Her voice came out a raw croak.

Lieutenant David jumped to bring her water. She sipped from the tube cautiously. Other captors had slipped truth drugs into simple sustenance. But then if these humans wanted to force her to reveal information they could include the serums in the cocktail of things dripping into her veins.

The first taste of water revealed nothing more noxious than the faint citrus taste added at the recycling plant. She drank again, more deeply.

And coughed most of it back up as her stomach rebelled.

Lieutenant David looked panicked. He pressed a summoning button frantically. "My apologies, Miss Adrial. I am not allowed to slap your back to help clear your throat. I'm sorry. Doc Halliday fears your bones are too fragile for rough treatment. I'm sorry. I dare not touch you to assist in any way. I'm sorry."

Adrial swallowed her smile along with some life-giving air. Her guard was half in love with her. Not the first time. She knew how to use him now to find the next key in her search. She'd delayed too long. She must continue her quest immediately.

The Messengers of the Gods had decreed.

Leave no trace of your passing.

Gently she placed her hand upon his to still his repeated summons. "The nurse will come in good time. Now tell me of the one who rescued me from the wreckage. Such a strange being with eight limbs, pincers instead of hands, able to hold air inside himself while traversing vacuum. Tell me how he brought me here to your safekeeping."

✦ ✦ ✦

Sissy sat heavily in the chair at Jake's right, across from Admiral Marella. All her hopes for relief from the press of the station against her senses swirled away.

The dogs sat silently at attention on either side of her. Monster edged beneath the table a bit, as if ready to grab the admiral's leg in his strong jaws to keep her in place.

"We're close to an agreement on the treaty." She didn't believe her own words.

"If you say so." The admiral leaned back. Her gaze drifted to Jake with affection. She looked feral and cunning.

Sissy stiffened, every hair on her body standing on end, like Cat when confronted with something new and scary. She knew in that instant that Jake and the admiral had been lovers. Jealousy flared along her spine, hot and explosive. She needed to lash out, wipe the satisfied smirk off the woman's face, as she wished she'd slapped Lady Jancee.

Remember your manners, her mother's voice said sharply in her memory.

Sissy almost looked around for the ghostly presence. Instead she took in a deep breath and mastered the emotions warring within her.

"And if I brought Lord Lukan to the pen within the hour, what excuse would you make to keep me away from this new planet?"

She heard Jake draw in a sharp breath that whistled lightly between his teeth. His fists clenched atop the table. The thin-bladed knife he wore inside his sleeve stood clearly outlined beneath the cloth of his black uniform.

Without a word, Admiral Marella pushed her chair back and stood. Her civilian trousers and jacket fell neatly into place without a wrinkle. Dog came alert, ears lifted, teeth bared, a low rumble in his chest.

Composed and haughty, the admiral left the room, not once looking back over her shoulder. As the door swished shut behind her, she spoke. "Jake, my office, ten minutes. Come alone."

"That is one person you don't want as an enemy, Sissy," Jake said quietly. "She's dangerous." He captured her hand with his own, squeezing it to emphasize his warning.

"More dangerous than you?" Sissy asked, returning the grip on his hand. She tried to hide her own fear. Whether fear of the admiral or fear at her own audacity she didn't know.

Jake gave out a short laugh, more a release of tension than true humor. "Not at the moment." He leaned back, released her and placed both of his hands behind his head. Far away from touching distance. "So what brings you to my conference room, Laudae Sissy?"

His relaxed pose didn't fool her. She'd seen him play this act too many times just before leaping into action with weapons flying and teeth bared. The dogs were less subtle and thus slightly less dangerous.

"I . . . I . . ." Words deserted her. Why had she come? "What exactly does hyperspace do to a body that a pregnant woman shouldn't travel?"

"Huh?" He snapped forward, hands once more on the table, jaw hanging open. "You aren't . . ."

"No, I am not." She should be insulted. He knew her. Knew her qualms about adopting the Temple attitude toward sex outside of a committed marriage. On the other hand, the slight was trivial compared to the joy in finding something, anything, that could surprise Jake.

"I ask on behalf of Lady Jancee. She really needs to go home, be among familiar people, in familiar surroundings."

So did Sissy. But she didn't have that luxury.

Jake exhaled deeply and lost a lot of his puffy indignation. "I'll ask. The ship's surgeon who came in with Pammy has more experience with that sort of thing than I do. I can't imagine Spacer females grounding themselves for a small thing like pregnancy. Some of them claim to have lived their entire lives aboard ship, never having set foot dirtside. A point of pride with them."

"Please do." She bowed her head shyly a moment. "Would you mind if I stayed here a bit when you go to meet Admiral Marella?" At the moment, the vibrations of only a single power plant penetrated her defenses. She caught its rhythm, allowed her body to breathe with it. Her heart beat a nice counterpoint.

Almost music. Almost synchronization.

"Stay as long as you want. But I'm not going to Pammy's office. I'm not at her beck and call anymore. Besides, I have too much to do. How about I bring some of my detail work in here. You can help me sort through graphs and accounting sheets. You're better at seeing patterns than I am." He yawned and stretched. "Some lunch would be nice too."

Sissy settled more comfortably in her chair. "Just like back on Harmony, where you taught me how to read memo doublespeak."

"But you were the one who found the pattern of repeated names on troop casualty rosters that Gregor faked in order to get reassignments where he wanted."

"We work well together, Jake." She dared touch his hand.

He turned his palm upward and clasped hers. Warmth and well-being spread through her faster than the fine wines Lord Lukan served at formal dinners. For the length of one hundred heartbeats she pretended they had the right to touch each other.

✦ ✦ ✦ ◇ ✦ ✦ ✦

CHAPTER SIXTEEN

A STEP SOUNDED OUTSIDE Adrial's door. She put aside her reader and rested her head limply against the pile of pillows behind her neck and back. As the frosted bio-plastic swooshed open, she composed her face into resigned endurance.

"Are you in pain, Adrial?" Doc Halliday asked. She hastened to the array of machines that pumped and dripped, measured and assessed.

"No more than any other time," Adrial sighed. "I think I should sleep now." Surreptitiously she flipped the document on her reader to show a series of meditations written by a High Priest of Harmony two hundred years ago.

"Not just yet. We need to talk." Doc Halliday pulled a stool over to the bedside and planted herself on it as if she intended to grow roots.

A stimulant hit Adrial's veins and forced her eyes open and her mind spinning. The machines reflected her response.

Too late to control them.

Doc Halliday looked behind and above Adrial to the screens filled with numbers. "Good. Your heart rate and respiration are closer to normal now. You need to breathe deeper, force oxygen into your system to promote healing."

As if Adrial didn't know that already, hadn't sped her recovery with a series of meditations that opened the flow of air throughout her body.

"I see you've been using the ultrasound to hasten the bone mending," the physician continued casually. Almost too casually.

"A marvelous device," Adrial replied weakly. She tried to figure out from her posture and the texture of her pupils what the older woman wanted.

She gave nothing away. Perhaps the doctor had learned control in the same school Adrial had.

Instantly she grew wary.

"What do you know about the Squid People who piloted the ship that brought you here?"

"Squid People?" Adrial feigned ignorance.

"Were you a stowaway that you never saw your pilots?" The doctor returned question for question. A good interrogator.

"I saw them. I did not know the term Squid." The stimulant kept pushing the truth out of Adrial. She could hedge but not lie. There must have been something else in that drug cocktail.

"So why did you choose their vessel, and what do you know about them?"

"They were coming here. I took passage away from where I was."

"And . . . ?"

"And they sought spiritual peace with The One who collects the lost and gives them purpose. I seek the same thing. I found Laudae Sissy. Do you think I could meet her?"

"Maybe. First we need to talk about your condition, Adrial."

"What is wrong?" she asked in alarm. Surely she would have found something drastically out of place during her meditations.

"Many things. Our scans indicate that you have been abused and raped many times."

Adrial relaxed. "Oh, that."

"Yes, that. We need to know who did this to you, to prevent them from continuing their crimes."

"It is no crime for the Law to torture their prisoners," she said quietly.

Doc Halliday stiffened and snorted in disgust. "That is a heinous crime on all the planets and stations I've visited. No one has that right, especially not the Law, who are pledged to protect and serve."

"The Law have lost the sacred rituals," Adrial replied. "The temples are profaned. They must be cleansed so that the rituals may be made sacred again."

"What temples? Which religion?"

"The Messengers of the Gods can't find the temples. Without a temple, the angels cannot touch their people and make them prosperous and plentiful." With that, Adrial chose to fall into unconsciousness, as if speaking so many words in a row exhausted the stimulant and left her weaker than ever.

✦   ✦   ✦

Two days later Jake relaxed into his old black uniform from his days on Harmony. The sturdy cloth with gel armor packs that could inflate in any number of strategic places molded to his body like a second skin, flowing with each movement and ample ease to stretch into awkward positions without resistance.

He stuffed weapons, handhelds, extra comms, minor tools, and electronic keys into the multitude of pockets on his thighs, arms, and chest. Even a few secret ones on his back. CSS fatigues weren't nearly so practical or comfortable.

Class As from either military were a pain in the neck.

"General Jake?" Mara's voice came over his private comm.

"Devlin here," he replied, wondering if he really needed a sixth throwing star. Better make it seven and keep the divine symmetry.

"Ambassador Telvino requests your presence in the diplomatic conference room, ASAP." She paused and cleared her throat. "Sir, what does ASAP mean?"

"It means get my ass down there ten minutes ago." He headed for the door. He was glad he'd found his old major's oak-leaf insignia for her, even though the governments hadn't confirmed her as his first officer or the promotion he requested for her. He had to drag out old battlefield promotion traditions to justify it to the ambassadors.

"I don't understand the origin of the word."

"An acronym. As Soon As Possible." Which meant he could legitimately override the trams to make sure one awaited him at the hub, and he could increase the speed to max. That little privilege saved him many minutes in waiting time as he moved about the station.

Jake almost ran into a Harmony corporal as he stepped off the tram and bounced toward the lift.

"Excuse me, sir. Laudae Sissy requested I remind you of your meeting in the comms wing tonight." With a formal bow he beamed a message from his comm to Jake's with a touch of his wrist. Then he remembered to salute before hurrying off to catch the tram Jake had just debarked.

"Guess I'm not the only one with too much to do and too many people demanding my time." He decided to enter the diplomatic conference room with more dignity than sliding down the circular staircase. He used the time on the lift mechanism to answer five messages that had piled up while he was en route. Two from Sissy, one each from the ambassadors, and a fifth from Doc Halliday. The last one had nothing to do with the meeting and wasn't urgent. He ignored her polite request to autopsy the Squid People in the crashed spaceship. That could wait.

Apparently the meeting couldn't.

"General Devlin," Sissy said from behind her formal veil and all-concealing robes before Jake had set half a foot inside the conference room. "Please explain in detail to Ambassador Lord Lukan the state of the war with the Maril. He does not comprehend the urgency in signing a treaty of alliance and mutual defense with the CSS."

Jake took a deep breath, noting that Lukan's son Garrin sat beside him, bristling with indignation. The young man, barely into his twenties, took offense at everything that involved contact outside Harmony. Telvino had a Marine lieutenant beside him, taking notes and accessing detailed records of previous meetings. Sissy had all six of her girls and two dogs arrayed about the room, observing the actions from every angle.

Pammy was notable by her absence.

"Map, recent battles with Maril and adjacent star systems," Jake called to the computer system.

"Authorization code and retinal scan required," the androgynous voice asked firmly but politely.

Alternately cursing the lengthy procedure to pry information from the machine and admiring the security, he went through the ritual, making sure he took no shortcuts. Sissy had set a formal tone. He intended to play along.

If he'd had the spectacles, he bet the computer would have acknowledged his right to the information without question.

Dozens of pinpoints of light flashed into the air at the end of the table to fill one third of the large room. Tiny letters appeared beneath the purple and blue lights, naming the star systems that belonged to Harmony and to the CSS. Green lights appeared around the edges, frontier worlds that traded with the CSS but did not belong to the Confederation. Yellow lights marked pirate worlds, the ones that had no affiliation and no respect for the laws of any of their "trading partners."

Jake counted twenty-two of the latter and whistled through his teeth. Last time he'd checked, there had been thirty-five.

Last, the Marilon Empire was revealed as a cluster of red that spread out and out again. They'd absorbed the twelve pirate worlds and seven of the frontier outposts. They surrounded Harmony's grouping of seven purple lights, leaving only a narrow corridor of protected access.

Telvino gasped as he too recognized the significance in the number changes.

"Explain this?" Lord Lukan asked. He rose and walked around the map, peering at colors and distances with curiosity.

Sissy reached out to the Harmonite Empire as if she could touch her home. Then her hand dropped abruptly back into her lap in great disappointment.

Jake explained the color coding. Lukan nodded.

"Meaningless," Garrin spat. "Harmony is safe. We know how to defend our borders. We have never needed help before. We do not need it now."

"Sir, if you will be patient a bit longer, I think you will begin to see what is happening on a broader scale." Jake nearly bit his tongue in two keeping himself from barking at the man as if he were the rawest recruit with a subpar IQ.

"Map, show position of Labyrinthe Stations," Sissy chimed in. Seven black bars appeared in seemingly random positions. "And the CSS military space stations." Another dozen black Xs appeared.

"Map, on the worlds most recently acquired by the Maril, show those absorbed into the empire and those wiped clean of inhabitants," Jake added, more intent on his own agenda.

Sissy gasped as five worlds blinked rapidly while dozens of others pulsed more slowly.

"Gentlemen, I have it on good authority that from the worlds the Maril have absorbed, they recruit troops to fill their expanded fleet," Jake said. His gut twisted a little at the thought of having to fight his own kind. "They have begun an intensive crossbreeding program with humans to insure loyalty of the next generation as well. Map, highlight recent battle activity."

Tiny pinpoints of light darted around the three outermost systems belonging to Harmony. Dozens more showed around the CSS space stations and the rim worlds, both in peaceful trade and pirate status.

"They . . . they're closing in on Harmony V, III, and II," Garrin gasped, half standing. He grew pale and wobbled. "Do we have enough troops to defend all three at once?" He looked to his father with bleak hope.

Lukan shook his head.

"Don't you see the pattern of occupation?" Sissy asked.

"What?" Jake whirled to face her, fully aware that she of all people would find a pattern where the most brilliant of strategists couldn't.

"The cleansed worlds . . . they . . . they are equally spaced among the Maril worlds. It's as if each one is the center of a grouping of equal numbers of systems."

"Damn. You're right. The absorbed worlds are outside that pattern. What's so special about these?" He pointed to them. "You said they were cleansed. Cleansed of people?"

"Behold the lands of our beginning. The feathered ones perform ritual cleansing before sanctification. The sacred breeding rituals must return." Sissy's voice sounded hollow, deeper than her usual timbre, full of magnificent authority.

Then her eyes rolled up. All six of her girls rushed to her side and guided her back into her chair. They encircled her, making a solid barrier between the High Priestess and prying eyes. The two dogs took up their own guard stance, ears cocked to alertness, noses working, ready to defend their lady to the death.

CHAPTER SEVENTEEN

MAC QUICKLY CLOSED DOWN the holo of the activity in the dip-lomatic conference wing. He listened to the activity beyond his closed door in MedBay. The hurrying footsteps passed him by. No one cared at the moment how he occupied his time. They'd never know how easy he found hacking through their image system to network with his own observation terminals and databases.

Tomorrow he faced surgery to complete the mending of his fried nerve endings. For the time being, he rested and observed, assured of his safety by a bevy of medical personnel led by the formidable Doc Halliday.

The habits of secrecy died hard. He kept the holovid off a while longer.

He had to think about what the star map revealed. Laudae Sissy had spotted the pattern seconds before he had. Patterns of Maril aggression, certainly. What the diplomats had not seen, but Mac had added at the last moment, was jump point locations.

No one truly understood the physics of the natural phenomena. He knew that most only led from here to there through hyperspace. A few precious ones could be manipulated by speed, trajectory, and timing to lead to dozens of locations.

Labyrinthe Corporation had built their stations near the latter. Except for the one near Harmony Prime. His mother and siblings had never managed to negotiate with that empire.

Biting his lower lip in trepidation, he pulled up the map once more. The battle locations still pulsed hot and white.

Two battles raged only a single jump from Labyrinthe Prime. Control that station and they controlled access to the entire galaxy.

For the first time in his life he knew fear for his siblings. If any one of the stations fell into enemy hands, the galaxy was lost.

On the other hand, if Labyrinthe Corporation worked together, built and armed an independent fleet, they could maintain peace and prosperous trade across a much broader sector of space than any one political alliance or empire could.

The First Contact Café was part of that network. He had to gain control over the station before Jake or Laudae Sissy spotted that pattern in the map.

He had to get out of MedBay and get to work. His lower limbs remained inert. He pushed his mind to override the damaged nerves. His back cramped into spasm after spasm of twisting muscle. Sharp pain, dull aches, and burning lances left him breathless and weak.

At the last second, before passing out, he sent a duplicate of the map to the reader built into the bedside table of his little bird.

✦　✦　✦

Sissy crept from her bed. The digital readout on the small nightstand showed two o'clock in the morning. Quietly she pulled on plain brown coveralls. She'd kept the coarse work clothes as a reminder of her origins and the people she served. She might be High Priestess now, but she belonged to more than just the highborn.

The dogs raised their muzzles from the nest of their paws, ears cocked in question.

"Shush." She held a finger to her lips. "Go back to sleep."

Monster stretched and followed her to the door. Hastily she shut him in. She felt her way through the complex of rooms toward the lobby in complete darkness. Her bare feet made no sound on the thick carpet.

She counted her steps, memorizing where the furniture should be. "Fragit!" she cursed as her toe stubbed against a chair. These rooms were bigger than her quarters in the damaged wing. Everything was just a tad off in her calculations.

She slowed and counted more carefully.

Eventually she escaped the suite into the circular lobby and the lift. Did the continuously moving mechanism run more slowly this late in the day? Maybe her own eagerness made the trip up to the tram seem longer.

She counted off the levels impatiently. Not content to watch the numbers click over on the floor, she had to peer out at each level and check who else remained awake. Only an occasional guard patrolled. None of them looked toward the constantly moving lift or noticed her.

At last she felt a lessening from the tug of gravity on her limbs. Two more levels and weight deserted her. She jumped free of the lift platform almost before it reached its zenith and moved laterally to begin its downward rotation.

Jake awaited her with a tram.

Her heart swelled at the sight of him. He looked tired, with his dark hair flopping in his eyes and wearing his crumpled black, everyday Harmony uniform with its myriad pockets.

A gentle push with her toes sent her soaring through the microgravity. He caught her with one arm and swung her around.

They both laughed. Paused. Gazed longingly at each other. Faces mere inches apart.

Mouths eager for a kiss.

And then he set her down inside the tram and keyed in the joint communications wing.

"You look tired, Jake," she said softly as her hand inched toward his. "You should be in bed. I can send my broadcast to Harmony by myself."

His fingers brushed hers. "I know you can. But I want to be there." He paused and squeezed her hand in reassurance and left their fingers entwined. "In case something goes wrong, or Lord Lukan discovers you."

"He is most protective of communications to Harmony, fearful of contamination from outside influences," she agreed.

"And he's a liberal," Jake chuckled.

"I wish Laud Gregor did not have such tight censorship on my official broadcasts," she sighed. "The Media caste is now independent and should be able to report the truth without interference."

"Governments have always influenced the media. Throughout history in every culture. The truth has always been a revolutionary concept carried out in secret." He looked down on her fondly.

She wished he'd touch her, do more than just look at her.

"What are you going to talk about this week?" he broke the silence.

"I need to remind people to check and recheck the original Covenant Stones, to make sure Laud Gregor and the High Council can't find excuses to change things again. We can't allow ignorance and secrecy to dictate our faith and our culture any longer."

"How's Penelope doing with integrating the schools?"

"I haven't heard." She ground her teeth in frustration. "I broadcast to the masses in secret. No one dares reply. I get only official announcements through proper channels."

"Meaning Laud Gregor edits them."

She nodded rather than speak the anger that threatened to erupt.

"Give it time, Sissy. It's only been a year. Earth took centuries to elimi-
nate racial prejudice. Humans need someone 'below' them to blame
rather than take responsibility for their own inadequacies."

"Have I known you only a year? Sometimes it seems we met yesterday.
Other times, like now, I feel as if I've known you through a dozen life-
times." She looked up at him, memorizing again the line of his cheek and
jaw, the sparkle in his eyes, the set of his shoulders . . .

"Maybe we have. Earth has a couple of religions that believe our souls
return time and again. Each reincarnation teaches us something. Maybe
we've met up numerous times in our pasts."

"That is an idea I'd like to research."

"I'll send you some books."

And just as he leaned down as if to kiss her, the tram stopped and the
doors opened on the communications wing with half a dozen CSS techs
waiting to board the car as they left at the end of their shift.

Jake grabbed Sissy's hand as he launched out of the tram in one long
leap to the lift. She barely had time to touch the glyph of Harmony on the
side of the car. They caught a platform just as it started downward. Sissy
allowed herself to relax, knowing Jake would watch for intruders. Even
exhausted, he'd always watched over her and her girls. She wanted to rest
her head against his chest as she rested her cares upon his shoulders.

All too soon they reached MG 15, where communications equipment
filled the entire level without partitions. Three CSS techs remained on
duty.

Jake led Sissy to an empty terminal beside a familiar corporal. She
nodded in silent acknowledgment. They'd met before, many times over
the last six months when he helped her speak to her people through a pirate radio station. Jake had insisted she never know their contact's name.
That way, if Lord Lukan caught them and demanded punishment, she
couldn't reveal his identity.

"Incoming from Harmony, My Laudae," Jake whispered. He looked
worried. "It's coming over our private channel." He pushed the tech aside
and assumed his position, taking command of the operation.

Silent words began scrolling across Sissy's screen. "Eyes Only. Laudae
Sissy. Eyes Only."

"Please key in your password and thumbprint, My Laudae," Jake said
curtly.

Sissy obeyed. She hunted out the keys for the string of numbers that
combined Jake's birth date with her own. The few crew around her politely averted their eyes for this protocol.

The scrolling message dissolved into Little Johnny's worried face. The head of the Media caste's son had shown a lot of initiative in sidestepping official restrictions.

She inserted an ear bud so no one else would hear the report.

"My Laudae," he whispered across the light-years. Static distorted his voice so that she almost didn't recognize it. "Laud Gregor has left Harmony Prime. Official reports say he's headed for a tour of the outer colonies. Mr. Guilliam sent me a delayed message. The High Priest is going to Labyrinthe VII, and he won't come home without you."

✦ ✦ ✦

"This isn't going to work, Jake," Pammy said a bit breathlessly the next day around noon. She followed closely as Jake dashed for the nearest lift.

Jake hoped she panted a bit because of his speed, not because she hoped he'd fall flat on his face at this newest crisis aboard the First Contact Café.

Then there was the crisis last night. From the paleness of Sissy's face and the stubborn set of her chin, he guessed something had happened on Harmony Prime.

What?

Why didn't Sissy trust him enough to tell him?

At the top of the lift, when the platform hesitated half a second before it moved horizontally and then began the downward rotation, he bent his knees, jumped forward and grabbed the door of the tram just as it closed.

Maybe, just maybe, Pammy would be that heartbeat too slow and have to wait for the next tram. He'd had enough of her dogging his footsteps at every move.

She acted almost as if she wanted him to fail—or admit failure and defer to her expertise.

"Can't know I've failed until I try," he called back to Pammy, trying to focus his attention on what awaited him rather than what happened last night.

Damn, she grabbed hold and slid into the tram at the last possible second. The automatic doors had to partially reopen rather than crush her. She even managed a brief touch to the Harmony glyph upon entry.

Sissy's little ritual had spread throughout the station. But the contents of that secret message from Harmony had not. He'd give one of his Badger Metal throwing stars to know what had caused her to blanch and then

change her message to the people of Harmony. Instead of urging people
to check and recheck the original Covenant Stones, she talked about trust
and opening channels of communication.

But she hadn't trusted him or told him what was in that message.

"You don't need one hundred Labyrinthe staff workers, Jake. Let them
go," Pammy broke into his musing halfway to wing eight.

"They have no guarantee of employment at the other end of their journey. I have no other employees to take over their jobs," he replied. "I
need someone who knows how this place works to get into the guts of the
propulsion system and find out why fuel consumption has increased five
percent over the last week."

"I'll get you a full staff. A trained staff. Just give me a few days."

"You've had three days, and I haven't seen the first sign of help coming
in. Not a request for docking space. Not a copy of a work contract. Not
even a rumor." Jake fixed a level gaze on her. "But I have had requests
from six shipping companies to stop here on their routes. They'll pay
double docking fees if I waive CSS customs. I need staff to cope with the
extra traffic. And I need to fix the propulsion system fast, before the fuel
drain eats any profits increased trade can bring."

"Those crystal stars on your collar have gone to your head, Jake. You
can't just order the universe to answer your pleas for help." She frowned
and crossed her arms. Amazing what zero G did for her breasts.

Stop that! he yelled to himself. *She's doing it deliberately to distract
me.*

"I didn't ask the universe for help. I asked you. And I asked Lord
Lukan. He's got a transport due to dock in three hours with the promise
of two dozen maintenance and computer techs. He's already given me
fifteen Workers who haven't been ennobled or lauded. I can taint them
with outside contact as much as I want. I need about three hundred more
people, Pammy. And that's a bare minimum."

"I'll get them for you. But these things take time. You need to concentrate on getting the three tons of Badger Metal in the Harmony ship's
hold onto the CSS ship waiting for it. We're losing ships to Maril attacks
and don't have anything to replace them. I won't send a fleet out without
Badger Metal hulls to protect from radiation and hyperspace distortion.
Have you ever been lost in hyperspace with failing instruments because
Maril plasma canons left holes in your shield plating?"

"Yes," Jake replied. Everything inside him threatened to freeze. He'd
faced certain death that day after a lightning raid on a Maril munitions
dump. "I got back alive and only a thousand klicks off target because I

stayed calm and trusted my gut to lead me in the right direction. I didn't panic and jerk my navigation around."

"The next squadron might not be so smart. Save your complaints about a crew and get that Badger Metal off-loaded."

"You want to take more time than I've got. And I can't shift that cargo without crew to shift it, no matter how much the CSS needs the Badger Metal. Now either I stop those Labyrinthe workers from leaving, or we shut this place down. Completely. And I don't think you are ready to settle on your new planet just yet. Or abandon this place to the Labyrinthe Corporation again. We need the First Contact Café to bolster CSS presence in this sector or we lose it to the Maril. Did you read my report about sightings on the fringe of this system?"

She shook her head. "Bored techs imagining data blips on dark watch."

"You know as well as I that our jump point will take a battle fleet just about anywhere in human occupied space," Jake continued. "The Maril see us as vulnerable and this jump point too valuable to bypass."

Something clanged in the back of his mind. Something about the star map he'd developed for Sissy . . .

The tram stopped abruptly. Jake almost lost his grip on the wall bracket. His feet flew out from under him. No problem in zero G. He flipped for proper orientation to the lift and pushed himself free the second the doors opened enough for his body to clear.

This time he did take the extra second for a finger kiss on the glyph—thanks for a safe journey, if not a solitary one.

His comm beeped as his feet settled on the lift platform. Pammy was just slow enough to have to take the next one.

"What?" he asked the comm.

"Labyrinthe Transport LC 8579 requests permission to cycle air locks and begin boarding passengers," came the respectful male voice at the other end. Not Mara. She had to sleep sometime.

A luxury no one afforded Jake.

"Permission denied," Jake growled. He was about to turn the unit off when it beeped again, a different tone. He didn't dare ignore it.

"Devlin," he said into the comm, not recognizing the origin of the signal.

"Lieutenant David here, sir. Harmony transport has requested docking as close to MedBay as possible, overriding all protocols."

"They're three hours early, must be a huge emergency. You still in MedBay?" Jake asked. This didn't sound good.

"Yes, sir."

"Get someone else to guard our guests and plant yourself at the air lock. I want you present every step of the way with whatever emergency they've got."

Aha! He had an idea about the content of Sissy's message last night. A highly placed and very sick passenger aboard that vessel. Who?

"My replacement isn't due for another three hours, sir," Lieutenant David hedged.

"Then find someone else you trust. Fast. And keep me informed."

"Doc Halliday will invoke patient privacy."

"Screw patient privacy. I need to know." He gulped three times, praying for patience. "Pammy, you hear that?" he called up the shaft.

"Yes."

"Want to go see what's up?"

"Yes. But I also need to keep track of you. Think of me as a limpet mine attached to your ass."

"Apt description," he muttered sotto voce.

"I heard that, Jake."

He jumped clear of the lift in the docking bay between light- and mid-G levels in the Labyrinthe wing. The docks on each wing took up a minimum of six levels in height to complete the transition between gravity designations above and below, as well as to hold bulky freight.

A sea of brown-robed, brown-skinned, big-eared people surged around the vast open area. This was a cargo bay with stacks of containers ready for transport, not a luxury passenger dock with padded chairs and concessions. The people milled around and around, jabbering in their ancient language they'd never allowed another race to speak. Few ever heard it.

"Does anyone here speak CSS standard?" Jake called above the constant susurration of sound from muted voices and shuffling feet.

A few hesitated, then continued in their anxious pacing.

"See, I told you, you wouldn't get anywhere," Pammy whispered in his ear from behind. "They don't want to communicate, so they won't."

Jake grabbed the sleeve of the first being he'd noticed hesitate at his words. "I offer you one and a half standard pay to stay for six weeks. Double that if you know how to fix the propulsion system," he said slowly and precisely.

The being looked at his pale hand on the dark brown robe as if it were a loathsome worm. Then his ears closed over his face, shutting Jake out.

From beneath the folds of skin came a whispered, "One and a half times nothing is nothing. Double that is still nothing. We leave."

"That's fifty CSS credits an hour," Jake protested.

"CSS credits are nothing. Our people on Labyrinthe Prime will not exchange them for good L dollars. We leave."

Jake slumped in defeat.

Pammy arched an eyebrow and smiled. "Told you so. Might as well open the doors and let them board."

$\blacklozenge \blacklozenge \blacklozenge \diamondsuit \blacklozenge \blacklozenge \blacklozenge$

CHAPTER EIGHTEEN

SISSY STARED AT THE BEWILDERING ARRAY of signs on the post beside the tram. "I think, girls, we need to expand our exploration of the station," she sighed. "We need to memorize each tram stop by more than . . . than . . ." How did one recognize the difference? The waiting areas leading to lifts all looked alike.

"The sign on the last tram stop said that MedBay was in this wing. The whole wing," Mary confirmed.

"So why does the sign at this station say that MedBay is two stops back?" Martha countered.

"Have we explored this wing?" Sissy asked. Her nose detected a hint of antiseptic. She'd spent a fair amount of time in the hospital back home, first clearing her lungs of dust from the quake, then for minor surgeries to replace the charcoal filters to continue the process.

Little Suzie began to cry. Sissy pulled her close. If the call from Med-Bay had seemed less urgent, she'd consider going back to her quarters and awaiting an escort. Presuming she could find her quarters again. Everything seemed turned around and upside down.

"You're an important person. Why can't they give you a comm like Jake's?" Bella asked.

"Because I'm not part of the station personnel," Sissy explained.

"Can't hurt to try exploring," Martha decided and somersaulted toward the lift. She landed neatly on a platform just as it transitioned across the top to begin the downward rotation.

"If they wanted you there so badly, they'd have sent someone for you," Mary agreed and followed Martha, just as adroitly.

"Come, girls." Sissy took Suzie's and Sharan's hands and walked/floated sedately to the lift. A nod to Sarah ensured that she'd escort Bella. Marsh and Ashel would follow, never letting Sissy get too far ahead of them.

The scent of chemicals and the unique odor of illness grew strong as they progressed downward. Mary signaled them off the lift at the last level of the light-G section.

Just behind Mary stood the square figure of Mr. Guilliam. He bowed slightly, most of his attention on the door behind him.

"What's wrong? Why are you here? When? How?" Spilled from Sissy's mouth.

"No time to explain. You are needed inside." He placed a hand at the small of her back and nudged her toward the closed door marked "CCU."

"Adrial?" Sissy didn't want to think of another patient who might require her presence so urgently.

"No, My Laudae. It's Laud Gregor. He had a heart attack in hyperspace. We barely found him in time."

"I don't understand . . ."

"Later, My Laudae. Right now, none of the Harmony physicians will operate without your written consent."

"Surely Penelope . . . she is his daughter."

"But in the Temple we do not always acknowledge family. Gregor certainly doesn't. You are the only one with the authority to allow them to proceed, and take responsibility should they fail."

Sissy gulped. "Who is operating?"

"The team of physicians from the Spacer vessels."

"I want Colonel Halliday helping," Sissy insisted. Jake had sung her praises as practical, efficient, and knowledgeable. Sissy wasn't certain the Spacer physicians had the experience to perform delicate surgery on a fragile heart.

She pushed open the swinging door. The heavy metal moved more freely in the lighter gravity than it would in a normal wing.

" 'Bout time someone with some sense showed up," the CSS physician, Colonel Halliday muttered as Sissy passed into the medical unit. "My Laudae." At the last minute Mariah Halliday nodded her head in a perfunctory bow. "Next problem is blood. No time to clone any, and your people won't let us use any transfusions except from Temple folk. Some nonsense about mutant caste marks." The physician rolled her eyes upward.

"Hemosynth?" Guilliam asked.

"Don't like to use it in open-heart surgery. Natural blood of exact blood-type match is best."

"Do what you have to do to save Laud Gregor. I grant you permission to use whatever blood you have that will work," Sissy said.

"Sign this." Doc Halliday shoved a clipboard with a single sheet of paper on it at her. The closely printed words ran together before Sissy's eyes. She had trouble sounding out three of the first ten words.

"Laudae Penelope is Laud Gregor's daughter. Will her blood type work?" Guilliam asked. He peered over Sissy's shoulder, reading every line of the document. "You can sign it," he whispered.

"Already tested her. She's not compatible. Tested the boy Caleb, too. The donor at the top of the list that I have on record for the best match is General Devlin. Three of the next five are also from CSS. I need a lot of blood for this surgery."

Guilliam backed up two steps. "Laud Gregor will not appreciate that. I'm not sure."

"We can't afford to let the High Priest of Harmony die because of some stupid prejudice. We may not like Laud Gregor, but he is one of a few fragile defenses we have against civil war and chaos back home." Sissy wanted to stamp her foot. Not in front of her girls. "Do it, Doctor Halliday. Get Jake and the other donors down here and start your surgery with the least amount of delay."

"Is that wise, My Laudae?" Guilliam asked. He bowed slightly.

"It may not be wise, but it is necessary."

"Then perhaps we should swear the entire surgical team and General Devlin and the other donors to secrecy," Guilliam said, already drafting the words on a handheld computer similar to Jake's. "I do not believe it wise to allow anyone outside this room to know the identity of the pa-tient. Not until I have in place the people to make a smooth transition of power in his prolonged absence from Harmony."

He looked over his shoulder as if suspecting eavesdroppers. "Laud Gregor authorized a Media person with six hover cams to cover events in the diplomatic wing," he whispered. "Beware of him. He reports to Laud Gregor first and Little Johnny second."

✦   ✦   ✦

Mac tested the medical gauze restraints on all eight of his limbs. The sticky webbing tightened with each twist until they nearly cut off his circulation.

His ears flapped involuntarily in frustration.

"You ain't going nowhere," the CSS guard chuckled from his post by the door. He sat in a straight chair, tipping it back so that it balanced on two legs. But his feet remained flat on the deck while the back of the chair rested against the bulkhead. Deceptively casual and relaxed.

Mac would not get the jump on him, even if he could escape the restraints. Doc Halliday and Physician John had told him he needed to keep still in order for his muscles and nerves to recover.

He'd awakened from their surgical drugs nearly twelve hours ago. More than enough time for the healing process to progress sufficiently to release him.

General Jake wanted him for questioning.

"The little bird?" Mac asked the guard, for the tenth time. "How does she fare?"

The guard shrugged. "Don't know and don't care. The only good Maril is a dead Maril—even if she is only half. I lost too many friends, family, and comrades in this war to ever want to see a live Maril," the guard snarled.

Mac kept his face bland when he truly wanted to slam two fists into the man's face, then rip his ears off with his two pincers.

Clearly he could not protect his little bird from this hospital bed. Nor could he implement plans for taking over the station management. He needed out. Now.

Twisting made the bandages cling tighter. He forced himself to relax his limbs. Better. The bandages withdrew a fraction. What would happen if he retracted his exoskeleton?

He concentrated on pulling his carapace back into his skin. The knife-sharp pain sent waves of dizziness across his awareness.

A little space remained between him and the restraints. He gritted his teeth and pulled again. A scream threatened to escape his throat. He fought it. One contraction, then another, rhythmically making himself smaller and smaller.

The Labyrinthian portion of his body was not made for this. His Arachnoid ancestors had perfected the technique for extreme emergencies. He welcomed the pain as a sign that his nerves had reconnected and as a symbol of his impending freedom. Two more contractions and the bandages sagged free of his skin.

One more excruciating wave of pain brought sweat to his brow and flashes of red light before his eyes. But his left secondary arm pulled free.

Mac relaxed his contortions to check on the guard. His attention seemed riveted on a bustle of activity in the corridor.

Doc Halliday shouted orders. Her firm and authoritative voice cut through the babble.

The guard stood and peered out the door. He swung his head back and forth trying to take in all the myriad people stomping about at once.

Mac used his pincer to cut the bandages on his remaining limbs.

In a single bound he leaped for the nearest ventilation duct.

"Hey, you, get back here," the guard called.

Mac ignored him and scuttled into the dark shaft and freedom. He aimed for his nearest terminal.

CHAPTER NINETEEN

JAKE HELD A SURGICAL PATCH to the vein at the crook of his elbow and applied pressure. All around him, the MedBay vibrated with activity.

"Mind telling me why we've been ordered to donate blood?" he asked the CSS med tech who made notations on his computer as he inserted Jake's blood into a machine.

"Emergency surgery," the tech said, blank-faced.

"Who?" Jake probed.

"Don't know. Sign this." The tech shoved a clipboard in front of Jake with an old-fashioned sheet of paper on it.

Jake scanned it. A lot of the medical vocabulary went over his head. "What am I signing?" he asked, alarmed that the entire transaction hadn't been recorded on the computer and had him affix his thumbprint to the screen—or signed the screen with a stylus. Much more efficient and less likely to get lost. Harder to forge, especially with a thumbprint and/or retinal scan.

He hadn't seen a form like this since he left Harmony almost a year ago.

The ship requesting emergency docking at MedBay had been from Harmony. Something in Little Johnny's message from Harmony had upset Sissy and made her change the subject of her broadcast.

Someone came in from Harmony. Someone with enough importance to turn the entire MedBay topsy-turvy.

"It's just verification that you gave blood today voluntarily and cannot donate again for ninety standard days." The tech never raised his head from the screen.

"What about this paragraph buried in the middle that says I can't mention to anyone except my private physician that I gave blood today?" That didn't sound right. For centuries donating blood gave a person bragging rights—part of the campaign to keep enough on hand for emergencies.

"I need to talk to Doc Halliday before I sign anything." He guessed she was his personal physician, if he needed one while stationed here.

"That's not possible." The tech still didn't look at him.

"Why not?"

"She's scrubbing for surgery as we speak."

"Then I'll use the time while waiting for her to speak to our two alien patients."

"Not possible. Doc Halliday can't perform surgery until all the donors sign their papers. Part of the new patient privacy laws.

"Since when?"

The tech shrugged. "I think the laws went into effect while you were on Harmony. If you haven't been in hospital since then, you had no reason to know."

That sounded like Harmony doublespeak.

"I think I smell Lord Lukan's hand in this business. I need to talk to him." Jake rose carefully from the recliner, well aware how woozy he'd feel after losing that much blood. The walls spun around him in one direction, the floor whirled the opposite way. He had to grab the edge of the tech's computer desk to keep from falling flat on his face.

"Drink this and lie back down." The tech handed him a glass of juice. "You won't be getting in to talk to Lukan for a while anyway."

"Why not?" Jake let his head sink back against the recliner, grateful that the rotating room slowed down, or his head caught up with it.

"He and Laudae Sissy are closeted with some bigwigs just come in from Harmony. There's a ship at the loading dock next level down waiting to make a turnaround jump back to Harmony. They're ready to take the entire delegation back with them."

Blackness crowded Jake's vision, the recliner seemed to sink into the heavy-grav section. *No!* They couldn't take his Sissy away from him.

He forced himself upright and wobbled through the maze of rooms to the lift. He'd do whatever he had to do, invoke whatever authority he could muster to keep her here.

He used his comm to summon a tram and ordered it to Control, double speed.

As the car sped away, he sank to the floor and leaned his head back, willing himself to stay conscious.

✦   ✦   ✦

"We have no choice, My Laudae," Lord Lukan said. He drummed the conference table with his fingertips in an arrhythmic pattern. "You have to return to Harmony. Today."

Sissy's heart soared for a moment. Home!

Then a shiver of anxiety began to tremble inside her. She had no home to return to, and little love for the officials who awaited her.

Lukan's fingers continued to drum.

She wanted to grab his hand and still his agitation.

She could not impose peace on his mind or soul any more than on her own. He had to find it for himself. Perhaps she could aid him in that quest, though, and hope it would help her at the same time.

A deep note formed in the back of her throat. She hummed it briefly, then found the chord that led into a light and airy song about spring flowers and first love.

Lukan's fingers found a pattern.

Sissy sighed with relief. Now she could banish chaos from her thoughts and say something coherent.

"My Lord, I need to stay here. This treaty with the CSS is essential to Harmony's safety in the galaxy at large. You saw the star map. The war closes in on us, on Harmony, on the CSS. We have to finish the treaty negotiations before any of us leave."

"We have no choice, My Laudae. With you here and Laud Gregor at death's door, there is no Temple presence on the High Council. My brother Bevan . . ." He shuddered slightly. Then he lifted his chin and straightened his spine. "My brother is extremely conservative. Since the defeat of the Maril at Harmony VI, he sees no reason to continue the alliance. Left in charge of the Council with no moderating voice to guide him, he will recall us and retreat to the laws and traditions in place before your ordination."

Sissy suddenly felt heavy and hot all over.

"Laudae Penelope, alternatives?" Sissy snapped.

The older woman looked up with bleak, red-rimmed eyes. "He's my father . . ."

Useless. Sissy turned to Mr. Guilliam, not an ordained priest but the one person who kept Crystal Temple operating in an orderly and efficient manner. He had no authority, but he had knowledge.

"Mr. Guilliam, do you have a roster of all priests of Harmony? I would choose someone to take over the administrative details and report accurately to me. Someone with enough spiritual sense to advise the High

Council and the heads of the other castes while Laud Gregor is detained on his mission to the outer colonies."

"I can get a complete roster if I might have access to communications and a computer for five minutes," he replied quietly.

"Granted," Sissy said.

"Just a minute, My Laudae," Lord Lukan interrupted. "Communications to and from Harmony must be strictly monitored to reduce the chance of contamination."

"You mean to keep the populace in ignorance. I trust Mr. Guilliam's discretion more than I trust . . . almost anyone else on this station." No sense in alienating the head of the delegation. Technically he had authority over every Harmonite citizen on station. Sissy sat in conference with him strictly as an adviser, to keep the word and the spirit of the negotiations in line with Temple teachings.

"We have to consider the damage to our culture. A short-term convenience of an alliance cannot be made more important than . . ."

"Excuse me, Lord Lukan, but our culture is already changing. Revelation of the *original* Covenant Tablets demonstrated just how much our laws and traditions changed over the last seven hundred years. We need this alliance if we hope to retain anything resembling our Covenant with Harmony," Sissy argued. She found her fists clenching and her feet arching with the need to smash and kick something.

"How long can we hold off the Maril at H5?" she continued hammering at his logic. "How long before the Maril smash through our fleet and capture our colony, use it as a launching pad to take the others one by one?" She let her voice raise and take on an edge. "The Maril have fought this war for over two hundred years. They will not end it because we wish it."

She drew a deep breath, fighting to maintain Harmony within when she knew the Goddess had deserted her.

"Harmony exists everywhere. We need only open our eyes and our hearts to find Her. Artificial restrictions and prejudice only keep Her out."

Who said that? Sissy didn't think the voice was hers. It reverberated and belled in clear tones that could not be mistaken as any voice but Harmony's.

Lord Lukan, Guilliam, and Penelope gaped at her. The dogs sat up, raised their muzzles, and howled.

Guilliam bowed low. "My Laudae, your wish is my command. I will have the roster to you within moments." He rushed out of the room, face alight with joy.

"My Laudae, you must return home. Harmony needs your gift of prophecy for all the people, not just this small delegation," Lukan said. He bowed from his sitting position.

"All of humanity needs my gift of prophecy," Sissy replied shakily. She felt incredibly light, as if the station had suddenly stopped spinning, taking the gravity with it. "I trust these negotiations to no one else."

"I beg your pardon, My Laudae, but the only *humans* exist within our empire. These CSS citizens are something less," Lord Lukan's son sneered.

"That is the kind of ignorant prejudice we are trying to erase," she fired back.

"But what are we going to tell the people?" Lukan asked. He waved his son to silence. "When word of Laud Gregor's condition leaks out—and it will with that Media person aboard and uncontrolled—the power struggle in the High Council and down through the ranks of the lesser castes will invite chaos and discord."

"We do what the Noble and Temple caste have always done. We keep the *other* castes—no one is lesser than another—in ignorance. That is how you have always enslaved the people. Ignorance and prejudice dictated from the smallest portion of our population." She rose, slowly, her hands flat on the table, elbows locked, to keep her head from spinning and her body from shaking.

"I shall give the Media person a story. Any story to keep him happy and away from MedBay," Lukan said quietly, eyes lowered to his hands. "That is how we have always handled them. But I still think you should return to Harmony. Leave Laudae Penelope here as your representative."

Sissy took a deep breath. "If you knew what I know about our origins and the creation of our society, you would fight even harder to keep this information secret, which means keeping me here. Turn me loose on Harmony without Laud Gregor to curb my tongue and with an independent Media to report my words, and the caste system would shatter against armed rebellion from five of the seven castes within weeks."

Mustering every ounce of willpower, she nodded to Lord Lukan and walked out of the room with the facade of authority and calm she'd learned to cover her true emotions.

Jake needed to know about this. She wondered where she'd find him for a private discussion.

Two steps into the lobby she had to bat away a hover cam and order it to find another victim to record. "An independent Media reporting the truth without censorship is a good thing," she reminded herself. "A little inconvenience doesn't outweigh the advantages."

The camera came back, following her onto the lift.

"However," she said harshly directly into the lens, "invasion of my privacy will not be tolerated!"

The camera backed off and left her alone at the next level.

Maybe she'd wait to inform Jake of the latest development.

✦ ✦ ✦ ◇ ✦ ✦ ✦

CHAPTER TWENTY

I CAN ONLY SPARE one comm unit." Jake looked sternly at the six girls clad in lavender coveralls. "So you all have to guard it well and never lose it."

He'd gathered the girls in the heavy-G gym where he usually worked out. Few came here, at least not before 0600 on the station morning. Sissy was occupied with something arcane in the Temple with Lord Lukan. She kept Marsh, Ashel, and Dog with her but not the girls and Monster.

The huge black dog prowled the gym, sniffing to see who had used each piece of equipment and when. Satisfied, he parked his wide hind end on Jake's foot and leaned.

Jake nearly staggered under the animal's weight.

"We will be very careful, Jake," Mary, the eldest, answered for all of them.

"You are to use it to report to me and me only. If I'm not available, then you hold that report until I am."

"Yes, Jake," they answered in chorus.

"And what are you to report to me?" Activity in the docking bay above told him that a transfer of food supplies from CSS worlds took place. Some of it would stay here on station. He had never realized how much food people ate until he had to provide for them. Most of the cargo, though, would move on to relieve rim worlds gearing up for siege by Maril battle wagons.

That same transport could spare him only a few extra fuel rods. The consumption rates had increased to seven percent above normal.

"We report anything that looks or feels out of place," Martha replied.

"Like the signs at the tram stops that are all mixed up," Sharan piped up.

"Show me that," Jake demanded, moving the girls toward the lift.

"We already fixed them," Suzie said quietly from behind Mary.

"Let's check them out anyway," Jake said. He took the hands of Sharan and Suzie, the two youngest, and stepped onto the next lift platform. He trusted the others to follow, herded by Monster. They rarely went anywhere alone. Always in a pack. Always exploring and therefore invisible. Maybe they could discover what was wrong with propulsion.

Jake held his breath as they rose through the docking bay. Too many chances for someone to look and notice him with the girls, but without Sissy. His cooption of their help needed to be secret. Or it wouldn't work.

Spies had to remain invisible. He'd learned that the hard way on Harmony.

A hover cam peeked into the lift. Jake beamed a coded message to it from his own com. It backed off convinced no one interesting used the lift. *Thank you, Mara, for that little piece of coding.*

"Keep the comm in your pocket, Mary," he said out the side of his mouth. "And if a hover com is near when you do use it, aim the on light toward the lens and push the red button."

She nodded and complied. Her fingers touched the cloth surrounding it frequently. He knew she wanted to fiddle with it, explore its capabilities, understand how it worked.

He didn't even know how it worked. Not really. Just the basic principles.

"I've set it to my private frequency. Don't change it," he ordered.

Mary, Martha, and Sarah, all looked at him with wide, innocent eyes. They held his gaze just a little too long. They were up to something.

"If you change one little thing, take it apart, do anything with it but report to me with it, I'll take it back and find someone else to do the dirty work."

"Yes, Jake," they chorused.

Yeah, right.

Soon enough they reached the microgravity of the station core. All six girls tumbled off the lift platforms, spinning and dancing without the restraints and limitations of gravity. Reveling in the freedom of weightlessness.

Jake envied them their innocence and adaptability. Their capacity for simple joy.

"These directions all look correct," Jake mused. Even as he spoke the lights on the post flashed. Screens darkened and new numbers and designations popped up. It happened so fast, if he hadn't been watching, he doubted anyone would have noticed that they were not at Harmony Spacer and Military Residential, access strictly limited. He knew he stood on the platform leading to CSS offices and group facilities. Only the smell of cooking soy loaf wafting up the lift shaft told him the kitchens and dining facilities were in this wing.

That reminded him he needed to get some engineers in to redesign the wings to cope with hull breach. They needed air lock doors closing off the lift and stairwell shafts. Another expense. Another day.

"Mara," he called Control.

"Yes, sir?"

"You notice a blip on any of your screens?"

A moment of near silence as she consulted with someone. "Just a nano of blankness. Everything came back normal. Must have just been a glitch or reset in the programming."

Were the glitches causing the fuel drain?

"Not everything came back normal. Signposts in the tram stations have changed. I need you to get techs out to check them all and fix the ones that are wrong. See if you can trace back the source. Look in propulsion first."

"On it." A long pause. He almost closed the connection. "Uh . . . sir? Is there a map of the station anywhere so we know what all the signs are *supposed* to say?"

Jake cursed long and fluently.

His six spies just giggled and went back to their dancing.

✦   ✦   ✦

Click. Click. Click. The soft sounds within the bulkheads caressed Adrial's ears. Dim lights of deep night. Few sounds in MedBay other than the constant drip and wheeze of lifesaving machines. And that out of place click.

Adrial had slept too many hours during the station's daytime routine to find rest when everyone else did. She spent most of the night reading, learning about her current environment and the people who inhabited it.

She had already memorized a map of the station she'd found on her reader. It looked more detailed and accurate than standard visitor directions to the most frequented destinations.

Click. Click. Click. The slow rotation of screws on the ventilation grate.

She checked her guard. She dozed in a chair outside Adrial's room.

Everyone supposed her in a drug-induced sleep now, as she was during most of the day. They had no way of knowing that her father's Angelic ancestors had been night hunters. She found the hours of darkness, whether dirtside or stationbound, soothing. A time to think, and plan, and learn.

A time to stretch and strengthen her muscles and bones in secret. A time to reprogram sensors and diagnostic scanners to look as though she had barely healed at all.

Something moved inside the bulkheads and ventilation shafts—someone who kept the same nocturnal hours she did and was out of place.

She moved her hand to the summoning button, cautiously. Her other hand clasped a Badger Metal knife she'd stolen from Lieutenant David. Just a little one that he rarely used and kept in his calf pocket. The being that moved secretively could be watching her.

At the last second she paused, waiting, wondering. Always better to observe first, assess the danger, find an escape, then act.

"Little Bird," a voice out of her dreams, or her nightmares, whispered.

She tuned her hearing to locate the source. There, in the shaft grating high in the left corner of the room. Another gift from her father's ancestors was sensitive hearing. She knew the voice belonged to the being who had rescued her from the Squid ship. He'd also moved her about the station several times, seeking a safe place for her to recover, not trusting MedBay.

"Little Bird, are you awake?"

"Yes." As she spoke she pulled the summoning button close to her body, beneath the light sheet that covered her to her chin. The gel floats didn't give her a lot of room to move, but she didn't really need them to protect her light bones any more. She'd made secret forays out of Med-Bay exploring the station.

Long ago she'd learned to leave no trace of her comings and goings. Security cameras responded to her commands without protest, showing the watchers what she wanted them to see.

"I would speak to you, Little Bird."

"Show yourself." She looked pointedly toward the doorway where the guard dozed.

The grating panel slid aside, and the being poked his strange head through. His large ears wiggled and twisted, capturing stray sounds and nuances. His flat nasal slits flared and retracted. Then he slid two arms with normal looking hands—four fingers, no opposable thumb—onto the wall. He seemed to grip the paint with those hands as he pulled his bulbous body through the narrow opening.

"How fare you?" he asked even before he touched the ground and stood upright. His extra limbs slipped into the deep folds of his clothing so that he looked closer to humanoid.

"I heal." No sense in letting him know any more than the medicos. Only she knew just how much strength she'd regained once they set her broken bones and repaired pierced organs. CSS medicine was far superior to what the Messengers of the Gods offered their prisoners.

"You need to know that I watch over you," the being said. "I will not allow the humans to harm you."

"Thank you."

"You also need to know that I have intercepted a distress signal from a Maril ship. I masked it very quickly. I do not think that Control received it."

"Maril?" Panic rose in waves from Adrial's belly. She had to get away, gather what information she could, and escape into the vastness of the galaxy. Easy enough to wipe the computers of any trace of her presence. Harder to erase memories.

"Do not fear." His hand rested atop hers where she was set to fling off the sheet. "Those aboard the ship will die before they reach here."

"It's a trap," she snapped and pushed him away. Her head swam for several seconds as she sat up, legs dangling over the sides of the bed. "They will use the humans' sense of justice and compassion to gain entrance here, then slaughter any who stand in their way to get me."

"This is no trap. I have monitored the ship. They are badly damaged, losing atmosphere. Pieces of their hull litter the path from the jump point to here. The humans will not know of their presence until they are all dead."

"How can I trust you?" Adrial didn't dare relax yet. She had to be ready to jump free and run.

"I will protect you, Little Bird. The Maril will not find you while I live." He jumped up and grabbed the vent opening. In seconds he'd scrambled into his hiding place and closed the grating. "Study the map of the galaxy on your reader," he whispered, the words fading away as he retreated.

Only the faintest trace of his scent lingered as proof that he'd even been there. "You are better at leaving no trace than I am. What can I learn from you?"

◆ ◆ ◆ ◇ ◆ ◆ ◆

CHAPTER TWENTY-ONE

LOVE MY HOME. I desperately need to return to Harmony. But I can't," Sissy cried to herself and her Goddess. "I can't trust these vital negotiations to anyone else. Not Penelope or Gil and especially not Lord Lukan, with Garrin whispering hatred into his ear."

She bowed her head in humiliation. "I can't leave Jake." That was the most compelling argument to her heart, the least important to her people.

She sank back onto the floor of the Temple, her back pressed against the altar. She'd spent so much time kneeling in prayer that her back ached and her knees felt raw. Her head still spun.

What to do about Laud Gregor? How could she justify staying at the First Contact Café when the High Priest ailed so terribly? He might never be strong enough to go home. Harmony would splinter and fracture with both the High Priest and High Priestess out of the empire.

She couldn't bear leaving Jake.

The people of Harmony would never allow her to be with Jake as she longed to be.

Seeing him every day, spending evenings with him in study and planning, was sweet torment. The thought of never seeing him again tore at her mind and heart. Yet her responsibilities to her people, to her Goddess, to her government threatened every hour to send her home.

She rested her head against the synthetic stone of the altar. Real stone dug from Harmony's bones was too heavy and expensive to ship to the space station. She longed for some tiny sacred connection to her home planet. The small crystals from her travel kit offered little solace in her need to set foot on her home world.

Slowly her eyes drifted closed as she pictured the funerary caves west of Harmony City. She drew in a deep breath as the caves breathed in at sunset, then let the air slide slowly out of her, as the caves did in the morning.

Again and again she imagined herself deep inside the caverns, grounding herself in the womb of Harmony, breathing with the Goddess.

Bit by bit she built the image in her mind of the cool air, the solid rock, the little rooms painted with murals of the creation, the niches filled with uncountable bones of her ancestors, and the aliens that had dwelled on Harmony before her people came there.

"Welcome," a gentle voice whispered to her as if she truly had entered the caves.

Her breathing fell into a sympathetic rhythm with the planet in her memory. She curled her fist around a rock covered with dirt and let it meld with her being.

And then she was flying high, soaring over the treetops. Her body ached from long hours at prayer and ritual thanksgiving, but her mind and soul had shed its burdens. The cliff face of the mountain offered her respite from her long journey with the Gods. She touched down lightly, folding her wing flaps beneath her arms, and sank into her warm aerie. Her younglings chirruped and gazed longingly over the edge toward the freedom of their first flight.

She had come full circle in the sacred breeding ritual. Her life had purpose now; her duty to the Gods and the government had been fulfilled. Soon she must return to work with her young in tow. Soon she must leave this sacred place.

Explosions startled her nearly back into flight. She spread her wings over the little ones, searching warily for the source of danger.

The surrounding mountain shuddered and groaned. Rocks fell all around her and her children. She huddled over the children, protecting them from the energy blast that struck the cliff face above her. She sent prayer after prayer skyward toward the Gods, questioning what she and the People had done to displease the newcomers so.

"We offered them succor and shared our shelters with them. We welcomed them with ceremony. Yet they turn on us and murder us by the thousands."

First one small stone, sharp and jagged, then several much larger ones slammed into her back. Pain ripped through her. Blood spurted. Her life drained away . . .

A sharp pain in Sissy's neck severed her connection to the waking nightmare.

"Harmony! Why do I dream of the war of attrition my people perpetuated against the Maril priests and mystics?" she cried, uncurling from her cramped fetal position.

*Were they only priests and mystics? Were their rituals so offensive to
you that you annihilated them?*

"I don't know. I wasn't there!"

You will be. You will understand.

"Is this a vision yet to come? What can I do to stop this?"

No answer.

◆ ◆ ◆

"My Angel, you have come to me at last!" Adrial held out her hands to
the High Priestess of Harmony, the keeper of lost ones.

Laudae Sissy clasped Adrial's hands warmly, as if she truly wanted to
be here with Adrial. The haunted depth of her eyes and the dark circles
surrounding them told Adrial that Sissy ran away from something else.

The two dogs that followed Laudae Sissy everywhere paused in the
doorway. Both raised their ears, looked to their mistress, and cautiously
sat. But their hind ends didn't quite meet the floor.

Adrial glared at the animals. She didn't like nonsentient creatures.
They could teach her nothing.

In response the dogs curled their lips, baring very long teeth. A deep
rumble crawled up from their chests to their throats.

Adrial pressed herself back into her bed, putting as much distance as
possible between her and the growling menace.

"Discord," Sissy sighed. "Please excuse the boys. They've been very
unsettled today." She got up to soothe them.

Just then a nurse with a lauded caste mark hurried along the corridor
and shooed the dogs away. She slid the door to Adrial's room closed as
she passed.

Peace settled on Adrial once more. Laudae Sissy had honored her with
her divine presence.

"I have brought you a portable reader with a number of books and
news access." Laudae Sissy smiled despite the worry in her posture. "You
won't be tied to the tabletop."

Adrial dismissed the gift with a wave of her hand. "Did you bring the
texts I requested? No one on Med staff thinks I should be bothering with
reading yet. The drugs still cloud my mind. You would be my savior if you
found even one of them, oh Sacred One."

Laudae Sissy withdrew her hands. "I wish you would not talk so, Adrial.
I am only a servant of the Gods. Not one of them."

"But you understand the will of the Gods, my beloved friend. You
speak for them. They speak through you." Now that Adrial was tempo-

rarily safe from the agents of the Maril, she needed to cultivate the resources at hand.

That was how she'd survived the relentless pursuit and her own driving need to find the path to Spiritual Purity.

A path that Laudae Sissy already walked.

"My education is sorely lacking, Adrial. I've not read any of the books you requested. But I did try to find the ones on your list. I found three of the fourteen. The rest are things my acolytes thought would entertain you."

In the past few weeks Adrial had secretly read every text on Harmony that Mac could find for her. She'd learned much, including how closely Harmony and Her divine family resembled the Maril patriarch D°glotikh—which translated to Balanced Discipline—and his consorts. She liked Harmony, her consort Empathy, their children Nurture and Unity, and the stepchildren they adopted, Anger, Fear, and Greed. Discord, the nastiest of the stepchildren, had been exiled. All natural parts of life seeking an ideal balance.

D°glotikh presided over his six consorts: Nurture, Unity, Pity, Vengeance, Discord, and Victory. They had banished Fear as the unwanted stepchild. Their balance looked only slightly different from Harmony's.

The resemblance must mean that she was getting closer to the end of her search. Sissy's repeated presence in her hospital room excited her more than any of the lovers she'd taken or been forced to accept in this endless quest. The Gods must forgive her for violating the most blessed of all rituals. They had sent messengers to give her this quest. She must find the path through any means possible.

Leave no trace of your passing.

"The Gods no longer speak through me," Sissy said quietly. "I have lost my connection to the planet Harmony and therefore to the Gods." The priestess looked down, studying her hands as if they held all the answers to life's questions.

"Give it time, my friend. I have known many prophets in my wanderings. Only the false ones have visions on a regular basis. You need to let the Gods find you here."

"I fear that Harmony has turned her back on me. She will not seek me in this tin can in the middle of space." Laudae Sissy blinked back tears.

There was something else, something Laudae Sissy didn't, or couldn't, say. Adrial needed to worm that bit of information out of her. It might be important.

"But there is a planet. The Med staff is all abuzz with rumors. We will go to this planet soon, you and I, and the Gods will find you once more. You shall preside over Their Temple, and I shall sit at your feet and learn from you." Warmth and strength flooded Adrial's body at this thought.

Laudae Sissy slid a chair close to Adrial's hospital bed and sat. She kept her face averted. Such shyness seemed unnatural in one gifted by the Gods and weighted with responsibility by her people.

"Moving to this new home seems far off," Laudae Sissy sighed. "So, tell me, what brought you here to the First Contact Café?" She brightened and fixed Adrial with a clear gaze.

"I . . . I . . . don't remember." Adrial turned her head away, staring at the blank wall.

"Do you remember why you left your first home? You've not told anyone here the name of your home."

"The Messengers of the Gods killed everyone else on Amity. My people had polluted the planet with their impure blood. The Messengers of the Gods spared me because my father was an Angel. But they could not allow me to remain because my blood is half impure. So they sent me into exile until I can remove the tainted blood by a special blessing from the Gods."

Adrial didn't want to think about that awful time. The noise of the first invasion, the fear from the explosions as block after block of the city vaporized. All her friends, her schoolmates, her mother gone in an instant.

The relentless pain and torture—

No, no, no, no, no. She wouldn't think of that. She must not contaminate her quest with that memory.

Her mind sidled into another, almost as disturbing but not forbidden.

Running home from school, near blind with panic. Early dismissal because of something dire on the news. She smelled fear on the skin of her teachers. Her friends bounced away from the building, ecstatic at the unexpected holiday. A few of the older ones, the ones near enough to adulthood to understand what was happening, held themselves tight and dashed for the safety of their homes.

Only there was no safety.

The bombs came, swift and merciless.

Adrial saw the smoke in the distance and smelled the death when the first ones struck the center of their town. The great belling boom of destruction sounded like the roar of God in a rage.

Panic. Confusion. Mindless running. An ache in her side, gasping for breath, knees turned to pudding. She didn't know where she ran to, or why, only that she had to get away. As far away from the city as she could get.

Don't stop. Don't look back. Just run and run and run until she fell flat on her face and could move no more.

Hours later, or was it days, she looked up in fright to find a great winged figure, all in black and white, looming over her. He picked her up by the collar of her ragged coat and shook her. Her head snapped back and forth with each jerk. Her arms and legs flailed for purchase. Something, anything to regain control of her body and stop this horrible pain lancing from the base of her spine into her skull.

Eventually she found refuge in blank blackness.

"Leave no trace of your passing." The anonymous words pounded through her veins with compulsion.

"Perhaps if you stilled yourself and meditated, your heart would open and you'd find the lessons already learned," Laudae Sissy said quietly.

Panic shook through Adrial's body. "No, I can't. I have to keep moving, keep looking. I'll know it when I find it. I haven't found it yet," she said too rapidly. Her fingers plucked anxiously at the light blanket over her body.

"Then tell me what you did today," Laudae Sissy said brightly. She patted Adrial's hands into stillness.

Adrial turned her head back to her new friend, smiling. Peace oozed outward from Laudae Sissy's touch. But only as far as Adrial's shoulders and knees. Her toes continued to twitch. Her mind whirled in wild calculation.

"I walked one hundred meters on the treadmill, this morning. Doc Halliday says she will move me to the mid-G level tomorrow. They have this marvelous machine that sounds like a purring cat. It strengthens my bones ever so quickly. I could not imagine so much healing in only three weeks." More healing and mobility than she let the Medicos think.

"That is good news."

"The phantom whispers to me in my sleep. He says I must not move. He says it's too soon, too dangerous. But he is an evil man. I do not trust him."

"Does this phantom speak to you often?" Laudae Sissy looked suddenly stiff and uncomfortable.

No one liked admitting the phantom existed.

Humans needed ghost stories for some reason, brief forays into the unknown, and then back on safe ground with disbelieving laughter.

"He comes into my room and watches me sleep almost every night.

But he only speaks to me when he does not like how they treat me."
No one would believe that. It sounded like a dream. The drugs induced
strange dreams in Adrial.

"The next time the phantom comes to you, ask him to speak to me. I
need to talk to him," Sissy said eagerly. "My acolytes have caught glimpses
of him. We need answers to some questions."

"I can't do that. He has forbidden me to mention him. I tell you in
strictest confidence. You are bound by your oaths as a priestess to protect
my secrets. He'll know if you tell anyone else, and then he'll punish me,
just like the Messengers of the Gods punish me. Do you think the Gods
sent him?"

She let her eyelids droop as if terribly fatigued. Then she babbled
nonsense words.

◆ ◆ ◆ ◇ ◆ ◆ ◆

CHAPTER TWENTY-TWO

"**A**LL ABLE-BODIED PERSONNEL to docking bay Supply HG!" Jake barked into his com. He pushed the button that would translate his words into three different languages. "We have refugees from Zarith V. Repeat, refugees. All medical personnel on standby. All able-bodied personnel to docking bay Supply HG. If you can carry a liter or fetch a blanket, do it!"

He ran up the stairs to the tram between his suite and Control. No time to lollygag on the lift. Blood pumped firmly through his thighs. As gravity lightened, his heart eased into the rhythm of his steps, no longer straining.

Adrenaline pushed him faster than he thought possible.

"Mara, what's the food situation? We've got close to a thousand people coming in." He tapped his foot waiting for the tram doors to open.

"Questionable," she barked in reply. He could almost see her hands flying over her terminals.

"Beg, borrow, buy, or steal whatever you can from any ships within two sectors. How we doing in opening a new wing? Two would be better."

"I got air flowing, pressure building, and heat trickling. Nothing is working fast enough. The propulsion system is draining power from all other tasks." An edge of panic crept into her usual calm. "Doc Halliday is complaining that the dock is too far from MedBay. And they're arriving in heavy G. Puts a lot of strain on injured bodies and on people carrying them."

"The ship can't maneuver well enough to get anywhere else. Had to stick them on the outermost wing on that end of the station," Jake grumbled. Mara knew that. She'd talked the pilot through the procedure.

"Do what you can, Mara. Drag in any help you can from the Spacers. They can move cots and arrange walls in EVA suits if they have to. We need quarters the moment Medical clears people. And don't let anyone give you grief. They'll answer to me if they do." At last the tram deigned to acknowledge that he and a dozen people from Control and the Admin wings waited for it.

Jake made a point of being first on, pausing two extra seconds to finger kiss the glyph of Harmony. The others, all in uniform from CSS or Harmony, followed suit. Deep frowns and anxious looks calmed with the simple ritual.

"General Devlin, I need to clear MedBay of ambulatory patients," Doc Halliday overrode all other communications.

"Parcel 'em out to any empty quarters. You know who to lock in, who to release, and who to drug insensible. I can't spare anyone to keep watch on our guests." He looked around at his audience. They all seemed too eager to know everything that transpired. "I've got two wings for anyone who doesn't need immediate treatment opening within the hour." *I hope.*

"I've got reports of blaster injuries, exposure, torture, dehydration, starvation, a whole medical text of conditions. You got any medicine stashed somewhere I don't know about?"

"No, I don't. Raid any ships in port."

"Do I have permission to try alternative medicine?"

A look of alarm passed around the cramped tram car.

"You can try any trick in your arsenal." That didn't help the nervousness in Jake's traveling companions.

"Good. I've got an intern who licensed in acupuncture before going to med school. Halliday out."

"General Devlin," Pammy sneered through the comm on the same channel as the physician, "do I need to remind you that 'alternative medicine' is severely frowned upon by CSS authorities."

"I'm sorry, Admiral Marella, your signal is breaking up. I can't hear you." He severed the link and keyed the full tram car to its destination at top speed.

"Wish I could do that with my sergeant," an anonymous voice whispered.

"So do I," Jake replied loud enough for all to hear.

A light giggle passed around, followed by quiet. They knew the boss rode with them. They needed to guard their tongues.

All of the tram passengers made sure they finger kissed Harmony as they piled out. Another tram dumped a similar number of passengers coming from the opposite direction. This one carried a few Labyrinthes as well as humans in civies and various uniforms. Jake parceled them out, sending some for blankets and stretchers, others to meet the medics. He went with the biggest and broadest-shouldered ones. The docking bay had heavy crates in heavy grav to shift out of the way. And only two antigrav carts.

Two ships. One thousand people. Zarith V reportedly had a population of fifteen million. Jake sincerely hoped more had fled in different directions. Maybe, just maybe, Zarith V was one of the worlds the Maril would absorb rather than cleanse.

The star map told him otherwise.

"Move these crates to the far side," he directed three men. "We have to clear the air locks, both passenger and cargo."

A stream of data came through his comm. He ignored a lot of it.

The bulkheads rocked, followed by a loud grinding of metal on metal. Jake grabbed hold of the nearest upright. His hand clasped cloth.

"Gil?" he stared at the man standing between him and the support beam. "I figured you'd show up sometime." He shook his friend's hand. They hadn't seen each other since . . . since weeks before Jake departed Harmony in a hurry.

"General?" Guilliam raised his eyebrows at the stars on Jake's collar. "I knew you'd figure out who had come to the First Contact Café from Harmony." He half grinned.

Another deck shiver wiped the expression from his face. Startled yelps sounded around the bay.

"Mara, what's going on?" he called into his comm. Blind. He was blind down here with no screens.

"Just a clumsy docking, sir. They're clamping on now. Air locks should cycle in ten seconds."

Almost before her words faded, air whooshed into the flexible tube between the station bulkhead and the ship hatch. It sounded like the wind breathing out of the funeral cave at dawn back on Harmony. A natural realignment of air pressure and temperature, Jake reassured himself.

Red lights flashed in an odd pattern around the lock.

"Keep working," Jake ordered his crew. "Nothing to see until the locks finish equalizing."

He cranked the lock the moment a green light blinked on the mechanism. Gil and another man in a Harmony uniform helped him haul the heavy hatch open. It felt crooked and sagged. They all cursed, Gil more fluently than the others, at the damage caused by the clumsy pilot on the ship.

The dim lights within the air lock revealed an empty gaping maw into the ship. A pale oval of a face appeared in the darkness. Then slowly it moved forward on ghostly silent feet. Its muddy, hooded robe that might once have been forest green swayed, giving hints of a tall figure.

Bit by bit the face took on definition. Only ten yards separated the two hatches, but the person seemed to take a week to traverse it. Male features, five days of beard, sunken eyes cloaked in dark circles. A cadaverously thin face and blackened teeth.

The figure stumbled. Halted. Blinked rapidly in bewilderment.

"You're safe here," Jake said softly. "We're here to help." He reached out a hand in greeting.

The man clasped it with bony fingers. His knees buckled. Gil rushed to support him with an arm about his waist.

"T'others," the man croaked.

"Drink this," Sissy ordered, appearing out of nowhere. She held a cup to the man's lips. He drank greedily. "Little bits at first. Take it slow. There's more."

Suddenly an island of calm surrounded her and her newest stray. The entire crew bowed their heads a moment in respectful prayer.

"T'others. Help t'others," he said wearily.

And then there were dozens of people from both sides, pushing and shoving through the air lock. The medics barreled back and forth with their gurneys. Strong men made temporary litters out of blankets. Everywhere came the cries for water.

Sissy and her girls answered the calls quickly and efficiently. Within moments Penelope and her girls added their own hands and soothing words.

"Should'a known Gil wouldn't be here without his wife," Jake mumbled to himself.

"Mara," Jake stepped aside as professionals did their work around him with noisy efficiency.

"What now?" she returned, too busy for politeness.

"We need water, Mara. Lots and lots of it." The reclamation and recycling system handled a stable population with a bit to spare for temporary guests. This influx would exhaust the system's reserves. In a hurry.

"And where am I supposed to get it?"

"I don't know. But a million liters is only going to touch the surface of what these people need."

"Do you care where I get it? Like maybe stealing from the planet below that we aren't supposed to touch in case we alter it's natural evolutionary process."

"Do what you have to do. Don't leave a trail. There's a small cargo shuttle docked between my suite and the HG levels. It has a tow hook."

"Um . . ."

"I'm sending someone to help. Someone who knows more about keeping secrets than you do. Someone who knows how to hide things in deep dark places no one else cares to go."

"There's no one better than me."

"I think there is. Gil!" he called over the babble. "Gil, I've got a job for you. Mara, if anyone asks tell them you found an empty wing prepared for water breathers, complete with a sea of their natural environment."

"Sir." Gil turned toward him, keeping an arm around a very pregnant woman who rubbed her belly as if ready to deliver right here, right now in the cargo bay. "I'm a bit busy, sir."

"Laudae Sissy can take over for you there. I need you elsewhere."

Once the water situation was settled and the refugees stable and depositions taken, he had another job only Gil could accomplish.

Like finding dozens of hidden listening posts Mac had stashed around the station. They needed to be destroyed. Well, most of them.

"None of these people are human. They're all barefaced trolls," Garrin reported to his father, Lord Lukan. His voice carried through the cargo bay without hindrance. "Our presence is not required here."

"Your stupidity is matched only by your laziness," Lord Lukan replied, also loud enough to be heard. "We are able-bodied. We can help those in distress."

"They are not worth . . ."

"They are worth a dozen of you!" Sissy rounded on him. "As High Priestess of all Harmony and her colonies, I order you to roll up your sleeves and work. You can at least pretend compassion." She turned her back on the Noble, deliberately, and blessed a wailing child by tracing the Harmony glyph on its forehead with her finger. Then she offered yet another cup of water to the baby and its older sibling.

Chastised but resentful, Garrin reluctantly threw a blanket around the shoulders of the shivering children.

Three hover cams recorded it all.

Another wave of walking wounded descended upon Jake. He lifted a child to his shoulder and half carried a woman to a waiting gurney and medic.

"Thank ye," she whispered through thin and cracked lips. "I didn't think I'd survive to see another human face."

"How long have you been fleeing the Maril?" Jake asked, handing her a cup of water from a tray atop a packing crate.

"Days, weeks. Can't tell. Six jumps through hyperspace evading." She lifted bleak eyes to him. "Not enough sleepy drugs for everyone. Too many ghosts crowding in. All t' ones we left behind." Tears leaked from her eyes.

Jake settled the wasted child, as light as a feather, next to her.

"Did . . . did the Maril take over the government, set up occupation?" He had to know what he was dealing with.

"Nay, sir. They killed all left on the ground. Bombed all the buildings to dust."

"Cleansing," Jake whispered. "How'd you get away?"

"We been under siege for weeks. A captain decided to take a risk and fight his way through the blockade. Some o'us chose t'run. Some chose to stay and fight it out." Fat tears rolled down her cheeks. Moisture she could ill afford to lose. "Me mate stayed."

He nodded for the medic to do what he needed to do.

Jake turned back to helping carry out the ones who couldjn't walk on their own.

With each step he cursed the winged creatures who started the war. He cursed their cleansing. And he cursed himself for not being out there on the front fighting them away from human space.

You vowed not to kill again, a voice in his head reminded him.

"This is different."

How?

✦ ✦ ✦ ◇ ✦ ✦ ✦

CHAPTER TWENTY-THREE

MAC LISTENED TO THE DISTRESS call from General Jake. He paused in traversing a maintenance tube. Refugees. His heart twisted in sympathy. He'd been a refugee all his life; running, hiding, scraping together an existence with stolen food, clothing, and air.

Should he turn around and help? With his strength and knowledge of the station he could help more than three others.

If he showed himself, they'd shoot him again, maybe kill him.

He had other chores, necessary chores, better accomplished in privacy. With all able bodies helping the refugees, no one would notice where he worked, or who he worked with.

He dropped from a maintenance tube into the heavy-G portion of the abandoned Harmony wing.

"You're late," Admiral Pamela Marella snarled from behind her EVA faceplate. The bulky suit masked her figure. She could be anyone in that disguise.

But Mac knew her scent and her voice from the night she had approached his bedside in the hospital. She needed his expertise. He needed out of the hospital.

She helped link his computer network to his bedside. He promised to help her with the autopsy. Favor for favor. Tidbit of information for tidbit of gossip.

"My movements around the station are not always linear. I must avoid detection," he replied cautiously.

"I appreciate that. Someday you must show me some of your routes." She turned to the bulky black box at her feet. "Help me set this up. I'm not used to heavy G."

Mac bristled at her lack of the respect he'd become used to in MedBay.

No "please." No "Mr. Mac." She wanted favors from him yet ordered him about like an underling. Or a lesser being.

He turned to retreat the way he'd come, not caring if he offended the admiral. What could she do to him his own mother had not? He could hide from her probes indefinitely. If necessary, he'd sneak aboard a ship bound for another station just to get away from her.

But he needed to stay. He was so close to gaining control of the station . . .

"I thought your curiosity would overcome your pride, Mac." She sounded unconcerned, but her body gave off a faint whiff of anxiety.

She needed him as much as he needed her goodwill. She respected people who dared to stand up to her.

He could play mind games with her all night.

"High rank does not relax the need for manners," he replied. "I'd like to direct you to the etiquette book compiled by my mother."

The spymaster ground her teeth.

"Would you please help me set up this autopsy table? I admit that I can't do everything by myself in heavy G with limited atmosphere."

Mac kept his back to her. "I can help elsewhere."

"Mr. Mac," she added just as he decided to resume his retreat.

"Very well, Admiral." In seconds he had the folding table open and braced on its six legs. Then he helped her carry the corpse of the Squid pilot out of the damaged cockpit.

The deep cold of space had prevented decay. Still, Mac smelled death. He shied away from it, fearing that this too would be his fate if he ever fell into the hands of his brother's people.

As the admiral made her first cut into the tough, rubbery skin of the alien, Mac murmured a prayer to Laudae Sissy's Goddess. He knew no other that might listen to such as he.

He wished he could sing the harmonies of the universe to give peace to the soul of this now extinct race.

"I wonder who came off the Harmony ship directly into CCU in Med-Bay," the admiral remarked casually.

She didn't smell relaxed. She needed this information.

"I never heard a name," Mac replied truthfully.

"But you know?"

"I can guess who an older balding human with a Temple caste mark and a fragile heart might be."

Pammy's eyebrows rose enough to show behind the distorting faceplate. "I can guess too. I can also guess why he came. All is not peaceful on Harmony. The HP needs the HPS to back up his politics."

Mac nodded. "I hope she does not go home with him. She brightens this dismal station."

Pammy snorted something and continued her autopsy.

While the spymaster removed organs, weighed, measured, and sampled them, all the while recording every move she made with her own hover cam—not one of the Media devices from Harmony—Mac removed himself to the cockpit and began working on understanding the ship's computers.

He allowed another of Pammy's hover cams to record everything he discovered.

They needed to know where the Squid had come from, what they knew, and why that graceful race had gone extinct, as his mother's race nearly did. What were the signals? How might such a terrible loss to the galaxy have been prevented? Who was next?

That thought made him stop and examine his thoughts a moment.

Extinction occurred when deaths increased and births decreased until insufficient numbers remained to breed and maintain a viable gene pool.

As he delved into the intricacies of the ship's computers, he let his mind run free in circles and loops and spirals inward.

A brief diagnostic of the ship revealed decay and malfunction from age and overuse without repair. No replacement parts for such an antique and arcane design.

No replacement Squid People. Because they had no home world to return to for breeding rituals. Because . . .

He breathed deeply and slipped outside a hatch to examine the hull. Badger Metal tiles all in place. Space radiation shouldn't have penetrated.

What if these water breathers were susceptible to a specific kind of radiation that the Badger Metal couldn't shield against?

What if . . . ?

✦   ✦   ✦

"I can't allow you to disrupt my patients," Doc Halliday said to Jake. She stood firmly in the entrance to MedBay, feet spread, hands on hips, determination making her a solid barrier between Jake and information.

She looked tired from her marathon of caring for the refugees.

"I need to talk to the captains of the refugee ships. I need to know what's going on out there," Jake explained gently. "They've got vital information that may help prevent a similar tragedy after the next battle or siege."

"Sorry. The first captain died during surgery. He took three full blaster hits at the beginning of the journey. I don't know how he stayed alive long enough to pilot through six jumps and a tricky docking." Defeat weighed heavily on the doctor's posture. "The second one suffered a head injury. If he wakes up, he may not have enough memory to help you."

"I'm sorry. For you and the men's families. While I'm here, is there anyone among the refugees I can talk to?"

"Not yet. They are all too shell-shocked to remember."

"For any of those willing and trained, I've got job openings in just about every category from cleaning and maintenance to propulsion engineer and Control tech."

"I'll pass the word along. Most of the refugees have nothing and nowhere to go. Families dead or missing. They might be grateful for work. I can use the space if you move them out to crew quarters."

"What about your other patients. Adrial . . ."

"Should still be drugged insensible. Per your orders." Doc Halliday lifted her chin and met his gaze defiantly.

"Adrial spoke to the Military I assigned to guard her not an hour ago. She listens to recorded music every waking moment . . ."

"Her reaction to drugs is a constant mystery. I never know what's working and how. Her obsession with music worries me. Her mind drifts. The only thing she focuses on is the music. If I can't get two coherent sentences out of her about her condition, you won't get anything worthwhile out her either." Doc Halliday shook her head.

"Adrial. Music," he mused. "Laudae Sissy is the most musical person I know. I want you to call her next time Adrial is coherent. Sissy should be able to make sense of her mystical nonsense." He longed for the spectacles his tech team still played with. With those, he could monitor heat signatures and heart rates in any room in the complex if he wanted.

Including the secret patient from Harmony he wasn't supposed to know about.

"No guarantees." Doc Halliday nodded her consent.

"What about Mac?"

"Mac?" she asked, as if she'd never heard the name. The stiffness in her smile betrayed her lack of innocence.

"The Arachnoid-Labyrinthe alien." Jake narrowed his eyes, trying to pry the truth out of her. "It's been more than a week since he dropped into MedBay unannounced, Doc."

"Broken bones and blaster wounds take a long time to heal."

"Can he talk?"

"You'll have to wait in line to ask him questions," she stalled.

"Why?" He edged a bit closer.

She didn't retreat or give him a fraction of an opening to push himself into the MedBay.

"In line behind me and half the med staff," she explained.

"And why can't you ask him questions?" Another step and he loomed over her. Her eyes were on a level with the crystal stars on his collar.

They didn't intimidate her.

"Because he disappeared within hours of surgery. No being should have recovered that quickly. He'll damage himself more by running around the station too soon."

✦   ✦   ✦

"Girls, take the dogs for a walk in the hydroponics garden," Sissy ordered, handing leashes to Mary and Martha.

"But . . ."

"And take Laudae Penelope's girls with you. Give them a tour of the station. Let the hover cams follow you."

Happy grins replaced stubborn protests.

Mary handed a leash to Bella. Then she looped her arm through Cassy's, the oldest of Penelope's acolytes. She looked up with open admiration and the kind of devotion only a thirteen-year-old can give a companion who had matured to the excellent age of sixteen. Lavender and pink clothes separated them more than age.

Martha also paired off with an older girl, leaving the youngest to clump in an ill-defined group, their pale clothing blending more than the older girls.

"Stay together," Penelope ordered a little nervously. "I don't want any of you getting lost."

"Alone at last," Sissy declared with relief as she plunked into a comfortable chair in her private parlor.

"They will be safe, won't they?" Penelope twitched in her own chair. She reached for a teacup on the low table between them. The crockery rattled, and a bit of liquid sloshed.

"My girls have prowled every inch of this station with and without me as escort. Nothing has ever happened."

"The criminal element . . ."

"This is a closed station, Penelope. If crime exists, it's nonviolent and petty. The girls are safe. The hover cam records everything. No one would dare hurt them even if they had a reason." She poured a fresh cup of tea for herself from the fat brown pot.

"I have trouble remembering this isn't Harmony City. Crime at home has tripled in recent months." Penelope stared into the depths of her cup.

"No one told me. What is going on?" Sissy sat up straight, alarmed.

"Children integrate easily, especially the littlest ones. They haven't learned to hate. Some Professional merchants have refused to sell to any but their own caste, Nobles, and Temple. There are long lines for food in smaller stores, where the larger ones are nearly empty of people but overflowing with goods. The hungriest have to resort to theft to stay alive."

"That is appalling! I'll draft an order . . ."

"The Professionals will merely close up shop. Several have rather than obey orders from the Temple."

"Who sends those orders?"

"Laud Gregor." Penelope's gaze wandered to the comm unit embedded in the wall. "I need to call MedBay, check on him."

"They will call here first if anything goes wrong. You need to relax and drink your tea. Don't make yourself sick with worry. We need you healthy." Sissy placed a comforting hand on her friend's arm. "What if the orders came from me, through my weekly broadcast?"

"I don't know. I just don't know anymore. The caste system needs to become less rigid. But sometimes I wish life could just go back to an orderly and unchanging routine." Penelope set her cup back on the table awkwardly. It wobbled a bit before settling in its saucer.

"I'll try that tonight. Then I'll follow up with a written message. Little Johnnie says I have a broad audience. I just hope they listen to me."

"They do. Every week I hear lengthy discussion about what Laudae Sissy said. On Holy Day everyone has your name on their lips. The people trust you, Sissy. They don't trust Gregor or Bevan."

"I need to go home." Sissy stared bleakly at the wall. She'd have to leave Jake behind.

"No, Sissy. You have to stay here. No one else understands the full picture, the scope of our needs like you do. You can listen to the universe better than anyone. Harmony is just one small piece of the big picture." Penelope sat forward, and anxiously grabbed hold of Sissy's hands, forcing her to look into her eyes and know the truth of her statement.

"Generations of lies and secrets are finally catching up with Harmony. I wish the transition to truth weren't so painful," Sissy whispered.

"So do I." Penelope sat back. Dark circles of exhaustion rimmed her eyes. Her once lustrous black hair hung limply about her shoulders.

"Sleep, my friend." Sissy rose and arranged a light blanket around Penelope. "Sleep now. Our problems will still be here when you wake."

Sissy paced her quarters, wishing she could go home and fix things with a wave of her hand. Wishing Jake could go with her to help and guide her. Wishing . . .

$$\spadesuit \; \spadesuit \; \spadesuit \; \diamondsuit \; \spadesuit \; \spadesuit \; \spadesuit$$

CHAPTER TWENTY-FOUR

"**H**OURS!" **JAKE'S ANGER** and fear exploded from him. "He disappeared within hours? That was three days ago."

Doc Halliday backed up a step. She had kept Mac heavily sedated for four days while she cloned enough blood for transfusions during surgery. Then twelve hours to repair nerve damage and another twelve for him to come out of the anesthesia.

"Why wasn't I told?" Jake breathed deeply, forcing his temper aside.

Major Jake Hannigan, loose-cannon pilot gave in to the need to hit things and people. General Jake Devlin was no longer that person. He'd learned to control himself. Mostly.

"Patient privacy," Mariah Halliday snapped in return. "I have to respect his right to refuse treatment. I also have to respect his right to recover where he chooses without broadcasting to the entire station. For all I know his species may require a private hibernation to heal. I doubt it. But I have to respect his right to try it."

And all the security cameras in MedBay were on a closed loop, accessible only to medical personnel with proper authorization. No one in Control could access them.

"Mara," Jake called into his comm unit.

"Yes, sir," she replied, prompt as usual. No trace of fatigue or frustration after the long night of rescues.

"Mara, I have just been informed that the alien left MedBay about three days ago. Please begin a search for anomalous heat signatures between bulkheads and in the maintenance tunnels."

"Searching, sir. This may take a while."

"Why?"

"Because Admiral Marella has coopted a large portion of our computer power for her own purposes. Compound that with the ailing propulsion system, my databases are almost inaccessible." The words were bland, but Jake sensed Mara's intense irritation behind them.

"Let Pammy be, but don't be afraid to leach some power away from her. Be careful you do it in small increments so she doesn't notice." He knew better than to hope anyone could monitor Pammy's work from a remote position. The spymaster knew how to layer secrets into otherwise normal looking communications and then cloak the whole in so much verbiage, anyone but the intended reader lost the meaning between subject and predicate.

"*Very* good, sir."

"I'm on my way to the penthouse. I presume our prisoner is still there."

"Working."

Two workers in bland gray coveralls entered the lift on the next level. One of them mutely handed Jake a small screen requiring his signature. Jake scanned the material, waiting for Mara to come back on-line. He pressed his thumb in the lower left corner and passed the work order for repairs to the plumbing on the new refugee wing back to the worker with a nod.

The two men crossed over the tram path on the footbridge to grab one going in the opposite direction from Jake.

"All reports from his guards indicate Mr. Labyrinthe is still at home with only his guards for company," Mara reported as the tram doors closed behind Jake.

A fragment of memory flashed before him. Mac refusing contact with his half brother. "Double-check that. I don't want the phantom sneaking in there and doing our guest harm."

"On it, sir. Only three heat signatures in the suite. All identified."

Jake breathed a sigh of relief. Seemed like lately he spent more time in the lifts or on the tram than any one place in the entire station. And he hadn't seen Sissy in almost fifteen hours. Tonight, when he met with her and the girls for lessons and strategy session, he'd ask her to interrogate Adrial with specific questions. Find out where she came from, why she happened to choose FCC to crash into.

He used the time in the tram to call directly into Sissy's office comms. No answer. She and the girls could be anywhere on the station, talking with anyone who crossed their paths, learning things no one thought to tell Jake, finding ways to help. The best spies in Jake's arsenal.

Mary or Martha would call him if something weird cropped up.

Strange that they'd not reported any new sightings of the phantom.

Jake was fairly certain the alien hadn't sneaked aboard any outgoing ships.

Once more he longed for the return of the spectacles. He could tap into any of Mara's searches with them.

The tram dumped him at the end of its run at the penthouse. He snagged a lift and dropped to the center of the wing, right outside Labby's door. Jake saluted the guards. Both barefaced and wearing CSS uniforms today. As much as he wanted to integrate the crew, he hadn't managed much sharing of shifts.

"I hope you are in a talkative mood today, Mr. Labyrinthe," Jake said without preamble.

"There is talk, and then there is talk. Would you like to discuss the weather in Harmony City?"

"How about we talk about the Labyrinthe Corporation and why they haven't replied to our reports and requests for your removal from the station?"

"I cannot account for my siblings." He looked Jake directly in the eye, frank and open.

"This is a valuable property. You are a valuable member of the corporation. They should want both of you back."

"Perhaps the messages never left the station." The alien's ears flopped forward, casting shadows on his face but not totally obscuring it. Labyrinthe said more with his ears than his words.

Jake had to think about that for a moment. Communications to the CSS and to Harmony City remained open and frequent. Jake held the veracity of the communications from Harmony City in question, but they happened.

"Interesting idea. Any thoughts on who might have hacked into the system and prevented messages to that one address from leaving the station?" Jake tried a disarming smile but had a feeling it looked more like a grimace.

If someone had deliberately blocked communications, Jake knew ways around it. And who to help him do it. Pammy had sent him messages while he was on Harmony under deep cover at a time when no communication penetrated the empire.

"The same person who turned off the maintenance bots when I'd ordered them powered down," Labby replied. "The same person who dismissed the entire Control crew during the midnight watch. The same person who disrupts traffic by changing signs." Labby returned the smile. On him it did look like a grimace.

"Our phantom again." Jake took a comfortable pose leaning against the wall.

"What about the one hundred workers who left here for Labyrinthe II? Surely they would have reported the changes here at the station."

"Maybe. Maybe not." Labby spread his hands and folded his ears to cover his face. "Few in power consider information from mere workers valuable or even true. Most of them have so little Labyrinthe blood in them, they are no longer considered persons." The last statement sounded muffled from behind the ears.

"Did you know that your half brother has disappeared again." Jake didn't move from his lax pose, but he tensed, ready to tackle Labby if he chose to bolt. The tip of his wrist knife tickled his palm comfortingly.

Labby's ears flew open, and his wrinkled brown skin turned a strange shade of gray. "I demand better protection," he said, turning his head back and forth, searching every shadow and corner. "Number Three could be anywhere." He began trembling, hardly able to sit upright.

"You seem mighty afraid of a phantom who does not exist. A phantom with a Labyrinthian name."

"I was told from birth that Number Three was a child's nightmare. What you call a monster under the bed to coerce the legitimate children into behaving. He has haunted me since infancy. You have to protect me." Labby fell to his knees, hands clasped in front of him in supplication.

"Don't know that we can protect you from a nightmare. But if we knew more about him and what he wants, maybe we could figure something out." Jake set his comm unit to record. Finally he was getting somewhere.

"He wants power. He wants control. He wants recognition as a child of A'bner Labyrinthe. He wants this station!"

"Admiral Marella to General Devlin," Jake's comm beeped.

"What?" His foot began an arrhythmic tapping. "I'm busy!"

"Not too busy for this, *General* Devlin," Pammy nearly chortled.

"What is more important than interrogation of a prisoner?"

"Leave it for an underling. *Champion's* sensors have picked up a ship in distress just inside the jump point. No distress signal, leaking air, and losing bits and pieces as it limps toward us. We think it came through with the two refugee ships but was too badly damaged to signal. I'm sending out fighters and a tug," Pammy said.

"Damn." Jake looked from Labby to his comm. "Meeting you in fighter bay in seven. I'm going with you."

"Unnecessary."

"If it gets me off this station and into a pilot's seat, it's necessary." He stomped to the door, paused and turned back.

"You." He pointed to the guards. "Move this prisoner to my old quarters in the CSS residential wing. Give him worker clothing. Hide him in plain sight. Do it quietly and record every word he says about his brother and the Labyrinthe Corporation. I expect him to speak volumes in return for his safety."

"Number Three is everywhere. He knows everything. I'm as good as dead!" Labby wailed as Jake dashed for the lift.

♦ ♦ ♦ ◇ ♦ ♦ ♦

CHAPTER TWENTY-FIVE

LAUD GREGOR, HIGH PRIEST of the Harmony Empire, pushed aside the tasteless mush the Med staff had left for his lunch.

"Guilliam!" he called. "Guilliam, where are you?" The effort of raising his voice pulled at the stitches that ran the length of his chest. Sharp pain followed the trail of the incision and left his head feeling fuzzy and undefined around the edges.

Too close to the memory of all of those ghosts pressing on him in hyperspace.

He rested his head against the piles of pillows and closed his eyes to regain a sense of normalcy.

"Mr. Guilliam and Laudae Penelope are in a meeting with Laudae Sissy, My Laud," Caleb replied from the doorway. Hastily the boy wiped a glob of red sauce from the corner of his mouth with a disposable tissue.

Gregor was willing to bet an extra week's stay in this thinly disguised prison that Caleb's lunch tasted a lot better than his own.

"May I assist you?" Caleb moved into the room somewhat clumsily. His feet had grown faster than his body and disturbed his balance. Typical of adolescents.

Gregor didn't want to wait for the boy to finish growing and turn into a semblance of an adult.

"I need some decent food," Gregor said, pushing the bowl of pap aside until it teetered on the edge of the bed table. Throwing the dish would take too much effort.

"I will check with your nurse, My Laud." Caleb ducked away.

Was that a smirk on his face?

"Who's in charge here, Caleb. Those lesser-caste nurses or your High Priest!"

No answer.

Moments later Sissy glided into the room carrying a bowl of soup. She also had a sheaf of papers tucked under her arm.

"Your doctors say that if you are well enough to complain about the food, you are well enough to try something more substantial, My Laud."

The aroma drifting from the steaming bowl made Gregor's stomach growl. He grabbed it from her hands, slopping a little, and dug in.

"Bah!" he nearly spat it out. "It needs salt."

"Your doctors say you must cut down on your salt," Caleb said quietly. He kept to the doorway, ready to bolt.

"Tasteless gruel," Gregor sneered.

"If you don't want it . . ." Sissy made to whisk the bowl away.

He pulled it close to his chest and tried another spoonful. Still watery and tasteless but better than the gruel.

"What have you brought me?" he asked between gulps.

"Copies of the latest version of the treaty negotiations with the CSS." She set the folder on the corner of the bedtable. "I thought they might interest you."

"Have you given away all our sovereignty and privacy?" Gregor sneered. He considered sending Sissy home alone and staying to take over the negotiations himself.

But who would run the High Council? He certainly didn't trust Sissy to manage without close supervision. She'd caused too much upheaval and unrest already with her progressive ideas about integration and re-turning to the original covenant.

"If Guilliam is in a meeting with you, why are you here and he's not?" Gregor asked, peering closely at his High Priestess.

She wore her usual purple, this time in slacks and a delicate print blouse. No jewelry. He didn't think he'd ever seen her in slacks before, unlike the other priestesses at Crystal Temple. Worker-caste women al-ways wore old-fashioned dresses with full skirts, unless they were actually working; then they wore brown coveralls.

He didn't like the informality of slacks on women and wanted them all back in dresses. At least when Sissy dictated that each priest and priestess could wear different colors—her predecessors insisted on everyone wearing the same green—Gregor could differentiate among them at a glance, without having to work at remembering what they looked like.

"We finished our meeting," Sissy replied. "Mr. Guilliam is now run-ning some errands for . . . Ja . . . for me." She tapped the folder, remind-ing him of why she'd come.

He kept his attention on her. Let her stew a bit, waiting on him. He'd waited on everyone else long enough here in the hospital.

Now if he could just get someone to disconnect all of the tubes and wires that chained him to machines and chemicals, he might be able to recover.

"What kind of errands?"

"We have decided that Laud Andrew, the current liaison with city officials, should take over some of your administrative work while you recuperate here." She tapped the papers again.

"Hmm." Gregor mused a moment. Andrew was a good choice. Assertive when he needed to be but also capable of blending in with the woodwork when wise. He knew when to defer to more senior members and when to invoke Temple authority.

"How long?" No sense in letting her think she'd done the right thing. Not right off anyway.

"Until the doctors assure me that you are recovered enough to withstand the stress of hyperspace *and* resume a reduced workload. You will have to defer many of your duties so that you can rest. They have repaired some of the damage to your heart. Some of it must be replaced, and they haven't the facilities to do that here. They did take tissue samples and have begun cloning a new heart, just in case." She lifted her chin and fixed her gaze upon him.

Inwardly Gregor cursed. What had happened to the shy and ignorant girl who never questioned anyone?

He'd trained her too well. Or she'd listened to that damned bodyguard, Jake.

"Is this cloning safe?" he asked. New technology always frightened him. This procedure sounded so alien he wasn't certain he'd be himself, complete and untainted, if he had a new heart.

"Doctor Halliday assures me it is the safest procedure for patients with as weak and damaged a heart as you have. There is no fear of rejecting a clone, whereas a transplant—if available, and that is highly unlikely—has added risks. Provided you are strong enough to endure the surgery. You'll have to eat properly and rest until they finish the cloning. Several weeks at least. You'll be better than new afterward."

He grunted, still not convinced.

Finally he could stand her silent expectancy no longer. "Andrew will do as well as anyone. He knows his place and respects my wishes. Unlike some I could name."

She raised her eyebrows, daring him to speak her name at the top of that list.

"I need something to lighten my day. Would you bring the twins to see me? I like to listen to their girlish chatter." He pasted an innocent smile on his face.

Sissy frowned at that. Then she nodded and retreated, leaving him with her notes on the treaty.

Her notes. Not his. As if she merely kept him informed and didn't expect comments and suggestions.

"I'll get control over you and Harmony again, Laudae Sissy. Don't expect to run free much longer." With a new heart he could remain in charge for many decades and not have to retire. He liked the sound of that. He'd need that much time to undo the damage Sissy had caused to their society and their religion.

He and he alone knew what was best for Harmony.

An angel all in white had come to him in the middle of the night and promised him he would regain power and control. She had promised in Harmony's name.

"Caleb!"

"Yes, My Laud?" The boy appeared in the doorway, once more wiping that damnable red sauce from his mouth.

"Bring me that Media person I authorized to work here. I think it's time we lauded his caste mark so he knows where his loyalties truly lie."

✦　✦　✦

Jake counted heads in the *Champion's* ready room. Nine other pilots donned their flight suits and helmets, adjusted sensors and life support.

"Ten feels unlucky," he muttered staring at his helmet. The little glyph of Harmony graced the side, right over his left ear, where She could whisper wisdom. "We should be seven in honor of You," he told the Goddess.

But this was a CSS mission, and in the secular CSS base ten ruled in all things. Multiples of a sacred seven belonged in the Temple.

No matter who watched over him today, he decided not to test his luck. He kissed two fingers and placed them gently over the glyph. "Guide us well today," he prayed.

He'd noticed about half the other pilots performing the same ritual.

Then he locked his helmet in place on his suit and led the men to their ships.

He made one last check of his personal comm. His security people reported "No sign of Labby." He'd bolted from protective custody. He, like his brother, had hidden himself well, and deep.

"Four people crewing the tug," Lieutenant Josephs told him over the pilots' private network. "That makes fourteen. We're still lucky in the numbers."

Maybe lucky enough for his security team to find Labby while Jake took a turn around the solar system.

He smiled at Josephs and held up a thumb in acknowledgment.

Seconds after belting in and putting all systems on ready he received the launch command from Pammy on the bridge of *Champion*.

A quick loop around the station oriented the squadron to the jump point. The stream of debris and leaking energy showed clearly on all the sensor screens.

"All ahead at two Gs, folks," Jake ordered and pushed his fighter forward. His face flattened, and his chest felt too heavy for his lungs under the acceleration.

He'd been absent too long. A lifetime ago, (was it only a year?) he'd endured three Gs for short periods without thinking about it. His workouts in heavy G helped his endurance. Still, he didn't think he could tolerate the stresses of a faster approach.

Someone had to take up the rear to escort the slower tug. Might as well be him.

Nine sleek fighters spread out around him.

"Why so slow, General?" Josephs asked. "You getting too old and fat for this work?"

"They may have promoted me to bureaucrat, but I can still outfly you youngsters. Next time you go out on patrol, I'll put you through paces you've never dreamed of." He discommed, hoping he hadn't opened his mouth and stuck his foot in it up to his knee.

Still, he missed the chatter and camaraderie among pilots.

"Sensors show heat signatures fading. Life signs gone," Pammy told him from her position aboard *Champion's* bridge. "Engine emissions indicate this ship is Maril. Approach with caution. Arm all weapons. They may have followed the refugees from Zarith V"

"If they're dead, Pammy, they can't shoot us," Jake snapped back.

"It could be a booby trap. Arm all weapons, I repeat, arm all weapons."

"You heard the boss, folks. Arm your weapons," Jake ordered. "But no one fires except on *my* command. Premature firing will cost you stripes

and pay. This is a Maril ship, relatively intact. We want enough of it left
to take it apart and study. Same goes for any bodies."

He didn't want to think about the last Maril ship he'd shot to pieces.
Granted it had only been a dummy flown on remote control by Pammy's
people. But the rest of the fleet thought a CSS spy had stolen it and
brought it home for study. Jake supposedly killed the spy as well.

That was the night Major Jake Hannigan, pilot, died, choking on his
own drunken vomit, and Lt. Colonel Jake Devlin, spy, was born.

This ship was real. Excitement wiggled up from Jake's belly. The CSS
had never had an intact Maril ship before. They'd never had enough of
a nav system to reverse engineer one and figure out how an entire fleet
could operate with telepathic precision.

Or was that merely avian flocking instincts?

"Pammy," Jake called the spymaster on a tight and private beam. "I'm
betting we find Badger Metal crystals in the nav system."

"I don't make sucker bets, Jake. Now watch that debris field for explosives as you approach. And just once play it safe and let a junior officer
be first aboard."

"Ah, Pammy, you take all the fun out of it."

"You're a general now, Jake. You are much more valuable sitting at a
desk than flying that death trap."

In answer, Jake put on more speed.

The long flight toward the jump point became more interesting as
they closed the distance with the intruding ship. Radiation levels rose
along with drifting obstacles that seemed to have erratic propulsion. The
fighter on the port flank lost a wing sensor, and the tug had to veer off
course to avoid a chunk of hull plating nearly as large as itself.

As much as the delay annoyed Jake, he forced the squadron to slow to
one-half G. He scanned his screens set at maximum magnification as well
as a real-time view.

"I can see the feathered markings, sir," Josephs squeaked anxiously
from the starboard tip. "They're green and white. Never heard of that
color scheme."

"Warships are all black and white," Jake confirmed. "The size and
lines suggest a light transport, maybe cargo, maybe troops. This thing
could be filled with armed warriors with special insulation to mask heat
signatures."

They slowed further, circling the ship again and again. "I detect no
ships weapons," Jake broadcast to his squadron as well as to Pammy back
on the *Champion*. Numbers piled up on his data screens beside scans

of the ship. Unfortunately, his equipment couldn't see inside. "You got anything interesting, Admiral Marella?"

"Nothing but two dead bodies. I suggest you tow it back to station before trying to enter."

"Negative on that. If the hold is full of troops with masked signatures, I don't want to take a chance on them invading *my* station. Josephs, lock on to the cockpit port and take a look inside."

"That's a tricky maneuver, sir. Easier to go in through the hold."

"You not up to that tricky maneuver they taught us in basic?" Jake quipped. It was difficult. Pilots needed a dozen tries to match up the hatches and docking clamps. Most gave up without completing it.

Jake had accomplished it in three back in the old days when he was hotshot pilot Major Hannigan. Back then, when he'd managed the docking maneuver, he'd never made it inside. A cursory glance through the window showed it lined with explosives. He'd backed off in a hurry.

Now he needed to demonstrate to these young show-offs what real precision maneuvers were all about.

"How about I lock on nose to nose and go EVA to peek inside?" Josephs countered.

Jake chuckled. That was the logical and safe solution.

Since when had he gone all cautious and logical?

"Back off, boy. I'll show you how it's done."

"Show-off," Pammy muttered on the private frequency.

"That's why you love me," Jake returned. "Just don't tell Laudae Sissy what an idiot I'm about to become."

"You know, General, this maneuver has only successfully been performed by a Major Hannigan?" Josephs added.

In the background Pammy swallowed an outburst of laughter. Did this guy suspect that General Jake Devlin was the legendary Major Hannigan and that his "death" had been engineered by Pammy when she recruited him as a spy?

"Too bad that guy died. Rumor has it he was crazier than a Harmonite on caffeine," Josephs finished his thought.

Jake had to swallow his splutter. Harmony had never allowed the importation of coffee or chocolate—too addictive the original colonists claimed. Can't control the masses if they have an addiction to feed. He'd watched Garrin, Lord Lukan's son, run around at full speed for hours after imbibing his first candy bar, followed by a cappuccino. Sure he got a lot of detail work done for a couple of hours. Then he'd crashed and slept for twice that long in total exhaustion.

"Watch and learn, boy," Jake barked. Then he took a deep breath and focused on the real-time view of his objective. His hands caressed the controls lovingly, coaxing them to follow his directions to the millimeter. Tiny increments of power, then shut off and coast. Slide closer, back off, adjust, slide in again.

And . . . touchdown! In five. Not as good as the old Jake. Still better than any of these children they called pilots these days.

He had to close his eyes and allow his suit system to wick the sweat out of his eyes. Still breathing too raggedly, he secured the docking clamps.

Shouts and whistles of triumph and congratulations cascaded over the comms. He even heard a bit of applause back in Control from Pammy. "I knew you still had it in you, Jake my boy. We'll celebrate in my quarters when you get back."

"You never know, Pammy." He'd find an excuse. Any excuse to keep from breaking his nightly date with Sissy.

"Time to go see what's happening aboard that ship," Jake muttered to himself. He ordered his ship to talk to the hatch of the other ship, neutralizing atmosphere and pressure between them.

Surprisingly, the Maril vessel accepted his orders and didn't require more than a few overrides to open.

He drew a blaster as the hatches slid aside. Eerie silence greeted him. And darkness. No running lights inside or out. The cockpit looked dead.

As dead as the Maril female with a cap of black feathers instead of hair locked in the arms of a human male. His skin and curly hair matched her black feathers, a New Numidian trader. Nothing else registered except their intimate, lovers' embrace. They'd died together when they could not live together.

He blinked back tears. Wondering if he and Sissy would have the courage to break free of the restrictions of their cultures and governments to run away together, face life or death together.

A flashing light on the comm panel finally caught his attention. A message scrolled across the screen in both CSS standard and Maril.

"Tell the lost one that Sanctuary can be found."

♦ ♦ ♦ ⟨⟩ ♦ ♦ ♦

CHAPTER TWENTY-SIX

"YOU ARE LOOKING FOR SOMEONE who is not here," Sissy said to Jake. They stood partway up the spiral staircase watching computer and maintenance technicians file off the latest ship to arrive from CSS territory.

Hover cams with both CSS and Harmony logos recorded the influx. Sissy had yet to actually see a member of the Media, only their ever present recording devices.

"I don't see any competent workers for one." Jake dismissed the mass of people with a gesture. At the same time he checked his comm.

"You expect whoever you are looking for to appear in your comm?"

Jake stifled a laugh and stuffed his hand in his pocket. The comm unit peeked above the line of his clothing, still readily available.

"Then tell me, who is Admiral Pamela Marella?" She tried to keep her tone casual.

"Um—she's a high-ranking CSS official assigned here to oversee military concerns in the treaty negotiations." He sneaked another peek at his comm unit, as if he could force an incoming call by will alone. "Where is the little bugger," he said so quietly she had to strain to listen.

"You're lying about Admiral Marella." Not about needing to find someone who eluded his troops. "Military supervision of the treaty was part of your job as liaison between the ambassadors."

"Huh? Oh, Pamela. That is the absolute truth!" Jake opened his eyes wide in horror. His hand went to his heart in an old gesture of avowal. The gesture put his comm in full view again. He checked it. "They've got to find him," he whispered.

Sissy chose to ignore that for her own agenda.

"Perhaps that is Pammy's official reason for being here. But she is more," Sissy pushed him. She knew Jake well. He could not keep the truth from her for long.

"You have your secrets, My Laudae, like the identity of the patient in critical care. We have ours." His face closed, and he looked down, toward the line of unwashed and threadbare men and women who shuffled through the loading bay between levels of an empty wing. Soon they would fill the small apartments in the mid-gravity levels above them. Soon after, they were supposed to deploy to duties about the station.

"Who is she that you depend upon her to find you a crew, and yet you do not trust her?"

"If I could tell you that without endangering us both, I'd tell you." This time he looked her in the eye with deep sincerity.

And something more.

"If you know nothing, then our enemies, both inside and outside our ranks, won't bother to kidnap and torture you for information." His face went blank again, hiding deep emotions. "Like they might do to . . ." He stuffed his hand into his pocket again, taking the comm out of his, and her, sight as he fixed a gentle gaze upon her.

She looked away first. If only . . .

But that could never be.

"Just as you cannot tell me who is the patient who needed so much blood for surgery," he continued. His eyes begged her to tell him. "I know he or she came off a Harmony ship. I saw some of the other passengers when we helped the refugees. I can guess."

"It is only a guess. You do not know!" she almost shouted. "That information will endanger more than just you and me," she continued with forced calm. "You have your secrets. I have mine. We will *not* exchange them. For our mutual protection."

"So we are at an impasse."

She turned away from him, swallowing deeply. The fate of the unnamed patient weighed heavily on her heart. "If they send me home, Jake, will you promise me to keep the pirate communication channel open? The people need to hear more than what governmental censors put on the Media. I don't think I could endure Crystal Temple without hearing from you."

A wave of sadness crossed his face. He looked so very vulnerable. Then it was gone in a flash, replaced with the stern military man who killed when necessary.

They both looked down at the new crew rather than at each other.

A Harmony hover cam inched toward them, lens circling for the best view. Someone directed it remotely rather than rely on automatic settings.

Jake's comm beeped. The camera came closer. He looked at his screen. A wave of disappointment washed over his face. He turned off the message cursing. "Too many places for him to hide."

"What has you so anxious?" Sissy asked. She wanted desperately to wipe the weariness from his face with a touch, a kiss, or just a word.

He looked away, gripping the railing with white-knuckled fierceness. "Another secret I can't tell you. A dangerous secret, and I won't put you at risk. I don't think I could continue living if something happened to you because of my secrets." Something like a poignant memory flitted through his eyes and then was gone.

"You'll leave indentations if you don't stop strangling the poor innocent piece of metal."

He yanked his hands away as if the railing burned him. Then he batted the watching camera away so that it turned toward the checkpoint at the air lock.

Below them, a CSS corporal in a gray-green uniform, carrying a blaster on his hip, stopped a worker from disembarking. Something about the information on his identity card.

Jake instantly became alert and descended two steps. "Control. Hack into Harmony hover cam three and record," he said quietly into his comm.

The corporal ran the worker's card through his reader a second time. He seemed satisfied with the results and waved the worker on.

The man quickly blended in to the milling crowd of his fellows.

"I do not trust the energy that flows around that man," Sissy said quietly. She noted the heaviness of his beard, as if he had not shaved this week, nor had his hair cut in many weeks. Grime seemed embedded in the lines around his eyes. His anonymous dark green tunic and trousers looked more ragged than most of the other newcomers.

Swirls of darkness seemed to follow him, as it did in the ancient paintings of Discord, the banished stepchild of Harmony and Empathy.

"What?" Jake asked. He turned half toward her but did not come up to her level.

"Something is amiss with that man. And many of the others. I would not give any of these people access to important and vulnerable places on this station." She had to close her eyes. The shadows crept closer. Her vision narrowed to a tunnel that connected her to Jake and nothing else.

"That's close enough to a vision for me," he grunted. "Tonight we go over all the work records of these people. I want to know which sewers Pammy found them in. I'd rather trust the refugees if Doc Halliday will ever release them."

"I suspect your Pammy found these people in prisons and asylums," Sissy whispered. "I have never seen auras of malice before."

Jake caught her, just before she fainted. Her last coherent thought was that he might not be enough to protect her this time.

✦　✦　✦

"Where have you hidden my brother?" Mac asked the images in his terminal. He watched the penthouse apartment. Hour after hour Number Seven moved from desk to reading chair, to dining table, to bed, and back again without change in routine. Not so much as a shift in menu or progress in the book he read.

Mac moved one of the remote hover cams closer to the locks and enhanced its heat detection. No one had punched in a code, and left remnants of their body temperature, in some time.

"Thank you, members of the Media, for the gift of extra eyes that don't lead directly back to me." He drummed his four fingers on his thigh, thinking about what he saw there. "You have tricked me, General Jake, repeating the recorded movements in a continuous loop."

He checked the time signature and date stamp. They advanced at a normal rate. "I salute your programmer, Jake. But now I know you have hidden him, I know where to look."

He scanned station activity for anything unusual. Patterns remained the same. People moved in and out of offices and quarters at a regular rate. The diplomats continued arguing over word choice in their treaty. Engineers tried to slow the propulsion system that kept his station in a stable orbit, exactly matching the forward movement of the station to the pull of the gravity from the planet below. If Mac could help them, he would, to protect the station. Those arcane machines were beyond even his understanding.

He watched medical staff guide his little bird through therapy. The trained professionals also moved in and out of a critical care room with purpose and closed mouths. Who did they hide? And who had died that Doc Halliday hid the body in deep freeze with triple locks. Mac could break the encoding. But not without leaving traces

He dismissed them from his search. Whoever required so much attention was in no condition to interfere with his plans. He needed to find Number Seven alive, not some uninteresting dead body.

He interrupted the good physician's search of databases for information on the Squid People. Mac smiled. In this he could rearrange Admiral Marella's agenda. He inserted a file into Doc Halliday's computer, a duplicate of all the information he'd discovered inside the crashed ship. The entire universe needed to know why the Squids went extinct, and how their nav system was tampered with. Pammy shouldn't keep it all to herself. Especially if she was guilty of that tampering.

Mac could still use the spymaster, but not if she continued her activities unchecked and without monitoring.

Armed guards moved about the station, poking their noses into odd places and returning to General Jake's old quarters. Someone had escaped their notice.

He knew they looked for him. But that search came from Control, seeking ways to find him with maintenance bots and heat signatures. Both methods he could override.

Number Seven had not the knowledge to perform such tricks. He didn't know the secret ways around the station as Mac did. Number Seven had to hide more openly.

Mac zoomed a camera in on the new crews. Dregs. Admiral Marella had cleared out the unemployed, drunks, and petty criminals from other stations to fill the ranks of Jake's staff. Why? Did she want Jake to fail as commander of this station?

Knowing the admiral as Mac had come to know her, he suspected something deeper. He scrolled through the entire list of new employees, their work records and criminal history. A pattern of sameness showed throughout. Nine out of ten profiles had been faked.

Who were these people?

An idea popped into his head, and he stared at two faces in particular. They looked familiar . . . He'd seen them on Labyrinthe Prime before the family had built Labyrinthe VII. He'd observed the newcomers closely on the original space station and decided they were spies for the CSS. Spies trying to gain complete plans of Labyrinthe Prime (the model for every succeeding station) so they could build their own for the CSS.

Every one of the new employees worked for Admiral Marella.

Perhaps a midnight visit to the spymaster was in order. After he found Number Seven.

Mac watched the new maintenance crew dismantle a power plant for a three-wing section due to open soon. Ah, that one with the blue stripe down the seam of his trousers carelessly threw pieces to the deck. And the one with a red bandanna covering his baldness cleaned the same piece over and over, looking busy, accomplishing nothing.

Then he saw a woman in a shapeless gray overall sneak behind a partition. She leaned heavily against the bulkhead while she drank from a flask secreted in a pocket.

Those three had legitimate records of frequent job changes, covered-up arrests, and time in something called rehab. If Mac bribed them to talk, he couldn't trust their information.

He shifted his attention to the common room on the dormitory level. Six men and women gathered around a table with the gaming cards humans seemed so fond of. They played a game called poker. Mac watched for a long time, learning some of the rules while he observed the players. Two men played with only half their attention, the other half fixed on a holovid of a ball game. One woman and one man looked serious, studying their cards and their opponents with care and equal attention. The other woman and man sweated and constantly counted their "chips." Gambling addicts.

Mac had seen similar traits in nearly every race that frequented any of the Labyrinthe stations. The games changed. The color of the money varied. The addiction remained.

Now he knew who he could bribe with money for their next game. He also knew which people would report his bribes to Admiral Marella and which would not.

His plans fell into place.

By the time he was done, Jake would hand him the station out of sheer frustration (provided they got the propulsion system working properly before the station broke orbit and drifted into infinity). Admiral Marella helped him with every incompetent slackard she brought in as staff.

But Mac would not assume his rightful place as master of this station until he found Number Seven and shipped him back to Labyrinthe Prime for humiliation and demotion.

"If I were Number Seven and needed to hide from General Jake, where would I go?"

The answer came to him.

"In plain sight."

$$\blacklozenge \ \blacklozenge \ \blacklozenge \ \diamondsuit \ \blacklozenge \ \blacklozenge \ \blacklozenge$$

CHAPTER TWENTY-SEVEN

"**D**OC HALLIDAY, I WONDER if your databases included anything about the Squid People?" Sissy asked. She'd found the physician in her office, just a few doors away from Gregor's room, after making a routine visit to Adrial that left her more confused than enlightened as to why and how she had chosen the ill-fated pilots to bring her to the First Contact Café.

"Funny you should ask," Mariah Halliday said around half a smile. "I was just looking them up myself. I think the only way General Devlin is going to let me do an autopsy on them is if I bombard him with information he doesn't have."

Sissy swallowed her distaste at the thought of willingly carving up the dead for study.

"I ask because I believe they deserve a funeral. I'd like to put together a ceremony based upon them and their culture, to honor them, to make a record of their passing." Sissy bowed her head, already composing prayers and hymns in her mind.

"That's nice of you. Come here and look what I found." Doc Halliday beckoned for Sissy to scoot the extra chair up beside her at the desktop terminal.

"It seems we are not the first to encounter the Squids," Sissy mused as she scanned long columns of data and detailed views of the computer interfaces, complete with labels for the different icons. "What's that?" She pointed to a tiny image, not so different from the simple glyph of Harmony.

"The label says translator," Mariah said peering closely and squinting her eyes. "I think it's supposed to represent some kind of fish."

"What happens if we touch it?"

"Don't know. This is a recording of the computer, not the actual one." She touched the miniature line drawing. Nothing happened.

They both shrugged and moved on.

"Whew," Mariah breathed through her teeth, creating a muted whistle. "Someone touched that icon during the recording. Look at this!"

"A journal?" Sissy asked. A string of numbers separated by a period centered across the top of the page. Then lines and lines of text, followed by a slightly different string of centered numbers and more text.

"That's what it looks like to me."

They both leaned closer, reading the personal diary of the navigator, the female of the pair.

Mariah scrolled to the beginning so they could read forward in time. They shared the loneliness and quiet despair of this loving couple, living out their days drifting from rim world to rim world, carrying whatever cargo they could. In every port they sought, hopelessly, for any rumor of any others of their kind. With each journey they became more and more aware of their own mortality.

"How sad." Sissy wiped away a telltale tear. "They knew months ago that this was their last trip."

"Yeah, and it's the same pair that brought Adrial here. This recording was made after the crash," Mariah grunted. "I think I need to tell General Jake we have this." She reached for the comm icon.

"Before you give him the opportunity to confiscate this, will you send a copy to my terminal?" Sissy stayed the older woman's hand.

"For you, yeah, I will. I know you won't abuse this. And . . . Laudae, I'd like to attend whatever service you perform for these people. They deserve our respect."

"Yes, they do. Our scientists also need to eventually look at this, and the ship. They had their own version of Badger Metal long before humans thought of it."

"And they didn't start to die off in large numbers until they changed to Badger Metal for their hull plating. I wonder if something in the manufacturing process of Badger Metal is human specific."

"The Squids began dying off at the same time they lost track of their home world," Sissy added. "We all need a home planet to ground us, to strengthen our ties to our Gods, to complete us."

"You might have something there, Laudae Sissy. Something as scientific as it is spiritual. There's a reason humans have always terraformed their new homes. We evolved on Earth in sympathy and symbiosis with the planet."

Sissy cocked her head in question.

"Every plant, animal, and mineral that evolves together on a world has a piece of each and all of those things in its makeup. We need the entire web of life to survive and thrive." Mariah kept her gaze on the journal. She tapped the entry that bemoaned the loss of the coordinates of the Squids' home. "When we move off-world, we lose some of those pieces. Parts of us die, never to be replaced or regrown. By moving out among the stars, we begin our slow death and devolution."

"Are humans dying too?" Sissy whispered in absolute fear.

"Not yet."

"But we too will one day go extinct, like the Squid People."

"Probably. But not for a while yet. We've been smarter than some races. We're still grounded on Earth and return frequently. We take big chunks of home with us and plant it wherever we go. Even here. The gardens use real Earth as a planting medium and seeds from home to grow our food."

"I think I need to go walk my dogs in the gardens."

"I'll tell Jake where he can find you."

✦ ✦ ✦

"What do you mean, you can't accept having your caste mark lauded? It's an honor, a distinction. Special!" Gregor screamed at the Media person standing beside his bed. He couldn't bring himself to look directly at the ugly black bar of a caste mark.

That one had belonged to the poor, the outcasts, criminals! The Media should have a Professional green triangle. They'd worn that caste mark proudly for generations. But since Sissy had revealed the original Covenant Tablets that made the Media a separate and independent caste, they'd all reverted to the ugly mark of the disposables.

Thankfully the man had left his obnoxious hover cam outside in the corridor. Gregor didn't care what his name was and hadn't asked.

"A ruling from the head of my caste, My Laud." The man bowed respectfully. The center of his unremarkable brown hair had thinned to a nearly bald spot. His unremarkable light brown eyes closed. His pale clothing seemed to blend into the walls. Few would notice him in a crowd. Fewer would find him if he didn't want to be noticed. A perfect reporter. "The Media must remain independent and loyal to the truth without interference. Therefore no augmentation of our caste marks. And we all must have our marks *upgraded* to the black bar." He smirked.

"I will not accept that," Gregor said. He pursed his lips, thinking, planning. His thoughts whirled in circles. Never, not once in fifteen years as

HP of Harmony and her six colonies, had anyone defied him so completely. And never so politely.

"The original Covenant establishes the Media as separate and independent, so that we are obligated to report the truth to all of the people," he said blandly. A pleasant smile grew around his words.

"What is your name, young man? I will notify your superiors of your impertinence." Pressure built in Gregor's chest as he ground out each distasteful word. He hated Big Johnny, the head of the caste and owner of the Harmony City Broadcasting facility. He hated dealing with him. Hated what he stood for. Hated his defiance that began long before the Media obtained separateness of caste.

The machine beside Gregor began beeping, rapidly.

His breathing sharpened.

"You will obey me, or I will break the Media, as I will break all the changes initiated by Laudae Sissy."

"My name is Simon da Samuel pa FCC," the man said upon another cursory bow, still smiling. "Feel free to repeat this entire conversation to the head of my caste, verbatim. I have it recorded." He held up a small device no bigger than his palm.

"I'll have your head . . ."

"You'll have nothing but a casket and a funeral if you don't calm down," Doc Halliday pronounced from the doorway. She bustled toward the array of machines around Gregor.

"I shall leave you to the kindly ministrations of the physician." Simon da Samuel bowed again, deeper this time, and backed out the door to his waiting hover cam.

"Kindly, my ass," Gregor cursed.

"My Laud, that's the nicest thing you've said to me," Doc Halliday said sweetly. "Now I'm going to increase your tranquilizer dosage and your vasodilator until your readings get back closer to normal. You may feel a little sleepy."

"Not yet. I need to make some notes about that obnoxious man."

"All reporters are obnoxious. It's part of their job."

"But . . ." Gregor drifted into an agitated twilight sleep. He thought he was awake, feeling his muscles twitch and his fingers itch to write down something important. He couldn't remember what.

A part of him dimly noted the physician answering a hail and darting away without adjusting his medications back to lower levels.

✦   ✦   ✦

Mac turned his attention to the few Labyrinthians who remained on station. All had shifted loyalty from the Corporation to General Jake. Which one was Number Seven?

He needed to view each worker up close to differentiate. Quickly he powered down his observation post and plotted a route to the most likely center of Labyrinthian activity.

Sixteen. He counted a mere sixteen (an unlucky number, there should be a multiple of seven) big-eared, brown-cloaked housekeepers scattered about, doing their jobs, making notes to pass on to General Jake later.

None of them was his brother.

An oddly gaited worker disappeared down a spiral staircase beside a lift to an unused level. He noted that the lift platforms moved too quickly. They did not complete the entire circuit of this wing. Had General Jake managed to replace the single construction lift with the triple conveyance that traveled a single gravity section and allowed safety bulkheads to close at the top of each?

The upper levels were fully accessible. Something was hidden in the lower, heavy-G levels.

Mac dared not use the lift or the open staircase to follow. But he knew other ways to access those levels.

His detour took too long. The worker had more than enough time to walk down those stairs to the levels below the lift circuit, complete his business and return without Mac seeing any of it. He cursed in his father's language of chitters and pops that he hadn't brought a portable computer—too easy to lose it and give General Jake or Pamela Marella access to the entire network.

Hurrying as fast as his eight limbs could take him through the narrow shafts and unused maintenance tunnels, he paused when he spotted the worker using a parallel maintenance tube to drink long from a flask and then catch a nap.

Mac could no longer hear the lift operating. He'd reached the second HG level of this wing that had no designation.

Darkness and shadows. His infrared vision registered anomalies. He had to risk exposure and discover the truth here.

As silently as he could, he opened the grating and climbed down the wall, head down, nose flaring for scent information.

He reared back.

Death.

He smelled death. And not a clean one.

Three cautious steps forward and he faced the truth. Number Seven hung from an exposed water pipe, a noose strangling his fleshy neck. His tongue lolled black and swollen. His glazed eyes stared blankly into the beyond.

A scrawled note in CSS standard hung on a placard from his shoulders. "Murderer!"

Too late. He'd come too late by hours to save his brother from an ignominious death. This was the execution of a criminal who had caused five deaths through negligence.

Five deaths that Mac had caused through his manipulations to make his brother look more slackard than he was.

The chatter of bright voices on the stairwell brought him out of his numb shock.

Sissy's six acolytes arranged themselves on the spiral. Six more in pink peered down from the level above. They stared at him, eyes wide in horror, mouths opened in silent screams. The oldest grabbed a comm unit from her pocket as her gaze riveted upon him.

Mac ran away.

✦ ✦ ✦ ◇ ✦ ✦ ✦

CHAPTER TWENTY-EIGHT

SISSY PACED JAKE'S OFFICE, the small area off the conference room where he was supposed to be but never was.

"Where is he?" she called to Mara in Control from the comm unit on the desktop.

"At the other end of his comm unit," came the disembodied voice. She sounded busy and harassed.

Sissy still didn't like remote communication across short distances, though she used it often enough on the station. At home her family happily visited their friends and family to share the news, borrow tools and clothing, or just to enjoy the company. In the crowded apartment complex attached to the factory, nothing and no one was ever far away.

At Crystal Temple, everyone used the telephones rather than chance invasions of privacy, or any sort of intimacy—except for casual sex initiated in the nude swimming pool.

"I need to talk to him face-to-face, Major Mara," Sissy insisted.

"Hit the blue button on the comm unit, My Laudae. It should summon him directly."

"Thank you, Mara. I won't take any more of your time."

"Not to worry, My Laudae. I always have time for you. Would that ship captains demanding precedence in the flight path spoke half so politely."

"I'll let you get back to them, Major Mara. And if any of them are from Harmony, tell them I said for them to mind their manners."

"Will do, My Laudae," she replied with enthusiasm.

Sissy glared at the touchpads embedded in the desktop. The blue button seemed to glare back at her, daring her to interrupt Jake in his demanding job. Reluctantly she pressed her thumb against the blue spot, the same color as a Noble's robes.

"What?" Jake growled almost immediately.

Sissy jumped back in surprise, almost expecting him to appear before her, like a holovid—another innovation she couldn't quite accept. They were too real; she liked watching flat screens and knowing that distance and time, and often reality, separated her from the portrayal.

"Jake, it's me," she said hesitantly.

"Sissy, what's wrong?" He sounded anxious. "Are you safe?"

"I'm fine," she replied, puzzled. Why wouldn't she be safe? "I've just come from Adrial and Doc Halliday. I have some information."

"On my way. Don't go anywhere without an escort. You or the girls."

"My information will wait if you're busy."

"I'm on my way back anyway. I've got to change clothes." Shouts in the background nearly drowned out his words. "Get all that evidence to Harmony Military. They've got a forensics expert and lab facilities," he called into the distance. "Yeah, I know they're paranoid. In this case I'm glad of it."

Sissy did not like the sound of that. "I'm in your office, Jake," she said quietly, wondering if she truly should let him get on with his work.

"I guessed as much for you to come through on this channel. Mara's the only other one authorized to use it."

She basked a moment in the quiet intimacy of his tone.

"I'll be there as soon as the trams allow. Don't go anywhere. I'm locking the doors to all but my key."

She paced, more than a little afraid at his tone and the questions he left unanswered.

And then he was there, in the same room with her, with a special smile he reserved just for her.

She grew warm all over.

Then she saw the blood on his uniform.

"Now what is so important you could not wait until this evening, or trust over the comm lines?" he asked, touching her shoulder as he perched on the edge of his desk, arms folded, long legs stretched out in front of him.

"I . . ." Was discussing the vast loneliness of the Squids so very important? She ducked her head blushing, seeking desperately for something else to talk about. "I spoke with Adrial this morning. Right after we left the new crew." Before she'd read the loving intimacy of two aliens, the last of their kind, who had loved each other completely for many, many decades. She wanted that same level of closeness with Jake. Ached to have him at her side, sharing her thoughts and dreams as well as her body.

She blushed, remembering how fulfilled she felt during her waking dream of a Maril on Harmony with new babies that completed a sacred breeding ritual.

"And?"

"Today Adrial seemed almost coherent. At least I think she parted with a few facts beyond her wandering thoughts about Gods and visions and angels."

"Really? Did you know that on ancient Earth she'd have been honored as a mad prophet?"

"Mad is the operative word here. I gather that she has been so mistreated that her only solace is in this quest for spirituality. But she keeps making the search more important than finding any stillness within her to allow the Gods to speak to her." She shuddered at her own waking dream. That was almost too much information from the Gods.

Her mind flashed to a stone ledge, candles and incense, a small fire behind which priests stood while a man made careful and gentle love with her. A part of her had been there with the Maril couple who had probably died at human hands five centuries before.

"Hmmm. Do you suppose that if Adrial ever allowed herself to be still, the memories are too painful to face?" Jake mused.

He didn't know how Sissy's thoughts had wandered, and she didn't want him to know. Yet.

"I believe so," she replied, yanking her thoughts back to the spoken topic.

"What did she tell you?"

Sissy recounted her last interview with Adrial.

"I'll set up a remote monitor while she sleeps, see if we can catch this phantom." Jake made a note on his desktop screen. "He seems our most likely suspect in the death of Labby, but . . . I don't know . . ."

"Mr. Labyrinthe is dead?" Blood rushed away from Sissy's head. So that was why Jake's uniform was so badly stained.

"Doc Halliday tells me Labby was dead several hours when your girls, backed up by Penelope's girls, found Mac staring at his dead body," he said sternly.

Sissy gasped in dismay, her hand covering her mouth as she choked away the need to retch. "They'll have nightmares."

"What I can't understand is why would Mac be standing in front of the body, acting shocked, if he was the murderer?" Jake moved about restlessly, tugging at the front buttons of his uniform blouse.

"If Mac risked himself to save Adrial, I do not think him capable of cold-blooded murder," Sissy mused.

Jake paused in stripping off his shirt and moved into a smaller room next to the office, leaving the door open. "Good point. I'll show you the recording of when he turned her over to the medics."

He emerged a moment later in a clean black uniform, still stuffing tools and weapons into the pockets. "Here, watch this." He touched an icon on his desk.

Flat images came to life in the polished surface. Sissy watched for several moments.

"Jake, can you repeat this?"

"Sure. I've looked at it several times because Mara thought it important. Something is wrong. I just can't figure it out.

Once more Sissy watched as the armed men confronted the alien being called Mac. They exchanged words. The guards threatened Mac. Adrial whispered something. Mac placed her on the gurney.

"There. Stop it there." Sissy pointed at the scene.

Jake reached around from behind her and hastily touched another icon. The images froze in place.

"Back it up a bit."

Jake obeyed.

"Stop." The images froze again.

"What am I looking at?" Jake asked peering over her shoulder, close enough that his body heat covered her entire back.

"Do you see how tenderly he carries her? How gently he puts her down? He almost kisses her forehead. That is not a murderous creature."

"Some of the worst mass murderers in our history have loved their mothers just as tenderly."

"Adrial is not his mother. She is a virtual stranger."

"You're right. I wonder if the forensics tech has found anything. Surface evidence gathering gave us precious little. Whoever murdered Labby left no DNA, no fingerprints, no trace at all. My gut instinct tells me that Mac wanted to humiliate his half brother, not murder him. We have to wait while the techs process what little information they found."

"I hope it is not too long. I shall prepare a Grief Blessing for him."

"I doubt he will have any mourners. Not even Mac will show up. Did you know that their mother had twenty-six children, each by a different father from a different species?"

Sissy shook her head, appalled and horribly fascinated by such a bizarre concept. Then she remembered the waking dream. A part of her felt completely fulfilled by the concept of a public breeding ritual. The Maril who had come to Harmony before the humans were not all mystics and priests. The ones who came for a short time and left were couples ready to have children.

She blushed and was glad Jake stood behind her and could not see her embarrassment.

"Labby told me that the Labyrinthe race was on the verge of extinction, couldn't breed among themselves anymore," Jake continued. "So they began taking spouses among other similar species. After a couple dozen generations it looks as though they can start breeding back with their own kind again. The workers are part of that experiment. A lot of them have subnormal intelligence." He mused a bit more on the information gleaned from Labyrinthe Seven while he paced the office restlessly. Most of the science of DNA breakdown and blending with other species to find a stable continuation of a people and culture went over Sissy's head.

And yet a few of the phrases rang a chord. Something about how easily she fit into a Maril body in the visions Harmony sent her made her wonder. She knew that the Maril had considered Harmony a spiritual outpost when humans first arrived. A place where conception of a child was a sacred ritual. Sissy's ancestors had murdered them one and all out of fear or loathing. She needed to think about it for a while.

The Squid People suffered extinction. She needed to think about the whys of that before sharing her thoughts as well.

"So Adrial comes from Amity? Where the hell is that?" Jake shook his head in puzzlement. Then he moved behind her again and brought up new screens on his computer. He set it to searching.

"I have never heard of such a place," Sissy admitted. "But then, until I came here, I'd never heard of nine tenths of the worlds inhabited by humans." She relinquished the chair to him and stepped behind him, peering over his shoulder. His fingers moved across the screens, highlighting this, discarding that.

"I need help with this." Jake leaned back in his chair, putting his face very near her arm.

She held her breath, not daring to hope he'd lean that extra inch to the right and rest against her.

With a deep inhale, he resumed his work on the screen, touching a comm button on the desktop, repeatedly. Finally he spoke. "Pammy, I'm shooting you some data. Will you run it through your search engines for me? Please." The last came as an afterthought. "She's not answering. Who knows when she'll listen to her messages."

"I'll leave you to your work," Sissy said reluctantly. Her feet remained firmly in place. "You might also send the information to Doc Halliday. She seems to have access to a lot of strange files."

"Do you have to go? I don't want you wandering about alone until we find the murderer, whether it's Mac or some unknown."

"I can stay for a while yet." She smiled, not caring if he was reluctant to let her go because he feared for her or because he was reluctant to let her go. Or just needed a respite from his duties.

"Good. I haven't eaten all day, barely had time for a piece of toast on the fly for breakfast. Join me. Please." He wandered toward his private sitting room adjacent to the office and conference room.

"I ate with the girls, before . . . before they went off exploring and found . . ." She gulped back her horror. "I should go to them."

"Penelope is with them all. So is Gil. They're dealing with it. Stay. Please. I . . . I need someone to distract *me* from all this unpleasantness."

"I'll have a cup of tea while you eat. Then I must get back to my girls."

"You can have coffee if you want." He flashed her a conspiratorial grin.

"Harmony's founders had reasons for leaving that addictive drug behind on Earth." She'd tried the bitter brew once at Jake's insistence and spat it out. Then he'd added cream and sugar, and she'd been lost, craving the rush of energy and good feelings as well as the rich taste at every turn.

"They left coffee behind as well as chocolate because they wanted complete control over the minds of their subjects, instead of allowing the lower castes to daydream about their next fix," Jake chuckled.

"When you put it that way, perhaps I owe it to the eventual breakup of the caste system to have coffee with you. Or better yet, some hot chocolate?" She looked up at him hopefully.

"Your wish is my command." He bowed formally, grinning widely. "While I eat, I'll tell you about our intercept of the latest pirate newscast out of Harmony City. Did you know that Laud Gregor was booed the last time he made a public appearance?"

"No," she gasped, appalled at such a display of disrespect for the office of High Priest, even if Laud Gregor's shortsighted view of the best path for the Harmonite Empire had earned him the dislike and distrust of the people.

"When was that?" she asked cautiously. Perhaps Laud Gregor's heart attack had been triggered by the unwelcome reception, and he languished in MedBay as a way to avoid going home.

"Three or four weeks ago. No one has seen him outside the Crystal Temple since. I also have it on good authority that Laudae Penelope has opened the first integrated school of Professional and Worker Children," Jake said.

"Now that is good news." Sissy had heard the same, from Penelope herself.

She settled in comfortably, eager for more news from home. The ache in her heart for those she'd lost and the Gods that had severed their connection to her only paled her delight a little. As long as she had these brief times to share with Jake, she could briefly forget about Adrial's wandering, the Squid's extinction, Mac's isolation from friends and family, the trauma to her girls at finding a dead body. Murder! Was there truly a murderer aboard? Who would be the next victim?

♦ ♦ ♦ ◇ ♦ ♦ ♦

CHAPTER TWENTY-NINE

"JAKE?" MARY HISSED through the comm.

He stopped the tram with a password override. "What's up, Mary?" he replied, forcing calm. *Please, don't let the girls have found another dead body!* Two more Labyrinthians had turned up strangled in other HG levels of the same wing as Labby's body.

The placard "Murderer" hung around Labby's neck—and the two other Control techs—were written in plain block letters in CSS standard, the same language used on Harmony, but they tended to produce more florid script.

Serial killers were usually smart enough to hide their trail. If this one chased anyone responsible for the death of the Harmony Workers, they'd go after any Temple or Noble. On Harmony, the top two castes had the power to execute anyone of a lesser caste without trial or justification. They were also responsible for keeping the other castes undereducated and ill-informed.

"Where are you?" Mary asked anxiously.

He didn't like her half-frightened, half-excited tone. "In the tram. Where are you?"

"Can you meet me at E5?"

"Engineering?" One of the wings in the same cluster as Control and the empty one where they'd found Labby. An identical engineering unit inhabited a wing grouped with Labby's penthouse. Redundancy to avoid sabotage. Except E5 held the propulsion unit that "pulled" the station forward and currently consumed more fuel than it should. The opposite unit "pushed" and ran as it should. The two together should keep the station in a stable orbit around the baby planet below them. If one went haywire, the orbit destabilized.

Higher fuel consumption. More speed. Slowly but surely the station was expanding its orbit and would eventually break free of the planet's gravitational attraction. They'd drift off into infinity until all the fuel was spent.

His heart beat double time, close to panic.

"Hurry."

He keyed in a new override, reversed direction at max speed.

The tram jockeyed over to a special lane. Immediate acceleration slammed him against the floor of the cubicle. He held onto one railing and hooked a foot into another. Just in time. The stops flew by faster than he could read the designations in the holo on the door. Then the car jerked to an abrupt halt that could have sent him through the ceiling as Zero G reasserted itself.

Mary awaited him on the transfer platform beside the top of the lift. Her lavender overalls and print blouse, the uniform the girls had adopted, looked a little rumpled and grimy. As the door slid open, she remote kissed Harmony and beckoned him forward with one hand, a finger from the other hand on her lips to indicate silence.

Jake's whole body stuttered. Why was Mary alone? The girls always traveled together. Lately they roamed with Penelope's older pink-clad acolytes. Safety in numbers.

He didn't want the girls out and about in less than a full complement of six.

A serial killer lurked aboard.

He waited until they were on the lift before raising his eyebrows in silent question. She shook her head. "Saboteur listening," she mouthed.

Discord! He suddenly wondered if the two anonymous workers and Labby might have known something about fixing the propulsion system. If so, then the saboteur would stop at nothing to destroy the station.

Jake began making notes on an evacuation plan. He figured at the current rate they'd need to start removing civilians in about three weeks. Sissy and her girls would be on the first ship out, no matter how much they protested.

As gravity increased on the lift, he felt as though his head was sinking into his gut.

They passed level after level of various and sundry engines and maintenance personnel quarters. One entire level was filled with maintenance bots, large and small for different purposes, in various stages of readiness. The mechanics working on them barely noted his passage on the lift.

Eventually they reached the level below the first docking bay—three levels combined. Seven drums equally spaced, each six meters tall and six meters in diameter filled the level. A gentle unison hum vibrated along the deck and up the bulkheads.

Five girls waited for them, their overalls and faces streaked with grease. They all looked more frightened than they had the night the Squid ship crashed into their home.

More frightened than when they faced horrible death by murder for the first time in their lives.

"What did you find?" he asked gently, so that he didn't scare them any more.

"Someone is listening," Mary whispered, pointing to one of the inevitable security cameras.

Jake found an abandoned, and mostly empty tool chest and rolled it beneath the camera. A boost, a reach, and the camera came off the bulkhead into his stretched hands. "It's a dummy. Nonoperational. Which means Control is being fed false coverage of this area from somewhere else. We're alone and unobserved."

Evidence that Mac was the saboteur? No one else on station had those kinds of skills.

Pammy does, his hind brain reminded him. *She hired the dregs of the galaxy to work the station.* Jake totted up in his head the number of men and women on the payroll with criminal records or obviously bleached records.

If the spymaster was behind the sabotage and murders, he'd take her down personally, and with grim pleasure.

Martha loosed a long breath. Then she visibly gathered her composure and motioned Jake to follow her up a ramp and around the sealed drum of one of the propulsion engines. From the top of the incline he had a clear view of the top of the machine. No seams. No visible rivets. No entry to the guts of the thing.

He knew that. He'd checked it himself when the fuel consumption was first noted.

Alien markings that looked like random tool scratches with no visible pattern ran around the top and bottom of the drum. Neither Pammy's nor Control's databases recognized the markings. Or they'd been reprogrammed not to recognize them.

Martha pointed to seven thin rods sticking out of the top at odd angles and varying lengths. "Speed controls. They are preset at specific distances to control something inside," she said.

"How'd you know that?" he asked.

"We asked," Mary replied, as if any dummy would do the same.

"We lifted Sharan up there, since she's the littlest," Martha continued. "She says the tops have been hammered, like someone rammed the rods deeper than they should. That's why the machine is running too fast. All of them have been hammered identically."

"How do you know this?" Jake asked, amazed.

"They sound different from the group at the other end of the station. We asked a Spacer engineer what the rods were for. He guessed. We only showed him the other ones in case you didn't want anyone to know something is wrong."

"Good girls." Now who did he call to fix the damned things? His own maintenance staff hadn't noticed anything wrong. Who could he trust? Who even knew how the things worked?

"That's why we called you," Suzie piped up. "Sharan and I together don't have enough strength to pull them back out again. We don't know how far to pull them even if we could."

Jake rolled the tool chest over to the vantage point. And used it to climb atop the machine, heedless of the dust and grease that stained his black daily uniform.

He pulled a folding knife with multiple tools attached from his thigh pocket. The miniature awl was too big to fit between the rod and the casement. So was the thinnest of the extra blades.

None of the tools left a scratch on the strange material.

He tried a Badger Metal stiletto from his sleeve. That left faint marks in the black surface, barely enough to see.

He stood up and grabbed hold of one of the rods with vague scratches and flattening on the tip. With legs spread wide for balance and knees bent for leverage he heaved upward.

The rod remained firmly in place. All those hours in the heavy-grav gym gave him no advantage.

"Whoever did this had a great deal of strength and special tools." He looked at the nearly empty tool chest. Were the missing pieces responsible for this? "Damn."

"General Jake?" Mary asked, not as appalled as he thought she should be at his language. "What can we do to help?"

"You've done your job. You reported something out of the ordinary. Now you need to go back to Laudae Sissy and get cleaned up for evening services."

"What are you going to do, General Jake?" Martha asked. She steadied the tool chest as he climbed down.

"Find someone who knows how this works."

"How?"

"I have no ef . . . idea. But I've got to do something fast."

✦   ✦   ✦

Mac hung upside down peering into the cold room below MedBay. Not hard to create a cold room for perishable storage. Just isolate the level and restrict the heating vents but not the atmosphere. Perishable dead bodies lasted a lot longer in the cold.

Doc Halliday and Physician John, the two most senior and experienced medics on station, or any of the ships docked there, examined, opened, and tested pieces of Number Seven. They compared weights and size to the two other Labyrinthe bodies they'd already cut apart and recorded.

Those two souls were bagged and tagged for shipment back to Labyrinthe Prime.

Mac had witnessed death many times over the decades of his life. Sometimes peaceful and natural. More times violent, ugly, and not natural. Life on the rim was harsh and often brutally short.

Watching this autopsy should not affect him. Yet, seeing his brother's organs weighed and measured, his blood drained and run through machines, seemed as if he watched his own death. He shared DNA with those lumps of flesh and once living tissue. His blood had similarities.

"I can't tell what I'm looking at because I have no baseline for comparison." Physician John shook his head. Behind his protective mask with its built-in filters, cameras, and spotlights, his face grimaced. "Every one of the three we've examined is different. Probably because of breeding with other species trying to stabilize the DNA."

"I'm in the same quandary. We have no other data on file," Doc Halliday also shook her head. "But I can tell that the noose didn't kill him. He was dead already when someone strung him up and placed that placard around his neck." She pointed to the lack of bruising around the ligature marks.

"What killed him?" Physician John peered more closely where she pointed.

"Blunt force trauma to the back of the head was also post mortem. Possibly to disguise this." She pointed to something Mac could not see.

The two of them crowded around the body—must think of it as only another body, not Number Seven—blocking Mac's view.

"A needle through the ear canal directly into the brain. Those huge ears are vulnerable," Doc Halliday said. "Probably crept up on him while he slept."

"Whoever did this must have a great deal of strength to drag the dead weight, unseen, to a different wing cluster and down to a heavy-G level," John muttered.

"It's the secrecy that bothers me. Mr. Labyrinthe fled safety from deep inside the CSS residential wing. Who knows where he hid. Possibly not far from where he was found." Doc Halliday joined him in poking and prodding. "The idea of a murderer being able to creep about so stealthily means there is either a major security breach or someone beyond our control to detect."

"Our phantom seems quite at home moving through the maintenance tunnels and ventilation shafts undetected," Physician John reminded her.

"He's the only one who is that knowledgeable of the station, and he's our chief suspect. I can't learn anything more here," Doc Halliday announced. "Tidy him up for shipment back to his own people. I need to know more about that Maril and her Numidian lover."

"My curiosity does not overcome my revulsion at the concept of two such different species as life partners." Physician John shuddered and turned to putting back all the bits and pieces of Number Seven they'd removed for examination.

"Be sure to record all weights and measurements as well as the placement of the organs. Closest thing to information we have about the Labyrinthians. I have a feeling we're going to have more and more contact with them over the next few years. Information is more valuable than Badger Metal at this point."

Physician John nodded and resumed his task.

Mac almost turned away, no longer interested in the grisly process.

"Huh?" Doc Halliday's exclamation stopped Mac in his tracks.

"The Maril is pregnant, and the baby's DNA looks totally human."

"That can't be." John reared his head up in surprise. "I'm coming to accept that you are as human as I, even if you have no caste mark and do not worship Harmony. The Numidian also seems a subspecies of humanity. But that female is more bird than woman."

"Not as much as you'd think." Doc Halliday held up a vial of blood and placed it in a machine. She studied the graph scrolling across the screen. "I need to talk to the brass about this."

"What do you see? We do not do much DNA research on Harmony. Just enough to keep the caste marks pure." John peered over her shoulder. His eyes didn't focus on anything in particular in the graphs.

"There." Doc Halliday pointed to a spot on the left of the screen. The squiggles and bars meant nothing to Mac.

"I don't see it." They meant nothing to John either.

"That's the avian genes trying to revert to human." Doc Halliday copied the file and shut down the machine. "This entire wing will be secured and guarded. I'm ordering full security and cameras. Not even the phantom is going to get in here until I get a geneticist in from the CSS." Her eyes flicked quickly toward Mac. She stared just long enough to let him know she knew he watched. "I mean it. This is too important to allow any corruption of the evidence." She turned her back on Mac and called Control.

"I get the message, Doc. I'll respect your secrets as long as I can for the safety of my station."

CHAPTER THIRTY

GREGOR GRIMACED as Paula du Penelope pu Crystal Temple and her twin Ginny du Penelope climbed up on either side of him in the hospital bed. They each flung an arm around his waist and the other over the top of his head in an awkward hug.

"Do you remember what I told you yesterday about caste marks?" he asked them somewhat breathlessly.

Ginny discovered that she lay atop his oxygen tube and shifted until air ran in and out of his lungs easily.

"Sorry, Grandfather," she whispered as she settled again.

Gregor hid his frown. Temple caste had no need for family names. The entire caste was one family—somewhat interbred. They should support each other, discipline each other, and band together against outsiders as smaller family groups did among the lesser castes.

"I remember, Grandfather," Paula whispered. "Every caste has a place in the divine plan. We humans should never question the Gods but should accept the separation of castes as sacred," she parroted the words exactly.

"Any variation in caste marks must be eliminated. Only pure caste marks reflect the glory of our Covenant with Harmony," Ginny finished the lesson.

"Your caste mark looks funny," Paula said. "It doesn't sparkle anymore."

"That is because Grandfather is very ill," Penelope, the girls' mother, said from the doorway. "He is too ill for you to bother him." She frowned deeply. Her red dress looked rumpled. Unheard of for the fashion conscious priestess Gregor knew. She also looked tired, with deep lines running down from her mouth and dark shadows beneath her eyes.

"The girls do not bother me. They remind me of the life and energy

of Harmony. They give me something to look forward to when I heal,"
Gregor said.

"You are not healed yet, Father."

Again with the family. Would she ever get over this new craze and
revert to normal?

"Go away, Penelope." He shooed her with a weak flutter of his hand.
He hoped the gesture looked dismissive rather than revealing how much
energy the twins' visit sapped from him. He longed for the white angel to
return with her stimulant patches. She always made him feel young and
virile again. "The girls and I have much to discuss. I need to know that
their education proceeds properly."

"You need to rest." Penelope snapped her fingers and the girls climbed
down from the bed and dashed to her side. They hugged her legs with
enthusiasm. "I am education director. I know my daughters have the best
education available."

"No, they don't. You do not tutor them in proper etiquette and tradition," he snarled. He needed to cough. Talking left his throat raw and
hurt his chest.

"We will discuss this when you are better, Father." She turned to go,
her daughters still clinging to her.

"Grandfather." Paula paused and turned.

"Accept Harmony . . ." Ginny said the next portion of the sentence.

"when She comes for you."

"We will pray . . ."

"and offer a Grief Blessing for . . ."

"all of Harmony."

"Girls . . ." Penelope looked as horrified as Gregor felt.

"We all die, Penelope. Best the girls learn it now. But I have no inten-
tion of dying soon. I have much to do yet. Most of it, cleaning up the
messes you and Guilliam and Sissy have made of my empire."

His daughter retreated with less than her usual grace, dragging the
girls with her.

Maybe now he could read the treaty notes Sissy had left for him. After
a nap. The twins really did tire him.

✦   ✦   ✦

"Lord Lukan, I must protest!" Jake said through gritted teeth.

He breathed deeply. In and out. Don't hold it. Let the anger flow
out.

Just as Sissy had taught him.

"Lord Lukan, Major Mara du Danna pu FCC has become an important part of my team. In the best interest of the Harmony delegation on First Contact Café, I strongly urge you to allow her to remain as my second-in-command."

"My government has never authorized *Lieutenant* Mara's promotion or her transfer," the Noble said calmly. He examined his fingernails, then shifted his attention to the holovid of the jump point that served as a window in the diplomatic conference room.

Only Lord Lukan's son and attaché, Garrin, served as witness to Jake's protest. He badly wanted Ambassador Telvino here. Lukan had refused Telvino's presence, citing this as strictly an internal matter.

"Sir, Major Mara is the only person on this station I trust to manage Control. She is competent, organized, and calm . . ."

"Lieutenant Mara cannot be allowed to move above or outside the controls of her caste." Garrin stood and faced Jake. His posture showed arrogance and contempt, from the lifted chin, to the slight sneer, to the shoulders half turned away. "She will return to Harmony for reassignment. If she is as competent and organized as you claim, she will certainly earn a promotion."

Lukan kept his back to Jake.

The ambassador and his son were in disagreement, Jake's only hope to keep Mara on station.

"I feel it important that my team employ both civilian and military, from both CSS and Harmony. I have no one to replace Mara."

"We do," Garrin said. "The Harmony transport arriving within the hour brings Spacer Major Roderick da Nevis pa FCC to become your second-in-command. The same transport will take Lieutenant Mara away, as well as a few other passengers from my delegation."

"I do not know this Major Roderick, sir. I do not know if he will blend well with my team. If you must rob me of Mara, at least grant me the privilege of approving or disapproving of Major Roderick before he is permanently stationed with me." Compromise. Compromise.

Jake had to remind himself that he was running a station now and not flying into a firefight with all cannons blazing.

"Granted," Lukan said abruptly, before his son could deny the request. "I understand the importance of trust and cooperation in a team. Admiral Marella knows this as well." He looked down his nose at Garrin.

What? Lukan gave Jake a coded message, obvious to the dullest wit in the room. Pammy had manipulated Mara's transfer. Or bribed someone. Or threatened. She had spies everywhere, and information.

So why was she sabotaging Jake? Endangering the entire station, murdering aliens, and now blackmailing ambassadors, he wouldn't put any of that past her. But why?

"I will escort Major Roderick to your office upon his arrival," Lukan continued. "If he proves unsuitable *in any way*, a replacement will be found." He stalked from the room.

Garrin hastened to follow him.

Compromise, Jake reminded himself. He'd earned a compromise.

But, oh, how he wished he could climb into a fighter and blast a dozen Maril—or Harmony—ships to smithereens.

He couldn't even find an excuse to fly patrol with the fighter companies from *Champion* and *Victory*.

✦ ✦ ✦

"But we want to play with Grandfather," the twins protested to Penelope as she dragged the girls into Sissy's private parlor.

"And I told you that Laud Gregor needs to rest," the girls' mother insisted. She shoved both girls into separate chairs.

"What happened?" Sissy asked looking up from the screen embedded in her desktop. Why did she find reading so much easier on the computer than on paper? Whatever the difference, she managed to keep up with the masses of documents requiring her signature much better here at the FCC than at home.

"Laud Gregor insists on drilling the girls with archaic lessons on the need to keep the caste system intact, as he thinks it used to be," Penelope snorted. "And I don't know how to undo his influence except by total separation."

The girls stared at their mother in mute defiance.

"They are as stubborn as you and Laud Gregor. I doubt separation will do anything other than firm up their resolution to follow him," Sissy said dismissively.

"Then there are the visions. How did your mother cope when you rolled up your eyes as if to faint and then poured forth strange images and portents?"

"I don't . . ." Maybe she did. Or used to. "Mama didn't know what I said was important. She mostly ignored my cute little sayings and went on with her day, taking care of five children younger than me."

An icon on her screen blinked red, quite rapidly.

She looked away. Often the little emergencies went away, or someone else handled them, if she ignored the alarm. When she looked back, it blinked more rapidly in a brighter and angrier tone. A little pinging sound accompanied it, harsh and insistent.

"What now?" She pressed her thumb on the blinking red light, knowing instinctively this was a private message requiring her personal identification.

"Laudae Sissy," a stranger in a Harmony uniform with Communications in the background appeared on the desktop. "I think you need to see this message from Harmony City." The person faded.

Images of buildings shaking and crumbling, fires racing through familiar streets near Crystal Temple, drenching rains with roll after roll of thunder and long forks of lightning that touched ground, filled her huge desk.

A small squeak escaped her throat.

"What?" Penelope dashed to her side, the twins right behind her.

"Discord reigns," the little girls said in unison.

"Your vision earlier—you don't need to prepare a Grief Blessing for Laud Gregor. You truly do need to prepare one for all of Harmony," Penelope said, a little too loudly, more than a little too harshly.

"I have to go home. Only I can calm Harmony's distress." Sissy rose from her chair. Her head grew light. She stumbled and caught herself against the desk. Her hand brushed another blinking red icon.

A new scene erupted before her eyes, this one of a massive tidal wave growing in the ocean, ready to crash into the coastline by the largest city on the Southern Continent.

"Death, death everywhere," she whispered, fully aware that she spoke her own words as well as those of her Goddess. "I have to be on the next ship home. I've been away too long."

Her heart wrenched between the need to take control, her fear of a very angry planet, and sadness at leaving Jake.

"No, Sissy, you can't." Penelope grabbed her arm in a fierce grip. Her knuckles turned white.

"I have to. No one else . . ."

"Paula and Ginny have your gift of prophecy and song. I will take them home. You have to stay here and get that treaty signed."

"But . . ."

"Don't you see, Harmony is now vulnerable to invasion," Penelope said, slowly and clearly, making certain Sissy understood each word, each phrase, each sentence. "The Maril are practically on our doorstep already. All our resources have to go into taking care of the dead and the injured, to finding shelter, food, and medicine for the displaced as winter closes in. You have to organize help from the CSS. They won't give it without the treaty!"

"My people need me at home." Part of what Penelope said filtered into her brain. Her heart twisted with her need to offer comfort and succor. She needed to sing the planet back to peace with itself.

"Sissy, the universe needs you. You don't just belong to Harmony anymore. You belong to everyone." Penelope's voice took on an echoey quality that frightened Sissy.

She stopped, leaning on the desk to support her wobbling knees. One deep breath, then two, then five. When she thought she could talk without crying or babbling incoherently, she touched a dormant blue icon.

"Jake, you need to see the news from Harmony City. Now. My people need a ship home. Now. I need contact with all CSS worlds willing to send food, medicine, building supplies, and volunteers. Consider the FCC command central for coordinating a major relief effort."

Another deep breath and she shifted channels to Lord Lukan. "We will sign the treaty today or I send you home in disgrace and negotiate on my own."

CHAPTER THIRTY-ONE

MAC SLOWED HIS PROGRESS through a passage between two wings. He'd heard something. A swish? A clink?

He couldn't place the quiet sound; he only knew that it had not come from him and did not belong here.

A thought awakened sensory pads on his secondary legs. Sniff, sniff. Extend the fine hairs like whiskers to pick up any stray change in air temperature and movement.

Ah! A human male crept behind him, cautious but not frightened.

He had a vulnerable terminal stationed close to here. He had to protect it from intruders.

Mac touched the screen on his handheld. All the lights and motion sensors in this passage went dark.

The human did not panic. He merely stopped and waited.

"I would know you, human," Mac whispered.

"As I would you, phantom," came the quiet reply.

"Why?" Mac twisted around, careful to avoid the powered tracks at the bottom of the tunnel, to face his pursuer.

"I grew up near an extensive cave system. I am quite at home underground. We have no ground to be under on this station. This is the closest I can come to it. I would know the one who seeks solace in the same way I do."

Was that a chuckle behind those words?

"I have heard you speak before, Harmonite."

"I have seen pictures of you. We have no spiders on Harmony. But they do on Earth. I wonder if your ancestors and mine had a friendly or adversarial relationship."

The slow speech, the inflections, the calmness in the voice belonged to only one man. "Mr. Guilliam of the Temple caste," Mac mused. "You surprise me."

"Oh?"

"You appear too meek to have the boldness to follow me."

"Appearances are masks in the light of day. Our true selves come out in the dark." He gestured to the expanse of black out beyond this maintenance tube.

Mac laughed out loud. "You sound like our Laudae Sissy when the Goddess takes control of her tongue. Are you another specimen such as she?"

"No, no, no, no. I'm not gifted by the Gods. Merely curious. Mac or phantom, whatever you are, did your ancestors also migrate from Earth?" The voice came closer.

Mac picked out the pale, round face, reading body temperatures and sound reflections more than sight.

"There are some who theorize my father's ancestors seeded some of their lesser get on your Earth to see if they could thrive. Eight legs are quite alien to all your other mammalian and insectoid life there. The spiders and crabs left on Earth multiplied, adapted, and evolved. But competition with humans was too fierce for the higher forms to return and claim the place for their own."

"Ah. That would explain much, especially the atavistic fear of your kind among humans. Even though we have no spiders on Harmony, my people still run away from the false cobwebs I lay as barriers to my hidden paths. Instinct. Do I have anything to fear from you, Mr. Mac?"

"Not at the moment." Mac decided he liked this man. Therefore, he could not stay and chat. He might reveal too much. So he contracted and twisted again, preparing to lead this human away from the terminal. He only brushed Mr. Guilliam's pale green shirt lightly in passing him.

"Can you spin webs?" Mr. Guilliam asked, breathless with a kind of awe.

"Sadly, no. My father's gene for extruding silk as a tether did not join in the mix of my life force. I have other means of constructing webs though. Mechanical means that are limited and inefficient."

"I'm sorry you cannot conceal your observation posts and terminals behind a web," Mr. Guilliam sighed. "That would be wonderful to see— to experience real web instead of the false stuff made from shredded sticky bandages I spread in hidden alcoves."

Mac kept silent. He too wondered what advantages he might have had with that inherited gift.

"I don't have a lot of time. A ship awaits me and my family. We must return to Harmony today. But I came to tell you that many people want to talk to you," Guilliam continued on a more normal note. "They intend you no harm. All they want is information."

"They must find these things out on their own. I am not an encyclopedia." Mac took three steps beyond Guilliam.

"Before you leave, may I know the origin of your name? Mac has Earther connotations. Son of someone."

Surprised at the human's ability to sense movements and the directions of those movements, Mac paused. "I have read much of your great thinkers and your history on Earth. I admire particularly the one called Machiavelli."

Mac lunged away at top speed, more frightened of this curious human than the ones with blasters and itchy trigger fingers.

✦ ✦ ✦

"Go! Go, go." Mary and Martha pushed Sissy off the top of the lift with all of their strength.

Heedless of her flying skirt, Sissy leaped. She grabbed hold of the tram door just as it began closing. With a quick twist of her body she flipped inside the car, careful to brush her fingers against Harmony as she passed. Breathlessly she thanked all seven Gods that she'd spent so much time with her girls exploring the station and practicing in Zero G.

"Destination, please?" the androgynous voice of the tram asked.

"Harmony Three," Sissy said, hoping the computer would decipher her broken words. She still fought for air. Not since before her ordination, when dust still filled her lungs and choked her every breath, had she found it so difficult to pull air into her.

"Harmony Three is a restricted-access area. Authorization code required," the computer informed her. The tram car remained firmly in place with the door closed.

Sissy's girls couldn't get in, even if they caught up with her. Discord, she was alone. They were alone. A murderer still lurked on the station!

"Authorization code: priority one, HPS one," Sissy choked out the necessary words for the new security precautions.

"Authorization code: priority one, HPS one accepted. Please repeat code for voiceprint verification."

Damn. More delay. Sometimes Jake was too careful in keeping the station safe. Sissy took a deep breath, which only made her cough. When the spasm passed, she spoke again, slowly and distinctly, praying the computer recognized her.

She couldn't be late. Just once she wished for the frantic speed with which Jake whisked about his duties rather than the deliberate pace of life on Harmony. She couldn't believe she'd needed three full hours in the comms level, begging, threatening, and bribing any ship within six sectors of Harmony Prime to divert their cargo.

"Voiceprint accepted." The tram eased forward at its normal sedate pace.

"Two wings. I only have to travel two wings. No sense risking a speed override." Not that she knew for certain her authorization code would change the tram's speed.

At last the car glided to a stop. The doors ground open only after all movement had ceased.

Sissy bounded out, then returned briefly to kiss Harmony for luck and to thank Her for the safe journey. The lift looked even slower than the tram. She opted for Jake's trick and perched sideways on the stair railing. With a little push, microgravity took over, and she slid down the spiral. At each level her weight and her speed increased. Going round and round the lift shaft made her dizzy. She dared not close her eyes lest she miss the loading bay between light and medium G.

She passed communications and computer operations so quickly no one looked up from their work. A reporter in the Media section waved to her and sent a hover cam to follow her. Damn. Too many people already knew that Penelope and Gil visited. Only a few logical jumps led to the conclusion that Gregor did too.

Her landing was tricky. Still, the lighter gravity here than a couple levels down helped her stumble without falling flat on her face.

Seven corridors off the lobby. Which one? She chose a narrow door, suitable for passengers but not loads of cargo.

A Military Sergeant recognized her distinctive purple dress and her array of caste marks. He saluted her and waved her through without question. But he stopped the hover cam.

Thank you, Harmony.

"The transport headed home?" she wheezed out.

"Right through here, My Laudae. They've already begun boarding. You only have a few moments." The sergeant ushered her around a security scanner and into a large lounge. Definitely a violation of the new security protocols. Sissy didn't care. In this case she needed speed.

Two lines of people threaded past more scanners and into the air locks.

Then she spotted Penelope's red outfit and the bevy of children and teenagers wearing pink surrounding her. Guilliam stood square and solid beside her in the light green that designated him an acolyte of Gregor.

Sissy sighed in relief. "My Laudae," she called.

Penelope turned. A huge smile lit her face and banished worry lines. "You made it," she whispered. "I didn't want to leave without saying good-bye."

They hugged tightly. Guilliam rested a comforting hand familiarly on her shoulder.

A hole seemed to develop in Sissy's midsection. Until that moment she hadn't realized how much she missed friends, adults she could talk to, peers who understood her life and work.

Jake understood, but on a different level. He couldn't share the day-to-day minutiae of her life. Her relationship with Jake was more than friendship and less at the same time.

Penelope fussed with a small personal bag. Their luggage would have been carried onto the space transport through another, wider air lock. "Do you have any instructions? Messages?

Sissy handed her a stack of printed messages. "Ten short statements. You may quote me. Deliver them over the radio or in person as you move about the city. I'll broadcast similar ones over the pirate radio station every night."

"Are there any new reports, My Laudae?" Guilliam asked.

Penelope looked up and fixed him with a bleak gaze.

"Nothing new," Sissy admitted. Hope was dying quickly within her. "The Media buildings are badly damaged. I don't know if they can receive or broadcast at all. Lord Lukan has sent messages to both the Spacers and the Military from Control and from the ships in dock. Different bands or frequencies or something."

"Don't tell my father what has happened," Penelope ordered. "The stress will kill him."

"He'll try to leave the hospital and go home too soon," Guilliam added. "He may be shortsighted, manipulative, arrogant, and a pain in the ass," he borrowed a phrase from Jake. "But he has always wanted what is best for Harmony. In that he is sincere."

"He can't see beyond taking our society and religion back to the state it was before . . . before . . ." Penelope waved a hand vaguely, and tears appeared in her eyes. "He'll see this as confirmation that any change is bad for Harmony. Because it is bad for him."

Sissy understood.

Penelope handed her bag to the oldest of her acolytes and shooed all of her girls through the air lock. Only then did she take a hankie from her pocket and dab her eyes.

"I have to go back to make sure Laud Andrew thinks for himself and doesn't follow Gregor's orders blindly," Guilliam said.

"He also has to find and destroy Gregor's orders to transfer us to a rural funerary Temple on the Southern Continent." Penelope grinned, but the worry lines around her eyes remained. "Harmony City needs us guiding the recovery. The people know us. They know we support you, Sissy. They'll follow our directions."

"I'm going to miss you," Sissy said quietly.

"All of Harmony misses you," Penelope said. "Come back to us soon."

"Not until after the final treaty is signed," Guilliam added.

"Maybe not then." Sissy bit her lip and looked away. Her eyes lighted on a small commotion at the security post.

Jake bullied his way past the protests of the guard. His caste mark and the black crystal stars on his collar were the only things that saved him from arrest.

"You have to get aboard now." Sissy pushed Penelope toward the air lock. "They're announcing last call."

Jake stretched his long legs and homed in on them like a bee to a fragrant flower.

She saw calculations spinning behind his eyes. By the time he reached them, he'd drawn the logical conclusions.

"Is he aboard?" Jake asked.

"No." Sissy replied. "Penelope and Guilliam return to deal with this crisis without him."

"Still in MedBay, too ill to transport after how many weeks? That does not bode well." He sounded angry. More than his voice belied his emotions. His shoulders tensed, and he searched the lounge anxiously.

"We have to keep his condition private because if Admiral Marella knew, she would tell Telvino and they would use this information to press an unfair advantage in our negotiations," Sissy returned.

"You're right. But she may already know." He seemed to deflate, only half listening, still searching for someone.

The phantom? The murderer?

For half a heartbeat Sissy was glad he still thought like a bodyguard. She'd taken a terrible chance coming here alone.

"Who are you looking for?" Guilliam asked hesitantly.

"Lukan has transferred my second-in-command back to Harmony without notice. I need to talk to her. I've written a letter of recommendation." Jake scanned the few remaining passengers.

"Jake, you of all people know how Harmony works. A recommendation from an outsider will do more harm than good." Guilliam held Jake's arm, as if to restrain him from dashing aboard the transport. "As it is, she has probably been judged tainted by contact with aliens and will be carefully scrutinized for many months before being allowed any degree of responsibility."

Jake gulped. "Yeah. I know. I'll miss several strong doses of your common sense, Gil."

"Next trip. We are needed at home," Guilliam said quietly. "I wish I could stay longer and help you search out your phantom. He and I have an affinity for dark enclosed places." His smile said he knew more but also kept a few secrets. "I have left some random notes and musings in an encrypted file in your office," he said more quietly.

"Final boarding call for all passengers on Harmony transport Prime 009567," a soothing voice came over the speaker system. "Anyone not aboard within two minutes will be locked out."

"We have to go." Penelope tugged at Guilliam's sleeve. "Harmony needs us more than Sissy and Jake right now." She turned and marched into the air lock with the haughty aplomb she assumed in her role as a senior Laudae.

"Good-bye." Sissy hugged Guilliam tightly. She'd spent too little time with him and Penelope while they were here.

"You've got the new codes for communications?" Jake asked cryptically.

Guilliam nodded. His throat worked, choking back strong emotions. "I'll let you know the situation at home as soon as I can find an operating transceiver. You need another priest to help you, Sissy. I'll send you someone good."

Sissy watched a long time after the air lock closed behind him.

"Pammy just sent me a message. A Maril trading group wants to talk, unofficially, no government ties they say. A drastic change after two hundred years of vicious warfare. They've tried very hard to just wipe us out. They arm their merchants like warships. Now this. They want to use this place as neutral ground to negotiate. I don't trust them and neither should you."

"It's a decoy. They've heard about the quakes on Harmony. They'll try to force your attention here on negotiations while they prepare for an invasion."

"Th . . . that sounded like it came from Harmony, not you."

"Maybe it did."

"Damn, I wish I had Mara around. She can monitor sixteen things at once. She'd be able to track that message to see if it truly came from Maril traders or a pirate enclave. Like there's a difference."

Sissy had to smile. "Perhaps the Goddess heard your prayer." She pointed to an oddly shaped shadow in a recess beyond the air lock. "I believe Major Mara deserted and disobeyed orders."

"Thank every God in the universe!" Jake grabbed Sissy's elbow and dragged her over toward that shadow with a bounce in his step and plans spinning behind his eyes.

◆ ◆ ◆ ◇ ◆ ◆ ◆

CHAPTER THIRTY-TWO

PAIN RIPPED THROUGH ADRIAL *as once again the Law found vio-lating her body amusing. A long time had passed since they had honored the sacred breeding rituals and kept recreational sex homosex-ual. They'd lost all the breeding sanctuaries decades before.*

Now they perverted the divine act as a way to force her to speak. She did not know what they wanted to hear.

Again and again they rammed shocking probes and parts of their own bodies into her. Nothing new. The Messengers of the Gods had been much more creative in testing her and preparing her before sending her on their quest for . . . for her own spiritual enlightenment.

She detached her mind from the pain. Her body no longer belonged to her. It was the toy of the Law.

"All we want to know is why?" the officer who observed her torture asked. He stood with arms crossed in front of his puffed chest. Feathered folds of skin draped below his arms like a half cloak.

The feathers and wing flaps looked too small, as if this male were morphing into another species. But his blue head crest flared with full plumage.

The other males also showed signs of melting into a more humanoid form. She had no time or attention to spare for the obvious question as yet again electricity arced from her womb to her head and radiated out to her extremities.

"Why what?" she choked out. "What do you think I've done?"

"You know what you've done. We know it. We have witnesses.

"Liars. One and all. I am different from you, an easy target. A . . ." she fished in her memory for a term they would understand. "I have become the fledgling cast out of the nest because I am smaller and weaker and cannot compete for sustenance."

"We have recordings of you fleeing the library with a single book in your possession moments before fire consumed the entire building, its contents, and over half the occupants."

"Recordings can be altered. I stole a valuable book. Nothing more. Does theft justify this intense a punishment?"

Another voice whispered to her, "Leave no trace of your passing. Destroy all evidence of your presence."

And so the interrogation continued. The torture. Until they tired of their game and threw her into a cold and austere prison cell, expecting her to die from her injuries as the poor victims of the fire had died.

Adrial jerked awake. That dream . . . she hadn't had that dream in many years. Why now? Why did it haunt her now?

Leave no trace of your passing.

✦   ✦   ✦

"Spacer Major Roderick da Nevis pa FCC at your service, My Laud." The uniformed man snapped a smart salute to Gregor, then bowed deeply from the waist. His yellow star caste mark had been ennobled but not lauded. He had no right to address the HP of all Harmony.

Gregor smiled a little. Laud Andrew had sent a respectful man. He knew who truly ruled Harmony and her delegation.

He doffed his reading glasses and marked his place in the book he skimmed. An old one, and a comforting one, written by another High Priest Gregor who had ruled Temple caste and the High Council over one hundred fifty years ago. Gregor of old had made the change to the Covenant with Harmony that negated the need for Temple caste to marry and divide their loyalties between caste and family.

Gregor of old had also lumped the Media into the Professional caste, taking away their power of independence. In their place he'd made a Poor caste, those who could not or would not work. Minor criminals had their caste marks downgraded to the Poor. Dissenters too. A convenient dumping ground for the unwanted. No one was obliged to feed, medicate, or care for the Poor. Many died of starvation and exposure, thus eliminating malcontents from an otherwise harmonious society.

"You are to be second-in-command here," Gregor stated the obvious. He had not specified which man was to replace the upstart Mara, only that she had to go. Admiral Marella had conveyed the message.

He fixed his gaze on the man, as if he cared intensely about this interview.

"Yes, My Laud. Presuming General Jake Devlin approves of my presence, after we've met." Major Roderick maintained his rigid attention stance.

Gregor decided to keep him stiff and awkward for a while. He did not encourage casual relations among the castes. This man was a tool, nothing more, nothing less.

"Major, you have your orders from the head of your caste."

"Yes, My Laud. I am to report to you before consulting with General Jake Devlin or Lord Lukan."

"Very good. You know that I do not need to know the registry of every ship that docks or the pay scale of every cargo handler. Only things that are unusual, odd cargoes to vague destinations, suspicious strangers, things that affect the senior members of the diplomatic delegations or the crew on the station," Gregor reminded him.

"Yes, My Laud."

"You are my eyes and ears on this station until I can be up and about again. Serve me well and I'll laud your caste mark and perhaps find you a promotion."

"Thank you, my Laud."

"You may go. I believe General Jake is expecting you."

"Yes, My Laud." He turned smartly as if to go, then paused. "My Laud, I have heard rumors of a phantom aboard. Is he one of your spies too?"

Gregor had to think a moment. Isolated and treated in secret, he'd heard next to nothing since waking up from surgery. The twins had been his most consistent confidantes, the others coming and going on their schedules, not his. Seven-year-old girls talked about other things than ghosts and monsters under their beds.

They knew nothing of the angel in white who came to him deep in the night. She spoke of journeys and spiritual healing, as an angel should, not station gossip.

Admiral Marella also came in the middle of the night. Three times now, without pattern.

"I do not employ a phantom, Major Roderick. But I would hear more of it as you learn about a strange being that inhabits this station. If you confront it, tell it I want to speak to it."

"Very good, My Laud." The solid door closed with a whoosh behind the major.

Gregor dialed up a holovid of the corridor outside his room, his only window on the world of the First Contact Café. Next time Major Roderick came to visit, he'd see if the man's computer skills allowed him to

find other views, like the infamous Control or the conference rooms of
the diplomatic wing.

Later. When he wasn't so tired.

✦   ✦   ✦

Jake drummed his fingers on the faux wood desk. He sidelined a vague
and antique reference to Zarthan III. Almost as soon as colony worlds
became available, an agricultural cult that denied the validity of mechani-
zation applied for a place the officials labeled Zarthan III. Its coordinates
were so far out they almost fell off the grid of jump points. Fifty years
later they mined their one and only jump point, changed the name to
Amity, and cut themselves off from Earth.

If, as Adrial claimed, the entire population had been wiped out by
Maril invaders fifteen years ago, who lived there now? Was it still habitable? If empty and abandoned, would it make a suitable home base for
the CSS?

He called up the star map, locating Amity by proximity to other systems and jump points. The map refused to give it a name. It was so far
out it didn't fall into the pattern of cleansed planets. Nor did it seem to
be on the route to anywhere.

An interesting path to follow if Adrial had remained at the top of his list
of things to investigate today. Major Roderick now occupied that place.

Jake read and reread the résumé displayed on the screen embedded
on the desk surface. He compared it to Mara's. He'd stashed her in his
old quarters in the CSS residential wing and issued her fatigues after Doc
Halliday removed the caste mark. She was working on the spectacles full
time now, trying to adapt them to human limitations and perceptions.

"Computer competency," he mumbled. "Competency by whose stan-
dards?" He hadn't found anyone more competent than Mara.

With the last statement he shifted his gaze to the compactly built
Spacer standing at attention in front of him. Major Roderick had a yellow star caste mark on his left cheek, bar beneath to indicate officer status, blue diamond outline showing his authority to deal with Nobles. Did
he listen to very conservative Lord Bevan on the High Council or the
liberal—liberal in comparison to Bevan—Lord Lukan?

Technically Bevan was head of the caste. But Bevan was on Harmony
Prime, a long way away.

Not a hint of a purple circle to the caste mark, which eliminated ties
to Sissy. Or Gregor.

"I was senior officer in charge of the computer systems on my last two ships, sir," Major Roderick replied to Jake's unasked question. He remained ramrod straight, as if he'd been born standing at attention.

Knowing the caste system, he might have been.

"A large part of the job as my second is sitting in Control, monitoring communications and traffic. A lot of those communications are encoded, encrypted, and in exotic languages. Are you prepared to delve into those communications for the safety of this station and all its inhabitants?"

"You mean spying, sir?"

"Yes."

"When necessary. I . . . um . . . downloaded a Maril translation program from HQ and studied it extensively. A strange, symbolic language. I can pick out a few primary nouns and verbs. I'll need a few more months to fully understand grammar and learn how they think."

Jake raised his eyebrows at that. "You hacked into HQ computers and stole an encrypted, top-secret program!"

"From a remote location, sir." The major allowed himself the faintest of grins.

Jake whistled through his teeth. This guy could be as good as Mara. If Jake could trust him. And being Spacer, he dealt with scientists on a daily basis. He'd know propulsion systems or know people who knew them.

They still had a month, maybe two, before the station broke orbit. Jake had upped his evacuation date to two weeks to make sure it took place in an orderly and peaceful manner.

He dared not share that plan yet. A stray word, a hint of potential danger, and the entire station populace would panic and desert the place, like rats leaving a sinking ship.

"This is not Harmony. We carry blasters here. You willing to take the dishonorable route and shoot an enemy rather than run him through with your sword?" Jake noted that the Spacer carried only a dagger on his hip.

"I'm Spacer caste. We are allowed blasters when dealing with lesser races."

"Meaning nonhumans. Not all of our enemies look different from us. We have a murderer running loose who could be anyone, alien or human, CSS or Harmony. Circumstantial evidence points to someone in the Harmony Worker force." And to the CSS spymaster.

Major Roderick swallowed deeply. "I will train with the blasters, as will any of Harmony's officers stationed here. But I would request cross training for CSS officers to use swords."

"Excellent point. We'll set it up. I'm trying to build a team here, Major.

Your loyalties have to be to the station and the team that tries to keep it running despite sabotage, criminal activity, phantoms living in the ducts, no budget, and coercion from both our governments. Do you understand that? Can you comply with that?"

And suddenly, he had an idea of how to deal with the thorny problem of Mara's desertion. The treaty that needed to be signed *now* would probably obligate him to turn her over to a Harmonite Spacer for prosecution.

"Yes, sir." He snapped his spine even straighter and saluted. "And may I add, sir, that I've heard rumors of the phantom. If I may, I think I know how to set a trap for him."

"He has access to our computer systems and security cameras. He's worked around every trap we've set for him. He also seems to have a genius for languages and codes. And he knows this station better than the people who designed and built it." Jake leaned back in his too comfortable chair and studied Roderick.

"He hasn't encountered one of my traps, sir."

"What do you have in mind?" Jake gestured toward the visitor's chair, inviting Roderick to sit.

Roderick nodded and planted his butt on the very edge of the chair, legs at right angles, as if he'd been built by a mathematician addicted to geometry and straight lines.

Quickly and succinctly, Roderick outlined a scheme so simple and yet so fiendish, Jake was reminded of some of his own youthful pranks.

"Stow your gear in the level above this one, Major, and report to Control in an hour. I'll meet you there."

"I thought I'd be housed with my own caste, sir."

"The FCC is your caste now. Can you live with that?"

"I think I must, sir."

"Good, then find me a propulsion engineer. Preferably a genius of a propulsion engineer."

✦ ✦ ✦ ✧ ✦ ✦ ✦

CHAPTER THIRTY-THREE

"LORD LUKAN," **JAKE WAYLAID** the ambassador en route to the latest treaty meeting. The man had aged a decade overnight. He and Sissy had worked well past breakfast time trying to organize and implement disaster relief for Harmony City.

Jake had given them a number of the Zarith V refugees as clerks, comm techs, and cooks to make sure they ate. They accomplished miracles in diverting independent ships. A lot more needed to be done but couldn't be until they officially signed the treaty with the CSS.

"Be quick, General Jake, I haven't much time."

"I have two documents for you to file in your official capacity as Ambassador from Harmony, sir."

Lukan raised his eyebrows in question.

Jake handed him two sheets of paper. "Computer versions are on file in my office, verified with thumbprints and retinal scans. You will note the signatures are witnessed by Admiral Marella and Ambassador Telvino.

"Curious." Then he read the top document. "This is outrageous. Unprecedented! And I'm certain totally illegal."

"On the contrary. I have a lawyer among the Zarith V refugees who assures me he can quote chapter and verse of precedent in a dozen different legal systems." Jake bit his cheeks to disguise his impudent grin. He had to make sure the ambassador took this issue very seriously. Mara's safety and life depended upon it.

Lukan flip the page and read the second document. "You can't be serious."

"I am. Major Mara is now barefaced. She has renounced her citizenship in the Harmony Empire and her position within her caste. I have granted her First Contact Café citizenship. As long as she stays onboard this station, you and your enforcers have no right to touch her. Any attempt to kidnap her for purposes of return to Harmony for prosecution will be met with resistance. My people are authorized to shoot to kill."

"You can't do this."

"I have done it. I have granted like citizenships to all of the Zarith V refugees who choose to stay here and work."

"You're setting up an independent state!"

"Maybe. We'll see how things work out."

"Major Roderick remains your second-in-command."

"For now. I have other work for *Major* Mara." Primarily those blasted spectacles that made the wearer dizzy and only clearly displayed one bit of data at a time. "You may consider the FCC totally neutral. All law-abiding races and cultures are welcome. Trade is duty free and free of customs inspection by anyone. Docking fees and rents pay our expenses."

Jake turned away whistling a jaunty tune Sissy's girls had taught him. "Oh, and, Ambassador, your rent on three and one half wings is due at the end of the month. The bankers of D'Or, the same ones used by the Labyrinthe Corporation have set up an independent account in the name of the FCC. I'll honor previous contracts, but if you wish to renegotiate, please make an appointment with Major Mara."

✦   ✦   ✦

Mac finished reading the last of the text on Adrial's reader. Ancient propaganda. All peace and harmony and doing no harm. She read philosophy so deep and convoluted, Mac couldn't begin to make sense of it. Not worth the energy to maintain on the reader. He considered deleting the books.

His little bird found joy and a kind of peace reading the meandering thoughts of long-dead philosophers. He should leave them for her.

She slept soundly in her narrow hospital bed. Physician John had moved her from light-G intensive care to mid-G rehab. Her bones had mostly mended; her strength did not. He'd read all of her scans and tests. Something seemed out of pattern with them. He didn't have the medical knowledge to know what.

Mac wandered the perimeter of her small room, as he did every night during the hours that humans slept. He had little need for sleep now that his nervous system had rerouted around the damaged areas. The blaster damage had caused him to lose only a little strength and agility in his secondary lower limbs.

"You need better food for thought, my little bird, if you are ever to achieve your quest," he muttered as he brushed a stray strand of starlight-pale hair off her face. He tucked the reader into the folds of his trousers. "I'll be back."

If he had the spectacles General Jake had stolen from Number Seven, Mac could have accomplished all his chores within a few seconds.

He bent as if to kiss Adrial's brow in farewell, thought better of it, and exited up the wall and through a duct.

At his primary terminal, hidden between levels in the Control wing, Mac accessed a database begun by his mother and continued by her many progeny. In her quest to control the universe through trade and offspring, she'd stored every work of literature from every race she could find. Mac transferred a few Earth documents to Adrial's reader, truly ancient pieces from the Hindu and Buddhist traditions.

She'd already stored and read most of the Maril documents. She knew as much or more about their culture and religion than most Maril. If the avians truly wanted to use Mac's station for negotiations, then Laudae Sissy needed this knowledge. He stored the tracts Adrial had translated into CSS standard in a separate file and forwarded it to the Temple terminal.

So what did he have that Adrial didn't? He'd always found his Arachnoid ancestors had an interesting sense of spirituality. They saw the universe as a giant web of energy. A tiny vibration on any strand affected all the others. Similar to but not the same as what Laudae Sissy preached each Holy Day. He dumped those documents into the reader.

Then a quick scroll through the index. What did Adrial need?

There! His favorite book of all. *Il Principe* by Niccolò Machiavelli. Best give her the Standard translation rather than the original Italian.

Now for his meeting with Pamela Marella and her team to seal the hull breach around the Squid ship with more than just ice. That was one person he hoped never got ahold of the spectacles. He also needed to examine the lab results from the autopsies on the corpses of the Squid People and their ancient but curiously efficient ship. He'd found their propulsion system vaguely similar to the arcane one used on the station. Interesting.

◆　◆　◆

"I'm not a geneticist, Jake," Doc Halliday said by way of opening. She'd accosted him in the tram between Control and a meeting to set up a second hydroponics garden and open promenade in Labby's now deserted wing.

"And that signifies?" Jake asked. He closed his eyes against the near constant fatigue. Oh, for one night of uninterrupted sleep. Just one. That's all he asked for.

"Stay awake, Jake. This is important." A slight sting on the back of his wrist told him Mariah had slapped a stimulant patch on him.

He yanked it off. Too easy to get addicted to those things. Jake had done a lot of questionable things in his life. Too much alcohol, fistfights, women. Oh, the women! But never drugs. He'd seen too many good pilots wash out when they relied on chemicals to think for them.

"Talk, Mariah. Make it fast." He handed the contaminated piece of webbing back to her, holding it by his fingernails—which needed trimming. He hadn't even had time lately to do that.

In response, Doc Halliday keyed an override to stop the tram between stations.

"Mariah?"

"I performed autopsies on the bodies you found in the derelict Maril ship. I ran the tests, didn't believe them, so I ran them again. And a third time to be sure."

"And . . . ?"

"The female was pregnant. From fetal development I'm guessing six maybe even seven months along. But the baby was incredibly small, too small to survive."

"Dwarfism? I though that had been eliminated from the gene pool centuries ago." But it still cropped up on rim worlds.

"Nope. I'm surprised she didn't spontaneously abort. She had Jarlanski's Syndrome."

"What's that?"

"An autoimmune disease we think evolved in humans due to water polluted by heavy metals. Causes miniature fetuses, spontaneous RH negative reactions to pregnancy when both the mother and baby are RH positive. In advanced stages it causes organ failure in odd clusters. We cured it in the twenty-second century."

Jake shrugged. Then the implication hit him hard between the eyes. "A Maril with a *human* autoimmune disease?"

"Yep. Found some other anomalies too. I think the Maril were once human, then they tinkered with their DNA to give them avian characteristics. Now that tinkering is breaking down. I don't know why. That's why they are trying to breed with humans on the rim rather than wipe them out." Mariah Halliday, a CSS colonel, a trauma surgeon on a battleship, looked scared.

"Since I got here, I've seen four species with DNA breakdown. The

Squids went extinct. The Labyrinthians found a way to crossbreed to stabilize their DNA. I think they are back to a point where they can breed with their own kind again. If the female Maril in the morgue is an indicator, then her people are in big trouble for a couple of generations."

"That's three."

"Harmony."

Jake went cold with dread. "The caste marks."

"If that's the only tinkering they did, they may be okay, if they stop messing around and just let the damn things go. Otherwise . . . ?"

"Who do you want to double-check your tests?" He straightened from his habitual lean against the tram walls.

"I want Nigel Farnsworth of the Royal College of Genetics, Cambridge. And I want him here. I'm not trusting any courier with my samples. Unless you want to personally take them back to Earth." She raised her eyebrows speculatively.

"Thanks for the compliment. But that's more Pammy's field."

"I don't trust her any more than I trust the Maril in battle."

This time Jake raised his eyebrows.

"Yeah, I know Pammy's the spymaster of the CSS. Gives me more than a couple of reasons not to trust her. She has her own agenda, and I'm not always sure it involves what's best for the CSS."

"I agree. Compose the letter requesting Farnsworth's transfer, and I'll cosign it with an ASAP from Telvino. But this discussion goes no further. Absolutely no one is to know what we know until we can confirm it. Not even Laudae Sissy." Though that would give her another excuse to break the caste system on Harmony.

"I agree. If Sissy has a secret this big, outsiders might not hesitate to coerce her into revealing it. She's vulnerable. And you are vulnerable if anything happens to her."

Jake silently agreed but didn't respond.

"Can I get to my meeting?" He checked his comm unit for the time. "I'll only be half an hour late."

"Okay." Mariah canceled her override. The tram slid slowly onward, then gathered speed.

"Any ideas on why the Maril tinkered with their DNA to begin with?"

"I'm guessing humans settled on a light-gravity world. First generation would have bounced around in near flight. Succeeding generations adapted with less bone density, leaner musculature, but because the light gravity was natural to them, they couldn't fly."

"And they wanted to," Jake mused. "Bind some feather genes to the hair mixes and invent a way to get the skin flaps to drape from the arms. Instant feathered glides."

"How long ago?" Mariah mused. She acted as if she didn't need the answer.

"We know that the Harmonites encountered a monastic holy order of Maril when they colonized seven hundred years ago. Harmony was in the second wave of exodus from Earth. On that time line, the Maril must have been one of the first human ventures in space. Probably cut off from communications with Earth soon after landing." The same wave that settled Amity, a closed world with human genes untainted by outside influences—human genes as close to the original configuration of the Maril as they could find. As good a place as any to begin crossbreeding.

Adrial.

"Is that why the Maril traders are making overtures to talk peace?" he mused.

Mariah pretended not to hear him. "Chirps and whistles carry farther than words while flying, so their language evolved too." She watched the stations numbers fly by. "We're looking at fifteen hundred years probably."

"The Harmony Military and Spacers have made great strides in decoding the language—the written form has some similarities to their own obsolete Temple writing—or maybe Harmony adapted to what was already there." Jake ignored his own speculation about possible peace talks. As far-fetched as the idea seemed, a year and a half ago he couldn't foresee negotiating with Harmony either.

Or falling in love with their High Priestess.

"The Maril writing is pictorial, like ancient hieroglyphs. The next logical jump is to assume it's also metaphorical, open to many interpretations. Damn, no wonder we've never been able to break it." Jake really wanted a good strong shot of whiskey. Maybe several of them.

The last time he'd gotten roaring drunk was the night Major Jake Hannigan died and Lt. Colonel Jeremiah Devlin rose out of the dead identity.

He took three deep breaths, letting each go slowly. "Harmony grant me peace of mind to think clearly and act wisely," he repeated over and over, as he'd seen Sissy and Gregor do many times.

"That's a good ritual. I'm going to see if it works for me next time I end up doing bizarre and borderline-ethical surgical procedures," Mariah chuckled as the tram settled to a stop. "Or autopsy aliens."

"To restore Harmony we need to go out there to the stars." Jilly's prophecy reminded him. Maybe Harmony came from the little things, the small rituals that linked back through tradition.

Jake made a point of remote kissing the glyph of Harmony on the tram. He needed all the peace and wisdom he could muster.

CHAPTER THIRTY-FOUR

"**C**OMMAS." **SISSY THREW THE STACK** of paper onto the conference table. "Eight months of meetings, an emergency of drastic proportions at home, and your only differences are punctuation!" She half stood, fists clenched on the table, and glared at the two ambassadors.

"My Laudae, because of your early educational limitations, you are perhaps unaware of how much a comma can change the meaning of a sentence," Garrin da Lukan pa Lukan/FCC said mildly.

Sissy fixed her gaze on Lord Lukan's son and primary assistant. "I know precisely how much punctuation affects the meaning of a sentence. In these cases they are meaningless. You are stalling. You don't want to sign a treaty of alliance, or trade, or anything." She shifted her attention to Lord Lukan. "You would rather Harmony City collapsed and died than accept help from outsiders."

"Laudae Sissy, I want this treaty as much as anyone," Lord Lukan protested. He held his hands in front of him, palms up. "We need the alliance. For many reasons."

"Then who gave you orders to wrap these negotiations in confusion until we are lost in a morass of punctuation?" She used Jake's words. They didn't need to know that. Jake chased different crises today. Something to do with a sabotaged power plant in the refugee quarters.

Briefly she wondered if Lord Lukan had learned of the hours she spent with Jake, either in his office or hers, going over the day's events, evaluating every nuance of relationships and interactions around the station. Holding hands and gazing into each other's eyes with longing. Aching to break every law against cross-caste and cross-culture relationships.

Would there be consequences if Lukan did know? And would he somehow misconstrue the facts to suit his purposes?

Out-of-caste relationships had become so distasteful to Harmony society that she didn't think breaking the caste system alone would bring about integration. The idea of the High Priestess of all Harmony becoming involved with an alien—even a human one—might depose her and send her into exile—never to return to Harmony again. Never to feel the sweetness of joining her mind, body, and soul within a funerary cave, the womb of the Goddess.

If her enemies didn't use it as an excuse to execute her. Within minutes of the quake they declared the disaster her fault for deserting her home in favor of talking to aliens.

Her enemies. She still had them back on Harmony. Those enemies kept her from returning and making a new home with a new family.

"Lord Lukan, if you want this treaty so badly, then who gives you orders not to sign?" She sat back down, letting her anger bleed out of her posture. The emotion still roiled.

Ambassador Telvino swiveled in his chair to more directly confront Lukan. "I thought you had the power to approve and sign?"

Admiral Marella, trying to become invisible in the far reaches of the wedge-shaped room, busied herself with her handheld computer.

Lukan had the grace to look embarrassed.

Sissy reached for the papers she had just cast aside. After a quick glance to make sure they had not been altered since she had brought them to the table this morning, she found a pen in her pocket and affixed her signature to the last page.

"Does this satisfy you, Ambassador Telvino? I accept this treaty."

"You have no authority!" Lukan pounded the table.

"As High Priestess, my vote outweighs all votes on the High Council. I would have to sign in the end. Why not the beginning?"

"You have separated yourself from the Goddess Harmony. The High Council no longer recognizes you as Her avatar," Garrin said quietly. His gaze slid away from her. "You caused the quake and monster storms. You leave us vulnerable to invasion while we fight to overcome . . ."

"Silence! You will not repeat that nonsense," Lukan ordered.

"I will not stand by while *she* gives away our entire heritage by enlisting outsiders to do what Harmony should do for herself. What we have always done for ourselves and our colonies. She's promising new Badger Metal hull plating to any ship that diverts supplies to Harmony Prime!"

"Harmony and her colonies no longer have enough resources to provide everything we need for a disaster of this scale," Lukan reminded his son. "Laudae Sissy has exchanged a valuable asset for help."

"She no longer has authority from the High Council to do this!" Garrin countered.

"My sources tell me that if the government no longer looks to me for guidance, the people still do," she returned. Flashes of her old insecurities ate away at her self-control. Over a year had passed since her ordination. Part of her still believed she belonged in Lord Chauncey's factory assembling navigation systems for spaceships.

"The people?" Garrin dismissed them with a wave. "The people have no say in this matter."

More and more Jake convinced her that she had the authority and personal power to act on what she knew to be right.

If only she had her connection to the Goddess and her sense of unity with a planet to confirm that authority!

"The people are the reason Harmony exists. Without the people, you would have no power, no one to rule. Without the people working every day, you would have no clothing, no pretty houses, no cars, nothing. You'd have to make it all yourself. I doubt, sir, that *you* would survive."

That was why the original settlers had created the caste system. They created slaves to serve them.

Sissy rose from her chair and tucked her hands into the sleeves of her robe. With a curt nod of her head she fixed her gaze on each person in the room in turn, including Admiral Marella, who tried to fade into the bulkhead.

"I expect a copy of this treaty, signed by Ambassador Telvino and Lord Lukan on my desk within the hour. If you delay in any way, I shall break this negotiation as I broke the government of Harmony. You will all be replaced by people willing to negotiate a viable treaty, people who do not have orders to stall and drag out the talks endlessly until some new crisis forces your hand. Do you understand me?"

Ambassador Telvino rose and bowed low. He grabbed the treaty and signed it with a flourish. Then he shoved the document in front of Lukan.

Garrin stayed his father's hand from adding his own signature. "My Lord, you cannot sign this document. It is vague and . . ."

"The only vagueness is in the changes you demand, Garrin," Sissy interrupted. "My Lord, do you sign your name or do I send you home?"

"I sign. As I should have signed weeks ago. You are right, My Laudae. We have orders filtered through many channels, but I think we both know their origin. I can no longer justify a delay. Harmony needs help. Now. Not at some undefined time in the future." He shook off his son's restraint and pulled his own pen out of a pocket in his formal blue robe, an old-fashioned pen with an elaborately carved wood barrel and a pointed nib. His signature dwarfed the other two in size and flourishes.

"It is done," Sissy sighed. "Shall we retire to the Temple for a blessing on this historic moment." Not a question, an order.

"Since you people take comfort in rituals for every action, I believe that appropriate," Telvino said. "You too, Admiral Marella. You can report back to the CSS afterward."

"Your presence is also required, Garrin," Lukan said. "We shall all inform our governments after we have said prayers of thanksgiving and lit incense and candle flame to bless the occasion."

Rituals. Rituals to complete every action.

A light flashed across Sissy's mind. Rituals reminded her of her connection with the divine. If she found rituals for small actions as well as major ones, perhaps she could reforge her connection to Harmony. Like remote kissing of the sigil of Harmony on the trams. Like lighting candles. Like blessing food before eating.

She did all those things and more.

Was the Goddess just beyond her reach, coming closer with each little connection?

At the last second, she grabbed the important document off the conference table. Her fingers barely reached it before Garrin or Admiral Marella could. "I shall take custody of this and make certain you all have valid copies." No sense in giving either of them the chance to alter it to their advantage.

✦   ✦   ✦

"You did not attend the treaty blessing ritual," Mac said flatly to Admiral Pamela Marella. He confronted her as she sneaked away from the conference room and headed toward the secret office she'd set up in the damaged and abandoned wing. At least the office was a secret to most of the station.

Mac had few doubts that the admiral had hidden her spy headquarters from Jake.

"I have no need for superstitious nonsense," she sneered. Her eyes flicked right and left, seeking a path around Mac's stolid presence between her and the lift.

"Nor I. But Laudae Sissy needs them. Since she is the glue that holds Harmony to the treaty, you should acknowledge her request for your presence."

"I don't have time for this. Get out of my way, Mac."

"Not until I know what you plan to do now that the treaty has been signed."

"That is not your business."

"If it affects the safety of this station and the people within it, then it is my business."

"This is *my* station. I do as I need to do to protect the CSS as a whole." Admiral Marella took one step sideways, then three forward. "That includes removing you from my path—from this station if necessary."

Mac blocked her with his body. As he shifted, he loosened his secondary limbs from the fabric confines of his clothing. "I think General Jake will argue that he controls this station. I will argue with you that it is mine by right of family as well as knowledge of the inner workings. I dare you to try removing either of us."

Mac made a mental list of information about Pammy and her spies that he could leak to the media on a dozen worlds.

"Get out of my way, beast." The spymaster pulled a miniblaster from the back waistband of her trousers.

Panic flared deep within Mac. The last time he'd been shot had nearly crippled him for life. Would he be lucky enough to escape major injury?

He doubted it.

His feet shuffled backward before he could think his next action through.

"We both know I can hurt you. Now get out of my way. I have forces to deploy and officials to inform about the treaty."

Mac noted the order of her chores. She'd get her spies in place before she informed her government.

Admiral Pamela Marella had her own agenda and loyalties. They did not always include what was best for anyone but her.

"I think you need to attend the others in Temple," Mac said, more firmly than his quaking insides felt.

"I agree, Pammy." General Jake appeared on the lift behind Mac.

"Jake, you don't understand," Pamela hedged.

"I think I do. Now either give me the gun or holster it."

Mac took the opportunity to sidle away down the corridor to the maintenance tube.

"Do it, Pammy."

"You can't order me around, Jake. I'm your boss. And I have the superior weapon."

"Superior to a Badger Metal stiletto?"

A quick look over his shoulder confirmed for Mac that somehow Jake had moved quickly enough to restrain Pammy's gun hand and thrust his pointed weapon against her throat.

General Jake was the only person on station who could handle the spymaster. Mac was more than happy to leave him to it.

"We will meet again, Mr. Mac, but for now you'd best get out of here before blood is spilled," General Jake said, keeping his gaze and weapon focused on Pammy. "Admiral, I believe our presence is required in Temple. Now come quietly or come in restraints. But you will attend when Laudae Sissy requests," Jake said with a similar quiet authority to the High Priestess.

"This is the last time we meet as allies, Admiral," Mac whispered as he disappeared. "Consider me your enemy until you leave my station."

◆ ◆ ◆ ◇ ◆ ◆ ◆

CHAPTER THIRTY-FIVE

JAKE STRETCHED AND YAWNED. The data charts on his desk all swam together before his eyes. Once more he wished for the spectacles to make order and sense of the shipping manifest and routes, the personnel dispositions, the fallout of the new treaty obligations, and the legal entanglements from granting citizenship to Mara and the refugees.

He had the next best thing: Sissy. She looked more overwhelmed than he felt.

"I need to stretch my legs, Sissy," Jake said quietly. He'd waited until she'd sent her girls to bed for the evening. They still had mountains of detail work to attend to, but it looked as though they had a steady chain of supplies lined up to help with disaster cleanup on Harmony Prime.

Their only reports of damage and casualties came from the ships in orbit around Harmony. Communications, power, water, sewers, everything was out or barely working in the city.

Sissy looked from him to the long list of memos on her desktop screen. She reached to activate a flashing icon by a new folder.

"No more work tonight, Sissy. Please. My head is reeling with facts and figures and plans and plots and schemes and . . . and just too much." He held his temples with his fingertips, as if the pressure would hold his brains inside his skull.

"Where would you like to walk?" She folded her hands in front of her, though her fingers twitched to search out that new file. "I hear that the starlight in the hydroponics dome is spectacular."

He'd never known her to pass up an opportunity for physical activity over reading reports. The sheer magnitude of the work of rebuilding Harmony Prime occupied her every waking thought.

"Not walk so much. I know a viewpoint where the stars are even more spectacular than the garden dome." He grinned like a schoolboy planning hooky.

She looked at him quizzically.

"I need to fly."

"Certainly we can stretch in the zero G levels." She stood up and looked around the perimeter of his desk for a pair of shoes.

"More than that. I have a private shuttle at my disposal. Come on, Sissy, let's go check out the new planet."

"I can't leave my girls that long . . ."

"It's only a single jump through hyperspace. We'll go there, fly one orbit, and come back. Four hours max."

A smile flashed across her face, lighting her eyes.

He almost saw a halo of enthusiasm radiating from her head.

"How did you get the coordiantes?" she whispered as if she expected secret listeners.

"There's more than one computer hacker on this station. I found that my passcode overrides top-secret clearances. Mara made sure of that before she—uh—changed positions." He couldn't help the smile that stretched his face so wide he felt as though his skin would crack.

She returned his grin. "Okay. I just have to find some shoes."

"Don't bother. I'll fix you up with a flight suit. Built-in boots." He grabbed her hand and dashed for the doorway and the lift before she could object further.

"This ship doesn't have a lot of jump power, but it will do for a short trip," Jake explained to Sissy as he ran down his preflight checklist. He used to do this automatically, running the routine and numbers in his head. His duties aboard the First Contact Café had kept him grounded for too long. He needed to double-check everything, make sure he didn't miss a vital glitch in any system. Besides, he had Sissy aboard. He'd not take any unnecessary chances with her safety.

"I've never flown in anything this small," she said, avidly watching his every move.

"It's bigger than the helicopters we used back on Harmony." Everything shipshape. He ran through the ignition sequence. A comforting rumble of raw power revitalized his entire body and mind.

"With a helicopter you have ground beneath you to catch you if you fall and air to breath if you open a window. This thing doesn't have any windows." She continued to look around, absorbing every bit of data.

"No windows, but we do have screens that will show real time any vista we need. Kind of hard to have windows in the cockpit when the cockpit is dead center of the ship—better protection against radiation on a ship this small and light."

"I like computer screens for reading." Sissy looked at the array of data spilling across the one in front of her seat at the copilot position. "But I prefer windows for looking out." She sighed. "I miss hearing the wind in the trees and feeling rain on my face, and seasons, and night and day."

"So do I, Sissy. So do I. Soon. We'll land on the planet soon, but for now we'll just do a flyby, and you can glimpse trees and rivers and meadows and such."

They shared a moment of silent understanding. Then the gut-wrenching shift as they dropped away from the station's gravity.

"We'll have microgravity from acceleration once we're clear of the station," Jake said.

She nodded, eyes glued to the images on her screen. Tentatively she touched an icon on the side. A rear view of the station expanded to fill the screen.

Jake did a quick loop to put him on the proper trajectory to the jump point. Then he punched up the speed. They were thrown back against their chairs with a crushing weight.

"I thought you said microgravity," she ground out. The light of adventure still sparkled in her eyes.

Jake kept the acceleration higher than normal for a bit longer, needing to feel the extremes after months of stagnation.

Too soon they reached the jump point. "Sleepy drugs in your handrest if you want them," he said. He hesitated over shoving his own hand into the rigid glove. As a solo pilot he needed to be awake. The ghosts he'd encountered the last time he stayed awake during hyperspace scared him.

"I . . . I don't need the drugs," Sissy replied quietly. She didn't look convinced.

Jake took a deep breath and clenched his jaw. "You can sleep. I'll stay awake."

"We'll watch during the long darkness and the empty and lonely paths together." She reached over and placed her hand atop his.

"Thank you." He shifted his palm to hold hers, then with his free hand punched in the sequence to jump to hyperspace.

Abruptly reality tilted to the right. Colors took a dramatic shift to the left. The screens went blank, taking the view of the stars away.

$$\blacklozenge \; \blacklozenge \; \blacklozenge \; \diamondsuit \; \blacklozenge \; \blacklozenge \; \blacklozenge$$

CHAPTER THIRTY-SIX

"WHAT DOES HYPERSPACE look like?" Sissy asked. She opened her eyes a slit and glanced at her blank screen.

"I don't know. Screens don't work. The few times I've had real-time views out a window, I've seen nothing but black. Or I've been so occupied with my ghosts I didn't take the time to notice. Friends report swirls of red energy against a black backdrop. Others say it's all white, as if all the energy of the universe combines."

"Hyperspace reflects what is deep within your soul."

He looked at her more closely. Her face had gone blank and slack, eyes closed. Her own swirl of multicolored energy made her glow all over.

A vision from her Goddess. If she'd only acknowledge it.

He'd barely formed that thought when the alarm chimed gently. "Coming out of hyperspace in two minutes. Antidotes to sleep drugs available," the computer told him.

Of course, two minutes computer time could be any stretch of time in hyperspace.

Sissy roused and shook herself, as if coming out of a deep sleep.

Another jolt to the gut and reality twisted back to where it belonged. Except, Jake had begun to think of the distortions in hyperspace as closer to reality than normal space.

Hyperspace reflects what is deep within your soul.

Truer words had never been said.

"Are we there already?" Sissy asked. She fixed her eyes on her screen as it burst to life again.

"We're about an hour out from the planet at two Gs. I can take it slower if you want." Jake busied himself with taking back control of the shuttle from the computer. "Odd to have a jump point within a solar system."

"Can we see the planet from here?"

He directed her to a magnified view of the inner planets, five of them, with another ten smaller ones on the outer reaches. The jump point had dumped them into the large gap between the two groups. She found the formula for zooming in on the fifth planet from the sun, a slightly larger version of Earth's yellow Sol.

"I can see a fair amount of blue water and brown and green land. White clouds here and there. It doesn't look so very different from Harmony," she gasped.

"Nor that different from Earth, or any other planet habitable by humans. We kind of take Earth with us in terraforming. This one has a little less water, a lot higher mountains. Arable land and forests mostly on the coastlines. Continent interiors tend toward desert."

"Mountains? Does that mean caves?" She held her breath.

"Don't know. Surveys are still preliminary." Jake divided his attention between flight controls on his own screen and the growing image on Sissy's. Soon the planet overflowed her screen. She keyed it to zoom back and keep the entire thing in view.

"Survey crew is on that big island in the northern hemisphere above the equator. Temperate climate from ocean breezes. A small mountain range inland from the southern coast. The rest is arable. Room for delegations to have separate embassies and a central core of buildings. We plan to keep the population small at first so that the island can support us with food and drinking water. Opening the rest of the planet to settlement will wait. We haven't done enough tests yet to determine long-term fertility of the land and the extent of natural resources. It's enough for a CSS headquarters. That's most important."

"Previous inhabitants?" she asked, tracing a chain of foothills rising from a broken coastline toward the mountains.

"I didn't see any reference to an archaeology report. Either we're the first, or any ruins are buried too deep for us to find with preliminaries."

"It's a pretty planet," Sissy said. "Jake, please, can we land? I need to *feel* land beneath my feet and wind in my face. I need to dip my hands in clean running water and taste the air."

Jake checked his chronometer. They were ahead of schedule. "Just a short stop. No more than ten minutes."

"Long enough to do an abbreviated ritual. I need to make this place my own."

✦   ✦   ✦

"It smells like home," Sissy whispered. "Lilacs!" Her nose twitched with the soft scents of spring flowers. A raindrop touched her cheek. Another plopped onto her head. She lifted her face to greet the elements. "But it vibrates differently. The sun sings a different song to the galaxy than Empathy and Harmony do."

The air tasted clean, had a texture of moisture and wind and dirt and . . . and life! Different but alive and vibrant.

"We can't linger, Sissy," Jake warned her.

"I know." She gathered the disappointment into a tight ball and tucked it away. "Soon, though. I'll come back soon."

"Don't go too far." Jake sounded worried. As he used to back on Harmony, when every shadow hid a potential assassin.

"There is nothing dangerous here, Jake. Your surveyors ruled out poisonous critters, predatory plants, and hostile natives." She stepped a little further away from the shelter of the boxy shuttle. With its stubby atmosphere wings, it looked alien in the lush paradise. Not a sharp angle in sight.

"When we build, we shall construct buildings with fluid lines and graceful arches, blending in and enhancing the landscape."

She drank in the sight of tall trees with broad leaves, bright flowers, the faint hum of insects and . . . and the chuckle of moving water.

She spun in place, arms out, glorying in the natural environment.

"It looks almost as if someone terraformed the planet," she said, marveling at how similar the plant life was to her home on Harmony.

"Yeah, it does. I wonder . . . Sissy, watch out!"

Her ill-fitting, heavy boots caught on uneven ground. She stumbled and plunged headlong into a clump of spiny shrubs.

"Oh, ouch," she moaned as she rolled away from the spikes that were as long as her hand was broad.

"Good thing you had the suit on," Jake said as he hauled her to her feet. He ran his hands down her body, brushing aside broken plant bits. "These things would penetrate normal clothes and go all the way in like a stiletto." He shook his head and frowned.

Sissy hid the long scratch on her palm from his gaze. They'd both left their heavy flight suit gloves in the shuttle. They didn't need protection from the mild climate.

A line of blood trickled from her clenched fist. A burning itch started at the center of her palm and spread to her wrist before she could think of anything to say.

"Sissy? Are you okay? You look mighty pale." He caught her around the waist.

"The spikes . . ." she mumbled as fire spread up her arm and down her body. Sweat followed the inflammation. Too hot. Hotter than noon under the bright sun in high summer.

Weakness followed the heat. Her head became far too heavy for her fragile neck muscles. She knelt down, placing her forehead on the cool ground.

Her heart hammered in her ears. Panic licked at her mind like a fire hungry for fuel.

Jake came down with her, cradling her gently against his side.

"Damn!" he spat, holding her wounded hand.

She didn't have the strength to reply. She could only stare at the rivulet of blood leaking into the cuff of her flight suit.

✦   ✦   ✦

"Fragit! Will someone please answer," Jake yelled into the comm.

Static. All he got between here and the FCC was static.

"Isn't anyone home?" This was as bad as the night the Squid ship crashed into the station and there was no one on duty in Control. He slammed his fist into the interface. Sharp pains ran from his little finger to his shoulder. Damn, he might have broken something.

Temper tantrums accomplish nothing, he reminded himself. The words had a strangely feminine quality inside his mind.

He had one last chance to save his beloved.

"Survey One, this is FCC One," Jake called through the shuttle's comm. "Survey One, do you read me?" He looked anxiously toward Sissy, stretched out on the cot in the cargo bay. She shivered and moaned, barely aware of anything but pain. Her entire body stiffened and then convulsed.

"Hey, FCC One, what you doing way out here?" came a relaxed male voice.

"Survey One, I have an injured passenger. She fell against a plant with long spikes."

"Oh, them blue hooks. Nasty things."

"Is it lethal?" Dread chilled him to the bone.

"Not usually. You know we ain't supposed to be talkin' to you. You ain't supposed to be down here yet either."

"I need help. My passenger is a very important person to the CSS and to Harmony. Can you send me a medic?"

Laughter greeted that request.

"Oh, God, what am I going to do?" he almost cried. He couldn't lose Sissy. It was all his fault. He never should have offered to take her off station. He should never have let her persuade him to land. All his fault.

His gut twisted with raw emotion.

The faint smell of incense that clung to her like a flower's perfume faded along with her life signs.

"Look, buddy, we're out on a two-week survival survey. Required. We have to live off the land for two weeks with no chance of rescue or contact with base. That's so we know for sure this place is okay for habitation. We're about a thousand klicks from you and no supplies," the voice finally explained.

"Shit!"

Sissy moaned again and twisted back and forth on the cot. Whatever gripped her mind and body drove deeper hooks into her, taking her beyond his reach.

"It's not all bad, buddy."

"It looks like bloody hell from my perspective."

"But it's all looks. You got a med kit with some antihistamines?"

"Let me look." Jake scrambled for the big white box with the red cross on the lid hidden beneath the fold-down cot where Sissy writhed. He spared a moment to touch her sweaty brow and brush away a damp tendril of dark hair. Her caste marks seemed to pulse and take on angry red tinges.

Not good.

The box held numerous vials and packets. He scanned and discarded one after another. Finally he came up with a fat packet of patches that promised instant relief from allergens.

"Got it," he crowed into the comm.

"Give her a double dose every two hours," the surveyor said. He sounded distracted, no longer interested in Jake and his problem. Not even curious about the very important passenger who shouldn't be dirtside at all.

"Double dose twice as often as recommended?" Jake squeaked. The packet contained dire warning about overdoses: hallucinations, elevated blood pressure that could lead to strokes and blindness, dehydration, etc., etc.

"Trust me on this, FCC One. The plant is nasty but not necessarily dangerous if you treat it. In eighteen to twenty-four hours she'll be back to normal. Oh, and don't take her through hyperspace until the swelling around the penetration point is gone. The sleepy drugs will compound the side effects of the antihistamines. She'll go insane. Seen it happen. Survey One out."

An ominous click and the line went dead.

"Wait . . ." Nothing. Jake reinitiated his call. Dead air. The survey crew had reverted to their self-imposed isolation.

"Damn stupid regs," Jake muttered. "Damn stupid me!"

He ripped the foil covering off of two patches, awkwardly with the rapidly swelling little finger of his left hand. Not knowing what else to do, he placed one patch on the wound and the other on her dancing caste marks.

Then he settled down to wait, wondering if he dared call home. If he could get through.

CHAPTER THIRTY-SEVEN

ADRIAL WALKED HESITANTLY with the aid of a cane. She made a big show of deliberately placing each foot flat on the floor as she stepped down the corridor to the MedBay lobby. She had to remind herself to favor her right leg by limping and balancing on the ball of that foot about every fourth step. No sense in betraying her true fitness to any observers. This space station was filled with observers.

She'd made this trek every day now for three days running. Doc Halliday wanted to move her down a level to higher gravity so that her bones would grow denser, better able to withstand stress and exercise.

With stronger bones she could venture farther afield in her quest for Spiritual Purity. So far she'd moved among the worlds colonized by the Maril, all less than half the gravity level of most human worlds. With stronger bones, she could go to Earth, home to her mother's people, and study with some of the experts in meditation.

Strange, none of the Messengers of the Gods had thought to try bone therapy in their teachings. They preferred bone breaking as a learning tool.

She'd found some wonderful teachings on her reader, books she hadn't known existed. Instead of seeking knowledge of the past, perhaps she needed to look inward a bit and organize all that she'd learned. Then perhaps in applying those teachings to her life she might elevate her spirit a bit to find the next step in her search.

That was what Laudae Sissy said she should do.

Leave no trace of your quest!

The deep psychological reminder severed the thought of going to Earth. She forgot her need to look inward. Out . . . she had to go out into the galaxy to find . . . Spiritual Purity. Nothing was more important than her quest. Not even her own health and well-being.

An odd flurry of movement ahead of her caught her wandering attention. A number of blue-coated orderlies, nurses, and doctors hovered around the doorway to another room.

A moment of *déjà vu* contorted her perceptions. She'd been here before. When? How?

"Get me a real physician, you barefaced pretender! If you can't find someone competent, then I will speak only through Laudae Sissy," a man shouted from within the room.

Barefaced! That epithet belonged to Harmony, where caste defined everything.

Only a high-powered man from Harmony would dare question the authority of a physician, even a barefaced one. Lesser classes were bred and educated to obedience and meekness.

Adrial had seen those traits in Sissy, the most powerful woman in the entire empire, and she deferred to everyone, asserting her authority only when pushed to extremes. Their almost daily talks had taught Adrial much about the High Priestess and Harmony.

Like the incident with the treaty. That story had circulated the entire station within moments. Normal Sissy, the young woman raised in Worker caste, would have listened and waited for the ambassadors to run out of stalling techniques and signed only when told to by the High Council. Pushed by her own need to organize help for her troubled planet, Laudae Sissy, High Priestess of all Harmony, avatar of the Goddess, had forced the issue and signed before the diplomats had finished arguing.

Adrial had been more reticent about her own past with both Laudae Sissy and the medics. Secrecy had become her chief survival tool.

She crept closer to the altercation, keeping to the shadows, letting her pale blue hospital robe blend in with the painted walls. Color and movement betrayed a lurker. She'd learned that long ago in her frequent flights from the Law.

Orderlies hurried toward the room with a gurney. They dashed right past Adrial without looking at her.

"You aren't taking me for more tests until a proper physician tells me why," said the angry male patient.

The orderlies bullied their way past the bevy of nurses gathered at the door. In backing out of the way, one of the women looked directly at Adrial. Her gaze slid past, then jerked back.

"You aren't supposed to be here!" The nurse, with a Harmony Professional and Spacer caste mark, bustled toward Adrial. Roughly she grabbed Adrial's arm and turned her away from the interesting activity. "You *can't* be here."

"But . . ."

"It's time for you to rest. You did quite enough walking this morning." With firmness in her step and her expression, the nurse nearly shoved Adrial back into her room. "Rest and stay put. That's an order." She closed and latched the door, then disappeared.

Adrial opened her reader to the latest newscasts from Harmony. What she saw and heard alarmed her.

✦ ✦ ✦

Mac made his slow circuit of the station. At each of his listening posts he paused. The powerful Laud in MedBay no longer interested him. His heart attack had rendered him useless in the power struggles of that empire. His influence would give Mac nothing in gaining control of his station.

He liked the idea of keeping the First Contact Café name. His siblings shuddered every time they heard the sobriquet. Mac wanted them as uncomfortable as possible.

Extreme quiet in the Temple Complex alerted him to something unusual. No acolytes bustling about replenishing incense burners, trimming candlewicks, practicing reading from the Covenant. He listened for Lady Jancee's strident voice chastising a servant or berating her husband over a point of trivial significance.

Silence.

The usual aura of burning incense and candle wax had faded. Not even the smell of fresh paint from the murals they all painted on the naked walls touched his sensors.

If Mac didn't know better, he'd assume the entire wing deserted and cold, awaiting activation.

He moved on, wondering where the Temple folk had gone. A crisis of great magnitude should send them to the Temple to pray. Since the devastation on Harmony Prime they'd all spent hours in Temple praying. Sissy made sure these folk put a lot of stock in prayer, setting as example her own hours on her knees before the altar.

What could have happened to send them elsewhere? He'd heard nothing alarming on normal station comms.

Quiet weeping cut through shouting voices one wing over. The sounds drew him to the conference wing where the CSS delegation shared communications and meeting rooms with Harmony. Sissy had set up miniature altars here, to pray for guidance during negotiations. Pockets of incense lingered here, barely.

"Telvino, if your upstart general has kidnapped our High Priestess for nefarious purposes I'll personally take his head," Lord Lukan shouted.

"Typical Harmony xenophobia. Always blame outsiders for your own inadequacies," Telvino snarled back.

Mac crept closer to the duct opening. This confrontation might lead him to discover a way to force these two factions to resign the station to his control.

"Jake would never hurt Laudae Sissy. He loves her," insisted Acolyte Mary.

"Maybe they eloped," whispered Acolyte Martha. A dreamy look softened her face as she looked beyond the limitations of the large conference room.

"Blasphemy!" Lady Jancee gasped. "Laudae Sissy is the avatar of our Goddess; such base behavior is beyond comprehension. An out-of-caste relationship is strictly forbidden. Hideous. *Disgusting*."

Mac grimaced at the voice lancing his sensitive ears like a surgical probe.

"My point exactly," Lord Lukan said quietly. "Laudae Sissy would not elope. She must have been kidnapped."

"The Media hover cams are everywhere. I'll check to see if one of them captured their departure," Admiral Marella said with a smirk.

Mac knew that she'd already found the record they sought. Her satisfaction told Mac the evidence was damning.

"General Devlin checked out a shuttle and filed a flight plan to the new planet," Ambassador Telvino said on a sigh, as if he'd repeated the statement many times. "It is not unreasonable to presume Laudae Sissy accompanied him for her own purposes. Who knows, maybe most of the populace of Harmony Prime will need resettlement or temporary sanctuary. Shuttles have accidents. Shuttles run low on fuel. Shuttles stall in hyperspace. Has anyone tried to contact the shuttle?"

Dead silence met that statement.

Mac scrambled back to his primary terminal. He needed to make certain communications did not reach that shuttle. Yet.

Then one more act of sabotage, maybe something to make the two CSS battleships docked here unable to support human life and unable to fly. Then he'd cut them loose from their moorings. Thus requiring a major effort to keep them out of navigational paths and fix them.

That should convince Harmony of Jake's unfitness to govern the station. The CSS would not accept any Harmonite to lead, since Harmony had not yet joined the CSS, only signed an alliance treaty. The Harmonites would accept no CSS citizen other than General Jake as station commander.

So Mac would offer his own services. On condition he get the spectacles back. He couldn't effectively run everything without them.

Soon. Oh, so soon. Mac would make certain his brother's dead body was on the next ship off station with a full report of his failures to their siblings. A very full report. No one would care if all of it was true.

Mother's etiquette book had no rule regarding truthfulness when falsehood, cloaked in a miasma of plausibility, accomplished mercenary ends.

$$\Large \text{+ + + } \diamondsuit \text{ + + +}$$

CHAPTER THIRTY-EIGHT

SMOOTH STONE WALLS rose up around Sissy. Glossy, polished rock reflected the benevolent light that bathed her in serenity. Mirror images of herself repeated down the tunnel in endless copies, each less defined, less solid than the last. She reached out, trying to gather up all of the pieces of herself.

The images kept marching away, following the natural rhythm of the land.

She tried to match her heartbeat to the pulse of life within the stones. Too fast. Her heart raced and pounded. She willed it to calm. Gradually the overwhelming speed slowed, stuttered, paused, then started up again melding with the life of the planet all around her.

She grew into something new, not quite her old self, not quite a child of this world.

Are you willing to sacrifice yourself to become one with me?

"Who said that?" Sissy asked, though no sound came from her throat.

Can you make the choice to become a part of me? Can you bring new life into this sacred place?

The cave around Sissy heaved a huge breath inward.

She knew this sensation. Sunset neared. The air outside was warmer than inside, so the cave brought in the warmth. At dawn it would breathe out.

She shared that slow breath of life.

Sunset? Which sunset?

Where was she that she knew a living land all around her? No space station possessed this kind of soul. Or voice.

"What do I call you?" she asked more politely. This time a tiny croak emerged from her dry mouth.

What you have always called me. We are all one. We have always been one. Each new life you create here is an extension of me, of us, of the universe.

"Harmony," Sissy whispered. "Do I speak with Harmony?"

That name will do, though We have many.

"Is it You Who used to speak through me?"

We still do, if you will but recognize it. You cannot become one with Us until you open your soul to the connected universe around you.

The cave walls thinned, became insubstantial. Light filtered through the living membrane. Then it was gone, and she knew darkness.

She was alone again. So terribly alone.

And the Goddess had withdrawn from her.

There was something she had to do . . .

✦　　✦　　✦

"Sissy, wake up now," Jake coaxed. He'd seen the flutter of her eyelids, heard the almost words escaping her mouth. His jackhammer heart throttled back to a steadier pace.

Beneath the antihistamine patch, her caste marks took on a new luster, shining with an inner light that shimmered against the normal crystal sparkle. Something strange was happening to his Sissy—something he couldn't explain, something that scared him to the bone.

Sissy twisted away from his gentle finger tracing the line of her cheek. She murmured something that sounded negative.

"Come on, my love. Wake up now. We have to get back to the station." He firmed his grip on her shoulder.

"No," she replied, very distinctly.

"Yes, Sissy. I know you're tired. I know your hand still hurts. But we have to go home." He grabbed both of her shoulders and pulled her upright. Her head lolled, and she kept her eyes closed.

Eighteen hours the survey team had said. Eighteen hours for the toxins to leave her body. He'd counted every minute of those eighteen hours along with the ship's chrono. She'd been unconscious for eighteen hours.

Lord Lukan and Ambassador Telvino must be frantic. If they hadn't torn the station apart looking for her, they'd tear it apart in frustration.

Jake hadn't been able to get a single message out or in. He presumed the isolation provisions for the survey team jammed communications.

"I can't leave," Sissy whispered.

"We have to go home," he insisted.

"The First Contact Café is not home." Her eyes flew open, and she fixed him with a stubborn gaze.

Uh-oh. He'd encountered that look before. At least a stubborn and determined Sissy wasn't unconscious, possibly dying.

"I once swore to protect you with my life, My Laudae. I didn't swear to let you throw yours away," he countered, just as determined. His fear for her overrode his need to do anything she wished.

"I can only survive with a living planet all around me. The station is soulless."

"I thought you covered that with a ritual when you first arrived?" He twisted her, forcibly so that her back rested against the bulkhead of the shuttle and her feet dangled off the cot.

"Not enough. I have to stay here, Jake. The Goddess has never spoken to me with as much clarity as She does here. I have to stay. I have to reforge my connections to Her." A fat tear welled up in the corner of her eye.

Damn.

"Later, Sissy. I promise I'll bring you back. But you've been very ill. I have to take you back and have the medical team check you out. What good is reconnecting with the Goddess if you die in the process?" This time he hauled her limp body to her feet and began frog-marching her toward the cockpit.

"If I die here, then I will truly be one with the universe," she sighed. But her eyes had sparked to life when she spotted greenery on the real-time cockpit screens. "If I die on the station, then all will be lost. My soul will be lost and left wandering alone, unconnected, separated from Harmony forever."

"You aren't going to die. Not yet anyway." Jake pushed her down in the copilot seat and strapped her in.

"My soul will be empty until I return, Jake. This planet is more my home than Harmony ever was. From this place I can reach out to the universe and find all the ways we are connected to each other and to the Goddess. All of us, every race, every planet." She leaned forward, gazing intently at the green meadow surrounding them.

"And you will make it your home. Just not quite yet." He strapped himself in and slammed the throttle open. He had to get her out of here fast. Before she woke up enough to take matters into her own hands.

He had no doubt she'd find a way to stay if he delayed a nanosecond longer.

✦ ✦ ✦

"My Laud, do you really want all of Harmony to know of your frail health, your inability to return to Crystal Temple for some weeks to come?" Major Roderick asked. "Keeping secret your presence on the First Contact Café is essential. I cannot authorize a Media person to come here to talk to you."

"The man I brought here will report what I tell him to report. He will also ask questions when I do not feed him a certain amount of carefully edited material. What have you told the Media?" At least he hoped the man had come to his senses after refusing lauding of his caste mark.

Silently he cursed Sissy for revealing the original Covenant Tablets, which showed the Media as a separate caste and made no mention of the poor. They kept printing the truth without Temple bleaching of the facts.

"You are on an extended tour of the colonies," Major Roderick explained. "My people in communications and your reporter here feed them stock and altered photos of the masses hailing and applauding you."

"How long before the people begin to question why they did not hear of my presence in the places I have been?" Gregor resisted the urge to reach for the oxygen feed. He'd show no weakness before this Spacer officer, even if the man had proved his loyalty to Temple.

"Another week. Perhaps two. The colonies you have visited have suffered major disruptions to communications due to sunspots and other natural phenomena. Only selected messages get through, all of them filtered through my people here." Major Roderick turned his head and coughed. A sure sign that if he told the truth, he did not tell it all, or he twisted it in some way.

Gregor allowed himself a tiny smile. "And what does General Jake have to say about all this?"

"What the general does not know in his absence will not hurt him." Major Roderick flashed a brief smile, then resumed his normal bland countenance as if it had never happened.

"Absent? General Jake absent? I don't believe it. That man is more persistent in his duty than any of our own Military."

"General Jake checked out a shuttle and filed a flight plan to the planet under consideration as a CSS headquarters. He is late in returning. Communications with him have been severed."

"Discord! I hope that man is finally out of my hair."

"You do not want that, My Laud."

"And why don't I?"

"We believe Laudae Sissy went with him."

Gregor grew cold. As much a nuisance as Sissy was, she and her prophecies were also valuable to him. He wanted her gone, but on his schedule. "How long?" he choked out.

"Nearly two full days. Laudae Sissy's acolytes believe they have eloped. A hover cam captured pictures of them holding hands and laughing as they entered the shuttle together."

The universe went white. Gregor clenched the mattress in a desperate attempt to remain conscious. His heart fluttered and beat weakly, erratically.

Somewhere an alarm beeped.

"She wouldn't dare marry out of caste, out of race. Word of this must reach no ears other than my own."

"Too late. That piece of news is on every screen and holovid on the station. Half the FCC is laying bets on when they will return and if they will wear mating rings."

Did the major's smile turn snide?

Gregor fought too hard for calm to spare time to puzzle it out.

"Get me documents to annul any marriage. Temple do not marry, and we do not make liaisons out of caste," he snarled.

"Does your authority extend to General Jake?"

"Damn it, man, I will make it extend! He wears a caste mark, a lauded caste mark. That makes him ours, no matter his citizenship."

A nurse bustled in, checking instruments and adjusting medication flow. She slapped a vasodilator patch onto the back of his hand. Instantly his breathing grew less labored. Then she reaffixed the oxygen tube into Gregor's nose.

"My Laud, I will leave you to rest." Major Roderick saluted and began backing out of the room.

"Send me Doc Halliday," Gregor ordered, even as he lay his head back against the elevated pillows.

"I thought you wanted nothing more to do with the CSS physicians." Major Roderick paused in his rapid exit.

"I have a chore for Doc Halliday that involves technology our physicians have not perfected."

The major lifted an eyebrow in query.

Gregor turned his face away, unwilling to share his scheme.

The only scheme that might save Harmony from Sissy's foolishness. Harmony had to survive and thrive. He lived for no other reason.

$\bullet\ \bullet\ \bullet\ \diamondsuit\ \bullet\ \bullet\ \bullet$

CHAPTER THIRTY-NINE

"JAKE, I NEED MORE HISTORY of my people," Sissy said quietly as they warped out of planetary orbit and sped toward the jump point.

"I gave you a bunch to put on Adrial's reader," he replied. He kept his hands on the controls and his eyes straight ahead.

"Those are lists of Temple and Noble leaders, spreadsheets of productivity and expansion. I need something . . . different." She too looked out the view screen at the blackness sprinkled with pinpricks of light. Stars. Other suns, many of them with planets. Some old, some new.

If she squinted her eyes just so, she caught hints of the energy connecting them all, connecting everything. Except herself. She sensed a void around her body, mind, and soul through which none of those connections could penetrate.

She needed something special to weave that energy into herself.

The Goddess of the planet she'd just left hinted at a way for her to do that. She stared at the seeping wound on her palm. More than just her blood and lymph secretions. The living blood of the plant and therefore the planet.

"How different?" Jake turned his attention back to her. He seemed to monitor the shuttle effortlessly, knowing precisely when to shift this dial, push forward on that graph. It all looked so simple beneath his strong capable hands, and yet so complex she knew she'd never learn to fly by herself.

"I need to know what my people thought about everyday life, how they coped with trials and celebrated joys."

"Social history."

"Sort of . . . I need to know the little rituals we did, how the common people maintained their connection to Harmony and the other Gods. How they avoided Discord and the other demons."

"Like when you kiss two fingers and then touch a glyph of Harmony on the tram doors? I found a glyph on my flight helmet." He touched a spot on the other side of his neck, mostly hidden by his suit. "I remote kiss it every time I take off. A wish for safe journey. Should have given you one."

She nodded. That was a ritual she'd made up. It just seemed to make sense. She pictured the glyph in her mind, a waxing and a waning quarter moon facing away from each other and between them a small circle with a line beneath. Humans becoming a part of the sky and extending to the universe.

"Don't know if anyone recorded that kind of information on Harmony. Gil would know. I can send him a message. But that may have to wait until a greater sense of order is restored in Harmony City."

"Thank you." She picked out an especially bright star on her view screen, one with a bluish tinge, willing her mind to reach out and touch it.

The void around her stretched a little but did not allow her to connect.

"Since your people came from my people, I can search Earth records for some of that. Might be faster than waiting for comms to reach Harmony."

"Would you?" Hope brightened in her mind.

"You can start with this one. Pick a star and look only at it."

"Yes." She fixed the bluish one in her mind.

"Then say: Star light, star bright, first star I see tonight, I wish I may, I wish I might, have the wish I wish tonight." He smiled and looked into the distance as if remembering something special.

"Can we see Empathy, the star that warms Harmony, from here?"

"Don't know. But when we get back, I'll pull it up on the star charts and let you see it on one of your windows."

She flashed him her biggest smile. "And what are you wishing, my friend?"

"Not supposed to tell." His eyes turned bright with moisture. "If you tell, it won't come true."

"I know what I wish for, but I don't think it will ever come true."

The quiet chime of the hyperspace alarm barely registered as she closed her eyes, permanently etching Jake's face in her memory.

"Closing your eyes won't keep the ghosts away," Jake said sadly.

"I have you to protect me."

With that thought, through her closed eyelids Sissy watched reality shift and twist.

She couldn't feel her body. Jake's hand within her own became an insubstantial shadow. Flesh on bone, all as translucent as the diagnostic scans in MedBay.

But there was another personality with them.

"Mama?"

"Is that who you truly wish to see in this space between here and there, now and then?" a little girl asked on a giggle. "If we are between, then we must be betwixt. And that means we are nixed."

"Jilly."

"Remember what I said as I died in your arms?" Jilly asked. She perched on the console in front of Sissy. The blank screens showed through her drifting lavender draperies.

"The answers are out here, among the stars," Sissy replied.

"The Covenant with Harmony can only be reforged out here. So what are you doing about it?"

"I went to the planet. I saw the Goddess."

"There is more. There is always more. You are the nexus, the point of energy that connects our people to the universe." Jilly began to fade.

Sissy tried to grab the mist, hold it there, as she wished so often she could hold onto the bright little girl and her silly jokes. "There is a blank spot around me. I can't grab hold . . ."

"Don't grab. Accept. It's like willing a kitten to come to you. Stop trying so hard. And tell the others that too. The universe is just one big joke, but you can't laugh until you step back and let the laughter come to you."

Klaxons signaled the return to normal space. Jilly disappeared into a trailing mist through the computer screen.

✦　　✦　　✦

Mac opened a window on his terminal. He'd found a new treatise in the CSS archives he wanted his little bird to read. Just a matter of a few keystrokes to transfer the text to her reader.

The last time he'd borrowed the device, he'd set it to receive remotely from this terminal.

While he had the reader open and receptive, he checked her progress in reading.

Fragit! She hadn't touched any of the material he'd given her. Instead she read and reread the Covenant with Harmony and the writings of their earliest teachers.

He should delete all of the Harmony garbage. Adrial had wasted enough time chasing mystical trails that led in circles and endangered her life every time she got close to the truth of the Maril. She needed to sharpen her wits and hone her innate ability to manipulate people to her own will.

Gods and religion had a place in keeping civilizations civilized, he supposed. But only for the gullible and naïve. The ones who willingly followed others. Leaders had to focus on more practical matters. He needed Adrial as his consort when he took control of the station. She needed to shift her concentration of study before then.

There, he'd adjusted her reading assignments, starred the ones he wanted her to study, just as Laudae Sissy did.

As he shifted away from the terminal, he detected a small sound. Something out of place in his hidden lair.

Four quick steps to his left brought him within easy reach of a duct.

Before he could reach to pull himself through the emergency escape, a human in a CSS military uniform pushed his head and shoulders through. He held a long blaster expertly.

At the same time, three more men in Harmony Military uniforms and caste marks shouldered open the primary door. They too carried energy weapons as well as long swords on their hips.

The man in the lead was the new second-in-command.

Mac raised all four of his arms in mute surrender. "How did you find me?" he asked almost in admiration.

"Locator in Miss Adrial's reader. The moment you sent her files, we had you," Major Roderick replied.

"Why must you arrest me?" Mac asked. He edged to his right. The trapdoor into the empty level below was buried under a pile of dirty clothing. Could he reach it before those blasters caught him? "I've done nothing to harm you."

"Maybe, maybe not. But you know more about that outlaw cargo ship that crashed into the diplomatic wing than anyone else. You were seen with the dead body of your brother—you had motive, means, and opportunity to murder him. But no physical evidence. No one else had a motive to kill two other Labyrinthine workers. You also have knowledge of the entire workings of this station and how to break or fix it. Come quietly and we'll talk. No pressure. No torture. Yet. We just need some information." Major Roderick turned his back quite casually, as if he expected Mac to follow without question.

Mac found the trapdoor latch with the pincer on his secondary leg. He worked it slowly, careful not to make any large movements or sudden noises.

"You could ask Lady Adrial . . ."

"Her," the major snorted. "She has the emotional maturity of a thirteen year old and the attention span of . . . of . . ."

"Of an ammonia breather," Mac finished for him.

Almost. He almost had the trapdoor ready to fling open.

"If you say so. Never met one of those before."

"My mother took an ammonia breather as one of her mates. My half sister by that relationship can actually string two coherent sentences together."

Major Roderick chuckled. But the laugh sounded false and forced. Then his eyes narrowed and his voice sharpened.

"You can forget about escaping. I've got another dozen men with blasters stationed below that door. The moment it opens, they start firing. Now are you going to come easy or hard?"

"I believe I shall come easy. This time. Tell me, Major, have you read *The Prince* by an Earther named Machiavelli?"

"Last night. I took it off Miss Adrial's reader. She wasn't interested in it at all."

✦ ✦ ✦ ◇ ✦ ✦ ✦

CHAPTER FORTY

ADRIAL SCANNED THE NEWS from Harmony time and again. She listened to speech after speech given by Laud Gregor, High Priest of all Harmony. He had a beautiful, well trained voice. He could cut through a noisy crowd and make himself heard in the far reaches of a stadium without amplification.

He had the same voice she'd heard down the hall yesterday. How could that be?

She knew him, knew she'd met him at least once, conversed with him. And yet she had no memory of the occurrences.

She looked more closely at each snippet of coverage. Laud Gregor did not look the same age in any two consecutive appearances.

The reporters, or those who fed the stories to the reporters, had used old broadcasts with new time and date stamps.

Her body grew chill with dread. Both Laud Gregor and Laudae Sissy had left the Harmonite Empire. The Goddess and Her family must be desperate in loneliness and mourning. Without the HP or HPS in residence the Gods had no one to anchor themselves to. That would explain the rumors of quake and volcanic eruptions she'd heard whispered about. The Gods desperately sought a way to force Laud Gregor and Laudae Sissy to return to Harmony so they could interact with the people through them. Gods could not speak to ordinary people directly.

She'd learned that on a dozen rim worlds that fought for survival without the aid of clergy and planetary deities.

Like the Squid People. They had another name for themselves, but no humanoid throat could work around the gargling squeals common to oceanic species.

Her memory took her back to falling through a doorway in the alleyway, back and back again before that to Biblio III, a planet devoted to scholarship. Humans had colonized the world and stayed on after the Messengers of the Gods had invaded. The winged soldiers had recognized the treasure of collected knowledge, in old-fashioned books and scrolls as well as digital texts.

Adrial had gone there, three stops, no four, after her exile from her home world.

She smelled again the dusty perfume of books, books, and more books stacked onto shelves a mile long and ten stories high, all encased in a building with many skylights and tall windows. Natural light was kinder on the eyes than artificial ones. Special filters protected the books from harmful direct light. A team of workers constantly monitored temperature and humidity inside and out to optimize the longevity of the books.

Motorized platforms moved up and down or along the shelves. She traveled slowly, drinking in the titles, dreaming of the wonders within each book.

A red volume, bound in ancient and cracking leather, seemed out of place. She jabbed her finger onto the control button as hard as she could. It creaked to a halt three meters beyond the book. She jerked the platform back and forth, up and down half a dozen times. She cursed and kicked the controls. In her eagerness she pushed the controls too hard, overshooting her aim. Finally she made it stop closer to the book. It stood out from the newer, shinier, and more subdued bindings.

Cautiously, she stood on tiptoe and reached up and up, pushing and grinding her shoulder joint until her fingertips brushed the precious book. Then she had to inch it forward enough with her fingernail hooked in the bottom of the spine until it teetered on the edge of the shelf.

At last it fell forward, and she caught it awkwardly against her thighs before it dropped to the platform. With the book cradled against her chest, she maneuvered the platform down to a reading table. That portion of the journey was easy; the platform was programmed to return to the ground as a fail-safe.

A caretaker handed her gloves to keep her skin from making direct contact with the ancient paper. She opened the cover and stared at the lovely typeface and delicate decorations on the title page. She didn't care that the book was written in a language she did not know. She cared only that it contained line drawings of every race known to the Labyrinthians. Races that had traveled far and collected wisdom from dozens of teachers from as many more races.

And there in the middle, on a center foldout page, she saw the Squid

People. She'd never seen anything so bizarre or so graceful in her life. Her eyes grew dry and gritty from staring at the drawing so long.

"Ah, yes, them," the caretaker sighed, looking over her shoulder. "They live in water and have developed special films for writing upon and indelible inks from their own bodies."

"Do they travel the stars?" she asked, tracing each black line reverently.

"Oh, my, yes. They have wonderfully designed ships, even if they are getting old, rusty, and unreliable. Their quarters are sealed off from the engines and cargo holds so that they can keep their saltwater environment separate. They can survive in atmosphere for a few hours, but they prefer not to."

"Who do they worship?" Adrial asked, eager to learn their prayers and rituals.

"No one knows. They are rarely seen and never speak of their home world. That translation device is wonderful, taps into brain synapses and interprets the meaning of words . . ." The librarian looked eager to wander off into technological babble.

"And what kinds of cargo do they transport?" Adrial asked, still fascinated by the intricacies of their anatomy. So simple and yet capable of so much with those long tentacles, some terminating in a pincer for grasping, others with sensitive pads for understanding.

"Anything that needs to move from here to there," the caretaker said with disapproval.

"Smugglers?" Adrial asked. She knew she'd need a smuggler or a pirate next time the Law caught up with her. Smugglers knew how to hide their tracks.

"Godless beings who worship only profit. They've destroyed their home world and several others along the way in their quest for more and more money. Just like the Labyrinthians. That is the only book known to be written in the language of Labyrinthe." A contradiction of his previous awe. Interesting. He knew more than he thought he did.

"How can they survive without a God and a planet to fix their place in the universe?" she asked warily.

"Labyrinthians live on and operate the best space stations in the galaxy. The Squids now live in their ships. No one knows for sure how they survive, if they propagate at all, only that their numbers decrease. Good riddance. They contribute little to the overall good since they won't share their translator or their texts. If they have any." He turned on his heel and left Adrial to peruse the book.

By the time she'd finished turning each page, she knew the Labyrinthe language and most of their collected knowledge.

And when she desperately needed to flee the Law and their prison, she'd stumbled on the last of the Squid People negotiating an illegal cargo destined for the First Contact Café.

The last of their kind. Few knew of their existence. Fewer would note their passing.

Leave no trace.

No one would remember Adrial when her time came to join the Gods. A part of her triumphed in succeeding at that deep command. She'd already set into motion a method for ensuring that no one remembered her presence here.

Now if she could just remember what she'd done and how, she could accelerate the plan if needed.

At the same time a deep aching loneliness brought unwanted tears to her eyes. She'd never have friends, a family, someone to love and be loved by.

That must be how Harmony and Her family felt with both the HP and HPS away from home.

She feared for Laudae Sissy and her people, lost and alone without an avatar to keep their Goddess at home. She needed to talk to the priestess.

Her message to the Temple wing met with silence. She repeated it every ten minutes for two hours without an answer.

$\bullet \bullet \bullet \diamond \bullet \bullet \bullet$

CHAPTER FORTY-ONE

JAKE'S COMM BOARD exploded with lights and noise. Beside him, Sissy winced.

Her face still looked pale, with dark circles almost purple enough to match her top caste mark marring her olive complexion.

"FCC Control, this is FCC One. Please jam the excess noise on my frequency. I can't dock this baby with people yelling at me. It's a delicate procedure, and I have to concentrate." He keyed in a code to get him a docking spot near MedBay. The increased speed of the station that gradually widened its orbit would make the docking trickier yet.

"Sorry, FCC One." The male voice of a subordinate officer from the CSS sounded like it winced too. "Lord Lukan isn't too happy with you right now. Ambassador Telvino and Admiral Marella have a few pieces of their minds to lay on you as well. They've all taken over the comm board."

"You can dock a garbage scow with your eyes closed, Jake!" Pammy screamed. The unflappable spymaster must really be upset to raise her voice in those strident tones.

"You done anything to stabilize the orbit of this tin can, Pammy? If not, shut up and let me do my job. Lieutenant Cortini, my orders super-sede theirs when it comes to running the station. Now can the chatter or I crash this shuttle with my VIP passenger aboard."

Three voices shouted in outrage. He couldn't tell one from the other. Not even in their abusive vocabulary.

"FCC Control, I'm cutting all comms. Just make sure that docking bay at MedBay is open and operative. My passenger needs assistance. Put a doc and orderlies with wheeled transport on standby." He slammed his fist against the board, making sure the others heard the thud before the frequency went silent again. His hand didn't like the abuse, but it didn't hurt as if it was broken, just beat up a bit. He could live with that; he'd endured worse.

He hoped they got the reference to Doc Halliday. He didn't want just anyone checking out his Sissy.

"Barely get a line open to the station again and the diplomats coopt it," he muttered.

"Jake, I don't need to go to MedBay. I'm fine now," Sissy insisted.

"No, you aren't. You look like you've been to hell and back." He let his frustration with the less than diplomatic diplomats color his voice with anger.

"Not hell. I think I went to heaven for a bit." She looked wistfully into a distance he couldn't see. "I need to go back."

"Heaven is too close to death for me. You're getting checked out by Doc Halliday or Physician John if you insist on one of your own with a lauded caste mark. They give me an okay on you before anyone else talks to you." He turned his attention to nudging the shuttle up to the bay door and aligning his entrance. He held his breath several times as he matched speeds faster than he was used to. The docking skids were wide enough to adjust to a less than perfect match. Jake prided himself on needing less margin of error than anyone.

"Lord Lukan will want to know why we were gone so long. There will be a scandal because you are out of caste," she said softly.

"He'll have to settle for my explanation. He's not going to berate you until after the doc clears you."

"What will you tell him?"

She turned those wide, pain-filled eyes to him.

"The truth."

"Is the truth enough?"

"It has to be."

He glided into the bay and touched down with only a bit of a sway and thump. He waited while the bay doors closed and the air lock cycled through before he freed himself of flight restraints. He'd barely terminated the final checklist when the hatch burst open, Pammy muscling aside the two diplomats to be first in.

"Where the hell have you been, Jake? You have no business disappearing for forty-eight hours and turning off all your comms," she said, hands on shapely hips, chin thrust forward belligerently.

"I thought you'd outgrown your loose cannon disrespect for authority, General Devlin," Telvino sneered.

"What kind of example have you set for your acolytes, My Laudae," Lord Lukan chimed in right on top of the other two protests.

Sissy slapped Jake's hand away from her own restraints. Then she proceeded to open them by herself, slowly, calmly.

"Lord Lukan, Temple has blithely ignored the relationship mores of the other castes for generations. You have no right to question my actions." She stood as she spoke. Her knees buckled a bit, and she swayed in place.

Jake caught her, just as he would have if he'd still been her bodyguard.

"Ambassador Telvino," Sissy continued as she found her balance—by holding on to the back of the copilot's seat. "As a former military man, you understand the value of following a direct order. General Devlin followed *my* orders." She stiffened her spine, every inch the High Priestess with the authority of life and death over an entire empire of seven planets. "And Admiral Marella, I suggest you look at the source of the interference rather than blame General Devlin for not communicating with you."

She closed her eyes and paled, as if ready to pass out again.

Jake wished he knew for sure if that was an act or not. He didn't think even she had that kind of chutzpah.

"Is there a medic out there?" he called loudly over the shoulders of the intruders. "We need a medic and transport, now!" He grabbed Sissy around the waist.

Her knees continued to sink toward the deck.

Deftly he scooped her up and pushed his way through the crowd.

"What happened out there, Jake?" Lord Lukan called, the only one of the trio truly concerned for Sissy.

"We ran into a spiny plant on our new planet. She had an allergic reaction."

"And now she's having backlash from the high dose of antihistamines," Physician John said. His green triangle caste mark had a new purple circle around it, along with the Spacer yellow star outline. Traces of a red square were embedded in there too. Not too far off Sissy's neat array.

Jake bit his lower lip, desperately willing Sissy to be healthy.

"I'm okay, Jake. I promise."

"I expect a High Priestess to keep her promises," he half grinned. He couldn't manage much more than that until he knew for sure that she'd recovered.

"I'll get better a lot faster if you take me back to the planet," she added with a touch of her usual spunk.

"Later. I promise."

"I expect my General Jake to keep his promises."

Physician John back kicked Pammy to get enough room to run a high-tech diagnostic tool over Sissy's brow and pulse points.

Pammy looked as though she was going to yell at the medic.

Jake quelled her with a glare. Her eyes went wide in disbelief.

"You won't get away with this impertinence, Jake," she hissed.

"Who you going to report me to, Pammy?" He flashed them all a cocky grin and relinquished his precious burden to an orderly with a gurney. "Last I heard, I'm accused of setting up the FCC as an independent state. You agreed with that so you could have the run of the place."

Then he stalked off to Control without a backward glance. He needed another look at the planet survey—the original one, not the one Pammy had given him after she'd had time to alter it. Somebody was going to pay for Sissy's injuries. He didn't much care who.

◆　◆　◆

"Ah, Physician Halliday," Gregor greeted the stocky woman standing in his doorway. "I am starved for company in this isolated corner of the station. Where am I, by the way?" He kept his voice light and conversational, though he had to force himself to keep looking at her bare face.

Didn't these CSS people know how revolting they appeared without the defining caste mark?

"Far removed from anywhere else," the CSS doctor replied curtly. "Now what is so important that you drag me away from my work, halfway to nowhere?"

"I understand that *my* HPS has returned. I need to know that she is safe."

"She'll be okay." Halliday kept looking over her shoulder, as if she needed to be elsewhere or feared she'd been followed.

"Excellent. I hope she is well enough to bear children *soon*."

Halliday returned his look quizzically.

Good. He hoped she was as ignorant of Temple customs as most of her people and his own.

"Physician Halliday, perhaps you do not know that on Harmony the High Priest and High Priestess must . . . um . . . mate. Temple caste is a very small and select group. Many of our children migrate to the Noble caste, the only mingling of castes tolerable. We must produce many children just to keep our ranks filled with properly educated clergy."

"And your point would be?" She moved two steps forward, curious despite her harried workload.

"I am in no condition to . . . um . . ."

"Yeah, yeah. Sex would put too much strain on your heart. Probably kill you. But what a way to go." She quirked a half smile. "You'll get your new heart in about two weeks. If you are lucky."

"Laudae Sissy was elevated to her position over a year ago. In a sense her ordination was also a marriage to me. She needs to bear my child, as proof to all of Harmony that Temple caste thrives and continues to serve them. We've delayed too long as it is. We both felt it better that she complete her education before she took on the responsibility for a child. The stability of our culture is now in jeopardy. We need your help to give us that child."

Sissy could not be allowed to bear Jake's baby and risk an improper caste mark.

Only Gregor's genes were strong enough to guarantee a true child of Temple. A true child he could raise to lead Temple caste and Harmony along the path Gregor knew to be true. Now if they'd just hurry up with that cloned heart so he could live long enough to bring his plans to fruition.

"How?" She wrinkled her brow suspiciously.

"Artificial . . . um . . ." he tried to look embarrassed. He knew enough of CSS sensibilities to recognize their discomfort with the topic.

"Insemination." She supplied him the word, just as Jake used to do for Sissy.

That grated on Gregor's nerves.

"We have little need for it on Harmony. Our physicians do not know how."

"I'm a trauma surgeon assigned to a military vessel. I don't know a lot about it either."

"But you have access to the information."

"Ye—es."

"You also have access to the technology to guarantee that the child will bear only a Temple caste mark on the proper left cheek."

"It's not that easy. Conception is chancy under the best of natural circumstances. Your specifications require a lot more than collecting sperm and shooting it into Laudae Sissy at the optimum moment. She'll need to take hormone therapy for months. Extraction of eggs, genetic manipulation, then reinsertion of fertilized eggs . . ."

Gregor grew cold.

"You do not understand. Laudae Sissy has recently begun a new and inappropriate relationship. I must take matters into my own hands."

"You want her to bear your child, you need her cooperation. I can't give that to you. You have to talk to her."

"She has this need to do things the natural way."

Halliday chuckled. "She has a need to do things her own way."

"There must be something you can do."

"I can assure you that Laudae Sissy did nothing you would be ashamed of while out gallivanting with General Devlin. I assure you. She's sick enough that she won't be doing much for a couple of days either. That's the best I can do for you. You are on your own for the rest of it. Now I've got to get back to real work." Abruptly she turned and vanished down the corridor, laughing to herself.

Gregor threw his water bottle at her departing back. It bounced against the closed door.

Then he had to drag himself out of bed to reclaim it. The effort left him panting and weak and seeing black spots in front of his eyes.

He needed a spy. Someone with two healthy legs who could move about the station, observing and listening. A live person who reported back to him, not a hover cam that returned to Media as a default. He also wanted someone who could bring him accurate news reports from Harmony.

As he plopped back onto the bed, his vision went all white. A radiant figure appeared beside him, her draperies glowing brightly.

His angel.

Her smile stabbed him deeply with emotions he barely recognized and filled him to overflowing with joy.

He felt strength return to his heart just looking at her. "My sanctuary. You offer me sanctuary," he whispered.

Then he felt the slight sting of a stimulant patch against his inner wrist.

"My Laud, you need to return to Harmony," she said. "You don't have time to wait for a new heart. The Goddess is alone, drifting. The planet is in upheaval, and many have died in quakes and storms and eruptions because both you and Laudae Sissy have deserted her. You and Laudae Sissy must return to give Harmony an anchor. Otherwise She cannot find your people. Her people."

Gregor's heart fluttered in sorrow.

CHAPTER FORTY-TWO

JAKE SLIPPED THE PRIVACY latch on his inner office door. Then he accessed the CSS database on Space Base III, the last station where he'd been permanently assigned. The last place he'd been known as Jake Hannigan. Admiral Telvino had commanded, and Pammy had recruited him as one of her spies from there.

He knew SB3's computer system and codes. Well, in the last two years, the techs had probably cycled through six sets of codes. But he knew those techs and their idiosyncrasies. Chances were, his two-year-out-of-date codes had come full circle and been activated again.

Nope, not those. How about the ones before that?

Partial entry to public services. Hmm. If Ron still ran the tactical team, he'd use the same three sets of secondary numbers . . .

Jake tapped his desk impatiently while the computers thought about his entry.

"This password will expire in forty-eight hours. Please change your password."

With a wicked grin, Jake set his own new password. Never know when he might have to do this again.

Bingo! He got past the first wall of security. He met a solid barrier at the next security level. Dan Michaels was good at day-to-day maintenance and winding his way through the maze of hardware. But he didn't have a lot of imagination. Thinking up new codes left him staring blankly and stammering. Jake reversed the numbers and slipped unnoticed into a barely protected archive.

Within seconds the pristine planet survey lay open in front of him.

He scanned the index for plant life. "Thorn of God" the xenobotanists had named the spiked plant. The survey crew called it "Blue hooks" based on appearance, bluish tinge to the leaves and a tiny hook on the end of each spike. Same difference. The sap caused severe allergic reactions, just as his contact had said. Chills, fever, hallucinations. Nearly everyone who encountered the ten-centimeter thorns built up resistance. A second penetration produced only headaches and sinus inflammation. No repeat hallucinations.

Jake would love to know what Sissy had seen while under the influence. He wondered if her previous affinity for the planet Harmony and tendency toward psychic visions would leave her sensitive to the Thorn of God.

"One in one thousand victims of Thorn of God will suffer a worse reaction with each exposure. We suspect multiple transfusions, filtering of the entire circulatory system, and artificial boosting of immune functions would be required upon the third exposure for those sensitive to the plant," the report read.

"I don't want to take that chance again," he muttered.

Then he pulled up the copy of the survey Pammy had given him. Thorn of God wasn't the only plant missing from the catalog. A few predatory carnivores had also walked off the official survey between Pammy's desk and his own.

Both copies indicated archaeology waited to inspect until after the survey crew survived their two weeks of living off the land. Jake didn't think that was standard procedure. On a project this sensitive, archaeology should have been in right behind atmosphere and zoology. The CSS really needed to make sure no one could make a prior claim to the planet.

"What are you up to, Pammy?"

He'd no sooner voiced the thought when his door chimed.

"I'm not here," he yelled and continued reading, comparing the two reports.

The door chimed again.

"What!" He hit the button for audio only.

"General Devlin, I have an interesting prisoner ready for interrogation," Major Roderick said politely. Officious, but polite.

"An interesting prisoner?" Jake mused. He knew of only one prisoner he wanted captured and questioned.

"Bring him in," he ordered, releasing the latch from his desktop.

Major Roderick pushed a misshapen figure before him. Large ears reminiscent of a small elephant in the encyclopedia of extinct mammals flapped forward covering a flat face with barely any nose. A swath of blue and buff fabric and three sets of handcuffs with an extra pair of ankle shackles identified the prisoner as the missing Arachnoid-Labyrinthe crossbreed.

"General Devlin, I'd like to introduce Mac, the phantom of the First Contact Café," Major Roderick said, pushing the stumbling figure forward once more. "He's got something to say about the cargo in the crashed Squid vessel."

"Oh? Like where it came from and why it was carrying an escapee from Maril Law Enforcement?"

Major Roderick raised his eyebrows at that.

"Doc Halliday noticed something odd about Adrial's clothes. They have sensors woven into the synthetic fabric. I did some checking. Only Maril equipment can detect them. Interesting concept. Cuts down on escapees. They have to strip naked to get away from the Law," Jake said. He pretended to give them only half his attention.

Doc Halliday had also reported many scars inside and outside Adrial's body. Evidence of past torture or at the very least repeated severe accidents. Then she'd remembered patient privacy and clammed up.

The words on the screen blurred as he surreptitiously scanned the alien standing before him. Without the handcuffs he could fold the extra limbs into his blousy trousers and shirt. To the uneducated observer, he'd look just like any other Labyrinthe with smaller ears and nose.

Mac remained ruthlessly silent.

"I find it interesting that within a nanosecond of shutting down his computer network, Shuttle One got communications restored," Major Roderick said. He toyed with the knife sheathed at his hip. Harmony officers rarely got used to carrying blasters or even projectile weapons.

After six months on Harmony, Jake still felt naked without at least one knife on his person.

"Interesting, indeed." Jake looked up from his screen. "Now, why would our phantom here want to jam my attempts to seek medical help for Laudae Sissy? She almost died."

Mac's face darkened a shade just before his ears came forward again, hiding him from close scrutiny.

Jake had seen Mac's half brother do the same thing too often to consider it a mask. More like a nervous tick that told him what poker hand he was really holding.

"Is Laudae Sissy okay?" Mac asked from behind his ears.

"Don't know yet. Physician John is still checking her out." Jake deliberately tapped his stylus against the desktop arrhythmically. He needed to keep this being upset and off-balance.

"I would never hurt the Laudae," Mac protested.

"She could have died from an allergic reaction to a plant she touched." Jake leaned forward, pinning Mac with his gaze. "I could have you up on manslaughter charges. Good thing I'm officially CSS; we'd only imprison you on a desert planet and work you death in the salt mines. If I resorted to Harmony's laws we'd take your head. Not a quick and easy death. They chain you to a block so you can't move anything more than your eyelids, alone in a room without windows. No one to keep you company or mourn you. Then you wait. A robot is programmed to swing a Badger Metal blade at a precise angle to take off your head. But the programming is random. The blow could come in a minute, or in an hour. You never know. You just wait, endlessly."

"There is a reason you have never encountered the 'Squid People,' as you call them," Mac said rapidly, folding his ears away from his mouth, just enough so that the words came out unmuffled.

"And that would be?" Jake toyed with a stylus, as if making corrections on the document before him. Actually, he merely marked passages in the original that had been eliminated in the copy.

"I believe the two autopsied by Admiral Marella and returned to continue floating in the abandoned wing were the last mated pair, elderly, beyond procreation. Their ship was also old, beyond repair. I intercepted a distress call at the jump point. They'd lost several major systems. I sent a copy of my report to Doc Halliday because she was curious enough to ask to do the autopsy Admiral Marella had already performed."

"And you didn't alert anyone to the danger the ship was in?" Jake shouted. He initiated a program to hack into Pammy's private files and Doc Halliday's. He wanted that autopsy. Now.

As he suspected, his robot extracted Doc Halliday's copy while still trying to break Pammy's security walls.

"There was no one to alert. And I thought that surely they were far enough away to divert from a direct hit on the station," Mac said quietly.

"Apparently not. You do realize that five people died because of that crash. Two of them children," Major Roderick sneered. He drew the longer of his two knives. The Badger Metal dagger, thirty centimeters long and sharp enough to sever an ear and several fingers and still retain enough edge to take the head.

"They would have lived if they'd obeyed the alarm and evacuated with the rest of your people," Mac protested. "Their own ignorance and fear kept them hiding in their quarters. So they died."

As much as Jake hated to admit it, Mac was right. Responsibility for those five deaths belonged to the Harmony caste system and their policy of keeping the lower classes as uneducated as possible. Don't even tell them enough to keep them safe. Workers are, after all, expendable. They produce too many children as it is.

Jake burned with outrage. Sissy wanted to break the caste system and let Discord rule the empire for a while. He should have let her do it when they had the chance. Instead Jake and Gil had persuaded her to make changes slowly, starting with integrating the schools and absorbing the Poor caste into the workforce rather than denying them the right to work because of a caste mark.

He had to cease dwelling on past wrongs and work on solving current problems. Like addressing the increasing speed of the station and why no one could figure out how the propulsion system worked, let alone how to fix it.

"Why were the Squid People coming here, unannounced, and without entry permits?" Major Roderick asked before Jake could address the concern uppermost in his mind.

"Check the cargo hold." Mac clamped his mouth shut and shifted his gaze to the jump point starscape in the window. "I should like to travel the space lanes," he added wistfully.

"You can leave the station any time after we finish this interview," Jake reassured him. "I'd like you gone so I don't have to keep suspecting you of murdering your brother and two other workers. Of perhaps murdering the entire station by disrupting the propulsion system."

Mac turned a bland face to him, no nervous tics, no change in skin color or elevated respiration. Even the dilation of his pupils remained unchanged.

"I wish I could help with the propulsion. But those engines were designed and built by a race you might call Dwarves. They are as secretive about their habitats as they are about the workings of their machines. My mother knew how to talk to them, what to bribe them with. She is dead." He shrugged and looked genuinely regretful. "I love this station. I would never do anything to permanently jeopardize its safety. You must seek another saboteur. Perhaps a Maril spy?"

"I accept that explanation. For now. What about your brother?"

"I wondered why I couldn't find Number Seven. By the time I did, someone else had taken justice into their own hands. I only wanted him humiliated and returned to our siblings as a failure—a worse crime to them than mere murder."

"What is so important about a hold full of plant-processing equipment?" Jake changed the subject back to the Squid ship, trying to keep Mac off-balance and therefore truthful. "It's not illegal. Turns any vegetation into nutritious texturized food."

Mac continued to stare out the window.

"What do you want, Mac?"

"I want my freedom."

"Why should I grant that? So you can return to your terminals and hack into all my systems, disrupt communications, traffic flow, and even the waste disposal? I can still charge you with attempted murder in the case of Laudae Sissy and manslaughter in the case of the crash. Though I am still considering charges of negligent homicide against your brother's record. I also have to deal with the propulsion problem before we break orbit and drift away into nothingness."

"Number Seven no longer lives. My siblings will discard all record of him and reopen negotiations directly with you. Send his body home as evidence of his failure. That will strengthen your position in the talks."

"The murderer may have killed the wrong person. No way to tell for sure since you all look alike." Jake flashed a mirthless grin. "Why should I send the body home if he is not Number Seven?"

"The body belongs to my half brother. I confirmed his identity. The others will not be recognized or noted by my siblings. I have my reasons for wanting the body returned."

"Sit down and tell me about them. While you're at it, you can tell me about the plant processors in the Squid hold and why they are so special."

"Plant processors do more than make food out of alien plant life."

Jake had to think about that one. Something . . . just on the edge of his memory. Gone.

The comm unit on his desk beeped.

He slapped it off.

It came back on more urgently.

"We have not finished this conversation," he said to both Major Roderick and Mac. Then he opened the line.

"General Devlin, Lieutenant Cortini in Control, sir."

"I know who you are. What?"

"Sir, I think you'd be wise to tune into the news channel from Harmony. This is the first broadcast since the quake disrupted things."

Jake dragged the blinking icon from the corner of the screen to the center. Then he fitted the earpiece so that only he could hear and turned away from the others. Something in the harshness of Cortini's voice told him this was bad news.

"Any out-of-caste relationship has to be considered rape." The speaker looked familiar. Jake had seen the middle-aged man stalk pridefully around Crystal Temple during his undercover months as Sissy's bodyguard. The purple caste mark sparkled, as did only those born and bred at the central religious complex. Except for Sissy. All her caste marks sparkled because of something special within her. And now they glowed with the light of Sanctuary.

"Rape carries the death penalty!" the priest continued. Laud Andrew. That was his name. Temporary replacement for Laud Gregor. But Jake wasn't supposed to know that. "We demand that this CSS spy be returned to Harmony for trial and execution."

Jake's gut sank.

"What is out-of-caste for Laudae Sissy?" asked a mild young man Jake knew well. Little Johnny, chief investigative reporter for the Harmony Broadcasting System and son of the owner of the largest media facility in the empire. He'd recently had his Professional green triangle altered to a vertical black bar as symbol of the unofficial acknowledgment that the Media was now its own caste. "Our High Priestess bears all seven caste marks. Which caste is out-of-caste for her?"

Relief lightened the heaviness in Jake's middle. Little Johnny was an ally. One of the good guys who recognized the need for change on Harmony.

"That man isn't even human," the priest hissed—literally drawing out the sibilant so he sounded like a snake. "He's a spy for the CSS. His caste mark is artificial. He chose to keep the caste mark when he returned to his people. That puts him under our jurisdiction," the priest snarled. He leaned forward so the hover cam concentrated only on him. "We know that underneath the pink skin and humanlike hair that all the CSS are reptilian, unhuman."

Little Johnny did something to push the camera back to a wider view.

"I was not aware that the CSS were anything but human. The most ancient murals in the funerary caves indicate . . ."

"Forgeries foisted upon us by the same CSS spy!" The priest's face darkened. A pulse throbbed in his temple.

"Careful, Andy, or you'll have a stroke," Jake murmured.

Where was Gil? Wasn't he supposed to keep things operating and under control during Gregor's absence?

This debate didn't sound under control.

Still, it was a discussion, broadcast throughout the empire. The first nonemergency telecast after the quake. Previously Crystal Temple would have just ordered Jake kidnapped and executed without the formality of a trial.

"In previous cases of out-of-caste rape brought to justice, the higher caste was always considered the aggressor," Little Johnny said. "But, then, cases of Noble or Temple involvement in out-of-caste relationships are never brought to justice, so we don't know how often they occur. Are you willing to alter the caste system and apply the same law to our High Priestess as to the rest of the empire? Will you arrest and try our beloved Laudae Sissy for this crime, if indeed a crime has been committed? Which has not been verified."

Jake forgot to breathe. Making Temple and Noble accountable to the law, the same as the lower castes, was a major step toward justice, a drastic change that needed to happen.

But not to his Sissy.

He could keep her safe from further plant attacks. He knew how to protect her from assassins.

But this!

He'd kidnap her and take her back to Earth before he'd let that happen.

Then again, the FCC was fast becoming independent. Harmony had no jurisdiction here. Neither did Earth or the Labyrinthe Corporation.

Hmmm.

✦ ✦ ✦ ◇ ✦ ✦ ✦

CHAPTER FORTY-THREE

SISSY SAT UP from the MedBay exam table. It seemed as though lately she'd spent more time in this wing than any other, visiting Adrial and Gregor, discussing Temple politics with Penelope and Guilliam. Now she wanted out, to go back to her girls and the dogs and just do normal everyday paperwork.

And go back to the planet. Her Sanctuary.

"You're breathing fine for now, My Laudae," Physician John said, making notes. "But we might consider changing the filter in your lungs before too long."

"Excuse me, Physician John, I need to talk to this patient," Doc Halliday said, entering the exam room without invitation. Two female nurses with Professional lauded caste marks flanked her. Sissy's two oldest acolytes followed, hands folded prayerfully and eyes downcast.

"Laudae Sissy is not your patient," Physician John edged between Sissy and the interloper.

"No, but General Devlin is, and there are things going down that can hurt my patient." Doc Halliday stood firm, hands on hips, feet braced. She looked ready for a fight, physical or verbal.

"I will talk to Doc Halliday," Sissy said.

"What is this about?" Physician John asked, still not moving from his protective stance.

"Girl talk," Doc Halliday replied, equally rooted in place.

"My patients have no secrets from me."

"There are some things women are reluctant to discuss with their doctors, especially if he's male."

Physician John blushed.

So did Sissy.

"You may leave, John," Sissy said quietly, drawing on all her lessons in excising her authority.

"My Laudae, I formally protest . . ." He swung to face her.

"You may leave. I have my acolytes and two lauded nurses to protect me if necessary," she replied more firmly.

Mouth pursed, eyes narrowed, he retreated to just the other side of the door.

"Close the door, Mary," Doc Halliday instructed the acolyte. "And make sure that obnoxious hover cam and the dogs stay out. I won't have dogs in my MedBay. Bad enough they shed and drool, contaminating the place, but they also snarl and bare their teeth at Adrial. Upsets her to the point of panic attacks."

"I'll turn off the security camera," Martha said. She proceeded to climb on a chair and press a tiny button on a small circle embedded in the wall that Sissy had thought was a place to plug in emergency lifesaving equipment.

"What is this about?" Sissy asked, maintaining the cool tone of one in control. Which she wasn't.

"I need to know exactly what happened while you were off carousing with General Devlin. Then, with your permission, I'd like to give you a physical examination." Doc Halliday stuck her hands into a sanitizer. She withdrew them, looking carefully at the flexible coating left behind.

Sissy recounted, for about the tenth time, how they'd touched down on the planet, she'd stumbled on the uneven ground because the boots of her flight suit were too big and clumsy. "I remember being too hot on the outside and chilled to the bone inside, dizzy, and then I passed out. I woke up about eighteen hours later and we came home."

"What did you see while you were out?" Martha asked breathlessly.

"What makes you think . . . ?"

"We know you," Mary said. "You had a vision."

"Your caste marks glow," Martha added. She reached out to touch Sissy's cheek, then withdrew her hand quickly, as if burned.

"If she had a vision, that's not important," Doc Halliday said. "I've read your chart. Jake slapped some antihistamine patches on you to counteract the plant poison. It worked. Your blood levels are almost back to normal, but you'll be a little fragile for a couple of days."

The nurses nodded agreement from their observing posts in the corners.

"What more do you need to know?" Sissy asked, suddenly apprehensive.

"Have you seen the news out of Harmony since you got back?" Martha asked.

"No. I've been here, no holovids, no flat-screen broadcasts."

"Watch this," Mary instructed. She flipped on a flat screen in the bed-side tabletop. Harmony didn't have holovids yet and broadcast only in two dimensions.

Sissy's mouth dropped in utter horror as the debate between Little Johnny and Laud Andrew replayed before her. Then she clamped her jaw shut in anger.

"How dare he accuse Jake of this."

"He's desperate, trying to hang on to the old ways," Mary said, drop-ping her gaze.

"He's mouthing Laud Gregor's words, fighting to discredit you and any changes you've managed," Martha confirmed. She looked fierce, ready to battle the galaxy—that was Mary's usual stance not Martha's.

"He's only provisional head of Crystal Temple until Laud Gregor re-turns or dies," Sissy mused. "He has to parrot Laud Gregor until he's confirmed HP. Only then can he say what he really thinks. I'm not sure I want to know what he really thinks. There is too much venom in his voice."

"There is one way to dispel this nonsense." Doc Halliday turned off the debate and nudged the table out of the way with her hip. "I suspect that you have never engaged in sexual relations with a man." Matter of fact. No room for embarrassment. Clinical detachment.

Sissy nodded, unable to speak of such a thing in front of so many witnesses.

"I was not raised Temple," she finally ground out.

"I don't know what that signifies. But I can determine if that is true and note it in the medical log. If this 'debate' goes any further, we'll have evidence that Jake did nothing but protect you. Do I have your permis-sion, My Laudae?"

"It's not so bad." Mary took Sissy's hand and squeezed tightly.

"Mary and I had it done before leaving Harmony," Martha added shyly.

"It's good medical practice, to check early and often, catch major prob-lems before they get too big to take care of," Doc Halliday added.

"I was raised Worker caste. We do not go to physicians unless we are very ill. We do not go to the hospital unless severely injured."

Doc Halliday made a derisive noise and grimaced. Then she straightened and put on her bland, professional face. "Do I have your permission to proceed, My Laudae?"

"Y . . . yes. If it will save Jake."

Doc Halliday chuckled. "The whole station knows you two are in love. That broadcast debate is the first clue I've had to why you can't admit it to each other. Glad I didn't join the betting pool on the date of your first kiss, the time of your elopement, or the state of a baby's caste mark. What are the current odds on the kiss?"

"Eighteen to one for. Twenty-five to one on various days this week," one of the nurses said on a chuckle.

Sissy blushed again. And again as she submitted to the humiliating probe. Mary and Martha held her hands tightly the whole time.

"For the record, I'm doing a full gynecological exam, screening for cancers, diseases, and unnatural conditions. That's something every woman needs done regularly. And you are clean and virginal, just as I thought. You can sit up now." Doc Halliday withdrew slightly and stuck her hands back in the sanitizer to strip away the protective glove. "You ladies can go elsewhere. I need to talk to Laudae Sissy about some dirty politics."

"Whatever you have to say to our Laudae, we need to hear," Mary said and Martha nodded agreement.

Sissy nodded. She didn't want to be alone. Doc Halliday's face looked too grim and forbidding.

"Nurses, I thank you for your help. You may go now. Take those tissue samples to the lab and run normal tests."

The two women bowed formally and departed with the sealed vials.

"What is so important that you need privacy?" Sissy finally asked, in control once more, now that she had dressed in fresh clothes the girls had brought.

"Another patient of Physician John's called me for a consult. A patient who isn't supposed to be on station."

Sissy nodded in acknowledgment. No sense in repeating names, in case there was more than one security camera in the area.

"He demanded I artificially inseminate you with his child. Without your consent or knowledge."

Sissy sat back down hard. Her breath caught in her throat. She longed for her inhaler. But she hadn't needed to carry one since coming aboard.

Martha and Mary moved to stand on either side of her, each with a supporting hand on her shoulder. "He wouldn't dare! And he's accusing Jake of rape?" Mary gasped.

"My thoughts exactly. I refused. This is something I would not do without your consent. I could not do it without your cooperation. But I thought you should know. He asked that I manipulate the fertilized egg to make certain the Temple caste mark dominates."

"Send him back to Harmony. Today," Sissy said. Her thoughts and voice hardened.

"Spaceflight would kill him."

"So?"

"Laudae," Martha gasped.

"Think, My Laudae," Mary added. "Here, you know what he's doing, who he's talking to. We reprogrammed one of the hover cams to sit outside his door and feed directly to our desktop. If he survived the trip home, you'd have no way to counter him."

"If he didn't survive, you'd have to deal with Laud Andrew. Can we be sure he'll think for himself. Or will he continue Laud Gregor's policies?" Martha said. "You don't know him."

"Where I come from, we have an old saying," Doc Halliday chuckled. "Keep your friends close, your enemies closer."

"Sun-tzu, an ancient philosopher. Most mistakenly think Machiavelli said it," Sissy confirmed the quote. "I have read bits of Machiavelli's writings. I found him fascinating and boring at the same time. Sun-tzu is more practical and mystical at the same time."

"What if Laud Andrew wants to discredit you at home so he can put his own puppet in your place?" Martha continued.

"You girls are right," Sissy said, feeling deflated. Now what? How did she fight rumor and innuendo?

She could go home. Not that Harmony felt like home anymore.

Penelope had felt that Sissy belonged to more than just Harmony. She belonged to the universe and was the only one who could keep Harmony connected to all the energies of life.

"I have a job to do here. Harmony must continue the alliance with the CSS in order to survive," she murmured.

If she went home, she'd have to leave Jake.

If she went home, she'd never complete her bond with the Goddess of the new planet. Sanctuary.

✦　✦　✦

"General Devlin, perhaps you should step down as commander of the FCC until this cloud of disgrace passes," Mac offered. His hearts glowed with possibilities.

"That might not be a bad idea," Major Roderick confirmed. His eyes brightened with ambition. His need to gain power made him vulnerable and blind to manipulation. A poor candidate to run the FCC.

Mac didn't need to study him closely to understand him. Humans were so easy to read, with formfitting clothing and tight skin, no exoskeleton. They had no way of hiding their emotions. Except maybe Admiral Pamela Marella. That made her too dangerous to manage the balancing act of keeping the FCC running.

"The FCC needs to remain neutral," Mac took back control of the conversation. "Neither CSS nor Harmony should run it."

"Assuming the station remains intact long enough to become a viable presence of trade and diplomacy. You, on the other hand, are loyal to no one but yourself," Jake finished for him, with a sneer.

"I can use the spectacles to full advantage. You can't." Mac bowed his head in acknowledgment, careful to fold his ears behind him. Humans liked looking a person in the eye when talking. They said that the eyes were windows to the soul. Mac had six layers of eyelids. With the first two lowered, he effectively blocked access to his soul. If he had one.

That was a point he'd never examined before. Perhaps Adrial and Laudae Sissy could enlighten him after he took possession of his station and had time to think beyond survival.

"You know this station better than anyone," Jake mused. "You could be an asset to me. To do more, you'd have to constantly and consistently interact with people. Develop relationships. Have any experience with that?"

Mac swallowed around a sudden blockage in his throat. He hadn't thought that far ahead. He needed to. And fast.

Jake reached for a comm button. "Cortini, get Major Mara up here ASAP."

"I can go places no other species can. Except the Dwarves who built the machinery. They have small bodies, but they are inordinately strong for their size," Mac continued his arguments. Maybe he needed a short apprenticeship in relationships before ousting General Jake.

"And you have a talent for working the computer systems to your advantage," Jake continued. "Perhaps the only one better than Mara."

"Yes." Mac decided to acknowledge Mara as near his equal. He could work with her. They thought along similar pathways. That could be his apprenticeship. And being female, Mara could aid him in his courtship of Adrial.

"Before I took over, you also effectively sabotaged every effort to expand trade and make this station profitable, to the point of endangering lives. I'd rather charge you with negligent homicide." Jake threw his stylus onto the desk. "I'll resign when the CSS moves to the new planet and not before. Major, take this being to a secure brig aboard the *Victory*, and keep him shackled with electronic locks so he can't escape."

"Sir, may I suggest we make Mac an ally, a spy. He could help us a lot," Mara said from the door. She flipped the spectacles about while holding one earpiece.

Mac studied her face, amazed at how different she looked with the removal of the caste mark. His thoughts jerked to a halt.

He'd fallen into the shortsighted human habit of looking at only one identifiable point and not the whole person. Now that he truly looked at Mara, in civilian gray blouse and trousers that looked almost like a uniform, with her cap of curls and bright eyes, she could be what the humans called cute.

"Mac has already proved himself untrustworthy. Get him out of my sight. I have a meeting with the ambassadors."

With a shrug, Major Roderick grabbed Mac by the collar and marched him out of the office.

Mara folded the spectacles and held them behind her back, well out of Mac's reach.

"What if I told you that Admiral Marella ordered the plant processors aboard the Squid ship. She'll use them to synthesize a drug from one of the plants on the new planet. A truth serum or a hallucinogenic that will drive the enemy insane," Mac shouted behind him. "Ask yourself if she has a motive to adjust the speed of the station and block contacts to find the Dwarves who can fix it."

"Stop," Jake ordered.

Major Roderick shuffled to a halt, still keeping his hands on Mac's shirt.

"Tell me more."

Mac looked at the major's hand and the shackles.

"Major Roderick, please inform the ambassadors that I will be a little late to their disciplinary hearing. Then take a crew in and recover all of the cargo on the Squid ship. Mara, look for any trace of these elusive Dwarves in any database you can hack into. You can work from here. Mac, you may sit, but the restraints stay until I know for sure you're telling me the truth."

"But, sir," Major Roderick protested.

"No buts. I gave you an order. I'll let you know if this conversation proves productive or leads to more dead ends."

"I will want the freedom of the station in return for this information," Mac offered.

"Will you wear a monitor so I can find you and talk to you at any time?"

Mac suppressed his smile. "Compromise," he told himself and General Jake. "If I have the spectacles, you can reach me through them and the implants they require."

"If Doc Halliday can pull the implants from Number Seven's corpse, I think I can implant them in Mac," Mara said hopefully. "I really want to work with Mac through the spectacles. I've started a preliminary design to adapt a similar unit to human limitations."

"You see, General Jake, compromise is better than war," Mac said. He held up his arms, mutely requesting removal of the handcuffs.

"I learned about compromise from Laudae Sissy. Now sit and talk."

"You know of course that many of the new crew imported by Admiral Marella are her spies . . ."

✦ ✦ ✦ ◇ ✦ ✦ ✦

CHAPTER FORTY-FOUR

GREGOR WATCHED his radiant angel glide forward. She smiled. The entire room seemed brighter. His heart beat stronger.

Then cold sweat dotted his brow, and his hands shook.

"I have just the thing for you, My Laud." The familiar sting of a stimulant patch on the inside of his wrist, right over the big vein. The muted colors of the MedBay became brighter, outlines more precise. And Adrial nearly sparkled in her white gown with her white hair and pale eyes.

"What is all the fuss about in the corridors?" Gregor asked. He couldn't take his eyes off the lovely woman. Tall and slim, her skin seemed translucent, and her pale hair caught the light in a glorious halo like moonlight on a clear night.

"Laudae Sissy has returned. The physicians are making certain she fares well. It seems she had an allergic reaction to something on the new planet. They are talking about the best way to replace the charcoal filters in her lungs." Adrial flitted about the room, touching this, shifting that. Never idle. Her emotions ran across her face as rapidly as her hands moved about every surface of the room.

She flits like a bird, Gregor thought, entranced by the image of a little white fledgling testing its wings, moving from branch to branch, berry to seed patch.

"Is Laudae Sissy all right?" Gregor sat up too quickly, making his head spin. "Nothing must happen to the HPS of all Harmony." He had to choke out the words as his lungs labored and his blood pressure fought to find a balance.

"Easy, My Laud. She fairs well. Harmony is not in jeopardy. Yet." She rested her hand lightly on his shoulder. An elegant, long-fingered hand that contained the power of restoring peace and well-being. Another stimulant patch hit the large vein in his neck.

"These are special combinations of drugs your physicians have never heard of." She caressed the patch, driving the medications deeper into his system. "They will make you stronger than the new heart they clone for you will."

For the first time in many years true desire coursed through his veins. So lovely. His angel was so lovely and ethereal, a lot like he'd envisioned his Goddess.

He cherished the warmth that radiated throughout his body from every place she touched him.

"If you assure me that Sissy fares well, then I can rest easy." He lay back heavily against his mound of pillows.

"Then come. It is time for you to begin walking about and regaining your strength. Soon you must either go home or travel to the new planet. Harmony needs you to ground yourself, otherwise She is set adrift. As this station is adrift."

"The station is firmly anchored in orbit," Gregor countered. "And Harmony is Harmony. She existed before time began. The presence or absence of one or two humans will not alter that." He smiled at her as she helped him off the bed.

His knees wobbled, reminding him that exploring his desire for Adrial was out of the question. She grabbed him about the waist until he steadied, and his joy soared. "What if I falter too far from the bed?"

"I have more drugs to get you back. Rebuilding your strength is most important. Harmony needs Her avatars to communicate with humans, to anchor Her in our lives. Only then will your home world cease its rebellion. I will let nothing happen to you until we find Harmony again."

"Interesting you should say that. Laudae Sissy's acolyte, the one who perished in a fire, said with her dying breath that Harmony can only be restored out here among the stars."

"Then I think we need to take you to the new planet. She must have meant for us to find that place."

✦　✦　✦

"Empty!" Jake exploded into his comm on the private frequency. "How can the Squid ship be empty. That wing is sealed."

"That's what we thought," Major Roderick replied. His voice came through distorted with a lot of background static. "Someone has been in here and removed the entire cargo from the Squid ship. Taken the bodies too. All we've got is a useless hulk half in and half out of our hull. The ice seal has been covered over with construction epoxy. It's permanent now."

Jake looked suspiciously at Mac. He'd removed the shackles in return for information on Adrial's movements into and out of Laud Gregor's suite. Now he considered putting them back.

"You know anything about this, Mac?" he asked, trying desperately to hang onto his temper. What he really wanted to do was slide his Badger Metal dagger between someone's ribs.

"Admiral Marella and I left the ship intact when she autopsied the bodies. I looked to make sure. We placed the Squids inside the forward cockpit. The admiral's team added the additional epoxy. I never saw their faces. I saved a record of it and sent a copy to Doc Halliday. You must look to who ordered the cargo for more answers than that," Mac said quietly. He rubbed the monitor affixed to the wrist of his secondary arm as if it chafed. It shouldn't. The molecular bond gluing it to the skin had proved completely unnoticeable and undetectable to humans.

Mac had to wear the monitor until they transferred Number Seven's implants into his teeth. Mara was certain she could put an extra tracker into one. Even now she was working with a dental tech extracting the tiny electronics from the corpse.

"Are you certain of the addressee on the cargo?"

Mac nodded and kept his ears away from his face so that Jake could look him in the eye. "Look at the record."

"I am." Jake had trouble dividing his attention between the jerky images and Mac.

"I inspected the entire ship, including cargo manifests, right after the accident," Mac said. "I needed to know that it presented no further damage to my . . . to the station."

An interesting slip. Mac considered the station his own. Jake needed to be wary of what the alien would do to take control away from Jake and the CSS. Would that be so bad?

For that matter he needed to be wary of what Major Roderick would do to put Harmony in control of the station.

This station is mine, Jake affirmed to himself.

An icon on his desktop blinked. He touched it and brought up an image of Admiral Pamela Marella sidling through the outer offices toward his inner sanctum. She wore overalls dyed the same gray as most of the bulkheads on the station. Her stealthy movements kept her to the inside wall, moving slowly beneath the normal security cameras but totally ignoring the ones Jake had newly installed by himself in the overhead lighting.

"Sloppy, Pammy. Sloppy for the spymaster." He looked up at Mac.

"Would you take an emergency exit but observe this conversation?" He had to offer the alien some measure of trust before expecting any back.

"Yes, my friend. I will watch and record in the best interest of the safety of *our* station." With those quiet words Mac pocketed the spectacles, extended all of his limbs, and scaled the wall to a vent grating. A quick flick of his pincers on the secondary arm removed the screws on the cover screen. Then he squeezed himself impossibly small and slipped into the duct. He pulled the cover closed and became invisible.

"I just hope you truly are on my side this time," Jake whispered to himself. "I don't think I know how to fight you if you aren't."

Pammy slid into his office without knocking.

"Welcome, Admiral Marella," Jake said without looking up from his desk.

"How . . . ?"

"You trained me well, spymaster. I know everything that happens on this station." Almost everything. Except for that damned propulsion system.

"I recruited and trained you for many reasons. Running this station is not one of them. I need you back in the field, Jake." She clung to the wall beside the door, observing every corner and shadow cautiously.

"Sorry, Pammy. I have other duties now. You'll have to recruit elsewhere. Like half the crew you brought in to help maintain this place." He immediately thought of Mac and shuddered. He really didn't want Mac and Pammy continuing as allies. Unless Jake could be sure Mac worked for him and reported everything Pammy said and did.

Nothing like spying on the spymaster.

"You do have value here if you can get me private offices with my own dock not subject to clearance from Control." She sat in the chair just vacated by Mac. Would she notice any residual body warmth in the synthetic wood? Interesting that she chose that rigid seat rather than the plasfoam one beside it that would conform to her body for a more comfortable position.

"Pick an empty wing and make it your own. I'll launder your rent payments so even one of your auditors won't notice it. But I can't give you privileges to come and go as you please. Might interfere with normal traffic. And traffic is picking up now that I've opened this place to expanding trade routes."

"Not good enough, Jake."

"I suggest you take the wing with the crashed Squid ship. I've heard rumors around station that it's haunted. Only the most desperate of lawbreakers will attempt to break my seals getting in there." He continued as if she hadn't spoken.

Pammy sat back, crossing her arms beneath her breasts and waited.

Jake knew the tactic. She knew how enticing he found her lush body. She knew he had little patience. She knew people back home who could pull his job out from under him.

She'd trained him too well. He'd discovered things far beyond her expectations, and he'd learned from Sissy how to dredge patience out his restlessness. He'd learned to love a sylph of a young woman who commanded through quiet authority rather than intimidation.

Pammy no longer had control of him. And that rankled her.

He leaned back and addressed the ceiling casually. "Have any trouble breaking my seals on that wing for an unauthorized autopsy, Pammy?"

"How did you know?" She sat forward, hands clenched tightly on his desktop. In a less concealing garment her bosom would be practically in his face.

"How much trouble?" he asked with a smug smile.

"Took me damned near an entire night to break your code, what with patrols every half hour—despite the emergency with the refugees—and the layers of encryption. Bad as deciphering Maril—which no human has managed."

"Maybe I need to increase patrols in that area." He flicked his stylus across the desktop as if making a note to himself. "And Harmony is halfway to cracking the Maril codes. I understand that our guest Adrial reads and understands it when she wants to. If you can get two coherent sentences out of her, feel free to interrogate her. What did you do with the bodies?"

"Sent them back home for study."

"I suppose you had no choice," he sighed with genuine regret. "Pity. I have it on good authority they were the last of their kind. They deserved a respectful funeral. Laudae Sissy wants to perform a Grief Blessing."

"There's no one left to mourn," Pammy snorted.

"The universe grieves for their extinction. Laudae Sissy seems to have a direct line of communication with the universe."

Another snort of derision from the spymaster. "They need to be studied. We need to know why such an intelligent species went extinct."

"If you say so. Interesting that the Labyrinthians also nearly went extinct, but they found new life interbreeding." *Thank you Doc Halliday for that little tidbit. Wonder why they didn't use water from their home planet in their cockpit?* "I suppose the Squids had difficulty finding compatible species who could breathe underwater. The Labyrinthians can breathe a variety of atmospheres."

"Enough, Jake. I need privacy and the freedom to come and go as I please. Give it to me or I'll get my own commander in here."

"Doubtful. Harmony won't agree. They only accepted me because I've lived on Harmony and chose to keep my caste mark. CSS agreed because I know Harmony better than anyone not born there, and I was in place and in charge when someone needed to take control. Saved them a bunch of trouble finding a suitable officer with diplomatic credentials and getting him here."

"That caste mark is getting you in trouble, Jake. The substitute High Priest claims it makes you subject to his authority."

"He'll have to fight Laudae Sissy if he files for my extradition. And I'm countering his legal authority over the caste mark with the FCC as an independent state. I'm here for the duration. I'll let you have an entire wing to yourself. Seal it any way you want. Keep as many personnel as you want. But you have to clear ships coming and going with Control. I can't have your flyboys darting in and out without checking to stay out of occupied flight paths."

"Traffic in and out of my dock are not logged. Anywhere. No trails."

"An 'eyes only' log that I delete each time I receive it."

"I set the encryption. Control can record but can't read. Only you can open it. And I change the pass codes randomly."

"If you must. But I'd feel safer setting the encryption myself. If my seals gave you trouble, very few others in civilized space could break them."

"My codes. And I don't pay rent."

"Your codes, and you pay rent like everyone else. And sign a lease. Also encrypted. That way if management ever changes hands, they can't kick you out for nonpayment. You can study the Squid ship minutely, but leave it in place until ownership of the FCC is finalized with Labyrinthe Prime. Then you can break it up for scrap *and* take responsibility for repairing the hull breach."

Pammy ground her teeth but finally nodded agreement. "Maybe I am better off with you out of the field. Who knows what kind of havoc you'd generate running loose."

"Who knows." He paused a moment, thinking desperately how to approach the next subject.

Straightforward and simple, he almost heard Sissy whisper to him.

"Ever heard of a race called Dwarves that build arcane machinery?"

"I might." She gave nothing away. She could either have contact information or be lying to stall and manipulate.

"Then I suggest you call in more favors and get some of them here within the week to fix the propulsion system. Otherwise we won't have a First Contact Café to fight over. Now if you'll excuse me, I have an appointment with the ambassadors. Then I'm meeting the Minister of Trade from Prometheus XII."

"Prometheus XII? The pirate haven of the galaxy?"

"Yep. The first place you sent me after recruiting me. The place where I watched my two comrades . . . my friends . . . die at the hands of those bastards."

Jake took a deep breath. Maybe he'd better skip the meeting with the ambassadors until he had control of his temper.

Putting on a calm face, he continued his explanation to Pammy. "The Marils have been threatening to take over Prometheus XII. Now the bloody pirates want to go legit and sign on with the CSS for protection. Figured they'd have more freedom with us as allies than absorbed forcefully into the Marillon Empire. They're coming to me because I outmaneuvered their pilots and got away with valuable information while on assignment for you. They respect me for being more of a pirate than they are." He couldn't help grinning at that.

"I'll remember that next time I need something from you. This place could replace Prometheus XII as a pirate haven. I have uses for smugglers and outlaws."

"Remember that when you write up your report on what you plan to do with those plant synthesizers. I presume it has something to do with a nasty little shrub called the Thorn of God."

She blanched as she made a hasty exit.

"And add any information you have on the Dwarves."

"I'll remember every word of this conversation at your disciplinary hearing with the ambassadors that began half an hour ago," she threw over her shoulder.

"Give my respects to the ambassadors. But I have more important things to do than listen to them whine. I answer to Laudae Sissy and God. Not to them."

"And me. You answer to me, Jake."

"Think again, Pammy." But she'd already left his office, silent and unnoticed.

Jake returned to the messages piling up on his desktop. "Fragit! I'm not your errand boy, Ambassador Telvino! No more than I am Pammy's."

CHAPTER FORTY-FIVE

SISSY SANK TO HER KNEES before the altar, grateful for five minutes to call her own. Twenty minutes ago she'd had the charcoal filter in her lungs replaced. Physician John wanted her resting in MedBay. Lord Lukan wanted her in conference with Ambassador Telvino. Jake wanted her with him, monitoring her every breath. The girls needed her. She had work to do organizing more relief supplies.

The list was endless.

In here with the candles burning, incense permeating the air, crystals humming, and new murals depicting the creation, no one would disturb her.

Just as she thought that, Monster, her big, shaggy, black dog, poked his muzzle beneath her hand.

She hugged him and ruffled his ears. That was the kind of interruption she liked. The two of them settled in to meditate. Dog, the shorthaired, brown mutt joined them and claimed her other hand.

"What am I to do about Laud Andrew's accusation?" she asked the universe and the dogs. "What am I to do about Laud Gregor?" she asked herself.

Two seconds later the door chime clanged softly once as someone opened the door, then rapidly a second chime as the door closed again.

Sissy held her breath, praying that whoever had sought to disturb her had left again. Doc Halliday had ordered her to rest. Undisturbed.

"My Laudae," a young woman pleaded. "I hate to interrupt your prayers . . ."

"Yes, Mary?" It had to be important if the eldest of Sissy's acolytes dared intrude.

"My Laudae, you have to tell General Jake that we should come along when you visit the planet again. We can't let you go without us. You need us."

Sissy let go a deep breath. "Nothing is decided. I don't even know when the next expedition . . ."

The door chimed again.

"My Laudae, you must intervene. Ambassador Telvino is trying to shut me out of the expedition to the new planet," Lord Lukan said. He stalked to loom over her.

Sissy kept her reverential position, though her knees began to ache.

"Ah, Lord Lukan, I see that you are in need of escaping the station and the increasing discomfort of your wife's pregnancy."

"That is not the case," he spluttered.

"Laudae Sissy, you can't let Laud Gregor go to the new planet. He's not fit for travel," Physician John and Doc Halliday said in unison. The door hadn't signaled closing and reopening, they must have come in hard upon Lukan's heels.

"Is there anyone on this station who doesn't want to go to the new planet?" she asked in exasperation.

"Me," Jake said wearily from the doorway. "Unfortunately, I'm the only one both governments trust to pilot the shuttle. I've got room for six plus Mac and Doc Halliday and the five marines I won't go without. That makes a total of fourteen. No dogs." He glared at the two animals pressed against Sissy's sides.

The mutts relaxed their ears and looked up at him, all cute and hopeful.

He shook his head and moved his gaze back to the ambassadors rather than succumb to the mute appeal. "Make up your minds, folks. The people Laudae Sissy authorizes will meet me in the shuttle bay below Control in one hour. One minute late, you get left behind. One person more than authorized and I scuttle the entire mission. And Pammy can't have any of my Marines."

He, at least, left. The others stayed and demanded that they be allowed on board. They shouted so loudly that the altar crystals hummed in Discord.

"Enough!" Sissy shouted.

"Doc Halliday, you and Laud Gregor may come and bring one helper, Lord Lukan, you and Ambassador Telvino will both come. No assistants, no attendants. I go. That's it. Any arguments and we all stay."

"That's only five," Mary whispered hopefully.

"I don't think we can forget Admiral Marella. She will come, invited or not, so we should plan for her ahead of time. Now get out of here, all of you and leave me to my prayers."

Sissy knelt once more and closed her eyes. She folded her hands together. "Harmony grant me peace and steadiness so that I may perceive Your wisdom in the course I take," she said, out loud. She usually whispered the opening prayer to herself.

One by one the others drifted away. Leaving her with the Discord they had raised and left vibrating against the walls like hammers against the hull.

✦　✦　✦

Adrial shifted her attention from Sissy to Mac, then briefly skimmed over the other occupants of the large shuttle. Seemingly everyone from the First Contact Café needed to check out the new planet, all at once, without anyone else being there "first."

Laud Gregor had insisted upon her presence—after only a little prompting on her part. He'd needed oxygen injections and special tranquilizers to get him through the short hop across hyperspace. (No one had bothered with sleepy drugs for the quick transfer.) Gregor's pale and clammy skin alarmed Doc Halliday more than Adrial.

Adrial knew the old man was tougher than he seemed. His mind even now spun with plots to get Sissy to return to Harmony voluntarily and thus come under his control once more.

Adrial needed to observe how each faction reacted to having real dirt beneath their feet and a planetary Goddess whispering to their souls, even if they didn't listen. "That's my role in life," she whispered to herself. "To watch and learn, not to participate. Only by learning can I achieve Spiritual Purity. Only by following the clues left for me by the Goddess and then erasing all trace of my passage and the clues so that no one can follow me."

Sissy sat before the window screen displaying their approach in real time.

"I've never set foot on a planet before," Mac said from right behind Sissy. The pincers on his secondary limbs clicked rapidly, the only sign of his emotions. The rest of his body seemed relaxed.

Adrial doubted the others could hear the slight noise. Admiral Marella kept looking at Mac with suspicion. But she looked at everyone that way. Trust did not come easily to that woman.

"Land there," Ambassador Telvino told General Jake, who piloted the shuttle. He keyed in the coordinates as well as pointing to a place on the map display.

Adrial admired how the station commander handled the shuttle with smooth grace. She'd never encountered so talented a pilot before. In all the years of her running from planet to planet aboard outlaw and smuggler vessels that had to use the best pilots to avoid capture, no one seemed to meld with their ships as Jake did. As Sissy seemed to meld with her crystal music.

Lord Lukan peered over Telvino's shoulder, noting the landing co-ordinates. Then they put their heads together, whispering in rapid half sentences.

"We're ten klicks from where Laudae Sissy and I landed," Jake said to everyone and no one. "Everyone keep an eye out for the spiny plant called blue hooks by the survey team because of the color of the foliage and the hook on the end of each spike. The botanists list it as Thorn of God. If it pricks you, the sap will give you hallucinations."

Adrial didn't care what Jake had to say. She tried to listen to the ambassadors but caught only a hushed word or two.

"Building site." "Water cleared." "Open and level." "Need Workers to farm."

She heard enough to surmise that Telvino directed General Jake to the site selected for building the new CSS headquarters.

General Jake set the shuttle down so smoothly, Adrial couldn't tell the moment they stopped flying and came to rest dirtside.

"Okay, everybody. We're prepared to spend the night. Ambassador Telvino and I will set up the plasfoam shelters with the help of our Military guards. The tents will become quarters for the construction crews later. While we are here, no one, absolutely no one, goes anywhere alone." He looked directly at Admiral Marella as he barked out the orders.

"You will have a minimum of three in each party. You may explore no more than one hour's walk in any direction; then you must return or call in. Anyone absent for more than two hours and ten minutes will be considered missing and injured. We will commence search and rescue procedures at that time. False alarms will result in confinement aboard the shuttle. If I send the 'all in' signal, I mean it. *Everyone* back to base camp with all due haste. The comms will guide you back." With that announcement he handed comm units to everyone, including Adrial and Mac.

A thrill of pride ran through Adrial. She'd never been trusted with expensive equipment like this before. No one had cared about her presence or absence. Or noted it.

Laud Gregor looked at the unit with disdain.

Doc Halliday slapped it onto his wrist. "You'll wear it and abide by basic safety rules, or I handcuff you to this seat for the duration," she said quietly. "I need to collect plants for analysis of potential medical purposes. I'm with Laudae Sissy and Adrial."

"I shall join you, honored Physician." Mac bowed formally.

A flare of jealousy, hot and prickly, flashed through Adrial. She needed Sissy to herself. If she had to add a third, she wanted Laud Gregor with her. Sissy would cling to Adrial rather than acknowledge Gregor's presence.

"Laud Gregor, you may stay in camp with General Devlin and myself," Ambassador Telvino said. "I know you need to rest."

"That leaves Lord Lukan and a Military with Admiral Marella." General Jake smiled at the woman. He looked smug and just a bit nasty. The Military wore a Harmony uniform, boasted an enobled red square caste mark, and carried a blaster and several bladed weapons. He'd not recognize the admiral as his superior. "Pammy, I trust you to take good care of the ambassador and not go off on your own private mission."

"Jake . . ." she said with a touch of warning.

"I don't care how well trained you are in wilderness survival. You stay with your group. I'm in charge. Violate the rules, and you'll suffer the same restrictions as Laud Gregor, handcuffed to the least comfortable jump seat in the shuttle."

"I don't think I like you anymore, Jake. You're too much like me," Admiral Marella spat. "You think too much. I hired you for your beauty not your brains."

"Sorry, Pammy. You got both." He flashed her one of his heart-melting smiles.

Now Adrial understood why Sissy loved him. If she had time for love, Adrial might just flirt with him a bit herself.

"Jake, leave the Military in camp and come with the ambassador and me," Admiral Marella said mildly. She shifted her posture to emphasize her sensuality.

"Rules are the pilot stays with the shuttle." Jake turned his back on her and began pointing out the crates of equipment he needed outside to the lowest-ranking Military.

"And when did our beloved Jake find so much interest in rules and safety," Telvino muttered. "I liked him better when I could bust him back to enlisted and slap him in the brig."

Interesting. Adrial filed that bit of interplay away for examination later. She noted Mac taking careful note as well.

Then Doc Halliday interrupted her musing by grabbing her hand and dragging her toward the hatch that slowly swung upward. "Come on, we've got a lot to do and not a lot of time to do it in."

"Jake, I am going to explore that cliff line to the west. It looks like it might contain caves," Sissy said excitedly.

"An hour out and an hour back. No more. Or I come looking for you in a temper. And you know you don't like me when my temper is up," General Jake replied. His fingers twitched nervously on the grip of his belt dagger.

Adrial sidled away from him. She'd known too many Law who liked playing with knives. Most of them didn't care who or what they found for a target. She had the scars to prove it.

"Before we separate, we need a moment of prayer," Sissy announced.

Adrial barely heard her voice, yet the intent of the words stabbed her mind with piercing clarity.

Sissy stood tall with arms spread, palms out in blessing. Despite her petite frame she suddenly dominated the scene, a glowing tower of divine authority. "Gods above and below, Goddess all around us, we ask Your blessing in this grand enterprise of exploration to found a new home; a place where worlds may share their plenty with those who lack; where peoples at odds with each other can negotiate compromise."

As she bowed her head, Laud Gregor sighed with weary impatience.

Adrial elbowed him to silence. Then they both stared in openmouthed awe as a benign aura glowed around Sissy's head.

"She has found what I seek," Adrial whispered.

"How do I fight that?" Gregor added. His face nearly crumpled in regret. "I'll find the tricks and gadgetry she manipulates. If I can't control her for the good of Harmony, I'll prove her a false prophet."

$\diamond$ $\diamond$ $\diamond$ $\diamond$ $\diamond$ $\diamond$ $\diamond$

CHAPTER FORTY-SIX

S **ISSY BARELY HEARD** Doc Halliday and Mac discussing strategy for gathering more plant samples. She wandered toward an intriguing shadow on the cliff face a few yards away.

Low-growing shrubs tugged at her pant legs. Clouds of pollen rose with her passing. She reveled in the subtle fragrances, so much gentler and more comfortable than the constant citrus tang to the artificial air on the station.

She sneezed heavily and didn't mind. The new filter should handle these pollens.

"Mac, will you climb that tree and gather samples?" Mariah Halliday stood at the base of a towering tree with frothy fronds for branches. "I need new bark from slender limbs, older and thicker bark from the trunk, new and mature leaves. You know how I like them labeled."

He'd gathered and labeled hundreds of plants in the last half hour, moving swiftly up and down trees, across branches, and through shrubbery more quickly and easily than any human.

Mac obliged by scrambling up the tree and disappearing into the blue-greenery. He seemed very comfortable for a person who'd never walked dirtside before. His willingness to climb high up in the canopy reflected the delight in his eyes at the opportunity to explore a level not as easily accessible to the humans.

Sissy let her fingers roam over inscribed marks around the arch of the natural cave that had been smoothed and rounded by intelligent hands. Tiny frissons of energy shot from her fingertips to her mind. Her heart pounded loudly in her ears. Air moved sharply and shallowly through her lungs. She forgot her need for an inhaler in her excitement.

A familiar series of curves and lines seemed to jump out at her from the jumble.

"Harmony," she breathed. "Harmony is here. And a new one . . ." She traced again and again the name of a companion Goddess, or possibly an augmentation of the simpler glyph for Harmony.

She placed her palm flat against the markings and closed her eyes in bliss. From one heartbeat to the next she shifted from here to there, now to then.

She saw herself inside a small cavern within the cave, lying flat on one of seven stone ledges arranged in a circle.

She'd been here before.

Seven flat rocks defined another circle at the center. Seven smudge pots on ledges sent the heady smoke of the Thorn of God upward in lazy spirals. The roof caught the smoke and pushed it back downward. She breathed deeply and dreamed of soaring high above the island continent upon her own feathered wings.

The Seven Gods joined her and whispered secrets into her mind.

You have come back at last to complete the sacred rituals. Soon we will have fledglings, specially blessed by the Gods to help our empire grow.

A benevolent and dreamy haze descended upon her mind and body. The energy of the universe reached out to enfold her, welcome her, send signals of this ceremony all across the galaxy to any receptive mind, sharing in the good luck and blessings. Her back arched in ecstasy, and she knew that new life began within her. She reached for her life mate in gratitude.

"Sanctuary," Adrial said, jolting Sissy back to reality. "Sanctuary grows out from Harmony, or Harmony grows in the core of Sanctuary; no two scholars agree. See how you can remove these few lines, and your Goddess becomes the center." She too stood entranced, fingers and chin trembling with excitement.

Sissy shook with the shock of abrupt separation from her vision. She couldn't seem to pry her hand away from the sigils carved into the living bones of the planetary Goddess.

"These marks are very old," Doc Halliday remarked. "We aren't the first intelligent beings to come here, but none have been here for a long, long time." She held up a gadget with a tiny screen. She'd used it before on plants. A very different graph appeared, with rising and falling lines in many different colors. Many more colors and lines than had appeared for plant study.

"What does this tell you?" Sissy asked, desperately trying to keep her teeth from chattering. She couldn't share her vision with these two. It was so intense, so right, and yet so wrong. She felt empty at the knowledge that she had participated in that ritual only remotely. No life blossomed in her womb.

She forced herself to study the information on the screen. Before Laud Gregor found her and elevated her to High Priestess, she'd spent most of her life from the age of twelve assembling interstellar navigation units. She knew how to read graphs and pictures. Written words took more work for her.

"I'm reading the elemental components of the rock, the algae, moss, and the natural aging patina. Combine them all and I can estimate that carving was done about one thousand Earth years ago."

"That's a long time." Sissy whistled through her teeth. More than three centuries before the original inhabitants of Harmony left Earth to found a new culture based on their religion. They were considered a not very respectable cult on Earth.

Worship of the Seven Gods had become the basis of a stable and peaceful society. Until recently. But like most artificial constructs (including the genetically engineered caste marks), eventually the social system of seven castes had begun breaking apart.

Mac swung down, gripping a branch about twice Sissy's height from the ground with his four lower limbs. He dropped a neat packet at Doc Halliday's feet. Then he disappeared back into the tree.

"One thousand Earth years ago was just after the time the Marils first ventured into space from their home world," Adrial added, as if she hadn't noticed the slight interruption. She continued feeling the writing. "These are consistent with the culture and religion of that time."

"How do you know so much?" Sissy asked. Suddenly she wasn't certain she should trust this woman. She seemed more alien than Mac with her ethereal thinness, her elongated fingers, oddly slanted eyes, and that nimbus of moonlight-pale hair floating around her head.

"I've bounced from planet to planet, studying the Messengers of the Gods. I had to learn to read their language and understand their religion—which is very history oriented. They revere their ancestors because they have joined the Gods in death."

That struck a chord within Sissy. How many funerals and Grief Blessings had she celebrated as she returned the dead to Harmony's womb so they could join with the Goddess? Every year her family made the long and arduous journey to the funerary caves to make offerings to the dead.

A breath of air passed her on its way inside the cave.

The caverns breathed, just as on Harmony.

"I need to go inside the cave. In here I can find my way back to Harmony through Sanctuary," Sissy said. She set her chin and took the first step beyond the archway before Doc Halliday grabbed her arm.

"That's not a good idea. Abandoned caves are ideal lairs for large animals of prey, small poisonous bats and insects, and who knows what else," the physician said clucking her tongue. Her fingers gripped Sissy's arm so tightly she felt bruises rising.

"There are ghosts here," Adrial said. She backed off rapidly, waving her hands in front of her face as if brushing aside a hunter's net or invisible spirits. Her entire body shook, and sweat broke out on her face. "Evil ghosts, hungry to rob you of your soul to replace the ones they lost." She turned and began running back the way they'd come. Her breath caught like sobs, or the beginning of screams of pain.

Mac dropped down in front of her, holding yet another packet. "General Jake says we must stay together," the alien said firmly. "But I agree, our time here has nearly expired. We should return to base camp."

Just then Sissy's comm unit began vibrating and beeping urgently. "All in," scrolled across the tiny screen, pulsing urgently, demanding her attention.

Jake. Her heart lifted a moment at the thought of him. Her life mate. The one she needed to complete the sacred rituals of Sanctuary. Then her mood sank as she realized she'd have to forgo exploration of this cave. Gently she kissed her fingertips and touched them to the markings. She sighed in regret as she turned to retrace her steps to base camp.

In the back of her mind she heard an echo of that sigh from deep within the cave.

CHAPTER FORTY-SEVEN

GREGOR PICKED HIS WAY around the rough circle Jake and Telvino had drawn as the boundary of base camp. Dirt and rocks, a few scrubby plants. His nose twitched with the need to sneeze out the dust.

Untamed and uncivilized. In his mind's eye he pictured a replica of the Crystal Temple gracing the center of the little plateau, with acres and acres of cultivated fields in the river valley below. He imagined the scent of mint and new-mown hay on the gentle breeze. Like a painter adding details, he embroidered the fragrance with a touch of salt from the nearby sea and cedar from the stand of trees at the perimeter of the camp. The vision became more real than the bleak vista before him. He stood entranced, gazing inward and smiling.

A magnificent retirement home took shape in his imagination, just there, on the edge of the river. Close enough to keep an eye on the politics of this new alliance, far enough away to have peace and quiet when he wanted it. And fish in the river. He wanted to spend hours of every day just sitting in a little boat, or on a dock, with a line drifting in the clear water.

"A perfect sanctuary," he said.

"Huh?" Jake looked up from where he set a complicated frame for an ugly temporary shelter. "Did you call this place Sanctuary?"

Telvino and the Military paused as well.

"Yes, I guess I did," Gregor admitted. "A place of peace and protection from the harsh realities of war and mixing with aliens, where the real work of forging alliances can be made."

"That's not exactly what Laudae Sissy said. But close enough. She's been calling it Sanctuary since we came here." Jake shrugged and returned to his work layering sheets of inert plastic over a basketwork frame.

A Military held the final sheet of catalyst ready to lay over the top.

Once in place, the two substances would do something to produce heat and foam, quickly expanding and then hardening into a solid insulated dome.

Ugly. No craftsmanship. No reverence for harmonizing the elements. But practical.

Gregor expected little else from the CSS. Godless creatures with no soul. Allowing each individual to choose his or her own God and method of worship or to choose to ignore all Gods—he shuddered at the thought—invited Chaos and Discord. No wonder they were at war. Harmony had maintained peace since the beginning of time by imposing order and structure upon all the castes.

A frisson of energy rippled through the ground and up through his feet. As if the Goddess awakened and stretched.

Sissy calls us.

Huh?

"That larger structure should go ten feet to the left," Gregor told Jake.

"Can't. The soil is too soft there, too close to the embankment. One good rain will wash it all down into the river," Jake replied absently. He wove two lengths of plastic framing into a third.

"The harmonious esthetics are out of balance. But I can't expect CSS barbarians to understand that."

Jake and Telvino ignored him.

The CSS manages an alliance that crosses fifteen member worlds and fifty trading alliances. You barely hold together seven, a feminine voice whispered into the back of his mind. She sounded like Sissy, but the accent was wrong.

He dismissed the idea as fatigue preying upon his overtaxed body.

"I need to sit, Ambassador Telvino."

"Two choices. Pull up a convenient rock or go back inside the shuttle," Jake said distractedly. He studied the instructions for stretching a frame for a larger structure.

Telvino buried his nose in the same diagram, ignoring Gregor as much as possible.

"Hrmf," Gregor snorted. He pulled out his handkerchief and dusted off a flat rock. A curiously flat rock. He hadn't spent much time out of doors in other than precisely laid out and maintained landscapes, but he thought rocks should be rougher and rounder in the wild.

Bright sunlight glistened against the spot he'd cleaned. Curves and lines jumped out at him, like ancient writing in the funerary caves.

Slowly he dropped to his knees, bracing himself heavily with his hands on the edges of the rock. He'd studied the glyphs as a child under his father's tutelage in the Temple library. That was when everyone expected him to follow in his father's footsteps. But Gregor had higher ambitions and worked hard to rise above the boring position of librarian.

Still, the early lessons lingered. Then last year when Sissy had undertaken a scientific and historic examination of the funerary caves, she'd discovered whole murals recording early life on Harmony. Entire stories had been compacted into colored glyphs, piling numerous abstract ideas into one panel.

Here he faced more evidence that Harmonites had been the first humans, not that they'd come from the same roots as the CSS.

He traced first one pictograph and then another, the roughness of the surface chafing and sensitizing his fingertips. The rippling in the ground he'd felt earlier intensified through the rock into his hands, awakening new ideas, broadening his awareness of the entire camp while concentrating his vision on the array of dancing figures. Quickly he sensed that the story began bottom right and moved back and forth across the stone. That was different from modern writing, but not unheard of in ancient texts in forgotten languages.

He recognized perhaps one image in seven.

This writing was truly ancient, possibly predating the earliest records on Harmony.

This is the beginning place, the Goddess told him. *This is where life begins.*

His heart began beating rapidly in his excitement. Blood pounded in his ears, and his skin grew clammy. He'd made possibly the greatest historical discovery of all time. Sanctuary was the home world of Harmony, not Earth. Harmony emerges only from Sanctuary. He had proof right here before his eyes. He had proof that humanity had split here, the higher beings going to Harmony, the disorganized cults wandering off to Earth and other places.

But why had they left? The planet was lush and the climate benign.

He leaned closer, trying to puzzle out the sections he did not recognize at first glance. His hands slid off the rock. Blindly he sought to brace himself on the ground.

"No, Laud Gregor! Don't put your hand there!" Jake yelled.

Gregor looked up confused. As he sought better balance his hand closed around the branch of a low shrub. It looked sturdy enough.

Sharp pain stabbed his palm and quickly shot upward to his eyes.

He looked down, surprised, as his focus narrowed and darkness crowded in from the edges. Blood welled up from the center of his palm and dripped copiously down his arm.

The scent of fresh mint grew stronger.

"Fascinating," he murmured, unable to yank his gaze away from his own life draining out of him.

Welcome to my Sanctuary. Join me in peace. Let the end of your life become the beginning of another.

A blinding white light crowded out the red blood in the center of his vision. Blackest darkness surrounded it all. The outline of a female clad in brilliant white robes with green undertones blowing in a celestial wind walked out of the brightness. She seemed to catch his wilting body and cradle his suddenly heavy limbs against her.

Why have you rejected me so often and for so long?

"I have never rejected you, Harmony." He didn't know if he'd spoken or not. He couldn't hear his words.

You sought power and control at the cost of other lives. You manipulated the Covenant for your own ends.

"I did what I thought best for all of Harmony—the mother planet and the six colonies."

Was it best for Harmony, or best for Gregor?

Shame filled him. What had he done to offend the Gods? He couldn't remember.

"Sissy? Should I have left her to die in the collapsing factory, or sent her to the asylum?"

Bringing Sissy to the people was the best thing you could have done for Harmony. For the galaxy. She has brought renewal to Our people.

Gregor found it hard to think. If he knew what he'd done to offend Harmony, he'd know how to atone.

For the gift of Sissy, We forgive you all. For bringing people back to this place, to the beginning place, we grant you blessing.

An amazing sense of peace filled Gregor's straining heart. At last, he'd found Harmony within Sanctuary. He wanted nothing more than to join with Her, to share the overwhelming peace with Her. To become one with the planet, the home of humanity.

"Laud Gregor, wake up. I need you to stay awake until Doc Halliday gets here," Jake ordered. He held Gregor's wounded hand high, slowing the drip, drip, drip of blood.

"My blood must feed Sanctuary. You must let me join with Her." He slurred his whisper, though the words sounded loud and clear in his mind.

"Don't you dare die on me. Stay with me, Gregor. Stay awake. We'll get you patched up and counter the allergic reaction with drugs. Just stay awake."

"Bury me here. I have found Sanctuary."

♦ ♦ ♦ ◇ ♦ ♦ ♦

CHAPTER FORTY-EIGHT

"OXYGEN. GIVE HIM OXYGEN injections and vasodilator patches,"
Doc Halliday ordered breathlessly over the comm. She sounded
as if she were running.

She couldn't get here fast enough for Jake.

He found the injection ampoules in the first aid kit and slapped two of
them into Gregor's chest directly above his heart. He put the patches on
the inside of his unaffected wrist.

"What about the antihistamines? They worked for Sissy." He debated
applying one to the wound.

"I don't know. His heart is so fragile, the shock may shut it down. I
thought he was stronger. He acted a lot stronger than the tests indicated."
The doc's words caught and faltered.

When she came back on-line, she sounded almost angry. "If he wasn't
getting better, then he was taking stimulants. Good lord, if he was taking
stimulants, he was killing himself."

"He's got a heck of a lot of toxins pouring through him. Isn't that more
dangerous than the antidote?" Jake looked around for any sign of the
physician. She should burst through the tree line at any moment according to his tracking system.

"Just give him more oxygen and keep him breathing until I can test his
blood. And clean the wound. Gently. Is it still bleeding?"

"No. But the hand and arm are a swollen bloody mess. The High Priest
of Harmony has lost a lot of blood."

"Damn. Blood thinners. Check his blood pressure with the
ultrasound."

"One hundred over seventy, eighty over sixty. It's plummeting." Panic
tightened Jake's throat.

"Lay the wounded arm on the ground below his heart. The toxins will have to work harder to reach vital organs. It might give us a vital few minutes. Is there a vial of Oxydigitalin?"

"No." Jake dumped the first aid bag and pawed through the drug kit.

"Get some from my bag. Inject it directly into the heart."

"Um . . . I don't know if I can do that."

"You've got to."

"He's looking mighty pale and clammy. I've got blue on the fingernails and around the lips," Jake reported.

"Pulse?"

"Rapid and thready. Breathing very shallow."

"Damnit all. Give him more oxygen. Then give him the Oxydigitalin. That should raise his blood pressure. You've got to keep him alive."

Still no sign of the doctor and her party. Nor of Pammy and Lord Lukan. At least Telvino had the sense to keep one Military occupied readying the shelters, staying out of the way. The other Military men ran back and forth to the shuttle for Jake. One of them brought the doctor's black bag. The injection pen of Oxydigitalin was empty, and there was no vial to refill it.

"Damnit, I know I put a full vial in before we left and added two replacements," Doc Halliday cursed. Still too far away.

Not knowing what else to do, Jake got the Military to make a bed out of emergency blankets and roll Gregor onto it.

The High Priest groaned something about joining with the Goddess.

The Military from Harmony paused long enough to make a circle of their thumbs and index fingers, with the rest of the hand splayed wide, the symbol of Harmony and the sun Empathy joining together.

"You aren't going to the Goddess, Gregor. Not yet. Not on my watch." Cursing Doc Halliday for taking so long, he slapped the antihistamine patch directly over the entry wound. "Sissy, forgive me if this is the wrong thing to do."

✦　✦　✦

Mac lifted Doc Halliday over a fallen tree trunk, then scrambled after her. She stumbled on the downside. Sensing the urgency in her instructions to Jake, he finally lifted her in his secondary arms and continued swinging through the dense forest with greater ease than she could manage on her shorter two legs.

"Can't you go any faster?" Doc Halliday asked. "Gregor is dying."

Behind him, Sissy and Adrial hurried in his wake. He didn't like the wet, wheezy quality in Sissy's breathing. It had no rhythm, a discordant resonance.

"I cannot carry you both at this speed," he said before increasing his pace. "Adrial, help the Laudae, make her slow down and breathe as deeply as possible."

Then he dropped to six legs, keeping the physician elevated above the ground cover shrubs. His limbs shifted, grasped, thrust aside, all obstacles in a straight line toward base camp. In just a few steps he could no longer hear Sissy and Adrial thrashing behind him.

Worry ate away at his speed. He couldn't abandon Sissy. He had to get Doc back with haste. Which was more important?

"She'll be okay longer than Laud Gregor will. Get me within sight of camp. Then you can go back for her," Doc said, as if she'd read his mind.

Decision made, he applied himself to moving as quickly as possible.

"You're a good person," Doc said, patting his chest when he finally deposited her at the edge of the meadow. "I can manage from here."

Mac didn't wait for further orders. He spun and dashed back the way he'd come.

Within the depths of the trees he lost all sense of direction. He had no familiar markings on metal ducts or the sound of the tram and lifts to orient himself. His path was obscured by the vibrant foliage that had sprung back. Sound seemed muffled by the soft, springy ground and creeping plants. He swiveled his ears seeking a trace of Laudae Sissy and Adrial.

Avian and insect life-forms chirped and chattered randomly. Was there a pattern or intelligence behind any of the communications or only pure instinct?

Finally he caught a hint of a labored breath. And yes, there, a voice singing something soft and soothing. A chirpy voice full of clicks and whistles. It sounded almost Maril in nature.

Adrial. She sang a hymn of gentle praise for one of her Goddesses.

Mac raced up the nearest tree and bounded through the canopy much faster than he could run along the ground. A kilometer, maybe two, took him to a spot above the two women. He clambered down the trunk, letting the suckers on his primary fingertips use the rough bark for traction.

Sissy's pale face scared him. Each of her breaths came shallowly. She winced in pain. The muscles in her throat bulged with tension.

He'd left her too long. The first person to ever show him consideration was dying before his eyes.

✦   ✦   ✦

"Laudae Sissy, you can't allow this Goddess to take you. I have so much more to learn from you. If you die now, I must return to the Law and allow them to take judgment against me. I must delay my enlightenment until my next life," Adrial cried.

She choked out another stanza of the hymn of death and regret. It should be a joyful celebration that Sissy's soul joined her ancestors. Instead, Adrial turned it into a dirge of regret for her own loss.

Mac rattling about in the branches above alerted her to his presence. She cursed when his movements broke her concentration and she forgot the next verse of the complicated hymn.

When he dropped in front of her, she faked a squeak of alarm and placed her hand over her chest as if to calm her racing heart. The soft moss and spongy leaf litter absorbed the sound of his impact.

"I will take Laudae Sissy to Doc Halliday for help," Mac said. "You must follow as quickly as possible." He reached out a primary hand and stroked her hair with a finger.

"Not . . . Doc," Sissy gasped. "Jake. You have to take me to Jake. He knows what . . ." The rest of the sentence got lost in her desperate search for air.

"I have to go, Adrial. Please follow and walk carefully." Mac scooped up the High Priestess and took off.

Adrial struggled to her feet. "That's not the right way, Mac," she called after his retreating figure.

"It is. Consult the coordinates on your comm unit." With that he hastened his pace beyond anything she could manage without hiking up her skirts and moving faster than dignity allowed.

"The coordinates of technology do not reflect the path of enlightenment," she quoted some long-dead mentor.

Mac had moved too far ahead to reply. Oh, well, she might as well go back to base camp. She'd learned what she needed to know about the inscriptions at the cave. This planet had been a spiritual home for the Maril, possibly the planet of their origin. More likely a place of retreat and meditation. One of many. For all their warlike tendencies, the Messengers of the Gods took great pride and comfort in their spirituality.

Or . . . Or . . . could it truly be one of the sacred ritual planets? She'd heard rumors that once upon a time the Maril considered the creation of a child the most blessed of all rituals, to be celebrated only in sacred caves on specially sanctified planets chosen by the Gods. Observed and carefully noted by priests and political leaders, augmented by incense and chants. Children born of such a conception became leaders both politically and spiritually.

Ordinary people took part in similar rituals closer to home in grand temples rather than within the womb of the Gods.

But the rituals had changed many generations ago, and the elite used the special temples now. Ordinary people went to neighborhood worship centers. The sanctuary planets for breeding and burial were all but forgotten.

Why?

Politics changed away from the need to improve the soul. Politics often got in the way of their enlightenment, and their spiritual homes became too expensive, or made them think of the consequences of their actions. So they abandoned them, only to found new ones during a later administration. They eventually abandoned those too.

Or, as happened on Harmony, the humans took over the planet, not knowing the meaning of the ritual caves. They tainted the entire planet with new rituals, new sacred spots.

She doubted the cave held any more information. The Maril had looted any books or scrolls long ago and housed them in libraries across the empire. She'd been to most of those.

The majority now lay in burned ruins useless to anyone else.

"On to the next teacher," she sighed. "I'm sorry Sissy is dying. She had a lot more to teach me."

CHAPTER FORTY-NINE

J**AKE TOOK ONE LOOK** at Sissy's limp form and cursed, long and loud. Telvino looked at him sharply. Doc Halliday raised her eyebrows then went back to whatever she needed to do to stabilize Laud Gregor.

Out of long habit Jake slapped the multitude of pockets in his old Harmony uniform, seeking an inhaler.

Ah! Tucked away in the calf pocket he encountered a hard lump. He fished out the inhaler he'd stashed there a year ago, before he left Harmony. A quick check showed him it still had a couple doses of medication. Out of date? Probably. Worth a try anyway.

Mac sank down onto his knees, still cradling Sissy against his body. He looked exhausted.

"I have to go back for Adrial," he said quietly.

"Rest a moment." Jake placed his hand heavily on the being's shoulder. "I've got Sissy."

Sitting cross-legged, he shifted her slight body to his own lap and shoved the inhaler between her blueing lips.

One shot.

He counted to sixty very slowly. His heart rose to his throat. "Harmony, don't let me be too late," he prayed.

No change. Shallow breaths, arrhythmical. Out of tune with the rest of her body.

A second shot. He pressed down harder on the plunger than he should. The dosage level dropped by two.

He nearly choked, afraid he'd given her too much. A backlash might kill her faster than the alien pollens and dust.

"What's wrong with her?" Doc Halliday asked, sparing them a glance from Gregor.

"She inhaled a hellish amount of dust and vaporized bio-plastic during a quake back on Harmony. The physicians implanted a charcoal filter to clear her lungs."

Doc nodded in approval of the procedure. "Physician John replaced it this morning. It was clogged from your last trip here. Shouldn't have filled up so quickly."

"She used an inhaler a lot back on Harmony, mostly when under stress. I haven't seen her use one since she got to FCC. This is an old one. Probably out of date."

"No dust or pollen in the station's artificial atmosphere," Doc replied. She signaled the Military to help her get Gregor raised to a forty-five degree angle.

The High Priest still looked ghastly, gray skin, thin eyelids closed, but he breathed.

"Your new heart isn't quite ready, My Laud," she said. "But I'm willing to take a chance on transplant the moment we arrive back at the station. Better a premature heart than a dead one."

In Jake's arms Sissy shuddered and gasped. She took three long wheezing breaths. Her pulse beat visibly too fast in her neck.

Jake yanked his attention back to her. He didn't really care if Gregor lived or died. But Sissy . . .

His Sissy . . .

"What's the medicine?" Doc Halliday asked. She began looking at Sissy as much as she watched Gregor. That must mean Gregor was stabilizing.

"I don't know. It's from Harmony." Jake shrugged.

Doc Halliday snapped her fingers and held her hand open. Jake tossed her the inhaler. She barely glanced at the label before nodding. "Best thing for her. Old-fashioned, but I can't think of anything better."

"A newer medicine might work better," Telvino offered tentatively.

"Not necessarily. Our drug companies stopped making that stuff thirty years ago simply because it *doesn't* go out of date, and they can't make as much profit from it." She tossed it back to Jake. "Give her this adrenaline patch, then another shot!"

"She's had three doses already." Back on Harmony, Sissy's physician had instructed him carefully in the precise dosage. If one didn't work, or backlashed, a second was more than adequate. Any more caused side effects more serious than the asthma.

"Do it. The medication needs to work double hard to combat *alien* pollens. Her immune system may be compromised. Do it, Jake, or lose her."

Jake closed his eyes and prayed as he slapped on the patch Telvino ripped open for him. With one last murmur to Harmony for help, he depressed the plunger.

Immediately, her breathing eased. Still too wet and shallow, but no longer painful. He counted to three between each breath, then a pause, a deeper one, and three more. A rhythm. The poetry of life. A bit of color crept back into her face. Her eyelids fluttered, closed, then opened again. She fixed her gaze on his face.

"You are stronger than you think, General Devlin. But you must forge your own path, free of the influence of those who seek to hold you back."

Her voice had that deep, echoey quality he'd come to expect when the Goddess possessed her.

Jake's heart stuttered, then beat strong and hard again. His fear melted a bit.

"That's my Sissy," he whispered.

"What? What did I say?" She opened her eyes further, fully conscious now and breathing almost normally.

Doc Halliday came over and checked Sissy's vitals with one of her electronic gadgets. "They're both as stable as we can make them with field patches. Now let's get off this godforsaken rock." She began packing her kit, gathering up all the discarded packaging from the portable meds.

"Oh, shit!" she screamed.

"What?" Jake demanded, not giving up Sissy to investigate.

Doc Halliday sniffed one of the discarded patches. "This isn't oxygen. It's a stimulant, probably a double dose by the smell."

"And?" Telvino grabbed the square of light blue tissue. He held it to his nose. Then he jerked away, pupils dilating rapidly.

"And, if someone mistakenly gave that to Laud Gregor, it could kill him." Doc Halliday moved faster at gathering the discarded wrappings. She inspected each before placing them into a sealable bag. Her lips pursed tight, and her movements became agitated.

"Talk to me, Doc," Jake coaxed, helping Sissy to sit higher, take responsibility for her own posture. Much as he hated letting her go, he knew he had to be ready to jump.

"All the wrappings are for oxygen, except for the one adrenaline you gave Sissy," Doc said very quietly. "Someone may have murdered the High Priest of Harmony by substituting the patch before we left."

"We need to get back to the FCC fast," Jake said. "I've got a forensic tech there who might be able to extract the who if not the why from that patch."

"The same person who murdered Mr. Labyrinthe? We still have a serial killer on the loose." Doc Halliday nodded and began directing the
Military to carry Gregor aboard. "We can't get spaceborne soon enough,"
she agreed.

"What about hyperspace turning victims of that plant insane?" he
asked, pointing for other people to continue the cleanup.

"I read the report—the real one, not the one Pammy altered. Lots of people go insane in hyperspace. Mostly because the energy currents turn their
thoughts inward, and they have to face their consciences. If Laud Gregor
survived his ghosts once, he'll do it again. I'll risk hyperspace over waiting
any longer than necessary to get him real drugs and that new heart."

"Ambassador Lukan and his party have not returned," Telvino said.
He sounded hesitant for the first time since Jake had known him.

"Pammy's with them," Jake replied. He pressed the all-in on his comm.
Every unit in camp beeped three times, repeated the three beeps six
times. "If she ignores that, it's her own fault."

"What about the two aliens?" Doc Halliday asked.

Jake hadn't noticed Mac slipping away. Sissy had occupied all of his
thoughts and attention. "Mac is smart enough to get back here or call in."
He wasn't so sure about Adrial. She, like Pammy, had her own agenda.

"There's Lord Lukan and his escort now," Telvino pointed toward the
river.

Jake peered over the edge of the plateau to watch the two men picking
their way uphill along a narrow game trail.

"Where's Admiral Marella?" he called as soon as they were within
earshot.

Lukan paused and looked over his shoulder. "She was right behind us
a few moments ago."

Telvino cursed more fluently than Jake.

"Pammy, get your ass back to base right now or I leave you behind,"
Jake broadcast on all frequencies.

"You wouldn't dare," a whisper came back on a tight privacy channel.

"You want privacy for your flyboys to come and go—let them come get
you. I've got two casualties who need MedBay an hour ago. Come back
now or stay and collect your psychedelic plants for the next week until I
can get someone to come back." He closed his comm.

"Let's get packed up. We leave the shelters, everything else goes
home," Telvino commanded. He followed his own orders, tucking his instruction readers back into their folders and throwing extra foam packets
into their crate.

Sissy waved weakly to Jake. He knelt beside her. "I'll carry you, My Laudae."

"Not just yet. Jake, I need a bit of this planet. A rock, some dirt, something to link me to the Goddess here." Her words came out slowly and deliberately with too many long breaths between.

"Make it a rock, and wash it clean of pollen before you let her touch it," Doc growled.

"Sissy," Jake said quietly, leaning as close to her as he dared. "The Goddess is everywhere. You taught me that. You don't need a physical link. You are the link."

"Not anymore." She looked away, trying to hide her tears.

"That's what Gregor led you to believe, My Laudae." He settled on the ground, legs crossed, holding her hand. "He's a useless old man with dreams of his youthful vigor and power. You've spoken prophecy any number of times since leaving Harmony. Including about ten minutes ago."

"I don't remember any of them."

"You didn't always when you were on Harmony. Trust me, Sissy. You are still the avatar of the Goddess. You're just suffering growing pains as you lead all of Harmony beyond their isolated fears and prejudices. *You* are reforging the Covenant with Harmony at the First Contact Café. Out among the stars, just as Jilly prophesied." He patted her hand and rose, using Gregor's rock as a brace.

The tiny raised markings seemed to jump out at him. He'd seen their like deep in the funerary caves on Harmony; in the oldest sections that had been used by Maril spiritual leaders before they were slaughtered or pushed out by the Harmony colonists.

Surreptitiously he recorded the markings with his comm unit. Not the best images, only two-dimensional instead of holovid. Enough to check against the survey.

Pammy had put a hold on the archaeologists coming. Did she know about some ruins or evidence of previous occupation. This could throw a laser screwdriver into the whole plan.

Or forge a new pathway to peace and diplomacy. Reforge the Covenant among the stars.

Sissy and her prophecies had started him thinking beyond his temper.

Damn. That prophecy may have been for him as much as for Sissy. He had a lot of work to do.

CHAPTER FIFTY

"THIS PLACE REMINDS ME too much of my home," Adrial said on a shudder. She leaned into Mac as if for protection. Surreptitiously she used the movement to turn off the beacon she'd just used on her comm link. She wasn't supposed to know how to use it on that particular frequency.

"How so?" Mac replied, looking around in admiration of the natural landscape. He walked slowly along a path only he could see. Adrial thought he looked as though he neared the limits of his strength and stamina. Still, he kept moving forward, guiding her and assisting her over the rough spots with an oddly charming courtesy.

Not since she had fled her childhood home had anyone helped her or cared for her. Always the exile. Always alone.

Leave no trace of your passing. Even in the memories of those she encountered.

She sighed with regret. She'd learned to like these people. Especially Sissy and Mac.

"The density of the forest," she replied to Mac's question, not willing to reveal the pain of her memories. She barely faced them herself.

"The survey assures us that no large carnivorous animals dwell within these forests," Mac said. He held out a primary hand—the one with actual fingers (four of them, no opposable thumb) instead of a pincer—to help her over a fallen tree trunk covered in moss.

"Are you sure we are on the right path?" she asked looking around in dismay. She didn't remember that pile of boulders, or the vine climbing that broad-leaved tree and choking the life from it. Animals weren't the only predators.

"This direction takes me where I need to go." He looked away.

"That's not what I asked you." Suddenly a spiritual path didn't matter as much as getting safely back to base camp. She'd accomplished what she needed to do after examining the glyphs at the cave mouth. "We shouldn't detour or delay. General Jake called the all-in."

"Do not worry. I will return you safely in time." He quickened his pace a bit, not nearly as much as she knew he was capable of.

"What are you looking for? This planet holds no more mysteries that interest me."

"But we brought a mystery with us that worries me." He stopped, scanning all directions with his ears wide and twisting to catch nuances she couldn't hope to detect. "Wait here a moment." Without further explanation, he jumped against an especially thick tree trunk and proceeded to climb.

In moments he returned to her side. "This way." He took her hand and pulled her ungently in a new direction, slightly to the left of their previous path.

She'd have headed off for base camp on her own if she thought she had a prayer of finding it. Sending that beacon had distorted the signal back to where she started from.

"What are you looking for?" she insisted, stopping short so he had to stop as well or drop her hand.

"Shhhh." He held up one finger to her lips in a universal signal for quiet. An oddly intimate gesture when accompanied by his lopsided smile.

"That's it? No explanation?"

"Hush, or we frighten her away."

"Her who?"

"I said quiet," he whispered in a harsher tone. The first severe words he'd ever said to her.

She obeyed out of shock.

Then he pointed toward a thinning in the forest. A bit of brighter light poured through the diffusing leaves. A clearing.

Adrial had to wonder whether it was natural or carved out by the Maril.

They crept forward a few steps, allowing the moist ground to mask the sounds of their movement.

An uneven open space lay before them, filled with tall grasses and some spiked plants. At one side stood Admiral Pamela Marella. She seemed deep in conversation with her comm. She spoke loudly in urgent tones. But she was too far away for Adrial to understand her one-sided conversation.

Adrial checked her own unit. The admiral wasn't using one of the standard frequencies within their group.

Mac cocked his ears to pick up words Adrial missed.

After a few moments Admiral Marella closed her comm and marched out the opposite side of the clearing.

Mac nodded and pointed back the way they had come.

"What was that all about?" Adrial asked when they were clear of the admiral's range.

"I do not understand all she says, but I must warn General Jake of this."

"Warn him of what?"

"Plans he will not like."

He said nothing more as he dragged Adrial rapidly through the woods.

She had no time to think, to plan, even to wonder how this would affect her quest.

✦   ✦   ✦

Sissy held the smooth rock Jake had found for her in her left hand, absently rubbing it with her thumb. Jake had chosen well. Shiny bits of color peeked through the rougher exterior. Sort of like the way the Goddess revealed bits and pieces of herself when you least expected it.

Could Jake be right about her connection to Harmony and Sanctuary? "All things are one, present at the time of the beginning of the Universe, continuing in ever evolving combinations of matter and energy." She quoted one of the texts that she had found on her reader.

In the beginning was God. God exploded and became the universe, Harmony whispered into the back of her mind. Or was that the ever present chiming along damaged nerve endings in her ears?

Jake lifted her into his arms and carried her into the shuttle, disrupting that thought. As much as she liked being held by Jake, she was getting tired of her fragility. She wanted to walk, to run, to explore this place on her own.

Gently, Jake reclined her seat, directly behind his pilot's chair, so that her feet came up and her head rested at a forty-five degree angle. Her breathing became easier almost as soon as the shuttle shut her off from the outside.

Doc Halliday directed the two Military to place Gregor across the aisle from Sissy and adjusted his seat to the same angle. The High Priest turned his face to the bulkhead, as if resigning from contact with other people as well as his position within the Temple hierarchy. The physician took a place between them, medical bag between her feet and half open.

Everyone else piled in and settled. Admiral Pamela Marella came last with a huge carrysack bulging oddly. She'd closed the top drawstring tightly so that none of her treasures peeked out.

The acrid, sweet, musky sap of the Thorn of God nearly overwhelmed Sissy's senses. In an eye blink Sissy saw again the seven niches around a fire ring, felt the satisfaction of a properly completed ritual that left new life growing within her, the lightness of soaring through the skies, then the heavy downward spiral as life changed, fleeing the relentless and uninformed march of the enemy.

Would that happen to her? If she brought change to Harmony, broke the caste system, did she also doom her people to a society without Temple guidance? Did she already represent the severance of the people from the Gods?

The edges of the shiny stone cut into her palm where she clutched it too tightly. She jolted awake, fully aware of the metallic smell of the shuttle and the taste of acid sap on her tongue.

"Doc Halliday?" she whispered, reaching out to touch the woman's arm. "Did you record the inscriptions we found?"

"Most certainly." She handed Sissy the electronic device.

Sissy stared at the squiggles and lines dancing across the screen in a graceful arc from right to left without truly seeing it. She already knew their secrets.

"Long, long ago the Maril used that cave as a place of dreaming with their Gods and with their ancestors. They all became one in a breeding ritual. Where life began in a blessed act, so it ended in another. We'll find their bones and murals inside, just as we did on Harmony. The place is sacred."

"We'll send trained scientists back to study. Maybe we can learn something useful about our enemy," Doc Halliday mused, taking back the reader.

"I must go with them," Sissy insisted. "They no longer seem like the enemy to me. More like a variation of ourselves."

Doc Halliday looked at her strangely, then jerked her gaze toward Jake. He shook his head slightly as he rapidly ran through preflight checks.

"Why did the Maril abandon this planet?" she asked no one in particular.

Had a few survivors come here from Harmony when humans forced them out of their spiritual homes?

Or had the avian creatures left here for Harmony?

She had to know more about their culture, their religion, and the actual time line of their movements.

If anyone within the CSS knew, it was Adrial. Sissy cringed at the thought of milking the self-centered creature for more information. How many convoluted circles must she follow to glean facts from her?

Then her heart sank as she realized that the CSS could not build here. They could not violate the Holy Island.

She had to content herself with a little piece of shiny rock.

CHAPTER FIFTY-ONE

ADRIAL CLOSED HER EYES. A tiny jolt to her entire nervous system signaled their entrance into hyperspace. She didn't understand why everyone fussed so about the jump that bypassed the normal time/space continuum.

Nothing strange had ever happened to her in the hundreds of jumps she'd done over the years, with or without sleepy drugs.

With a sigh of contempt for the lesser beings who feared hyperspace, she opened her eyes and looked around.

Strange. The bulkheads seemed to thin to translucence. Her companions became skeletons; softer tissue glowed as pale afterimages. She'd never witnessed this before.

She hoped this was yet one more clue on her path to Spiritual Purity.

As she watched, a thin wisp of life rose up from Laud Gregor's body. No surprise. Jake must have used the double-dose stimulant patch on him that she'd substituted for one of the antihistamines. The drugs would propel his heart to beat far too rapidly and strongly for the damaged muscle to support. A necessary precaution. She never knew when she'd have to disable an enemy. Best to have a supply of odd weapons at hand.

She tucked the purloined vials of Oxydigitalin deeper between the seat cushions. By the time someone found them, few would remember she had sat in that particular seat, a different one from the journey to the planet.

She did not regret the priest's passing. He had no true spirituality and couldn't teach her anything important. He'd cut himself off from Harmony long before coming to the First Contact Café.

That is what you think. What you think is not always the truth. Laud

Gregor's shade stood over her. Deep holes in his skull where the eyes should be became wells absorbing all light.

Layer after layer of her defenses peeled away, pouring into those black holes, until every soul that had died at her hands stood before her.

Including Mac's brother Number Seven. And the two Control techs she'd mistaken for him, who'd been absent from their posts the night of the crash.

She hugged herself, feeling naked and vulnerable for the first time in many years. Dozens of men, women, and children ranged around her, until they crowded out her perceptions of anything else.

"Go away," she cried, hiding her eyes beneath her arms.

She could not blot out their accusing presence.

Why? they asked, each in turn, until their voices grew and compounded. The question pressed against her like the most sophisticated pressure chamber designed for torture by the Law.

Why?

She shook her head. The question and the ghosts remained.

"It was necessary," she choked out.

Why?

"The Messengers of the Gods commanded me!"

Did they?

"Of course they did. They said I had to find Spiritual Purity. All of you stood in the way of my quest."

Is that what they said, or what you wanted them to say to justify your actions?

"Leave no trace, they said. Even in the memories of those who teach me. My quest must be secret."

Is that truly what they said. Or how you interpreted it?

Before she could form a reply or drop into the forgetfulness that had sustained her for so long, the ship's klaxon announced the jump back to normal space.

Chaos erupted around her as Doc Halliday discovered Laud Gregor's soul had left him.

Adrial wanted to scream that he was standing right beside her. *Please, oh, please, come get him.*

The hallucinations faded one by one. Laud Gregor was the last to leave. The image of his burning black eye holes lingered longest.

Only their questions remained echoing through her mind.

Why?

✦   ✦   ✦

The music of the stars connects everything, is everything, a different tune for each people, a floating mist told Jake two heartbeats before leaving hyperspace. *Use the music to save them all.*

Wonder and awe sent waves of energy from him into the half-formed shape that might have been feminine. The voice echoing in his head sounded feminine.

Normal space jolted his mind and body. He broke free of distortions, visions, and an almost tune drifting through his mind.

The message lingered. Questions arose.

He forced himself to get his charges back to the station safe and sound.

The ship's computer wanted to wrest docking control away from him. He couldn't let it. The station was moving too fast, in the wrong trajectory for the programming to handle. He gritted his teeth and prayed no one would get hurt.

Scrapes and bumps. Six tries, each one farther off the mark than the last. Finally, desperate, he closed his eyes and let his body feel the ship and how it wanted to move. The controls flowed smoothly beneath his hands.

Jerk, grind. Screams of alarm. Movement ceased. The shuttle dropped into the bay and tilted wildly. More screams. He leaned into the stabilizer.

They righted.

Jake slumped against his restraints, exhausted. He sensed movement around him, had to let his passengers take care of themselves for a moment.

Finally he had the energy to open a comm to Control.

"Anything important happen while I was gone?" He sat very still in his pilot's chair while the others bustled off.

Pammy was first to disembark with her bag of plants. She had her head bent into her comm unit and ignored everything else.

Sissy's girls swarmed in and then out again, comforting her, supporting her, guiding her back to their quarters for rest. Sissy clung to the inhaler like a lifeline. At the last second she looked over her shoulder toward Jake.

"I'll find you," he mouthed.

She nodded, trusting him, as she had always trusted him.

Then she was gone.

Lord Lukan and Telvino left with their heads bent together, discussing how to break the news to Harmony that their HP had died and their HPS refused to go home to conduct the funeral.

Doc Halliday stayed behind to supervise the removal of Gregor's corpse.

But Gregor didn't leave with his body.

The translucent outline of the High Priest stood before Jake with a puzzled expression on his face.

Jake had watched him die. He'd seen how Gregor and a bunch of other ghosts crowded around Adrial. Gregor had led them. He stood tall, a commanding presence in his green clothing, more solid than the other spirits.

But Jake wasn't privy to the conversation.

That was the nature of hyperspace ghosts. Each experience was private and individual, between a live person and those he or she had lost.

The ghosts weren't supposed to survive the jump back to normal space.

The message from the Goddess still resonated in his head. So did the High Priest.

Music was the key. He had to save them all with music? He couldn't sing a note. But he knew someone who sang like an angel. And often sang with them.

Gregor looked longingly at the inert body inside a black bag as the doc and her assistants wheeled it off the shuttle. Then his gaze returned to Jake.

"Why are you here?" Jake finally asked when they were alone. His comm board blinked with all kinds of lights demanding his attention.

He wanted to talk to real people, not this vague shadow.

The ghost shrugged his shoulders.

Maybe he couldn't speak outside of hyperspace.

Maybe he was just a figment of Jake's imagination, born of stress, fatigue, worry, and a total drain of adrenaline from his system.

That must be it.

He hit the comm icon from Major Roderick. "What happened?"

"Major diplomatic crisis. You've got to get up to Control now."

"On my way. Orbital status?" He tried to keep his tone casual, as if that question were routine.

"Trajectory and speed holding. But, sir, this diplomatic thing is more critical. Don't bring anyone else with you. I've got Mara working from your office." The major's voice shook with dread, excitement, and ambition.

Jake hadn't thought anything could upset the man's controlled demeanor. Maybe he just hadn't had time to plot how to turn this crisis to his advantage.

"On my way. Send Cortini down to MedBay; we've got a crisis there too. And close all outside communication, especially to and from Harmony, until I authorize differently. Heck, close down the whole board except to incoming ships. Jam everything else. And no one leaves unless cleared by me. Not Lord Lukan or Telvino and especially not Admiral Marella and her crews."

"Yes, sir. Your crisis is not as big as this one. If Laud Gregor died, this would overshadow it. Nothing could be this big."

"Oh, yeah?" Jake growled.

The ghost followed him as he jumped down from the shuttle and bolted for the lift.

Did deceased Laud Gregor count as someone who must be left behind?

"Discord, I hope I'm the only one who can see you."

Laud Gregor didn't say anything.

Jake shrugged and let the rotating platforms carry him up to the tram.

Disconcerting to see the ghost rising with him, facing him, within the shaft but not on the platform.

"What the hell do you want?"

No reply.

Jake decided to ignore him. Maybe he'd go away when they put his body in cryo before shipping him home.

Damn, but Sissy should go with them to conduct the funeral and Grief Blessing. Harmony needed her special touch to heal after a loss of this magnitude on top of the planetary upheaval.

If she returned to Harmony, she might never come back to him. "I'll find you, wherever you go, my Sissy," he muttered to himself.

Laud Gregor frowned and raised a fist.

"Screw you, you're dead."

The tram ride to Control seemed to take forever. Every time Jake shifted to avoid looking at the spirit, Gregor shifted too. Always in his face, his angry silence demanding something. Jake just couldn't figure out what.

He continued to almost hear celestial music in the back of his head. Music that seemed to vibrate in harmony with the metal bulkheads and decks.

Ideas began forming.

He leaped off the tram before the doors had slid all the way open. Gregor matched his pace, as if tied to him by an umbilical cord.

"Can't you go haunt someone else? Someone like Sissy, who can deal with it. Or Lord Lukan, who could use some advice about now."

No answer.

When he stepped off the lift into Control, the ghost seemed to fade a bit, become digitized static.

Jake held his breath, hoping all the electronics disrupted the spiritual energy and banished it.

No such luck. Three heartbeats later Gregor jelled back into his translucent form, perhaps a little paler, but not much. His green clothing stood out against the gray walls.

"Sir, you need to read this," Major Roderick rose from his computer terminal and pointed toward a message scrolling across the screen. If he could see the ghost of his HP, he said nothing. All his concern centered on the jumble of indecipherable glyphs.

"That's Maril!" Jake said, taking the seat. He picked out a couple of symbols he'd learned in the funerary caves on Harmony and seen repeated on the flat stone on Sanctuary. The previous message from rogue traders had come in broken and badly constructed CSS standard.

"There's a . . . a crude translation below it. Like they really want . . . want to communicate but have an . . . an imperfect knowledge of our . . . our language," Roderick stammered.

Jake watched the words in standard letters rise to the center of the screen.

MUST MAKE WORDS. YOU KILL GOD.

Surreptitiously, Jake compared the message with the glyphs he'd recorded on his comm. Similar symbols. Not all the same. The rock carvings were simpler, cleaner, almost primitive.

Gregor shook his head violently in denial of the obvious message on the screen.

But that was Gregor, alive as well as dead. He saw only what he wanted to.

"That make any sense to you, sir?" Roderick chewed his lower lip.

"Not much, but I get the drift." Or maybe the tune.

"Get someone to pull the translator program off the Squid ship. We're going to need it. Soon."

♦ ♦ ♦ ◇ ♦ ♦ ♦

CHAPTER FIFTY-TWO

S ISSY SAT PATIENTLY on a hard chair in her public office while Physician John checked her pulse, blood pressure, temperature, and who
knew what else. He'd adopted the CSS electronic scanners eagerly. The
old mechanical instruments from Harmony took too long and were subject to individual interpretation and error.

"I'm going to replace the charcoal filter again," he said.

"I don't want more surgery," Sissy insisted. A hint of a wheeze remained in her breathing. "I'll be fine once I've had a hot shower and
some sleep."

"I'll use fiberoptics. Go in through the same tiny incision. You'll be
awake, but tranquilized. An hour."

She thought for a moment. Then shook her head. "I don't have an
hour to spare right now. And I have to think clearly. No tranquilizers.
Maybe tomorrow, or the next day."

"Those are alien pollens that triggered your asthma attack. If General
Jake had been one minute later with the inhaler, no amount of medication could help you. We've got to clear your lungs as soon as possible.
Your immune system is compromised." Physician John consulted his all-
in-one gadget.

"Not today."

"You can stay awake the whole time. Special glues to close the incision.
No stitches, minimal pain, back on your feet in two hours. I can coun-
teract the tranquilizers once I'm done." He sounded more and more like
Doc Halliday.

Sissy wanted to giggle at how quickly her people adapted to foreign
ways. She suddenly understood why Harmony had closed off all contact
fifty years ago. She didn't like the isolation or think it wise, but she understood the fear and need to retrench.

Retrench or abandon the quest. Was that the message of Sanctuary? Change carried as much bad as good.

"You won't be out of contact with Harmony at all." Physician John flashed her a grin.

She wondered if he had recorded her thoughts on his gadget and needed to reassure her that technology didn't change his faith.

"I have too much to do." The death of Laud Gregor, while not unforeseen given his heart condition, left a huge gap in Harmony politics. A gap only she could fill. Otherwise she risked civil war and the destruction of all the good on her home world as well as the hated caste system.

"You will never be able to leave the dust-free, pollen-free artificial atmosphere of a station or spaceship if you don't have this surgery," Physician John warned. "I would restrict your movements in the station gardens as well. You cannot risk alien pollens. The proteins . . ." he wandered off into a long dissertation Sissy didn't understand. Just like Doc Halliday.

"Harmony Prime may be the only world you can visit if you don't get a new filter and have it changed frequently," Physician John finished.

Sissy stopped short, half standing. She plopped down again. "That is unacceptable."

"I agree. Let me take you back to MedBay. I'll do it immediately." Physician John bowed formally, then extended his arm in an offer of escort.

A warning whistle buzzed through the comm system throughout the Temple complex.

"Will Laudae Sissy please honor station management with her immediate presence in Control." Not a request, a demand.

Sissy ignored Physician John and touched the blinking icon on her desktop. "Laudae Sissy to General Jake Devlin."

"Sissy, I need you, now," Jake's disembodied voice filled the room. He sounded desperate.

She tested her lungs with a deep breath. Oh, how she'd come to loathe the citrus-flavored air with a metallic aftertaste. Her brief immersion in a real atmosphere scented delicately by native plants served as a reminder of what she'd sacrificed in coming here.

"Physician John, we must delay your procedure." She touched the comm system again. "I must change these filthy and pollen-laden clothes, General. We will join you very shortly."

"That had better be a royal 'We.' This is urgent and your eyes only. I don't care what you are wearing. Just get up here." He cut the connection abruptly without so much as a polite sign off. The station etiquette book, endorsed and enforced by Jake, required a sign off.

◆ ◆ ◆

"I saw," Mac said quietly as he crept up behind Adrial. She stood in the docking bay reception area next to where they'd landed, turning right and then left again in uncertainty.

She jumped and cringed at his words.

He watched her chin quiver and her eyes dart about, never resting for more than a heartbeat. Avoiding his gaze altogether.

"I did not want to see," Mac continued. "My kind is not haunted by our past in hyperspace. Today I was haunted by *your* past."

"I do not know what you're talking about," Adrial replied. She wrapped her arms about herself and hugged tightly, keeping the truth in so that only her lies could escape. "I saw no one of import during the jump."

"Yes, you did. I watched Laud Gregor's shade speak to you. He was joined by many others. I understand that you have lost your entire family to war with the Marils. But why would Laud Gregor seek you out at the moment of his death? He should haunt Laudae Sissy if anyone." Mac shifted so that he could grab her should she run in any direction.

He had no doubt she would run at the first opportunity. She always did.

That saddened him. He so wanted her to turn to him instead.

"I did not kill Laud Gregor, if that is what you are implying. Why should I kill him?"

"I don't know. You tell me." He edged closer even though her subtle perfume threatened to swamp his senses and remove his self-control.

"I had no reason to kill him. Through him I finally saw the imbalance in the universe that prevented me from finding Spiritual Purity." She released her death grip upon herself and faced him squarely. Her eyes cleared.

She lied, but she firmly believed her own lies.

"And what is that imbalance?"

"Laudae Sissy. She has to return to Harmony. Without her, the Mother Goddess is lost, adrift, alone. She cannot speak to Her people without Her avatar. Laudae Sissy has to return to Harmony. Only then can she interpret what the Goddess has to say to me."

Mac bowed his head in acknowledgment. She made sense to him. But did what she say make sense to the universe?

◆ ◆ ◆

Nothing made sense. Gregor drifted about Jake's private office without purpose. Every time he tried to leave, to rejoin his body and find final peace, something yanked him back to Jake's side, like a bouncing tether.

If Harmony decreed he must continue on this plane without his body, why in Discord's name wouldn't She allow him to get on with the work!

This half existence had no purpose.

None that you can see, a soft feminine voice whispered to him on the artificial air currents. *Only you can bring Harmony through your death, where you could not in life.*

That sounded suspiciously like something Sissy would say.

But his HPS was nowhere in sight. Jake had called her to join him up here. She was on the way. But even when touched by the Goddess, Sissy could not speak through half the station without a comm unit.

You know what you must do if only you allow yourself to look.

Now that made no sense at all.

You have always wanted what is best for Harmony. Now look to see who can best achieve that without the prejudice you nurtured your entire life. What is best for Gregor may not be what is best for Harmony.

Gregor decided to ignore that for now. He contented himself with reading the Maril message over Jake's shoulder. If only his code breaker still lived, Gregor would point Jake toward someone who read the secret language that had no roots with anything human.

Alas, Gregor had murdered the man because he'd figured out that the people of the CSS were as human as he was. At the time, Gregor's actions had seemed prudent. Secrets had to be kept for the protection of all Harmony.

For the protection of My people or for preservation of your power.

"Oh, shut up. You are becoming annoying."

No sound escaped his lips.

Not even Jake noticed that he'd spoken.

Gregor slammed one fist into the other in frustration. What did he have to do?

You know.

Sissy entered the suite and hurried toward Jake.

"Can you read any of this? Get a more accurate translation?" Jake asked Sissy.

Something hummed inside Gregor. Ah. His continuation had something to do with that message or its interpretation.

"A few words." Sissy pointed toward an array of stick figures. "That looks like someone kneeling in prayer."

"Got that one right off. We saw something similar in the caves." He wrapped his arm about her waist and drew her closer.

"You have no right to touch her!" Gregor screamed.

Sissy batted at her ear as if a fly had buzzed too close. Then she leaned her head against the top of Jake's as if she belonged there. As if they had become comfortable touching each other over many months.

He needed to sound alarms back on Harmony. Sissy could not be allowed to ally herself to this man with his false caste mark. His *lesser* caste mark. Who could witness this? Who would listen.

Who could hear him?

"What about this one?" Sissy pointed to another glyph. "It looks like that spiky plant and a fire. Burning the Thorn of God?"

"I don't see it." Jake tipped his head sideways and shook it.

"I . . . I saw something in a vision," she said quietly.

"Told you so." He flashed her a big grin.

They looked at each other a long silent moment with deep longing.

Gregor turned his head away in disgust. Repulsive watching people of different castes together.

What is a caste?

"Oh, shut up."

Sissy bit her lip and looked at the message once more. "I think Adrial can read this."

Jake slumped. "As much as I hate to include any outsiders, I do believe you are right. Mara and Roderick didn't get much further than you. I'll send Security to fetch her. I don't want anything broadcast through the station at this point."

"I think Mac can help control her. He might help interpret the message too."

Jake nodded agreement. "I'll call him through the spectacles. He can escort Adrial here. Too bad we'll have to postpone moving to Sanctuary. Mac will make a good leader on the FCC. Eventually."

"Adrial is more likely to come with him than allow Security to dictate her movements."

"The first moment we can get away from Control, I have another job for you." Jake looked up at her with hope, expectations, and emotions Gregor didn't want to have to examine.

But the words of the Goddess in his ear kept reminding him that perhaps something he hated was best for Harmony.

Not this. Anything but this!

"Oh?" Sissy lifted her head to look more closely at Jake's expression. But she did not move away from his gentle grasp.

Gregor pushed himself between the two, to separate them once and for all. His body passed right through them both with no more notice than a slight cold shiver from each of them.

"I think you might be able to correct a problem in Engineering, find the right notes to make some parts resonate properly so they can be returned to normal positions."

"Sounds interesting." She wrapped her arm around his neck and dropped her head back on top of his.

"Jake, I discovered some things about Maril culture and history during my visions," Sissy said hesitantly.

Jake looked up at her, mutely giving her permission to continue. Gregor moved closer, the better to hear and learn. This information could help settle the question of his continued spirit existence.

"Sanctuary, and I think Harmony too, were sacred to them."

"Spiritual retreats," Jake said. "We knew that."

"More than that. The ritual caves represented the beginning and end of life. Coming from the ancestors and rejoining them."

"Birthing and funeral centers. Makes sense." Jake pushed icons around his desk, always keeping the Maril message center and dominant.

Gregor was sick of looking at it, not knowing the exact meaning of each glyph.

"Not birthing. Conception. It was a sacred ritual, too important to risk on a casual encounter or random timing."

Gregor approved of that, especially for the limited numbers in Temple.

Jake stilled. "There's something I haven't told you. And you cannot repeat this to anyone yet." He continued so quietly he might almost have whispered. A strange tale of the Maril deliberately shedding their humanity in favor of avian bodies, instincts, and language. Then he added the most damning information of all: The DNA tinkering was breaking down, much like the caste marks on Harmony but on a more drastic scale.

Gregor grew cold, colder than the chill funerary caves.

"That explains so much," Sissy crowed. "When humans destroyed their ritual center on Harmony, the Maril withdrew from other vulnerable sacred places, erasing most of the evidence of their purpose, so they wouldn't be tainted as they considered Harmony to be defiled."

"We know that happened about five hundred years ago. Why did the

Maril wait another three hundred to begin a war of attrition against humans?" Jake looked very tired.

Gregor felt more tired. Yet he couldn't leave, couldn't rest as he deserved to.

"Politics and religion don't always mix," Sissy said on a grin. "At the time, religious fervor may have taken a back seat to practicality. Then the DNA breakdown became more prevalent. People turned to the priests for answers. If their religious leaders are in power now, they are seeking to resanctify their Sanctuaries, to bring the breeding rituals back as a way of stopping the mutations."

"They cleanse only the planets that were Sanctuaries. That's the pattern you saw in the star map."

"That is why they are crossbreeding, trying to stabilize before they tinker with their DNA again to reestablish their avian characteristics," Sissy finished for him. "Adrial was one of the first experiments, to see if they could still breed. Amity was later cleansed. Maybe it was a Sanctuary at one time and her conception the first of the reclaimed rituals. That makes her special to them."

Gregor tried to leave. He didn't want to hear any more of this speculation. Bad enough the CSS tried to gain more power and influence in the galaxy by claiming Harmony came from Earth. Now they wanted to "prove" that the Maril did too. Would they stop at nothing to make science more important than faith?

"That's why Adrial was chosen for some arcane mission," Jake said.

"To find the first Sanctuary." Sissy's exhale whistled with surprise. It also sounded wet and wheezy, as if she still suffered from taking in too much alien pollen. "Jake, she did it. And she sent a message. That's why the Maril contacted us today. Adrial called them."

"So did you."

In the back of his mind Gregor heard the Goddess sigh, *Finally*.

CHAPTER FIFTY-THREE

SISSY LOOKED AT JAKE SPECULATIVELY.
Jake nearly glowed from the inside because he'd figured out something before she did.

Gregor looked as though he'd like to explode, or crumple in tears. Jake couldn't figure out which.

"Think about it." Jake touched Sissy's nose in an affectionate gesture. "You touched the carvings on the cave. You had a vision. I'm betting you sent a psychic signal to your counterparts on Maril."

Both Sissy and Gregor shook their heads in denial.

"Think about it. Mac has Adrial now." Jake touched an icon on the screen. "I hope she's sane enough to interpret this message so that we can understand it. She talks in circles."

"The language is in circles. Remember the spiral of the creation story in the caves?"

"Yes!" Jake looked at the middle of the Maril message and began tracing the glyphs in a spiral, clockwise, from the center out. Each tiny pictograph spread out a bit so that it no longer looked like human text in lines and columns. "Adrial speaks in spirals, not circles. Because she's been trained by Maril priests! But that doesn't explain why she was wearing Maril prison clothes when she got here."

Gregor hummed and sizzled. The first noise he'd made. Jake knew without a doubt he'd gotten something right. Gregor confirmed it.

I bet Adrial holds clues to his ghostly existence.

Or maybe she held more information about where this message came from and how the Maril discovered the CSS planned occupation of Sanctuary.

Jake had to get her isolated and in custody before she did anything else that might jeopardize the station.

✦ ✦ ✦

Adrial stared, stunned at the message scrolling around the screen of Jake's terminal in his private office. She hadn't the clear mindedness to look for an alternate meaning in the words. She had to tell the truth, no matter how much it bewildered her.

Mac, the ghosts, all of those people she could no longer run away from, made her think too much. She could no longer retreat into forget-fulness or flight.

"When Laudae Sissy touched the glyphs by the ritual cave, she set off a psychic signal to their priests. They wish a meeting and offer a language tutorial to facilitate negotiations. Failure to respond within the passage of a day will be assumed as a declaration of war. They prepare battle wagons for violation of their most sacred beginning place," she read out loud.

The Messengers of the Gods would take care of eliminating the mem-ories of her stay here. If she escaped in time, they'd allow her to continue her progress toward Spiritual Purity.

Jake jumped to his feet from the chair beside her. He paced anxiously around and around the desk like a dog herding woolly beasts. "Mara, have you got that translator off the Squid ship," he called into his wrist comm.

"You have no need of that archaic device. I can translate for you," Adrial offered, knowing she wouldn't be here long enough to do that.

Jake glared. "Mara, that is our top priority. The Maril are sending a tutorial to help us along."

"Working on it," came a muffled reply.

"Control, get Telvino and Lukan up here, now," he spoke crisply into the comm without pause.

"Sir, the ambassadors are in closed conference," the voice from Con-trol replied.

"I don't care. This is more important. Tell them to get their asses up here or get left out of the biggest diplomatic coup of the century." He slapped the desktop to close the link.

"You need a language expert to compose a tutorial to exchange with them," Laudae Sissy said.

"I can do it," Adrial insisted. Suddenly that chore became important.

"Right. I bet Pammy has someone on tap." Jake spoke as if he hadn't heard Adrial. As if she didn't exist. Or he couldn't remember her. He aimed a fist toward the comm again.

"Jake . . . do you really want to involve her?" Sissy asked.

"I have to. She'll find out anyway. Wouldn't surprise me if she knew already."

Adrial let the conversation flow around her. She had to think and plan. Her thoughts swirled and looped back upon themselves.

Mac watched her silently, carefully, from a place near the door. He would remember her passing.

"They are coming for me," she whispered to herself.

"Are you so important that the Maril are willing to talk peace with their greatest enemies just to apprehend you?" Mac whispered into her ear as he moved silently and swiftly to her side.

Leave no trace of your passing.

"I have to leave." She stood and smoothed her white gown, not the one with the sensors woven into it, the new one with white embroidery at the hem and cuffs that Sissy had given her. The gown with many deep and hidden pockets and wide sleeves to secrete special tools.

"You aren't going anywhere until we get a reply sent off," Jake said. He shifted his pacing to stand between her and the door.

Why did he suddenly remember her. He was supposed to forget. They all were. She couldn't leave them alive if they remembered!

"But I have to . . . um . . . use the necessary." She took one step toward the exit. In her mind she already had her few belongings packed and had negotiated passage on a ship. There was a cargo vessel bound for Labyrinthe Prime tonight. Would the captain give her space in the hold in exchange for sex? Probably not. She'd have to find another form of currency. Unfortunately, Mac's race only worshiped money. She'd have to trust the damaged propulsion system to erase all evidence of her passing here.

"In there." Jake nodded his head toward the innermost rooms of his private quarters.

She already knew she'd find no exit from there. The vents? Not without Mac's help.

He seemed more interested in moving icons around the oversized spectacles that covered half his face.

Adrial dashed into the inner rooms. The moment she had privacy, she whipped out the comm unit Jake had given her on Sanctuary. Telvino was supposed to collect it, but in the chaos of Gregor's death, she'd hidden it.

She opened a frequency to a Promethean Pirate scout nosing around the edge of this solar system.

Sissy's small hand closed around hers, effectively closing the frequency. "You can't run again, Adrial," she said softly.

"They will kill me! I'll never find Spiritual Purity. I'll never commune with the Gods. All my searching will be for nothing." She wrenched her hands free of Sissy's strong grip. The comm unit remained in Sissy's possession.

"Sometimes you have to face the enemy to get to the right path."

Sissy's voice had that odd disembodied quality again.

Adrial began to shake. Her teeth chattered.

"Shouldn't you take your own advice?" she shot back to the High Priestess.

Sissy gasped. "Perhaps you are right. But that does not solve your problem."

"Do not stand in my way, Laudae Sissy. Please do not be the one to impede me."

"Why?"

"Because I like you. I shall regret your death. The Gods always make sure those who stand in my way die."

✦　　✦　　✦

Sissy drew in a sharp breath. The air reached only the shallow surface of her lungs. She felt her body closing down in its desperate search for air.

On the edge of her next inhalation came a whiff of the acrid, sweet smell of the Thorn of God.

"Is it the Gods who kill, or you, Adrial?" she asked, already knowing the answer. Her words came out softly, barely audible. All she could manage.

"I . . . I . . ." Adrial's eyes lost focus, and her chin trembled. A fat tear appeared at the corner of her eye. With each stammer she inched around Sissy toward the door.

Ploys. All ploys to get her way, Sissy reminded herself.

She braced herself against the flood of emotion coming from the woman. Fear, anxiety, pain.

For half a moment a flash of memory not her own passed through her. She knew the intense agony of endless torture. She crumpled in on herself from the pain, until it became a part of her. She didn't know if she'd feel whole again without the agony invading her bones. And through it all a commanding voice repeated over and over again:

"Tell no one of your purpose. Tell no one that you seek the planet of Sanctuary. Our spiritual home. The first and most important of our ritual sites. Tell no one. You know the signal when you find it."

Then an electrical jolt through their bodies to reinforce the message.

She straightened from her shared pain. She understood now. Misinterpretation. Hundreds of deaths caused by a misinterpretation of a language that worked in spirals and metaphors.

Misinterpretation gave Adrial the clear conscience to become truly dangerous to anyone she perceived in her path.

Fear sharpened Sissy's perceptions. A hot rush of adrenaline gave her more room in her chest for breathing. She made sure she kept a good distance between herself and Adrial.

One step backward, two, a third took her into the office.

"The Gods always put the weapons in my hands," Adrial finally said. Her eyes narrowed in cold calculation.

A stick bearing three thorns, each longer than Sissy's hand, appeared in Adrial's hand.

"Harmony protect me," Sissy whispered as her breathing closed down again.

Adrial looked at the thorns with wide, puzzled eyes, as if she hadn't known that she had pulled it out of her sleeve.

"Sissy!" Jake shouted.

Sissy sensed him dashing to her side.

"Don't touch her!" Adrial shouted. "The Messengers of the Gods commanded me to . . . to find . . ." Her words drifted off. Confusion clouded her sharp features. "I can't tell you what they commanded."

"What did they command?" Mac asked. Somehow he'd managed to climb the wall behind Adrial.

"I have to find the truth." Adrial's face cleared and sharpened. "I can't let anything stand in my way. You are in my way, Laudae. You see, Sanctuary gave me this plant to protect myself from you. She knew you'd try to prevent me from finding Her."

Sissy backed up again. Blackness crowded the edges of her vision. Adrial in her white on white dress, her moonlit hair in a soft halo around her pale face, seemed to glow as bright as any sun.

Jake kept pace with her. His hand hovered over the dagger at his belt.

"The weapon is exactly suited to the High Priestess. She is very sensitive to it," Mac said soothingly.

"That's right," Adrial agreed. "Sanctuary wouldn't have given me this branch if She didn't know I'd need it against you, Laudae Sissy." She waved the branch around wildly.

The scent of the raw sap filled every opening and crevice in Sissy. It ate away at her physical defenses and her mind.

Adrial, Mac, even Jake multiplied into three or four copies of them-selves. The multiple views moved together and separately, here, there, and everywhere at the same time.

Her balance shifted with the images. Her head reeled.

She had to close her eyes to regain some sense of reality.

Afterimages burned into her eyelids told her precisely where everyone stood. She heard each one breathe in a different cadence, smelled their emotions.

Adrial gave off the same pheromones as a wolf on the hunt, the scent of prey drawing her forward.

"Adrial," Mac whispered. "The Goddess didn't provide you with weapons. You did. Sanctuary and Harmony would never order you to kill. You have killed innocent people, many innocent people simply because you no longer needed them. You have left a trail of dead bodies across the galaxy."

"Why did you kill Mac's brother?" Jake asked, edging in front of Sissy.

"Because he hurt Sissy! The Goddess loved all the people killed and injured by his negligence." No reference to how the crash had caused those deaths and injuries.

"And now you want to kill Sissy. Is that because only you have the right to kill?" Mac asked. His brown skin paled, then suffused with blood. "Are you a God that you have the right to kill—to murder?"

"But the Messengers of the Gods commanded! I must . . . I must . . ."

"You must do what?" Sissy asked. "What did the Messengers in all their black-feathered glory command you?"

"Maril Warriors?" Jake mouthed to Sissy.

Sissy nodded.

"They . . . they told me I must seek the path to spiritual oneness with the universe. Only I could move through both the Maril and the Human worlds. Only I could read all the texts in both languages," Adrial stated proudly, as if she had to drag the exact words from deep inside her memory.

"My mother said my father was an angel. I inherited the ability to find Spiritual Purity from him."

Images clicked inside Sissy's mind. The stone beds inside the cave, the smudge pots with the burning plants that induced visions.

"The Maril language is highly symbolic. Translations are not always exact," Sissy said quietly. The array of glyphs dancing around the arched opening of the cave played before her mind's eye in perfect order. Each one contained a multitude of meanings and interpretations. "Think carefully, Adrial. What did the Messengers of the Gods really command you to do? They were warriors, not priests. What did they have the authority to demand of you?"

"The path . . ."

"Dig deeper in your mind, Adrial," Jake added. He had his dagger half out of its sheath.

"The path to the lost place of spiritual oneness," Adrial ground out each word.

"The lost world of Sanctuary," Sissy said. "The beginning place. The blessed cave where procreation became a sacred ritual." Her embarrassment at any discussion of sex slid away. This was not her ritual, she did not have to partake. And yet it seemed so special. So right for the Gods to participate.

"Yes!" Adrial cried. "Those words exactly. I must find the lost world of Sanctuary."

Jake nodded, comprehension widening his eyes. "All the holy people were set adrift to wander the stars without support or succor from their home world," he said. "That was how your father came to Amity."

"My father was an angel!" Adrial insisted.

"An angel who came before the Warriors. The Maril were afraid of us," Sissy said quietly. Her breathing sharpened, became shallower, more painful to draw in. If only Adrial would drop the branch with its poisonous sap!

"But they don't fear you any more," Adrial continued on for her. "They know how to defeat you in battle, how to find the lost sanctuaries. But not the first one, the most beloved. They need Sanctuary again. The Gods have sent plagues against them because they have broken the path of Spiritual Purity. Only on Sanctuary can they find their Gods again and heal. Only the rituals of Sanctuary will allow them to breed true again. I must not let anyone stand in my way. And I must leave no trace of my presence, not even in the memories of those who help me."

She smiled smugly, having recovered the memory.

Sissy knew she spoke truly. Her aura held a comfortable glow.

"They kept me for days in isolation, repeating the same words over and over to make certain I would remember." Adrial continued. "Beating the words into me. Cutting me so that my blood knew my mission as well as my mind."

Sissy almost cried at the torture this lost soul had endured. No wonder she'd warped the command for her own self-preservation, trying desperately to hang on to something of herself above and beyond their commands.

"The mixed couple, a human male and a female Maril who died trying to come to First Contact Café, were following you, Adrial," Jake said. His eyes went a bit vague as he thought hard. "Their dying message was, 'Tell the lost one that Sanctuary can be found.' "

"And you have found Sanctuary, Adrial," Mac added. He had moved with incredible swiftness to stand beside her. A flutter within his clothing betrayed the extension of his secondary arms with their pincer claws.

"You have completed your mission, Adrial. You have found Sanctuary," Sissy said. She had to keep Adrial's attention focused forward, away from Mac.

"You don't need to kill again," Jake prompted. "You called the Maril and told them the coordinates of the planet and the CSS plans to build there."

"I touched the cave message. Their priests linked to my mind. My visions of what happened within the caves came from them. They needed me to know so I would leave the place without further tainting," Sissy concluded.

"But I have not found my own Spiritual Purity." Adrial looked back and forth frantically. "My mission is not complete."

"That was not your mission," Sissy reminded her.

"It was. It is. It has to be, otherwise . . . otherwise what I did . . ." She looked about wildly, totally lost. "What will I do?"

Then her eyes narrowed to mere slits as she focused on Sissy. "You betrayed me. I came to you for help in my quest, and you failed me! You have to die." She brandished the Thorn of God, almost shoving it into Sissy's face.

Sissy backed away from the toxic sap dripping from the ends of the thorns.

"Surely Harmony and Sanctuary are appalled at your actions, Adrial," Jake said slamming his dagger back into its sheath. "How will the Goddess deal with you when you murder her avatar? Murder Sissy and you murder the Gods themselves!"

"No!" Adrial screeched. "Stop talking, you are confusing me." She covered her eyes with her free hand, still holding the branch out.

But she spread her fingers so she could peer through them.

"What the hell do you mean *ordering* me here, Jake?" Admiral Marella demanded from the doorway.

Everyone looked up startled at the intrusion.

Air whooshed past Sissy. A sharp scrape to her arm through the cloth of her favorite purple dress.

Heart-stopping fear brought the room into sharp focus. A quick check showed some pulled threads in her sleeve, but the thorn had not broken her skin.

Mac grabbed the branch from Adrial's hand with his claws.

Adrial's long skirts disappeared through the doorway. Mac scuttled up to an open vent and squeezed through it. The two Marines who had stood guard outside the door blinked in confusion from the floor where they sprawled.

Sissy's knees gave out.

Jake caught her and held her close. She clung to him, in relief, and gratitude, and something much more.

"What would I do without you, Jake?"

"I love you, Sissy. I'll be here for you always. You have to know that."

"Yes, my love. I do know that."

"As much as I want to stand here all day and just hold you, I've got to catch Adrial."

"Go. We'll talk later."

He set her into his oversized armchair.

"We'll figure something out." She clutched his hand in a moment of desperation. "Somehow. I won't let a little thing like a caste mark keep us apart any longer."

"I'll hold you to that." He kissed her quickly, then ran out in Adrial's wake.

"I hope there's more to this than the pretty pickle of you two finally admitting you're in love," Admiral Marella said, hands on hips, a scowl on her face.

"Oh, there is. Let me show you." Sissy directed the spymaster to the Maril message.

"Holy shit!"

"That about covers it." Sissy sank back in the chair and trembled with relief and new concerns.

$$\text{◆ ◆ ◆ ◇ ◆ ◆ ◆}$$

CHAPTER FIFTY-FOUR

ADRIAL RAN. No time to plan. No energy to think. She had to get out of this place. Now. Before . . .

Before the Messengers of the Gods found her and exacted vengeance for her failure.

All for naught. All of her pain, the anxiety, the meticulous learning, the running.

Compulsion, deeply imbedded fell away. She'd found Sanctuary for the Maril.

But she'd failed miserably in her own quest.

The deaths. Every being who had died at her hands flashed before her mind. Innocents caught in the backlash of her obsession with secrecy. People who had helped her, shared in her quest for knowledge. Gone. All gone.

How many had she killed?

She'd lost count years ago.

Had any of them been necessary?

Yes! Her psyche screamed. "I had to survive." She justified slaying the Law who hid his blue feathers to fool her, then tricked her into littering so he could arrest her. She had to kill him to get out of prison. He'd been the first.

But burning the entire library and all the people inside when a forgotten text had given her vital clues and she couldn't risk anyone else finding it? She could have just destroyed the book, not the entire library. Or taken it with her.

And the Squid People. Their ship would have made the trip safely if Adrial hadn't sabotaged the nav system. They could have found a haven at the First Contact Café. Five innocent Workers, including children, had died too.

There had been others. Too many others to remember each individually.

But their faces pressed against her memory, clearly defined, their faces trapped in their final agony.

Deep pain ripped through her inner being.

She'd been so wrong. She didn't deserve to live.

Frantically she searched the lift and tram spaces for something, anything that would end her pain.

No weapon or poison came to hand. She passed a maintenance tube on her way to a lower level of an empty wing. If only she could get outside, space would kill her. In space she'd finally become one with the universe.

The Goddess Harmony would accept her sacrifice in atonement for her sins.

She aimed her steps for the cargo bay between habitat levels.

Peace at last. A few more moments, a step into the icy vacuum, followed by one last burst of intense, glorious pain, and her quest would end. Only her death would atone for all the mistakes she'd made, all the lives she'd needlessly taken.

"No." Mac dropped beside her, just as she began keying in the manual override of the air lock.

"Get out of my way," she cried, hot tears blurring her vision. Two more strings of code. Then she'd be free.

"Or what? Will you kill me too?"

"No," she gasped. "No. I can't kill anymore." Her hand paused over the air lock.

"You can't kill yourself either."

"It's the only way I can atone." She calculated the number of steps she needed to reach the doors as they opened into the air lock, the heartbeats of time needed to punch in the last codes. Mac would survive in the dark vacuum of space. She need not worry about him.

"Will your death bring back any of those you've murdered?"

She stopped short, halfway into the lock.

"They have all joined their Gods. They are beyond me now."

"Killing yourself will not make up for your mistakes. Only helping the living will begin to do that."

"Help? How do I do that? Who would trust me after what I've done." A slightly different angle gave her line of sight to the air lock. All she needed was two steps and a series of six numbers on the panel inside.

But the air lock took time to cycle. She couldn't leave the bulkhead open behind her. The entire wing would lose atmosphere, killing even more people.

"Trust has to be earned. Helping others is not always obvious. You have to search as deeply for what they need as you searched for clues to the lost planet."

"I can't do it. It's too hard." Only one way to ease the ache in her heart that threatened to choke her. Let it break. Let every bone and organ inside her break.

It couldn't hurt any worse.

One long leap past him. Her hands landed on the spinning lock. She dropped her full weight on at it as she landed, trying desperately to close him out before the second lock fully opened to the vacuum of space.

Mac's hand grabbed her waist, trying to drag her away as he locked his pincer claws around a handhold inside the lock.

Too late. Klaxons sounded. The bulkhead doors closed quickly. The cargo doors began their slow grind open.

Air rushed out the tiny opening, dragging them forward. The blackness beyond beckoned her. The glimmer of a star shone brightly in the vastness. Empathy, Harmony's sun. It promised her release.

She went limp, letting the equalizing air and pressure carry her outward.

Mac's grip on her arm tightened. Then his other primaries enfolded her.

"I can't let you die. I love you too much, my Adrial. My wounded little bird," he shouted over the noise of the alarms and increasing wind.

Love?

Something deep in her belly warmed and stretched.

The doors slid further open. She could pass between them now.

"I have to atone," she wailed, reaching a hand toward the end of the pain.

"Dying accomplishes nothing."

"It is my justice."

"Justice or running away yet again? Justice is finding ways to make up for your mistakes, helping others in their time of need. Becoming as beautiful inside as you are outside."

"Let me go. I don't know how to do . . . I can't."

The alarm died. The doors stood fully open, wide enough to pass a lift cart laden with cargo through them.

So easy to just drift away and die.

"I'll help you."

The warm thing in her belly grew bigger. It slid tendrils of life through her veins, encapsulating her heart and easing the pain.

"We'll travel the galaxy together, giving aid, or teaching, or just quiet moments of prayer where it's needed. You and Sissy have taught me how much I value other beings. You have given me reason for existence beyond this station."

"I . . ." Words failed her. She had no air to fill her lungs. She had nothing left except the vision of his broad face in front of her. "Air . . ." she choked out.

His mouth came down on hers, passing his air reserves, life, and a reason for living back into her.

$$\diamond \; \diamond \; \diamond \; \diamondsuit \; \diamond \; \diamond \; \diamond$$

CHAPTER FIFTY-FIVE

"JAKE, WHAT HAPPENED?" Sissy rose from her chair and grabbed Jake as he stumbled toward her.

Ashen pale, eyes darting wildly without focus, he leaned heavily on her.

She welcomed his weight even as she strained to keep them both upright. Slowly she allowed herself to sink to her knees, dragging him with her. He looked as though he needed a long session of prayer and meditation.

"They . . . I think they committed suicide together," he gasped, letting his head loll forward. "I couldn't get to them before the bulkhead closed. My override wouldn't open it in time.

Sissy gasped and held her heart in horror. Her teeth wanted to chatter. She clamped them closed because Jake needed her strong and sensible.

"Mac can survive vacuum," she finally whispered harshly.

"But can she?"

"He saved her once before by giving her his extra air and protecting her body. We can only pray they made it to one of the ships in time."

He nodded mutely. "He left the spectacles behind, on the lift. He knew he wasn't coming back."

A long silence stretched between them. Neither needed to break it with useless words. Their hands crept toward each other and clung. For those moments Sissy felt herself joined to this man, the man she loved above all others, completely, spiritually. They pressed their foreheads together in mutual understanding.

"We've one more chore to do. Then we can rest. Talk. Find a path to the future," he whispered. His lips sought hers briefly.

Too briefly.

"What do you need me to do?"

"Sing the propulsion engines back into Harmony." He quirked her a half grin.

"I don't know anything about engines," she protested.

"You sang a whole planet back to Harmony to calm a quake," he said, still grinning.

"But that was a living planet!"

"So, this shouldn't be as hard. Not as big anyway. All part of the universe. We are all bits and pieces of Harmony. You taught me that."

"I . . . guess . . ." She thought about it for a moment. "I'll need the girls. Mary and Martha at least."

"All six of them. Maybe the dogs too. This is going to take a bit of trial and error until we understand the nature of the beast."

Still holding her hand, he rose and led her back toward her quarters. Sissy wasn't surprised to find the six acolytes, two dogs, three cats, and a ferret awaiting them. Those girls knew everything that happened on the station.

Together they all trooped through the lifts and tram to E5.

Sissy walked around and around each of the seven huge drums, listening to them, feeling their vibrations. Soaking in their Discord and their need to regain Harmony.

The dogs followed her, ears cocked, noses working.

"There is no way to get into the mechanisms that I can find," Jake said, following her closely, with the girls right behind him. "But I think, if we can get those rods humming in concert with the drum casing, we should be able to adjust them and get the station back on track. I've got my people in Control monitoring everything. They'll tell us when we've done it right."

"I'll know when we've done it right."

"I just can't figure out how Adrial had the strength to do this—or had the knowledge of what to do." He shook his head, staring at the rods sticking out at odd angles.

"She had the strength and intuition of several extra warped personalities combined," Sissy replied. "The visions . . ."

"Every one of those personalities became part of her need to leave no trace of her passing, even in the memories of those who helped her." Jake looked as if he needed to cry. Or hit something. Hard.

Putting all of his strength into this chore, accomplishing the impossible, should help smooth his temper. Doing it in concert with her and the girls would help balance his mind and spirit even more.

"She was so fascinated by music, some of it must have crept into her subconscious," Sissy said.

"She found the music but not the Harmony," Jake confirmed. "A different tune for each race."

"Suzie, Sharan, climb up with Jake and keep a careful eye on the rods. You should see a slight change of color, or a scratch, or something when he pulls them out to the former length. Sarah and Bella, please take the descant. Mary and Martha, find the alto harmony. I'll take the primary hymn. A different race set the rods. The music will resonate to a different planet and Goddess."

Sissy drew a deep breath, settling her thoughts, grounding her perceptions in the station as a whole.

"Jake, I'll need one of your Badger Metal blades," she held out her hand, knowing he'd comply.

When the cool ceramic metal alloy lay flat across her palm, she hummed a note toward it. Instantly the matrix in the tool shivered in response.

Jake stared at his knife in wonder. Then he laughed long and hard.

"What's so funny?"

"I finally get it. I know why we couldn't reverse engineer Badger Metal. It's not the combination of elements or heat and pressure. It's sonics! As the alloy knits together, it's blasted with predetermined sounds. The music of the universe is woven into the alloy."

"The music of the universe is woven into all of us. Just different tunes. I wonder if each race needs a different set of . . . sonics . . . for Badger Metal to truly protect them in space?" Sissy mused.

"Each race has different sensitivities to the radiation of space, as they have different nutritional needs based on their home world evolution. They need different harmonies in the Badger Metal hull plating to properly protect them. That's why the Squids began dying. They switched to human Badger Metal. The Maril changed their sensitivities when they tinkered with their DNA!"

Sissy rapped the humming blade against the drum's exterior, caught the clanging note, held it, then pushed it upward into a soaring hymn of praise for the wonder of the space station that became a crossroad for trade and diplomacy. For the neutral location that granted her a chance to be with Jake.

Her girls joined in, bringinng the music into a grander harmony.

Jake's boots banging against the metal disrupted the music a bit. But she added that tentative discord into the mix and found a place for it in the new universe of the propulsion engine and the music and the thrumming of the Badger Metal in her hand, in Jake's insignia stars, and the other weapons he carried.

Sissy felt the mechanism respond, needing to join in her song. Jake's shout of triumph as he wiggled the first rod into a new position became just one more piece of the scattered universe seeking a home within the puzzle of life.

Over and over she sang the hymn, adding bits and pieces as Jake moved each rod into place, correcting the wrong, enhancing the right.

Her body and mind grew limp with fatigue. Still she found the music, found solace and continuance in it. She sang and sang until there were no more songs to sing, no more chords to complete.

A subtle note of triumph and thanks continued humming through the air and the entire station. All the power plants moved into Harmony with the corrected propulsion engines.

Jake jumped down from the last drum, wrapped her in his arms, and kissed her with his entire soul. "We belong together, my Sissy. We'll find a way."

"Harmony will guide us. Just as I trust Her to guide Mac and Adrial to a new life together."

✦ ✦ ✦ ◇ ✦ ✦ ✦

EPILOGUE

JAKE STOOD BACK and watched the subdued throng of passengers waiting for clearance to enter their Harmony-bound transport. No one dared board until the VIPs arrived and took their august places.

The ghost of Laud Gregor kept silent vigil beside him.

"You going to attend your own funeral, My Laud?" Jake asked sotto voce.

Gregor shrugged. Complacent in death as he hadn't been in life. He'd even added his own ghostly hum to the ceremony of getting the propulsion engines back on track.

"If you're waiting for me to apprehend Adrial, you have a long wait coming. I have no idea if they survived."

His sensors and patrols had found no bodies floating in space.

They must have survived. Jake wasn't about to give up hope that the strange pair of aliens had found refuge in time. Mac knew how to hide from every sensor ever invented. Adrial had learned more than a few tricks from him and had taught him a few of her own probably.

Jake's green class A uniform itched and nearly choked him. In all of human history, no one had ever designed a comfortable class A. Repeatedly he touched the cool black crystal stars on his upright collar. A tingle of anticipation ran through his fingertips each time, followed by an almost chime of melodic bells in the back of his mind.

That was the Badger Metal woven into the crystal matrix. That was the music of the universe finding a home.

In all the concessions both Harmony and the CSS had made, the formulas for Badger Metal to plate spaceship hulls and black crystals to improve ship-to-ship communication were not among them. They were Harmony's primary bargaining chip. They had already begun working on variations tailored to each race.

Jake wanted them to keep the monopoly. For Sissy's sake. For his own.

In this restless hour of waiting to send High Priest Gregor home for burial, Jake felt as if he belonged as much to Harmony as he did the CSS.

The thought of Badger Metal blades available to one and all scared him.

The more people who had the formulas, the more easily the Maril could steal them. The avian aliens might want to talk now, but they were still officially at war with both the CSS and Harmony. He and his people had endured too much pain, loss, and hardship during the war to immediately forgive or welcome them.

To trust them.

A rustle of movement around the lift alerted him. A cortege of Harmonite Military officers stepped off the rotating platforms, followed by a green-draped casket on a lift cart.

Everyone stilled and bowed.

Jake had to do the same. He couldn't help himself. Gregor had been shortsighted, ruthless, arrogant, and selfish. But he'd remained true to his convictions in running the Temple and the government.

The ghost raised his eyebrows in surprise at Jake's show of respect.

"You're dead. You can't hurt Sissy anymore," Jake replied to the unvoiced question.

Gregor smirked.

"Just try it and I'll get every psychic and priest in the galaxy to exorcise you, send you back where you belong."

That didn't faze the ghost in the least.

Then Sissy appeared on the lift, framed by the mechanism's archway. Her black regalia, complete with obscuring veil, shimmered in the shadows.

She stepped free, followed by her six acolytes in their corresponding gray brocaded robes. The brighter light of the reception area banished some of the mystery she projected but not her quiet authority.

"As awesome as ever," Jake told the ghost.

Gregor nodded.

Sissy turned her head, finding Jake with her gaze. She held out a delicate hand.

Drawn to her like a magnet, he covered the distance between them in a few long strides. His hand slipped around hers, belonging there.

Gregor looked back and forth between Jake and the body being loaded into a special compartment aboard the ship. He took half a step to follow himself, then jerked back to hover behind Jake's shoulder.

Great. Jake wasn't going to banish this ghost as easily as he'd hoped.

"I won't stay away from you any longer than I have to," Sissy said loud enough for anyone who cared to hear.

"I await your return, impatiently. This place won't be the same without you. I won't be whole without you." Jake bowed over their clasped hands, raised them and kissed her palm.

Sissy tilted her head back so the bead strands fell away from her face. "I have to do this, Jake."

"Harmony needs you. I just hope She can spare you very quickly."

Impulsively she threw her arms around him in a tight hug.

Jake rested his cheek against the heavy padding of her headdress, wishing he could touch more of her.

A soft chiming behind him announced the ship was ready to receive passengers.

He had to let her go. He already ached all over with loneliness and missing her.

"Have you got your inhaler handy?" he asked.

"Yes." She put enough distance between them to fish the gadget out of her sleeve. Still, she kept one hand on his chest, as reluctant to separate as he.

"Mary and Martha, do you have backup inhalers?" He let his left hand linger on Sissy's back, rubbing the silky fabric compulsively.

"Yes, Jake," all six acolytes replied in unison. Each of the girls held up identical inhalers. The dosage meter on the ends showed them all full.

"Then I guess there is nothing to keep you . . . to keep . . ." He couldn't say the rest. Couldn't let her go so easily. Desperate, he pulled her close again. He closed his eyes against the wet lump in his throat.

Someone cleared his throat sternly from behind Sissy.

Lord Lukan and Lady Jancee stood there, frowning in disapproval. Garrin turned his back so he didn't have to watch the blasphemy of their High Priestess holding an out-of-caste alien so intimately.

Jake tried to put some distance between himself and Sissy.

"The Jake I fell in love with would not conform so readily," she whispered, clinging as tightly as ever.

With a cockeyed grin, Jake lowered his head and kissed her soundly. Instantly her mouth softened beneath his.

She tasted so sweet, so warm and welcoming, as lovely as he'd dreamed.

He pressed the kiss deeper, molding his body to hers, cherishing the feel of her pressed against him. Even through way too many layers of clothing.

The sound of many hands clapping roused Jake from his enthrallment. The sound grew louder, accompanied by many whoops of joy that echoed about the stark loading bay.

"You've made your point," Lukan said. "You two intend to fight tradition to the very end. And it seems you have the support of too many of my people for me to block you."

Jake eased away from the temptation of Sissy's mouth. His gaze never left hers.

Out of the corner of his eye, he watched credit chits exchange hands. He wondered briefly what the odds on the bets had been.

Then he decided he didn't care.

"I'm leaving my son as my deputy while I'm on Harmony," Lukan continued. "He will look after my wife in the final weeks of her pregnancy. Should she go into labor before my return, I expect only properly authorized and lauded physicians and nurses to attend her."

Jake nodded.

"But I'm sending his older sister to balance his actions and attitudes as soon as I can. She will have final say in all decisions dealing with the CSS."

Garrin and Jancee glared at him but said nothing.

"It's time to go, Laudae," Lukan said sternly.

"A moment more."

He tsked in exasperation. "The empire awaits you. Our government is at a standstill—no one works, no one does anything but await your pleasure."

With one last squeeze of hands, Sissy stepped back and dropped her face so that the strands of glass beads and crystals fell into place. Then she glided toward the air lock, graceful, calm, in charge.

Jake waited a long time after the bay had cleared of passengers and well-wishers.

Gregor waited beside him.

He watched the monitors until the ship had backed away from the dock. He watched as it slid farther and farther away from the station. He watched as it sped toward the jump point.

He watched long after it had disappeared into hyperspace with a blur of motion and shift out of reality.

He watched while Gregor paced wide circles around him.

At last, when he knew in his heart that Sissy could not return to him today, he stepped aboard the lift and rose through level after level until he reached the tram.

He let the vehicle take him to another wing, a single wing, not close enough to any others to be part of a cluster. Recently, workers had prepared the light-G levels for a new diplomatic wing. Then they had hastily deserted the place.

Jake took the lift silently down to the first docking bay. Alone, as instructed, though he knew his Marines waited quietly and fully armed in the maintenance tubes. Backing him up should anything go wrong.

He prayed they weren't as trigger-happy as he wanted to be. How could they trust the new ambassadors? All of the CSS personnel had lost someone in the war. The need for vengeance was strong among them.

A new ship with odd markings mimicking red and black feathers was just matching hatch to dock. A flexible arm locked the two together. The same air lock that Adrial and Mac had disappeared through.

Moments later the bulkhead cycled open, and three Maril emerged, gliding gracefully across the metal deck. Ruby red feathers crowned their heads in flamboyant upright crests. Long surcoats matched their feathers. Stark black uniforms clothed the rest of their lithe bodies.

The one in the middle chirped something.

Jake cocked his head, puzzled. Then he passed them a small device Mara had put together with the Squid translator. He pointed to a matching one and inserted it into his ear. The Maril mimicked the action, finding an almost invisible ear hidden among his red feathers.

Instantly the chirps clarified into stilted words.

"We come in peace."

Jake put his wariness behind him, available but not obvious.

Sissy had taught him there had to be a better way than war. She fought against traditions that held society so tightly it could not grow. He pushed aside his need for the war that had lasted hundreds of years.

"I welcome you in peace," he replied and bowed deeply.